WHERE ROWANS INTERTWINE

MARGARET GRANT

PUBLISHED BY

MYNYDD LLWYDIARTH

PRESS

To dear Jean,
For all our tomorrows,
Blessings, love & light.
Margaret Grant   2015

To my wonderful family.
My heart soars
by means
of your
love and support.

CONTENTS

✽

ACKNOWLEDGEMENTS

⌘

I would firstly like to thank my wonderful family, who nurtured me through the writing of this novel; especially Claire Grant, my daughter, who had the patience to do the first edit, my parents, Jim and Ada Hufton, for their encouragement and faith in me, and my son, Andrew Grant, who cooked many a meal to keep me going. Most of all I would like to thank my long suffering soul-mate and husband, Gordon Grant, who provided me with the cover photograph, kept me well supplied with research material from Bangor University library and who nursed and financed me through a severely disabling part of my life.

Also, without the nurture and prayer of my local Baha'i Faith Community, I think I would have certainly given up when the going got tough. The sacred scriptures revealed by Baha'u'llah give such structure and goal to one's life. What I would have done without that spiritual food and inspiration, I cannot fathom? More information on the Baha'i Faith can be found at www.bahai.org.

I would like to thank Vivienne Candlish for introducing me to Reiki healing, my Reiki masters, Kristin Bonney and Soyin Tang, and Kerry Caldock for introducing me to medical herbalism; each of them crucial to my recovery and for giving me background material for the heroine's healing skills.

In matters of historical research I would like to thank Brian Jones for his advice and knowledge of the Roman occupation of North Wales; Bangor University for the use of its reference library; Gwynedd Museum Bangor; Segontium Fort Caernarfon; Oriel Ynys Môn, Llangefni and Deva Roman Experience, Chester, for their wonderful artefacts and historical information. I would like to thank the people of Anglesey; some of whom I found to be truly descended from Druids and Romans; or maybe both?

Grateful thanks go to Claire Peall for her knowledge of horse behaviour and to Ruth Prosser for the second detailed edit. Thanks are also due to Larry Ewing, President of Bergamot Brass Works, Incorporated, Wisconsin, for providing one of their buckle designs, using the Celtic symbol of entwined lovers in the Tree of Life for the front cover.

This novel would never have got to publication without the encouragement of Chris Cullen, local archivist; and novelist Melanie Kerr, whose patient guidance and knowledge of the self-publishing process was crucial. Thanks a million Melanie for teaching me so much! Grateful thanks also to Stef at Writeintoprint for the ebook formatting; Yvonne Betancourt at ebook-format.com for a patient paperback format; my niece, Laura Rogers, for introducing me to Wordpress and helping me set up my website and to Kertu Laur from Safarista Designs for helping me redesign the jacket.

Last but not least I would like to thank my muse Ceridwen, who inspired, corrected and guided the content of the novel, so that it would reflect more truthfully, the essence of her life story.

Preface

⌘

Before you begin your journey into the past, perhaps you would like to orient yourself to the island of Mona (Anglesey, or Ynys Môn as it is known today). If you look at a current map of North Wales, you will see the island is linked to the mainland by two bridges. During the Roman Occupation of Britain around 230 A.D. those did not exist of course. Access from the mainland to the island was either across the treacherous Lavan sands at low tide, or by ferry boat. Menai Bridge was known as Dindaethwy (Fortress of the Daethwy). Beaumaris was known as Cerrig y Gwyddyl, and Llanddona on the north east coast was the site of Din Silwy, the fortress lorded over by the chieftain Eithig in the story.

Inland and a little to the west of Din Silwy is Mynydd Llwydiarth (Purple Mountain), the site of Cae Gwynion, the ancient holy place of the Druids. Below the mountain to the south, in the environs of the current B5109 would have been the settlement of Tan Yr Aur in the story.

During the third century A.D. there was a Roman naval base near Caer Y Twr at the site of Holyhead. It would have been crucial to repelling Irish raiders from across the sea, but also a better supply port than Dindaethwy, which could only accommodate small craft. Supplies coming and going to Deva (Chester) would have come in here as well as at Segontium.

On the mainland of North Wales, there is not much left to see but the footings of the old Roman fortress of Segontium, near to Caernarfon town centre. But, if you are in the vicinity, do take the opportunity to look at this ancient archeological site in the trust of Cadw (the Welsh equivalent of the National Trust.)

There would also have been a ferry crossing from Mona to Caer yn Arfon and the Roman fortress at Segontium, from somewhere near Brynsiencyn. Part of a Roman warehouse, a Roman road and Samian pottery shards have been found at this site, now named Caer Leb. Abermenai, at the very southernmost tip of Anglesey, was also used as a ferry point, linking the island to the mainland.

Abergwyngregyn (Aber) on the mainland coast between Llanfairfechan and Bangor operated some sort of ferryboat over to Cerrig y Gwyddyl (Beaumaris) from ancient times right up until the 19th century. However, it is well worth the magical climb up from the village of Aber into the Rhaeadr Valley, where wild ponies are often curious enough to accompany you along the way. Towards the top of the climb you will be directed south eastwards to witness the dramatic force of the Aber Falls depicted at the end of the story.

No visit to North Wales is complete, however, without taking in the wonderful vista from the highest mountain of Yr Wyddfa, or Snowdon as it is known by most of us. If, on a clear day, you take the easy route up by train from Llanberis and at the summit look across northwest to Anglesey, you will see Mynydd Llwydiarth, the forested setting for this tale of Mona's past.

Besides the Welsh names you will come across several strange words in the text. *Geas* is an ancient druid word, which means 'against all culturally proper conduct' and a *sending* is a form of a telepathically sent vision or message. I understand it to be the means by which we communicated before we developed word language, so it is a very old form of communication.

A *glamour* is a form of enchantment, where something is transformed or hidden from view. You could say that this happens nowadays when we pretend we are something we are not. It is a form of deceitfulness in that sense - a masking, a bewitching and beguiling in another.

Deosil means working right to left in a circle pattern (clockwise) and *widdershins* means working left to right in a circle (anti-clockwise). This is used in folk dances and in the

Nature worship of pagan rites to this day.

A *commote* is a tract of land owned and worked in common by a Celtic tribe. It could be interpreted as an administrative district in today's terms, which makes up part of a *cantref* or county.

Nain means grandmother, *Taid* means grandfather and *Cariad* means dearest or darling. *Adref* means homeward and *hiraeth* means longing for the homeland. I never really understood the latter expression of hiraeth, until we had to leave our beautiful, mountain home on Anglesey in exchange for the South Yorkshire Moors, when my husband took up a chair at Sheffield University. How my heart longed for Mynydd Llwydiarth and its peacefulness, where I had regained my health and felt a deep sense of belonging. For me there was such heart wrenching in the leaving and a new spiritual challenge. I did come to know what *hiraeth* really meant.

The *principia* was the administrative and religious centre and most important building in any Roman fort. It was situated mid point, where the main streets of the *via praetoria* and the *via principalis* crossed. You will see the outlines of such in the stone footings at Segontium near Caernarfon.

'An *aquilifer* was a senior standard bearer carrying the eagle standard of a Roman legion. This was the most important possession of the legion and its loss was a terrible disgrace. The aquila emblem generally had up-raised wings surrounded by a laurel wreath. It was mounted on a narrow trapezoidal base, on a pole that was held aloft. The *aquilifer's* position was accordingly one of enormous prestige, and he was ranked immediately below the centurions and above the optiones, receiving twice the pay of an ordinary legionary.'(Brunt 1950)

The *praetorium* was the commander's house, where the officers would assemble for instructions and tactical discussions. The Roman *basilica* was a large roofed hall erected for transacting business and disposing of legal matters. As early as the time of Augustus Caesar, in the first century, a public *basilica* for transacting business had been part of any settlement that considered itself a city; and so, towards the end of the story, we visit one at Deva, the great Roman Fortress of Chester.

The Welsh language is very lyrical and the Welsh call it 'the language of Heaven.' It is phonetic and easy to read aloud, once you know the alphabet and some of the pronunciation rules. If you would like to research these, you could begin by visiting:

bbc.co.uk/wales/livinginwales/sites/howdoisay/alphabet

Characters in 'Where Rowans Intertwine'

⌘

Ceridwen (Keridwen): A young nineteen year old maiden, trainee priestess and healer to the Celwri tribe, who lives in the environs of **Mynydd Llwydiarth**, (Purple Mountain) on the island of **Mona**, (Anglesey) off the coast of **Cymru**, (Wales).

She has conscientiously studied her Druid arts at the knee of her grandmother, in the hut at **Cae Gwynion** (Holy Ground) since she was given for the training at five years old. She is burgeoning with the naive confidence of the young at the beginning of the story. She is beautiful; her fair skin speckled with faint freckles; her grey-blue eyes mysterious and deep in the soft oval of her face; her burnished copper hair tamed into her braids. She has natural grace and a sweet voice for chanting.

Ceridwen allows the stirring energy of Spring to course through her veins and bring her closer to the Earth Goddess whose name she bears. She knows that it is not only her five physical senses, which are awakening, but her spiritual ones. Her new powers excite her, but she is well trained and not foolish enough to misuse them. Her main weakness is that she has so absorbed the tales of the bards she despises all that is Roman. Her attitude, although understandable, is not the way of the Druid.

Nanw (Nanoo): Ceridwen's grandmother and patient tutor, who lives at the hut on the holy site at **Cae Gwynion**. Once beautiful, she is now getting bent and frail, although her wits are still sharp. She is conscious that she is not long for this world and has, of late, been intensifying Ceridwen's training. She is dignified, noble of soul and wise; keeps a guarded tongue and uses it with love and diplomacy; trying to emulate her late husband, **Cadoc**, a seer and priest, who was well respected by the tribe. Nanw's advice is never at fault and always towards the path of good. She is wise enough to know that bitterness most hurts its owner. Always by her side is **Mwg** (Moog) her inscrutable black cat.

Gwilym (Gwilim): Ceridwen's thickset, middle-aged father and headman at **Tan Yr Aur**, the farmstead in the valley below Mynydd Llwydiarth. His business is raising horses for his own family's profit and growing crops to pay the Roman taxes. He has a dogged determination and an ethic of hard work, which he displays as an example to his three sons and bondsmen. He has no scruples about keeping both the Romans and the neighbouring Celtic warriors sweet, for his motive in life is to do whatever is best to serve his family's interests; but there is a limit beyond which he will not be pushed.

He is fond of his wife, **Marged**, but not demonstrative. Rather than pick an argument, he is content to let Marged run the farmstead in her own way. His favourite child is Ceridwen, but he tries hard to disguise this, being a proud father. He is well liked by his bondsmen, who recognise a good living when they have one and are content to be loyal to Gwilym.

Marged: Gwilym's wife and mother to Ceridwen. She is more renowned for her directness than her diplomacy, but she is well intentioned. She organises the daily life of the farmstead at Tan Yr Aur with relentless energy, ever practical and concerned about feeding the farmsteaders. There is never an air of peacefulness around Marged, for she is never at ease herself unless she is busy.

Coll: Ceridwen's brother, who lives at Tan Yr Aur, is an impetuous, highly skilled horse trainer in his early twenties, whose acrobatics upon a horse reveal his Celtic penchant for showmanship. Auburn haired and hot blooded, he hates the injustices of their chief, **Eithig** and finds it hard not to retaliate physically. Ceridwen is the one person in the family who can calm him and make him see the priorities.

Owain (Owine): Ceridwen's eldest brother, who although being shy, is just as skilled with the horses. He brings a steady temperament to everything he tackles, which endears him both to the animals and children on the farmstead at Tan Yr Aur. Although courageous, he thinks before he acts. He is as yet unmarried, although he is in his late twenties.

Hedfan (Hedvan): Ceridwen's twelve-year old brother, who is both fleet of foot and swift on horseback. He is the adventurous messenger boy, riding or running between the settlements in their corner of the island. It is his burning ambition one day to own the beautiful white mare, **Gwyngariad**. He is impatient to be a man.

Ness: Ceridwen's only sister, who initially shows love and tenderness for her brood of children at Tan Yr Aur. **Rhodri, Daf** and **Rhys** are her young boys and **Rhonwen** her little daughter; but she is six months pregnant with her next child at the start of the story. Being a parent has been fun so far, with so many eyes to keep an eye on them all at the farmstead.

Madog: Ness's utterly loyal husband, who can always be relied upon to provide tabor and drum music for the festivals. He is also excellent at mock battles. His friend and bondsman, **Cullen** provides the traditional pipe and horn music.

Eithig (Aythig): Unscrupulous chieftain of the Celwri, who lives with his warriors in the barricaded village of **Din Silwy** on the headland to the east of Mynydd Llwydiarth. Ceridwen has the measure of him when she says, 'He is a prisoner of the sensual, without sensibility or manners. He may be strong and courageous, but he is addicted to power and satiating desire. He smells of sweat and vainglory.'

He has inherited his position from his father, who had been a respected and elected chieftain before him. Now that the Samhain elections are a foregone conclusion, Eithig rules by fear and intimidation. The grim set of his face and his bulging eyes strike terror into many of his subjects. The tribe awaits a saviour.

Betw (Betoo): An ageing aunt of Eithig's; ample and warm hearted, with the gift of 'the sight' and a valued member of the coven at the Holy Place (Cae Gwynion). She is leaned on for her experience once Nanw is gone. She waits at Din Silwy for her opportunity to help oust Eithig, whom she suspects has been abusing **Einir**, his young sister.

Meromic: A young Roman auxiliary from the hill fort on the crest of Mynydd Llwydiarth, who is helped by Nanw and Ceridwen. He had spent an idyllic childhood on the seashores of Aremorica, but was captured along with his sister and sent to a slave market in Arvernia. When he was nine years old he was parted from his sister, **Fiommar**. He became friendly with the Roman legate, who bought him and set him free. He joined the Roman army. It is the only family he knows. He still looks for Fiommar and hopes to find her again. Ceridwen reminds him of her and there begins his loyalty to her.

Marcus: A skilled Roman surgeon stationed at the mainland fortress of **Segontium**, who has suffered the last two years with depression and grief after his wife **Leona** and baby **Crispian** were crushed in a building accident. He is in his mid twenties with a neat beard and sun bronzed cheeks. He is of medium height and weight, broad shouldered, with the taut muscles of constant army training. He has a straight aquiline nose, a generous mouth, dark eyes and white teeth, is meticulous about self-hygiene and does his best to obliterate his grief by working conscientiously. He hides his emotions from his men, but **Dith**, his assistant, can usually read him. Marcus's hard professional exterior disguises a sensitive man beneath. He never really knew the love of his parents, but he is anxious to belong and to be a good father himself. He feels cheated by the Gods at his loss.

Vipsanius: A clear headed and decisive commandant at the Roman fortress of **Segontium**; popular with his men and good at trading and negotiating with the **Ordovicans** who live at **Porth Arfon**, the sea town below the fortress. He counts Marcus as one of his best friends and theirs is an easy camaraderie despite the difference in rank. He is married to **Rhiannon**.

Rhiannon: Attractive, red haired, young daughter of the chieftain **Lord Geraint** of **Porth Arfon** who lives with her husband, Vipsanius, in the commandant's house at Segontium. She adores **Vipsanius** and is learning to be a commandant's wife, taught by **Flavia**.

Flavia: wife of **Hortensius**, a centurion who lives with his family close to the commandant's house to provide support for Rhiannon and Vipsanius. They are also very friendly with Marcus, whose professional visits turned into social ones when he married **Leona**, Flavia's servant. Since Leona's death they have missed his visits.

Dith: Marcus's good-natured assistant at the infirmary at Segontium. A huge man, capable of the very heavy duties needed in lifting sick men, he is totally devoted to Marcus and once rescued him from slavery. His idolatry and possessiveness of Marcus sets him up for disappointment and jealousy, but he would never do anything to harm Marcus, despite his own feelings. He feels inadequate in that he has not been able to learn to read.

Quintus: a tall curt-tongued centurion, who bitterly resents his new posting with his eighty men, to the outpost hillfort at Mynydd Llwydiarth. His uniform helps to give him his feeling of self-importance and he wears it imperiously. He has little knowledge of the local people and customs; yet despite his ignorance, he is determined to make his disciplinarian's mark upon the area. He brooks no challenge to his authority and would never admit to a mistake.

Lady Tangwen of Dreffos: A rich widow living at the moated farmstead of **Dreffos**. Her eldest son, **Iowerth**, (Eeowerth) was to have coupled with Ceridwen this Beltane, but he was thrown from his horse and killed. She is left with a younger son, **Ieuan** (Yayan). She enjoys her part in the coven, a council of local women who consult together about the local customs and rites at Cae Gwynion.

Einir (Aynir): The young teenage sister of Eithig, whose mother died when she was born. Eithig abuses her both verbally and sexually, but she is too terrified by his threats to tell the womenfolk at Din Silwy. She lives in terror of displeasing him and awaits her chance to find a way out of her situation. She longs to be the princess of legends and wear beautiful clothes, but Eithig allows her little materially.

Elin: Granddaughter to Old Betw. A romantic naive teenager, who has fallen in love with **Cullen**, the piper from Tan Yr Aur.

Ffynan (Finan): A ten year old, thin, spindly boy whose father, the bard to the commote, died in mysterious circumstances. Ffynan has taken the role of bard upon himself and his delicate musician's fingers are at one with his lyre. As yet, his unbroken voice is sweet and his poetry clever for one so young. He lives at Din Silwy and has been taken under the kindly wing of Old Betw.

Edwyn (Edwin): A compulsive liar, who is desperate for fame and recognition. This young warrior, who lives at Din Silwy, would initially stop at nothing to become Eithig's favourite. Already he has ingratiated himself by saving his chieftain's life on more than one occasion. He allows himself to do Eithig's bidding without question, but there is a conscience there ready to disturb him if he would but reflect. He hopes to bed with Einir at Beltane with a view to becoming her husband. She is a princess after all.

Huw The Giant: A huge henchman of Eithig's, capable of lifting most men in the air and splattering them. No one has come out better than he in any combat.

Lord Meurig (Mayrig): A mature, portly and sensible chieftain of the Daethwy tribe, hailing from **Dindaethwy**, the village on the island of Mona, nearest by ferry to the mainland. He tolerates Eithig, but would like to see him conquered. He is married to **Gwenifer** of **Cerrig y Gwyddyl**, a member of the *commote* coven.

Lord Geraint: Chieftain of the **Arfon Ordovicans** at the mainland harbour town of **Porth Arfon** below the Roman fortress of Segontium. His people rely upon him to negotiate their deals with the Romans and their welfare depends on his trading skills and his steady diplomacy. He is genuinely fond of his son-in-law, Vipsanius and the Roman doctor, Marcus, for he has no live sons of his own. He is thick set and sturdy, riding an equally stocky black hunter. He has a quiet authority over his men, which comes from the conviction that he is doing the best for his people. He is married to **Lady Branwen**.

Lady Branwen: A protective mother who did not agree with her daughter's marriage to the Roman commandant at Segontium, but who is wise enough to keep tongues from wagging by outwardly supporting her husband, Lord Geraint. She misses her daughter's company now she is at Segontium.

She can be practical, decisive and warm hearted in a crisis.

Old Mali: A shrewd, gnarled old hermit woman, who trained with Nanw many years ago. She now ekes out a meagre existence telling fortunes in the mirror of her well at **Ffynnon Glan** upon Mona. She is careless of hygiene, but meticulous about rooting out information. She wears a thick, brown woollen, thorn-torn tunic. Her matted hair stands in a white bushy crown about her head. Her beady eyes peer above a sharp hooked nose, reminding one of a magpie.

Uncle Tullius: An over-fed, hard-nosed, barrel shaped, wine merchant, who plies his trade between the ports of the Roman Empire. He is Marcus's father's brother and grows his vines on his estate above the port of Ostia near Rome. His shrewd, calculating eyes almost disappear into the ample folds of his huge face, but this in turn does not hide the hard line of his mouth and the chiselled set of his square jaw. He seems to have influence with **Eugenus Aelius**, the Roman legate at Deva, (Chester) headquarters of the Twentieth Legion.

Eugenus Aelius: A proud legate of the Twentieth Legion at **Deva**, who sees himself as representative of **Emperor Severus Alexander**. He is cold and calculating, but polite to his visitors. He is proud of the legate's palace at Deva and enjoys demonstrating its splendour, as does his wife **Aurora**.

⌘ ⌘ ⌘

WHERE ROWANS INTERTWINE

CHAPTER I

⌘

THE FORAGE

It had been no comfort that the culprits had been flogged to death. Was it only three Springs ago since the wall collapsed, three Springs since his young wife and suckling babe had been crushed by the falling masonry? Some idiots were supposed to have recently repaired a breach in the courtyard wall at the fort, a Roman stronghold with a human flaw. Bad workmanship! How had such a thing come to pass?

His hand fingered the pugio at his side, its small blade biting in to the swell of his fingers, mirroring the anger biting into his soul. He knew he must refocus. He knew he must begin to dwell on something uplifting; must exchange the bitterness and grief, that habitually welled in his soul, for something which would enable him to do his army surgeon's job as professionally as he had been trained to do it.

Marcus allowed the rhythmical swaying of the pony beneath him to lull him into a more relaxed state. It had been a hard morning's ride out from Segontium, the main Roman fort in the area. They had crossed the Straits to Mona in hired ferry boats, manned by local tribesmen who knew the dangers of the Spring tides, the swells and thrusts of the great confluence of water and the sinking sands. The horses had swum across and, apart from several tense moments when the last horse had fought shy of the water and had nearly capsized the ferryboat, there had been no sign of danger.

Legionary life had been quieter of late, with more building

work to supervise than skirmishes to settle. Apart from some bone setting, Marcus's surgical skills had not been greatly in demand. Thus, when Vipsanius, his closest friend and cohort commander, had suggested forage into Mona to trade for new horses, he had been eager to temper the restlessness, which had seized him with the onset of Spring. A journey to the legendary island of the Druids would take his mind from the stirring memories. Mm...Perhaps?

A surgeon with the Roman legions must have a stomach for gore, but the sight of the crushed and mutilated bodies of the two people he most loved still haunted him. At the time of the accident it had sickened Marcus to the core and he had taken fever himself and almost died.

Yet here he was, with memories and pain rekindling, and no permanent way to shut them out. How he envied Vipsanius and the rest of the garrison. Vipsanius had recently married a chieftain's daughter, who ran the domestic affairs of the commandant's house at Segontium as though she had been bred to it. Many of the soldiers were unofficially married to the trades-people, who had gathered in the environs of the sea-fortress to take advantage of the opportunity of a good living. And equally as many enjoyed a casual romance, or paid for the favours of the unprotected women, enforced to make their living the only way they knew how.

Most legionaries had left behind sisters or a mother in the homeland, a worry and a responsibility; but it seemed to Marcus that no one else was bathing in his sort of torment; a great chasm of emptiness that gnawed at him, whenever he had an opportunity to reflect.

Why had the Gods given him the sweet ecstasy of Leona, only to snatch her away again? He had tried so hard to play his role in life. He must appear in control at all times; a professional with a calling, able to deal with the brutalities of life by cutting off his emotions before they grew into disabling forces. But Leona had reached into that part of him that no one else had ever had privy to. He had known the first time he had observed her draw water from the fort well that she would have the power to unnerve him.

Their courtship had been brief and their marriage very convenient, as Leona was able to continue service with the wife of the centurion Hortensius. Their sleeping quarters had been a simple room forming part of the quadrangle of the commandant's house at Segontium. At one time there had only been room for the men at arms, but, as more and more troops had been pulled out to the North, it had been much safer and more convenient to house the officers' women at close quarters.

In his mind's eye Marcus could see Leona now, cradling Crispian in her arms, the tiny fingers stroking the silk of her breast, as the babe suckled contentedly. He constantly tried to substitute this picture of them, whenever the darker memory of their mangled bodies returned to torment him. He clutched automatically at his breast to make sure that the locket, on its leather thong, still hung around his neck. Inside its hinge of Celtic bronze hid a tress of Leona's glossy, dark hair, entwined with a downy curling lock of Crispian's.

Marcus marvelled how the bravery of men could take in the valour of combat; the tasks of hunting and slaughtering; the physical pain of torture, amputation, being maimed – all with plenty of yelling and cursing; yet the pain of seeing a lock of hair could bring a man to tears.

He never opened the locket unless in private and he wondered how his comrades would view this army surgeon of strong stomach, if they could witness his private grieving.

He had been lagging behind a little, absorbed with his own thoughts. It was time to catch up with the rest of the party as they neared the settlement of Dindaethwy. They would rest the horses, take some refreshment themselves and take the lie of the land.

Dith, Marcus's assistant, had been sent ahead to warn the Daethwy that they came for peaceful trade. There was no point making these tribespeople edgier than usual. Consequently, there was already a good crowd gathered in the central settlement clearing. People had emerged from their huts with goods to exchange, excited at having the opportunity to barter with the legionaries.

3

There was new bread hot from the ovens, Celtic strong barley brew that caught the breath as it was gulped down, lengths of chequered woollen weave to make a handsome blanket or keep the draught from the door. Someone had made a poor attempt to copy the imported Samian pottery. There was an array of clay bowls and amphorae decorated with bulls and Roman Gods, but the potter had made a better job of his traditional Celtic designs of intricate swirls and patterns.

Marcus left Dith to negotiate the exchange of an amphora of Gallic wine for a warm horse-blanket and found himself drawn to the glowing fires and bellows of the smithy.

'The Gods be with you in your work. May I watch a craftsman at his trade?' Marcus queried in his best attempt at Brythonic.

The smith nodded assent without encouragement. He was paid to produce metal goods, not provide entertainment for these Roman intruders. He worked hard on the bellows for a few more minutes until the charcoal of his forge glowed brighter than ever. He was working on a sword commissioned by Eithig, chieftain of the Celwri. It was illegal to bear arms. He wondered what the Roman would have to say as he fashioned the showpiece.

'It looks quite special, the sword you are making?' Marcus made it more of a query than a comment.

'It's a ceremonial sword, for the election of the chief of the Celwri tribe's inauguration...a foregone conclusion these days. There's no one willing to challenge Eithig. The leadership has been in his family for generations. The elections are a formality that's all.'

'A ceremonial sword you say. I suppose it may be honed to a sharp blade?'

'That's as it may be! But when it leaves my smithy it shall conform to legal proportions. It is no affair of mine what a man may do to fashion weapons after they leave my forge!'

Beads of perspiration were dripping from his half naked body as he worked the metal with his tongs and hammer, but it wasn't only the heat and effort of the work, which contorted his face. He hated the petty Roman rules, which everyone knew you had to turn a blind eye towards in order to exist.

How could a man survive without hunting weapons and knives with which to cut meat and eat food? How could things be fashioned without sharp and dangerous implements? Everyone had to compromise and 'not bearing arms' was interpreted in the main as not carrying a shield and sword overtly; although most men travelling carried a dagger at the belt and a sword, sickle or axe in the saddle baggage.

Marcus had no intention of stirring trouble for the smith and his family. He had come to find good horses and enjoy the precious time away from the bustle of the fort.

'How will you finish the hilt?' he ventured, sensing the man's unease and wanting to reassure him that he wasn't about to have him arrested.

'With this stag's horn inset with amber. My wife will finish it well with her fine touch, so that it will feel smooth as a babe's skin in the hand.'

The smith had begun to relax and feel that Marcus had genuine interest in his work; but the now friendlier interchange was disturbed by a commotion in the main clearing.

A man had emerged from the main hut. He was dressed in a grander manner than the workaday rags of the Daethwy – a deep purple tunic, leather breeches and a colourful tartan cloak pinned to his shoulders with golden brooches. A brightly burnished golden torc drew attention to the thick sinews of his throat. He towered head and shoulders above the boy whom he was kicking along the dusty thoroughfare. A crowd quickly gathered, enjoying the spectacle and appreciative that it was no boy of theirs being punished by the chieftain visitor.

Eithig was hurling abuse at the boy messenger. Hadn't he been promised the white mare three Moons ago? What did the boy mean by 'She isn't ready for you yet, Sire?' Did those brothers of his call themselves horse trainers? They were wet nursed amateurs! If they would deliver the mare he would train her himself!

Much as the boy might dodge and roll from the onslaught it almost seemed as though the crowd were against him. They moved aside as the hefty chieftain railed and kicked. No one dared intervene. Not even the Roman legionaries, in the throes of their bartering negotiations, seemed eager to intervene.

It all seemed to happen so quickly. Looking back, Marcus felt he might have prevented the burning, but the boy was careering towards the forge so fast that, even though Marcus leapt to prevent it, the boy fell heavily against the anvil.

The boy's yells turned to a tortured scream as his shoulder singed. Marcus ran to pick him up bodily and plunged the boy into a trough of water.

'Help me!' he urged the smith. 'Hold his head above the water for me. You! Hold his legs still for me,' Marcus motioned to the forge apprentice.

It seemed an age before they moved to help him, too frightened of a show of support for Roman against a chieftain. But eventually compassion for the boy won out.

'Let him lick his own wounds and take the message back to those beggarly brothers of his that I'll have that mare by next Full Moon, or see it as an act of treason against their chief!' Eithig seethed, breathing hard after his kicking and railing at Hedfan, the boy messenger from Tan Yr Aur.

'This boy is in no fit state to take any message back to his people. You have seen to that!' Marcus's anger spewed from his mouth without diplomacy.

'I think it wise that we should let these tribes-people settle their own little disputes, Marcus. Time to involve the judiciary when there are larger things at stake, don't you think?' It was Vipsanius reprimanding him and taking charge of the situation. 'I'm sorry if my surgeon offended you in any way, Lord Eithig. His sentiments come with his skills as an excellent healer. I can vouch. We shall leave the boy in his good hands, shall we, and share a meal together as Lord Meurig planned?' Vipsanius posed it as a question, knowing that it would save face for the Celwrian chieftain.

For a moment Marcus thought that trouble would flare again as he met the gaze of his opponent. There was no submission in the gaze he met; only a challenge; but it seemed that it was to be met at some time in the future. For now the Roman officers and the leader of the Celwri followed Meurig, Chieftain of the Daethwy, into his hut to sample Celtic hospitality at its best.

Vipsanius sent a messenger back to Segontium. The forage for new horses might take longer than planned due to his 'meeting the needs of a sensitive situation.' He had wanted to press on and reach a farmstead with good horses for sale by nightfall, but it would be considered *geas* to reject the offer of hospitality given. It was an opportunity to meet, with not only one, but two chieftains and was not to be missed. They were wont to drink their barley brew undiluted and might reveal important aspects of their future plans in their efforts to impress him.

Marcus, meanwhile, had the boy transferred to the smith's family hut. He dressed the wound himself and was relieved to see that, because of his swift action, the blistering had been minimal. But half an hour of being immersed in freezing cold water and the shock of the brutal beating had rendered Hedfan, the boy messenger, a shivering and confused wreck.

Dith was well trained to these situations and knew well how to provide his master with the best support. Dith was all brawn and no brain, but had earned his own self-respect at the hands of a caring teacher. If a body needed lifting, washing, holding, feeding, warming, Dith could follow instructions to the letter. In return he had the security of Marcus's constant approval and a sense of self-dignity that his own family were never able to provide for him. His loyalty was never in question. He was prepared to die for this master.

He had been on the scene as soon as he heard the commotion and had run for the saddlebag supplies of unction and linen bandages. Between them they soon had Hedfan more comfortable and he was able to sip a warming brew of hot mead spiced with reviving herbs.

'Ceridwen! I want Ceridwen!' the boy was gasping between gulps. 'I want her. I need her!' His distress mounted.

'Quiet, now, boy. You must rest a while. We must see how you are in the morning. We might be able to take you home in a litter,' Marcus soothed, finishing the neat bandaging of the shoulder by wrapping it securely around the boy's chest.

'Ceridwen would take the burning away. I need her hands on me...to take the burning away.' Much as Hedfan had tried to be brave, the injustice and brutality of his injuries overwhelmed him and the tears now began to roll without control. Then he began to sob. Dith and Marcus held him for a good five minutes until the sobbing eased to an occasional, involuntary, convulsive intake of breath.

'Coll and Owain, my brothers, they breed and train horses. They work a large patch of land to the North, near Mynydd Llwydiarth, The Purple Mountain. They have raised Gwyngariad, this white mare, from a foal. She can be gentle; but she is spirited. She is not yet completely obedient. Coll says she will not behave for Lord Eithig. He is cruel to his animals. He had his last horse hacked to pieces, because it threw him in the mire and lost him some pride. We can't let Gwyngariad go to him until she is completely obedient. He'll end up butchering her in one of his bad moods. She's my favourite creature.'

'Is not Ceridwen your favourite creature?' Marcus soothed as he gently bathed the boy's brow.

'She's my favourite person in the whole world. She's beautiful, and good. She's my elder sister. She's in training to my grandmother as our priestess and healer. She puts her hands on you and you feel better. She gives you a herb drink, or an ointment and a prayer to say to her Goddess and you feel better. I feel better just being near her. Please can I go to her?'

'I've told you. We will see if you are fit to travel in the morning. If your brothers are horse dealers, then we may be able to persuade Vipsanius to take a look at Mynydd Llwydiarth, your Purple Mountain. Try to get some sleep. If you can rest, you will heal all the quicker,' murmured Marcus reassuringly.

'Sir, my name is Hedfan. It is a special name, because I can run fast. They say I have the wings of the wind. What shall I call you?'

'Call me Marcus, and this is my assistant, Dith. He will sleep by you tonight. Goodnight.'

'Thank you, Marcus! You're not too bad as Romans go.'

'And you're not too bad for a brave Celtic warrior.' Marcus smiled a farewell and was gone to join in the hospitality as best he could. He had not meant to make any enemies on this forage, but his sense of unease about Eithig would not leave him.

⌘ ⌘ ⌘

CHAPTER II

⌘

CAE GWYNION
THE HOLY PLACE

The breeze was so gentle that day, a caressing promise of Spring to come. As Ceridwen trod the heather, gathering kindling in her apron, the scent of newness seemed to be released all around her. For the first time in months she threw off her purple woollen cloak and lay down on the mountain, determined to take a well-earned rest from climbing and collecting.

She breathed the heady freshness of the day, a mixture of sea and mountain air with the scent of pine, oak, heather, gorse and fern all around her. This was her favourite spot; a clearing on a rocky outcrop of the mountain, warmed by the noonday Sun and sheltered from the Irish Sea. From this vantage point Ceridwen could truly imagine she was powerful, like the Goddess whose name she bore.

Although only five hundred feet above sea level, the vista from this part of the island was incredible. It was as though she could reach out and touch the sacred summit of Yr Wyddfa, the highest mountain on the mainland, and the Lleyn, stretching like the great body of a dragon, its barbed lashing tail the southernmost tip of the peninsula to the South. The forested valleys below, dotted here and there with a farmstead, or newly planted fields and grazing lands, seemed sleepily accepting of their subservience to the mountains of Eryri.

Ceridwen watched the mist rising from the straits, a brief band of tidal water cutting off the island of Mona from the mainland of Eryri. As she did so, she fancied she saw the spirits of her Druid ancestors, slaughtered by Agricola and his Roman military machine, arising from their watery graves to defend once more the Druid stronghold of Mona.

She knew she must be silent and keep to herself the deep scar of resentment she held for these Roman invaders, whose Gods had proved mightier than all the ancient Druid wisdom and who now took what they needed from the land; their copper, their gold, their corn, their meat, to feed the dwindling garrisons.

Resistance had proved futile and unprofitable. The Romans had much to offer; employment, trade and a way of life, which some of the Celtic chieftains were unashamedly copying. The Celtic nouveau riche had a way of alienating themselves from their local tribes-people by building spacious villas with tiled floors, bathhouses and slaves to take care of the daily upkeep; but there was still a core of stubborn chieftains, too proud to capitulate. They kept their fortresses well manned with warriors; enough to keep the Roman garrison on the mainland at Segontium, near the mouth of the Seiont, on its toes.

Ceridwen found herself tensing, irritated by the thought of her kinsman Eithig, the young, hotheaded chieftain of the Celwri. Lacking the inherent wisdom of his father, he enjoyed playing cat and mouse with the Roman legionaries based along the coastal hill forts. Ceridwen suspected that he would go too far one of these days and stir real trouble for the local tribes-people, who were trying to keep a low profile and get on with the task of feeding their families and nurturing the land.

She had to hand it to her father and brothers. They were past masters at negotiating deals with either side. As long as their trade in mountain ponies and corn did not suffer, they were wont to make a show of sympathising with either side, in an effort to keep the peace.

'No point sulking,' her father Gwilym would say to the younger menfolk. 'We may as well profit from the Romans being here, as kick up a fuss and end with our tribe annihilated.'

She could see them now, working on the tract of land shared by the tribe in the valley below; her brothers Coll and Owain reining in one of their frisky mountain ponies, which would soon be broken in sufficiently to ride; her father, Gwilym, ploughing a long furrow for the spelt wheat, driving old faithful Tergmud in front of him, halting the old ox now and again to realign the furrow ploughed by the wooden ard.

He was breathing heavily now, wiping the sweat from his brow with the back of his hand. Although strong enough for his age, his muscles thickened and taut with a lifetime of physical labour, he was finding the daily toil beginning to take its toll.

The lads would have to manage more of the farming, instead of concentrating on breeding and training their ponies. After all, they kept an expanding slave family to help with the never-ending tasks, which their growing enterprise demanded. They should be able to manage if he were to take more of a supervisory role. He would just make sure of the measure of the first furrow; then leave the rest of the field to the bondsmen. He had to show them there was life in the old dog yet.

Ceridwen smiled with amusement. Even from this distance her father's dogged determination showed in the grim line of his body and sheer effort he was putting into the task. He certainly set an example to the young ones. He seemed to thrive on hard work; yet he sometimes proved to be such an exacting taskmaster that no one felt they could compete to his standard. It was as though he strove to stave off his journey into old age by keeping up such momentum.

As the midday Sun grew hotter, Ceridwen knew that they would head back to Tan Yr Aur, the farmstead with its group of circular huts in an enclosure of blackthorn and wattle. They would sit under the thatched awning of the main hut and be served cold spring-water and mint, barley cakes and honey. Her mother, Marged, would fuss around the men like a clucking hen and they would joke and gossip together, planning what they might do to teach Eithig a sound lesson.

As priestess of the Celwri tribe and guardian of Cae Gwynion, the Holy Place, her grandmother, Old Nanw, kept a keen eye on their antics and gave counsel where she knew the situation could easily get out of hand. But Nanw was getting

13

no younger and gradually Ceridwen, as her grandmother's apprentice, would take over the work of leading the worship at the festival rites, of performing pathworkings and spells, of healings and herb medicine.

At the age of five, Ceridwen had left the farmstead of Tan Yr Aur in the fertile valley below and had become a constant companion to her grandmother, whose hut nestled close to the holy ground at Cae Gwynion on Mynydd Llwydiarth, or Purple Mountain as the rocky outcrop, nestling in a band of birch, oak, ash and rowan, was known.

Life with Old Nanw was so different to the urgency of life on the farmstead. There was still plenty to do at Cae Gwynion, but there were only two mouths to feed. Between planting vegetables and herbs, repairing the leaking thatch and tending the goats, geese and chickens, there was time for chanting and repeating old spells. There was time to use hands in the time-honoured way, time to soothe old grievances, revenge old grudges, foretell the fortunes of the passer-by, tell old history to furtive pilgrims, and most joyously, since the onset of Ceridwen's days of fertility at thirteen, she had been allowed to help with the birthings.

Occasionally Ceridwen was filled with regret that she had left the bustle of the farmstead for the quiet of the hut at Cae Gwynion, but most of the time its sheer peacefulness was food and drink to her. Whereas Marged, her mother, had to be highly organised in the daily running of the farmstead, handing out instructions with the efficiency and authority of a Roman general, Old Nanw would rise, wash and pray in an unhurried fashion and, once they had got the fire stirred and glowing healthily, she and Ceridwen would consult together about the structure of their day.

Today they had risen at dawn and had begun by sweeping the interior of the cottage, laying fresh sand and dried sweet smelling herbs on the rock floor, asking a blessing on their cleansing work from the Goddess. When the work was finished, they had shared a bowl of barley gruel, which had been slowly simmering in a large iron pot slung over the fire since the night before. Then Ceridwen had drawn water from the deep well behind the cottage and put it in the large clay retaining pot by the threshold.

Old Nanw had set off for the farmstead with some remedy for an ague, plaguing one of the bondswomen at Tan Yr Aur; whilst Ceridwen had subdivided what seemed to be a hundred perennial herbs, and bedded them into a new patch of recently dug and composted earth. It was one of those jobs, which should have been done at Samhain in the Autumn to give the roots a good start over Winter, but they had been busy with birthings and an epidemic of rashes and those had had to take priority.

A few days earlier Coll and Owain had been up to turn over the midden, establish a new midden area and dig out a fresh patch for Nanw's precious herbs; for although there was a plentiful crop of useful plants growing wild on Mynydd Llwydiarth, it was much easier to have them to hand in abundance and variety near to the hut.

By noon Ceridwen had become in need of a change of activity and had decided to walk the mountain collecting wood. She had ambled through the Ancient Burial Ground, asking for the strength and wisdom of her predecessors as she wove a path over the mounds of earth covered tombs, where urns bearing the ashes of her people were interred.

She doubted whether she would have the courage to pass alone in this place at dead of night unaccompanied, but in the strong sunlight, bedecked with bright yellow gorse, the serenity of this sacred spot seemed to fill her with its beauty; rising from the earth energy, through her feet, moving through the core of her body and out towards the sky, with its wheeling birds playing on the wind.

She came to the Holy Oak Grove on the breast of the mountain. The budding branches of newly established oaks, struggling to make a statement about forever, swayed courageously in the light breeze. Two hundred years ago it had been the centre of Druid learning, a secret place for learning secrets, a place of dedication to the Gods, a place of worship and healing. Now, although the *commote* used it regularly for festivals, there was a forlorn abandoned feeling to the place that had at one time pulsed with the daily chanting of the Druid novices and their teachers.

After the massacre of the Druids on the Straits of Menai, the Roman invasion of Mona had sought to obliterate any trace of the Ancient Order. The grove of ancient oaks was one of several on the island, which had been levelled in an attempt to eradicate the power centres of the Druids.

The timber was used to rebuild the structure of an old hill fort on the summit of Mynydd Llwydiarth, where a small Roman garrison was installed to watch for Irish raiders invading from the sea, or insurrection of the rural tribes-people from the land below. But Druid thinking could not die. It was too much a part of the farming year. The feasts and festivals continued... the rites...the patterns of healing...the magic...the customs. These could not be killed off as efficiently as people.

As the fear of insurrection had waned and the Celtic and Roman peoples began to live side by side, some even intermarrying, the two cultures rubbed along well enough; finding similarities in their Gods and festivals; tolerating each other for the sake of survival and trade, and occasionally, when needs must, celebrating their feasts together.

There were ways of preserving customs; handing down the old traditions by word of mouth; chanting the old wisdom using runes and rhymes, so that the little ones absorbed their rhythm and melody at the breast and played them as games whilst still children.

Ceridwen had learned her lessons well. She had a love of chant and a mind as sharp as an arrow. Her memory rarely failed her and by four years of age she had been able to join in the festival chants and dancing as though she had learned them in some previous life.

When Nanw had claimed her as her successor, she felt in her bones it was her destiny. To be the hub of the wheel of their tribal society meant empowerment, dedication and hopefully the growth of wisdom accompanied by assured humility.

Ceridwen stretched luxuriously in the warm Spring sunshine. To be young; to be healthy; to be part of all this beauty; to be at one with it all; surely this is why she had been given life; to appreciate her everlasting essence; to nurture it and help others to nurture theirs? She was feeling the responsibility of her station without the heaviness of burden, for she was but nineteen. Reaching out for maturity was an exciting part of life's adventure.

She gazed at the wisps of white cloud spread gently over the blue of the Spring sky. A pair of buzzards was playing on the warm air currents, effortlessly suspended with their great wings outstretched in total trust of being carried higher and higher into the warm sunlight.

'We should trust in the Goddess as these marvellous creatures trust in the winds,' thought Ceridwen. 'When we are at one with all things there is such peace and beauty here on Earth.' She must try to remember the teaching of the Old Religion whenever the resentment and hatred in her heart began to burn...*Hatred never ceases by the arrows of hatred. It shall be conquered only by the darts of love.* She began to chant it and play with the melody until it was carried on the breeze and reached the creatures around her. It was as though the mountain itself was responding to the prayer, yearning for the love and dedication it had witnessed in times gone by.

Ceridwen danced as she chanted so that the lines and rhythm of her body helped the chant to swell and flow. It was a gift of love to her Goddess, the Mother Goddess who gave birth to all that is beautiful. A bramble caught at her leg like a jealous maiden, who had not yet learned to dance. Ceridwen bent to wipe the scratch with her own spittle.

'Yes, even you are beautiful when you give us your flowers and fruits at the end of the Summer.' She was determined that nothing would take this benevolent mood away from her on such an exquisite day. But as always, when one is confident that something will last forever, she was immediately tested.

Was that a glint of sunshine flashing on burnished metal below her? There was movement near to where the spring found its path through the rocks towards the underground source of the well at Cae Gwynion. Could it be a foot soldier from the Roman based hill fort over the mountain ridge behind her? What was he up to...poisoning the stream perhaps, or just intruding?

Ceridwen felt hot anger well up inside her and, dropping the kindling, she hurled herself down the mountain, missing her footing more than once, scratching her bare legs this time on the sharp gorse.

She scrambled to where she had fancied she saw the glinting, wary now in case she should be attacked from the rear, but, whoever it was, was now pushing up through the bracken and heather well above her, wearing, as she had suspected, the helmet of a Roman legionary. Whatever he was doing he had left evidence behind him, for a soft pigskin bag, which had seen better days, lay in the path of the stream.

It was heavy and sodden as she pulled it clear of the water. With difficulty she loosened the drawstring and seeing the contents fell sick to the stomach. 'Ye Gods! Have you Romans no respect for life. Must you always kill what is beautiful! I hate...!' she paused and checked her tirade, which had begun to echo back to her from the other side of the valley. Priestesses in training were supposed to gain control of their emotions and see best how to mend all things.

She steadied her breathing and cleansed her mind with a prayer. Gently she drew each tiny furry body from the bag, each with the tight-shut eyes of the newly born and the relaxed soft limpness of the newly dead. She drew all six kittens into her apron and sat peacefully on a mossy stone, sending their spirits towards the Great Earth Mother. Her own outrage must wait. She must recycle their life force into something equally beautiful.

It was then Ceridwen felt the familiar throbbing in her hands, the call of life force upon life force. One of the kittens was stirring, responding to the great Love Energy flowing from the Earth, through Ceridwen's body and out through her gently positioned hands. A sweet miracle! The joy of being part of such healing was surely a sign from the Goddess that she was doing well with her training, confirmation that this was her true calling.

Instinctively she lifted the tiny vulnerable body nearer to her left breast, where the kitten might hear the beating rhythm of her heart. The stream flowed almost soundlessly over the stones and the breeze died to stillness, as if Nature were holding her breath.

The familiar tingling energy in her cupped hands grew steadily and heat, like that of the warm Sun, began to stir the tiny silken form in her hands. For a moment both kitten and maiden were unified in a great glowing. The kitten sneezed and, taking in a gasp of air, began to breathe regularly and normally.

It nuzzled close to her woollen tunic, and for the first time she was able to appreciate its exquisite tortoiseshell coat, the white star on its breast, its four white 'mittens' and the tiny clinging claws. Gratitude for the life of this beautiful creature welled in her throat and eyes.

⌘ ⌘ ⌘

CHAPTER III

⌘

MYNYDD LLWYDIARTH
PURPLE MOUNTAIN

When Hedfan did not return from his mission the day before, Coll came up to Cae Gwynion from the homestead at Tan Yr Aur to ask advice of Nanw and Ceridwen. They had both been busy preparing the festival clearing for the Spring Rites, when they had heard the strange cry of a buzzard overhead. It warned of danger. They had prepared for it by offerings of sweet herbs and flowers at the Goddess's altar, and chanted a prayer for protection.

'Ceridwen, look into the fire and tell me what you see?' Nanw was handing over more and more responsibility to her granddaughter as her time of transition to the next world drew near.

'I can see Hedfan. His eyes plead with me to hold him in my hands.'

'Hold that picture of him in your mind.' Nanw came behind her and held Ceridwen's hands in a cupped position before her eyes like the shape of an oval window. 'Be like a hollow reed which allows the winds of blessings to flow through it. Do not use your own power, or you will dilute and sully the healing magic. Breathe him a breath of the Goddess. Be a mere link in the chain of good.'

'I can see him more clearly. I can feel a cooling stream flowing between us. He is becoming calm. Poor Hedfan! He has been so terrified. Now he feels protected, reassured. He will not let me take my hands away.'

'Be guided by that strong feeling. Leave your hands there as long as they remain linked to Hedfan,' Nanw advised.

'His demand is becoming weaker. Is he dying, Grandmother?'

'No. Dying is a growing of power, not a waning. He does not need your hands. He is probably in a healing sleep. Let us repeat the rites of protection. I sense he is to the South. We shall direct our energies there.'

When Coll arrived, panting at the threshold of the hut, the two women had a roaring fire within. They had finished their task. It was now in the hands of the Gods. The hut smelled of sweet herb smoke and hot broth. He shared a meal with them around the fire and was reassured that, for the present, Hedfan was safe and that there was no need for him and his kinsmen to ride out on a rescue mission. He was feeling guilty now that he had sent Hedfan with such a message. Eithig's temper was becoming renowned. He should have gone himself.

'Nanw, Grandmother, will Eithig always be elected to be our chieftain? I need to know by what deeds he will succeed or fail and whether I am to be part of his fate?'

'I read revenge in you, Coll. But you must be wise. Our tribe needs young men like you to work and protect us. It would be false wisdom to challenge him and be killed. We all know his great strength in combat. We must wait. One will come who is wiser and stronger than he. For the moment he must serve us as he can, and we must accept it gracefully.'

'He does not serve us like a true king or chieftain. He pays no heed to the advice of the elders. He rules by fear and that goes against all you have taught us about consultation and balanced action.' Coll tore at his bannock as though he would tear out the heart of a man.

'Be at peace, my grandson. Patience will change our fortunes. Offer a prayer to your Goddess that she will give you the wisdom to know when to speak out. Meanwhile re-channel your anger. It could do us a great disservice.' Nanw stirred the fire with her iron tongs and nodded to Ceridwen.

Ceridwen had been able to soothe her brother's quick temper since she was tiny. 'Let me comb your hair Coll and you can tell me your heart.' When she teased out the tangled hair with her wide wooden comb, it was as if the emotion knotted in his chest disappeared and was replaced by clarity of thought and purpose. How could he resist the invitation of his younger sister? She knew more about him than any other, for as yet he had no wife. He shifted round and yielded his head to her lap. He would sleep here until dawn, enjoying a sweet respite from his responsibilities at the farmstead. Owain would see to the horses tonight. As he gave in to overwhelming exhaustion, the glow of the embers and Ceridwen's gentle stroking of his head, he heard her say, 'You know Hedfan is in safe hands. Know it and keep it.' And, as though in response to his trusting, a small, silken kitten came to nestle in the crook of his arm.

Nanw and Ceridwen made their acknowledgement to the rise of the Moon at the threshold of the hut. She was riding silver shod tonight, with clouds driven by the south-westerly winds, now hiding, now revealing, now veiling her beauty.

The two women stood spellbound for a moment and then as the wind caught at their tunics, they shivered and turned to truss up the door. They both shared a moment of silent amusement as they took in the incongruity of Coll's huge frame curled around the tiny trusting ball of fur. Luce was doing well on goat's milk. One of the females was in kid and her first milk seemed to suit the tortoiseshell scamp. They had used a pigskin teat and experimented with different sizings of the hole until they had found a way of suckling the kitten successfully. Only Mwg, Nanw's sedate male cat, seemed disconcerted by the new presence at Cae Gwynion. He chose to ignore her completely and would walk away in jealous disdain, if he caught anyone so much as glancing at her.

He was curled up on Nanw's straw pallet awaiting her attentions; time to share Nanw with no other. He sensed Nanw could forgive him anything as long as he kept her feet warm each night.

Ceridwen watched until Nanw was settled, banked down the fire and wrapped herself in a swathe of new homespun fresh from the looms at Tan Yr Aur. Tomorrow, she knew, would bring a new set of challenges. For the time being she must sleep.

Vipsanius was eager for his horse hunting detail to set out from Dindaethwy. One evening trying to avoid offending the volatile chieftain Eithig and the shrewd probing of Lord Meurig was testing enough. The hidden agenda of the festivities proved to be to create the impression that, without actually breaking Roman law, the countless small tribes of the whole region were united in their feeling for being Ordovicans, with a culture of song, dance and religious fervour to outshine that of any Roman.

They had bemused the Romans by plying them with a local brew, guaranteed to make your head spin within minutes. There had been dancing in whirling circles, and later, as the fires died, there had been mournful tales, sung by young and old, of the great exploits of their forebears: songs sung so soulfully to the accompaniment of a simple hand held harp, tabor and reed pipe, that, even though Vipsanius could not understand much of the ancient Brythonic language, he found himself moved to tears. There was a tight longing in his heart for the home country, the comforting sounds of his own language and the heat of the Sun warming his bones. But, at this moment of vulnerability, he suddenly became his most professional; for he knew he must be on his guard.

He had been relieved to see Marcus enter the main hut and make his way between the carousing mêlée. He had brought two goblets of spring-water. 'Here, drink this. It will help you get your head back a little,' Marcus breathed knowingly.

'How is the boy?'

'Sleeping now and comfortable; but he's eager to get back to the safety of his own homestead. His family has a talent for training horses. Perhaps we can kill two birds with one stone and accompany him home.'

'Do you think it diplomatically wise?'

'Vipsanius, Rome is supposed to rule here. Lord Eithig's behaviour was barbaric and would have been punished if we had been at home.' Marcus was smiling through clenched teeth to give the impression to the company around them that they were sharing a joke.

Vipsanius motioned Marcus to break apart from the group

so that their whisperings might not be overheard. 'I had hoped to feel master here, Marcus, but these tribes learn quickly to play us at our own games. We must tread very carefully.'

'Carefully, agreed. But by token of doing nothing we make a nonsense of our laws. Our Emperors have fallen by abusing their sacred role. We must not be seen to approve of such unjust cruelty. By taking home the child we are showing our disapproval of injustice without openly castigating Lord Eithig. The majority of those tribes-people witnessing his temper yesterday are with us, Vipsanius. They are just too frightened to knock Eithig from that pedestal of his. They are frightened of what his henchmen might get up to.'

'You have a point, Marcus. The majority of the Daethwy tribe would sympathise with the boy; but there is no way they would destroy the trading links with the Celwri by openly disapproving of a chieftain's behaviour. They are more likely to employ the services of a priestess to weave a spell of impotency around him.' Vipsanius sipped at the spring-water. Then, staring at the continuing revelry around them, he came to his decision.

'We are not at home and one does not stir a hornet's nest for the sake of a child. Nor does one challenge the authority of a local chieftain, unless he is undermining the greater authority of Rome. We shall make no formal complaint. We shall go to this 'Tan Yr Aur' they speak of for our horses and take the boy along...That is if he is well enough to travel. This must be censure enough for Eithig.' Vipsanius rose and began to take leave of his host and hostess.

'Thanks to the Gods for our opportune meeting! Thanks to your husbandmen for the excellent food, and thanks to your tribe for the warmth of your welcome. We shall be gone early in the morning to Tan Yr Aur where you say we shall find good horses.'

'Indeed you will find no better steed than those trained by the men of Tan Yr Aur,' replied Lord Meurig, heaving himself to his feet, his portly belly swaying amusingly as he regained his balance. 'Their skills in rearing and riding their horses may be compared to the best you may have in the amphitheatres of Rome.' This was declared with an enthusiasm born of nostalgia for his own youthful, daring feats on horseback, using mountain ponies reared at the hands of Gwilym.

'As Gwilym's son is injured, you will need a scout to take you along the easiest route across the island to the North.' This was the only censure Meurig was going to direct to Lord Eithig. Enough that he should know of Meurig's trust in the family and that, despite Eithig's views to the contrary, he had total confidence in their ability to rear and train the most vital of beasts.

The comments were all but totally lost on him, however; for Eithig was well on his way to a drunken stupor, ogling the tantalising drooping eyelids of Meurig's youngest daughter, who had recently discovered the heady effect she had upon men. She stroked the strings of her harp with enough intensity to set the most cool-headed male on fire.

'We shall depart at sunrise and aid Hedfan back to his family, if he is well enough to travel.' With a nod of respect to the chieftains and their attendants, Vipsanius made his exit to his own tent, where he would sleep, well guarded by his own men.

Marcus followed him out, but returned to the smith's hut to keep an eye on Hedfan and allow Dith some relaxation. They too would take it in turns to keep watch, for they were not naive enough to presume that outward appearances of friendliness meant safety.

The following morn dawned crisp and cold, with a hint of ground frost and shafts of early morning light breaking under the clouds to reveal the bulk of the mainland rising from the cool tides of the Straits. The Romans did not pause to light their own breakfast fires as usual, but contented themselves with a quick splash of water from the beach and a piece of bread from the previous day's rations. The tents were packed on the horses and a cart hired to transport Hedfan and some goods, which the Daethwy wished to trade with the Celwri.

Marcus knew that Hedfan would find lying in the cart intolerable; so he had rigged up a hammock, which could swing freely between the top and rear of the cart. In that way the jostling on the rough tracks could be minimised and if the path became too narrow for the cart, then it could be left and the hammock made into a litter.

Hedfan was stiff and sore this morning and the burn on his shoulder smarted and throbbed alternately; but Dith had done a good job on cushioning it with sheep's fleece between the linen bandages and Hedfan felt he must grin and bear the pain of the journey, if only to see his family all the sooner. It was made more tolerable by Twm, the Daethwy scout and messenger. He was only two years older than Hedfan and rode his pony alongside the cart, giving directions from a position behind the spearhead of the party. He had so many amusing tales to tell about skirmishes between the tribespeople, about dodging the Roman tax system, smuggling booty from one coast to another. All was done with an excessive amount of embellishment, but succeeded in whiling away the journey time for Hedfan and gave him something other than his pain to concentrate upon.

Coll helped the women with their morning duties. He axed some wood for the fire and laid it under the awning for future use. He skinned a hare and set it to roast over the spit. They would take it as an offering to the homestead, when they had finished the daily tasks here at Cae Gwynion. There were goats to be milked and tethered, herbs to be crushed and jarred, and warm clothes to be put on for the short journey down into the valley.

Both Nanw and Ceridwen fastened jars of herbs and ointments to their belts at intervals, so that the pots would not crack against each other; something for Gwilym's aching joints, something to soothe a babe in colic, a potion for amorous doings and an expectorant for the usual marshland cough.

Ceridwen made a sling for Luce, the tortoiseshell kitten, for as yet she was too young to leave to her own devices. She eased her into it with less care than she intended. She was scratched and bitten in return.

Nanw took a stout ash walking stick and Coll slung the partially cooked hare, still on its roasting stick, over the back of his dappled grey mare. The three set off for Tan Yr Aur; Coll leading his pony, confident that the restlessness of the horses there and the cries of the ravens in nearby trees augured that there would soon be visitors with news of Hedfan.

⌘ ⌘ ⌘

CHAPTER IV

⌘

THE ENEMY WITHIN

Marged had slept fitfully and pestered the men to go out looking for Hedfan, but it would seem they had more faith in Nanw and Ceridwen than she and, when a spiral of blue smoke had come from the Nanw's augural fire in the festival clearing, they had known he was safe and that they must wait for news.

Around noon they were rewarded for their patience by hearing the cries of young Twm of the Daethwy, galloping at top speed on his bay pony. Vipsanius had wisely sent him ahead to warn of their arrival, so that it would not alarm the farmsteaders. Twm was then to ride ahead to the headland fort on Mynydd Llwydiarth, where the detail was to make camp that evening. There was relief all round that Hedfan was alive and would mend, and the womenfolk rushed around preparing an extra soft bed and some nourishing broth.

Twm was given a gift of a new pigskin water bag for his efforts and enjoyed his moment of glory being spoiled and cosseted by the girls. He ate and drank and bade farewell before there was even a sign of the Romans' arrival. Mixed with concern for Hedfan was a general excitement. The Romans soldiers were coming to trade. Marged was busy giving orders for extra food to be provided and for people to bring out their surplus wares.

Ceridwen found herself burning with resentment. She would have to thank Romans for taking care of her brother. There was the added indignity that their own chieftain had inflicted the injury upon Hedfan and slighted their community.

'How can people be so forgetful of our history and trade with these invaders? Look at our family and our bondsmen, Grandmother. They are all scurrying around like ants, preparing to welcome the very people who tried to annihilate our Druid culture, to kill the very heart of our nation.'

'Ceridwen, that was two hundred years ago! It is important for you to learn our history and keep it alive in the minds of our people, but you must also apply spiritual law to this. Hatred can only breed hatred. In some ways, the Romans have helped us to maintain order. Our commotes have not pillaged each other's territory for almost a generation. We have not had all-out warfare between our tribes since before you were born. We need to band together and save our strength for troubles ahead. There have been reports of Irish raiders to the South. They may turn their attention to our small island.

'Coll and Owain have been disturbing your serenity,' Nanw continued. 'They are as masterful at playing their parts of being friendly with the Romans, as they are at disguising their hatred for their own chieftain. But do not let their eyes be your eyes. See with your own.' Old Nanw had finished untying the medicine pots from her belt and had stacked them in Marged's chest behind the hanging blanket, which gave her and Gwilym some measure of privacy in the roundhouse. She accepted Ceridwen's offering of broth and sat for a few moments on the lid of the chest whilst Ceridwen knelt by the centre fire soothing Luce.

'I know what hatred can do. I counsel Coll and Owain against it, when it burns in me. It seems that I am as bad in my duplicity as I am irritated by it in others,' she sighed, trying to make sense of the conflicting emotions by smoothing the fur of the young animal on her lap.

'You are on the path of serenity if you can recognise the source of your own troubling, my youngling. Ask the Goddess. She will give you the opportunity to conquer your prejudice, for that is the disease of your heart.'

'But with these thoughts burning in me, how can I be worthy to become priestess of my people?' Ceridwen protested.

'The Goddess does not ask us to be anything other than human when we serve Her. All she asks is that we recognise the promptings of our lower nature and encourage our higher nature to take the lead. It is how we grow. The thorn in your flesh will be turned into your salve in due course, for it will endow you with the capacity to unfold and to recognise the flaw in others. As you learn the remedy, so you shall lead others, who are ready to learn the same lesson and who tread a similar path.'

'But what of now, when screams of anger torture my throat and I dare not voice my thoughts for fear of the damage they will wreak?'

'Cry your anger to the howling wind. Spit the burning thoughts into the flame of the fire. Drown the monster inside you with Holy water from the spring. Replace the space you create with thoughts that you can live with in harmony; thoughts which you choose to dwell in you. You must master your thoughts and not allow them to be master of you, for that is the worst form of slavery.'

The noise of riders arriving and shouts of welcome made both women rise to their feet. But despite Nanw's advice, Ceridwen found herself immediately bristling at the sight of the Roman detail.

'It seems as though I have the opportunity to use your counsel immediately. I shall fill my mind with only thoughts of Hedfan.' Ceridwen passed the sleeping bundle of Luce into the eager waiting hands of her young niece, Rhonwen. Then she smoothed down her tunic and ran outside into the rough clearing, where Gwilym, Coll and Owain were gently transferring Hedfan from the hammock on the cart to the main roundhouse. Old Nanw now took her place to welcome him over the threshold, her arms outstretched in blessing.

'Be careful! Don't touch that shoulder!' Marged fussed. But it was impossible to do the transition from their arms to the freshly made up pallet bed without making him wince with pain. Ceridwen took up a position supporting his head on her knees and Nanw took up her position at his feet, but they did not commence the peacefulness of their hand healing work until he had drunk his fill of the goblet of water held out to him by Marged.

He was too weary to tell the tale of yesterday's woe. Vipsanius did it for him, telling it factually without embellishment; for it needed none to make clear the stark cruelty of their chieftain.

'No doubt you will choose another to lead you at your next elections?' Vipsanius's conclusion hung in the air like a condemnation of their weakness. They shifted uncomfortably from foot to foot and looked to Gwilym to be their spokesman.

He surprised them all by saying, 'There are many qualities to be looked for in a leader. No one person can hope to display all. In Lord Eithig we have a fearless man of combat. His courage and strength brook no criticism. We know of no other who would match him in the field. But at times of peace we turn our backs on our warriors and prefer wise and diplomatic eldership. Before we dispense with him, we must be able to replace him with equal or better, and I know of no such person.'

'The Goddess will send us a new leader, of that I am sure. Who knows, he may be amongst us now.' Nanw was conscious for a fleeting moment of allowing her gaze to rest upon Marcus, but she knew it to be unwise and threw her gaze around the hut to encompass them all.

'We have discharged our duty towards your son, Sir. May we now come to the main purpose for our visit to Mona? We have been instructed to buy fifty new horses.'

Vipsanius left with the menfolk and a string of curious children to inspect the contents of the blackthorn corral and discuss trading terms. Only Marcus remained with Dith to tell the women how he had already treated Hedfan and to encourage them to keep on with the same regime. They nodded silent assent, for they had begun their work with their healing hands and had no wish to disturb the energy they had created.

'Thank you, Sir! You have done well for Hedfan,' Nanw whispered sincerely as a signal of dismissal; but for a moment Marcus was completely unable to move. His eyes were riveted to Ceridwen's hands. They were Leona's hands; the same long, tapering fingers; the same oval nails; the same caressing sensitive fingertips. He swallowed and she raised her gaze to his as she sensed his direction of focus.

It was not Leona's, but a face just as beautiful in its own right. Her eyes were a deep, grey blue, questioning and absorbing all things, with a thirst for life learning that he had only seen in small children; yet it was not an innocent gaze, which she cast upon him. It guarded its own secrets. Ceridwen's hair, caught in a single braid down her back, shone with golden lights. It was neither blonde, nor red, nor brown, but reminded him of burnished copper; tendrils of untamable curl nestling against her unusually flushed cheek. He was tempted to stroke back the hair, feel the silk of her skin against his hand, but knew he dare not. For two years there had been no awareness of beauty in his life. He thanked the Gods that he had wakened again, even though beauty, like grief, had her own pain.

'I will leave you in peace, ladies. However, we are to be housed for several days at the fort and, if I may be of any further service to you, please do not hesitate to ask.' Marcus turned on his heel to leave them, followed by Dith; but as they went Old Nanw became certain their paths would cross on the morrow.

Ceridwen had risen before dawn. She was restless and eager to finish with her morning tasks at Cae Gwynion, so that she could go down to Tan Yr Aur to see Hedfan again. Old Nanw stirred stiffly, the cold setting into her.

'Let me get the fire going before you rise. Stay under the blankets until the whole room is warmed and I can bring you a warm drink,' Ceridwen soothed, not wanting to disturb her grandmother before her usual rising time. Nanw smiled gratefully and let Ceridwen take over. Soon she would be free of this stiff aching baggage she carried around with her. She felt her time of calling was near. Then Ceridwen would have to manage without her constant supervision.

The girl had such a lovely presence. She carried serenity with her. Her movements were graceful, yet unhurriedly efficient. Her healing arts had yet to be extended, but she could manage to assist and prescribe for most of the common ailments. She had the sight, which would develop naturally with use and she had the touch, which was stronger than Nanw's already and renowned in the *commote* for its soothing and healing power.

Ceridwen seemed to have the innate knack of taking the heat out of quarrelsome moments, of calming emotions to a more tolerant and tolerable level. Nanw could not help but feel that Ceridwen would make a better chieftain than they had, but she would not be able to spread her energies that far.

If Ceridwen were to couple with someone who would make a good chieftain, would that be a better alternative? Nanw left the thought in the hands of the Gods for them to sort and manage and drifted into a state of comfortable dozing.

The Spring Rites would be upon them in two days. The festival clearing was almost ready, but Ceridwen needed to gather Spring flowers and herbs for the incense fire. It seemed that by doing these simple duties she could blot out the turmoil in her mind and soul. She had promised Nanw that she would try hard to dispel the hatred, which often overwhelmed her when in the company of Romans.

She had thought that this particular spiritual battle was half way to being won, when she found a thought of gratefulness creeping into her mind at finding Hedfan had been so well cared for; but she hated herself for that gratefulness. Even worse, she began to suspect Nanw of casting some sort of spell upon her; a spell over which she had no control; for why else would she feel this great longing to see the Roman doctor again? Why else should she be harbouring thoughts so alien to her tribal loyalty? She bent to gather the first violets into her basket.

'Your task is a sweet one.'

At the sound of his gentle, rich voice she froze. For a moment she wondered if her longing had conjured Marcus's voice in her head, but as she turned, he stood gazing at her, smiling, drinking in the pleasure of her presence. His teeth showed white against the pale olive of his clean-shaven cheeks, his neat clipped beard outlining the strength of his jaw. His lips were neither too tight, nor too full to take sincerity away from his smile. His deep brown eyes twinkled secretively under the shadow of his full, dark brows and head of natural waves. She did not speak, but stood still in momentary confusion.

'I thought I would take the opportunity of learning something about your local medicines. Perhaps you could show me what you grow and how you make up some of your potions?' Marcus was eyeing her with kindly amusement, misreading her confusion as shyness.

'I think not, Sir. My grandmother guards the secrets of her healing arts and entrusts them to no one but myself. The medicines will be handed down to the next generation of priestesses, through me.' Ceridwen had gained her composure by this time and had adopted a peremptory tone.

'I understand your reasons for guarding your secrets well; for if they were to fall into the wrong hands they could kill as well as heal. Many of the herbs you deal with are poisonous when taken in ill-advised doses. However, I am a doctor and bound by my oath to Mithras to treasure life. Perhaps I could exchange some knowledge with you, so that the good we do may expand?'

'You must speak with my grandmother, then.' It was a dismissal and she carried on gathering, turning her back to him. But she had dropped a bunch of wild violets at her feet. Marcus bent to retrieve them.

'Ceridwen,' he murmured.

No one had spoken her name like that before. It was reverent, as though he spoke of something precious. Momentarily disarmed, she faced him, meeting his eyes. They bathed for a fleeting moment in a light of pure knowing, their souls recognising in the other a destiny of sorts.

'Thank you.' Ceridwen stretched out her hand to take the flowers. Marcus had to resist the overwhelming compulsion to wind them into her hair, hold the beautiful oval of her face in his hands and kiss her disdain away. But he knew that nothing could immediately wipe away the barrier she was erecting between them. He would have to tread carefully or, like a nervous wild mare, she would be lost to him forever.

'I will finish my task here and be down to Cae Gwynion presently. My grandmother will have risen by now and I'm sure she will be glad to receive you.'

'I will be gone, then,' he said.

She heard the reluctance in Marcus's voice, but dare not face him again before she had completely composed herself. He began walking down towards the hut, but could not help stealing a look behind him to watch her at her work. She moved with such effortless grace. Then she seemed to snatch angrily at the tendrils of green. She must have been really offended that he had asked to learn of her work. Perhaps the old priestess would react in a similar fashion.

Nanw was washed and dressed, busy already, tending the cauldron of broth over the fire. She welcomed him with her wrinkled smile, her eyes shining brightly with memories. She recognised the forces, which drew Marcus and Ceridwen together, even if they themselves did not yet recognise fully the power that had them in its grip. The magnetism which she saw drawing them together was no spell of hers, but one of the Goddess's.

It would be a courtship fraught with tensions - emotional tensions of culture and loyalties. But would their personalities be able to withstand their testing? Would the attraction wane when the circumstances proved hard? This she did not know, but harboured a hope that the dying prophecy of her husband, Cadoc, would be fulfilled: *When the noble bloods of Rome and Druid mingle, as our rowans intertwine, then peace and honour will come with us to dine.*

Marcus stood on the threshold. He did not have the height of Coll or Owain, but he was tall enough to be imposing with his muscular frame and shock of wavy, dark hair. The short leather tunic he wore exposed part of his lower thigh, his shins and sandalled feet. He had washed and smelled fresh and although his hands were roughened with work, his nails had been cleaned. Something to commend him, thought Nanw. She motioned him to come and sit by her, enjoying his nearness as it reminded her of another time, another man.

They talked easily of their healing work and Marcus found her in no way secretive about the contents of the potions. It was the amounts she seemed vague about until she showed him the set of copper measuring pots, which had been handed down from one generation to another for many hundreds of years. Since he had no equivalent measuring devices, he understood why she was reluctant to share the knowledge, even though he was her Roman counterpart. Old Nanw agreed to share some information on proportions, however, and they had just begun to make a puree with honey and comfrey when Ceridwen returned.

She gave a wry smile as she watched their two heads bent together in concentration. Old Nanw had such patience with the young. Perhaps Ceridwen might develop it with age. She hoped so, but no doubt this Roman had wheedled his way into Nanw's good commendation by showing interest in the intricacies of her medicine skills. If he thought that, by such a show, he was going to achieve the same with her, he was mistaken.

Ceridwen set about feeding Luce. The pigskin bladder and teat had to be filled with fresh goat's milk, tied securely to prevent leaking and fed to her patiently. As soon as Luce smelled the milk, she stirred from her snuggling under some blankets and stretched her limbs, before shaking eagerly and precariously waddling across to where her mistress was holding the teat. She climbed upon Ceridwen's knee and guzzled gratefully.

Marcus, busying himself with putting more ash logs upon the fire, watched her from the corner of his eye. Her tenderness with the young animal reminded him so much of Leona's mothering. It called forth in him a great surge of involuntary protectiveness.

'You have a way with animals,' he said with an attempt at a winning smile.

Ceridwen wanted to say starchily, 'You have a way with women,' but stopped herself in time. Instead she said. 'They have come to me since I was a child. Even the wild creatures when they are in pain do not reject the love of a human hand. But I cannot say I enjoy the cattle killings before the Winter. I am obliged as priestess to calm each beast before it is swiftly killed for meat. It is a duty deemed necessary, for I give blessing and thanks for the life of the animal and they say it makes the meat sweeter, but I would rather stomach a birth than such a sacrifice.'

'The unpleasant duties of our professions are balanced a great deal by the good we can achieve. I shall sample your meat tonight, for my men have been invited to a fest at Tan Yr Aur. We finish our horse dealing this eve and return to the fort at Segontium the morrow.'

Ceridwen was searching for some excuse to avoid another encounter with the Roman. She found that in his presence her usual poise and sharp wit seemed to give way to what she could only describe as a form of imbecility. She became tongue tied and nervous in trying to cover her inner turmoil and anger. She did not want to spoil the trading opportunities for her *commote* by giving vent to her personal resentment; nor did she wish to reveal the overwhelming desire she had to be near him, to hear his voice, to touch him with as much familiarity as she did her animals.

It was Nanw who responded by saying, 'It will be an honour for our tribe to host a fest for you this evening. The sale of the horses will stand us in good stead for the coming year. We shall both be there to enjoy the festivities and bless the transaction. But, before you leave, come here early in the morning and you shall have some of the healing plants and seeds fresh from our medicinal plot.'

'Segontium will grow them with fond memories.' Marcus knelt and gently fondled the kitten now curled peacefully in Ceridwen's lap. He lifted his gaze to hers and found himself staring into her lovely eyes. For a moment he thought he saw a glimmer of longing, but it swiftly shifted to a hard insolent stare. He stood up and took his leave uncomfortably, copying their custom of touching the forehead with both hands and then offering a blessing to them both as he said, 'The Gods be with you.'

There seemed a strange emptiness in the hut once he had left and a silence, which hung between the old woman and the young for a long time before Nanw said, 'Black the bread becomes when left too long by the fire.'

'What spell is this that you weave on me, *Nain*? I cannot understand why the Goddess would give me such an enchantment to improve my character. It is too uncomfortable by nature to be of Her doing?'

'The discomfort comes from your inner battle, not from the test itself. I have cast no spell, except to hope that you may find one to love you as your grandfather once loved me. I see a very strong physical attraction between you and the Roman surgeon, but only time and your response to circumstance will tell if you will grow together in mind and spirit.'

A denial began to thread its way in a serpentine way along Ceridwen's throat, but she knew that Nanw would recognise the lie; so her response was to kill it and take a new tack.

'How did you and *Taid* grow in mind and spirit?'

Nanw had many tales to tell about Cadoc, her husband. Most of them illustrated his wit, or his wisdom, but so far she had revealed little about their relationship. Ceridwen was intrigued.

'At first we found our relationship was extremely physical. The instinct to procreate was uppermost in our minds, but we also had much in common. We loved sitting by the fire and talking of the purpose of life and how we could make things better for the *commote*. Sometimes when we made love it felt as though our life essence was mingling instead of our being two separate people. Then we found that, as we grew to know each other's minds, we could often be with each other for long periods and know the other's feelings and thoughts. When he died I thought I would break in two, but I find we still talk and think together. Occasionally, when the conditions are auspicious, our spirits mingle and unify fleetingly. The sexual attraction, which drew us together in the first place, served its purpose very well, but we now have an intercourse, which seems to transcend this world. It seems that not all souls have such blessing in this life. My desire is that you shall find such a soul mate.'

'You cannot think that the Roman may be he?' gasped Ceridwen incredulously. 'I hate Rome. I hate Romans and all they stand for! How could I find a soul mate amongst those I despise?'

'How do we heal a gaping wound? By drawing both sides together, that their proximity may unite them. I am human. I am fallible. Perhaps I am mistaken to feel the possibility of your union; but until the bloods of noble Celt and Roman are mingled, we are destined to remain suspicious enemies. There are many who are issue of union between Celt and Roman, but the relationships of the parents are tenuous, perhaps between slave and master. There have been few born within the security of true marriage. Do not reject this opportunity to weld our two peoples together. But neither do it from a sense of duty, if your heart be not in it.'

'You are talking as though you are sure that Marcus will want to take me for his wife, when we have met so briefly.' Ceridwen was aware that it was the first time she had spoken his name and she surprised herself that it did not feel like venom in her mouth. 'Even were I to come to like him, I cannot see that our lives could run together; for I must stay with my people and he must serve his legion.'

'Perhaps the Gods are wiser than us in unfolding our destiny. I'm sure that if you lay the problem at the feet of our Goddess and he should take his yearning to the altar of his God, then between them they will work out a feasible path for you both,' Old Nanw laughed, shaking her head at the mistrust of the younger generation. 'Come, we have work to do outside.' And with that she disappeared to the vegetable garden to focus on something entirely practical.

⌘ ⌘ ⌘

CHAPTER V

⌘

THE FEST

Marged and Gwilym had been busy with the other homestead families making preparations for the fest since sunrise. There were fires in the five small reed-thatched roundhouses to tend, where cauldrons of broth with vegetables, barley and the chopped remains of last Winter's salt beef had been set to boil and small fowl would be roasted.

There was a huge spit fire, hung over with a wooden awning to keep off the rain in the central clearing, where a lamb, which had fallen and broken its neck the previous day, was to be roasted and where, alas, the two fattest of Hen Hygar's piglets were to meet a sizzling fate on the same turnspit. Side by side the piglets and the lamb would be turned gently by one of the boys, until every mouth in the settlement would be watering in anticipation.

Gwilym was busy supervising the rescuing of the mead barrels from the cold pit. A good deal, such as the sale of fifty horses, must be sealed with the best food and drink they had to offer.

There were five families altogether living within the confines of the Tan Yr Aur blackthorn barricade, more useful for keeping children and animals in than enemies out. Marged and Gwilym were the elders in the community and occupied the largest roundhouse along with Owain, Coll and Hedfan.

Their eldest daughter Ness, with her husband Madog, lived in the second hut along with Rhodri, Rhonwen, Daf and Rhys, their brood of four, the fifth showing good evidence that it was on the way.

They had originally farmed with Madog's father to the West, but raiders from the sea had murdered him, along with his workers in the fields, and fired the farmstead.

Madog's mother and sister, Olwenna and Angharad, had fled with them to the farmstead at Tan Yr Aur; pooling what little resources they had left with Marged and Gwilym. They occupied the third hut along with their great weaving looms.

The bonds people consisted now of two families, who thought of themselves more as farmsteaders and members of the wider *commote* rather than slaves. True, their ancestors had been enslaved from the remains of a Scots raiding party, but they had intermarried with other tribespeople and whilst there was a secure living on the farmstead and everything was done for the common good, what was the point of 'escaping' to a homeland, which offered less comfort?

Gwilym's family had originally settled in the valley below Purple Mountain, glad of the natural springs flowing into the lake on the breast of its rocky outcrops and the river, which wound its way through the marshland to the cleared forest belt. Here was a soil to till with reward for the working. Here was wood for fuel and timber, limestone for rock walls and rich fertile soil, made by the leaf fall of hundreds of years of ash, birch and oak. Here it was good to raise grain and goat and progeny.

Despite the shackle of the Roman taxes, they profited and branched out into raising horses on the rich pasture they could provide.

Coll and Owain had been taught all they knew about horse rearing from Cadalgan, who once boasted that he had been thrall to a master of horse from the legion at Deva. He had been a bondsman at Tan Yr Aur for almost thirty years and had had almost sole charge of the two young men as they grew. On his deathbed they had promised him that they would continue his work. Indeed the old man would have been more than proud to see the outcome of his years of tutoring.

Coll, the younger of the two brothers by six years, was full of energy and a wild impetuosity, which frequently got him into trouble. However, it was his wide engaging grin, as broad as his shoulders, which more often than not redeemed him from censure. He had a special way with the ladies and found the twinkling of an eye could soften the face of old and young alike, whenever he overstepped the mark.

The horses adored him. Not for him the quiet, placid beasts who were dependable as a rock like Owain; but a high spirited mount, which responded to the clamour of their mock battles and chariot races with the same eager addiction to competition, that thrilled the veins of the master who rode them.

Today was an opportunity to show all they had been taught. They had planned a spectacle, which the Romans would not forget in a hurry, a spectacle, which would show Celtic superiority in some quarter at least.

As soon as the party of legionaries arrived, as agreed, an hour before sunset, they would be garlanded and welcomed by the children with a warming home brew. Then they would be led to the bank outside the farmstead hedging, overlooking a flat stretch of road, which eventually wound its way Eastwards to the port of Cerrig y Gwyddyl two leagues away.

Coll and Owain had organised chariot races, designed not only to show off the sturdy spirit of their horses, but to give the young men an opportunity to display a whole range of daring tricks, accomplished from the platforms of the moving chariots and onto the backs of their galloping steeds. Madog and Coll were to stage a mock combat on horseback and there would be a challenge of a race with the Roman visitors. Coll held no uncertainty about the identity of the more superior horsemen and was laughing confidently with his companions, whilst Marged panicked about there being enough food to go round.

Ceridwen's first task on arrival had been to calm her mother and reassure her that everyone was playing their part to the full; then she must find Hedfan and dress his wounds if need be.

She found him in Olwenna and Angharad's hut, playing aimlessly with a spindle and whorling the wool into knots around his hands. He did not look up as she entered; but knowing it was her said dejectedly, 'I'm not coming to the fest. I have been deprived of honouring my tribe. I cannot ride in the races with wounds so new.'

'You have honoured your tribe by bearing your wounds bravely and by bringing us this trade. If it had not been for you the legionaries might have taken their trade elsewhere. It would be good to have you there when we seal the bargain.' Ceridwen was hoping a little persuasion would work, but seeing it had little effect on Hedfan's present despondency she decided to try a new tack.

'I have secret knowledge for you to cheer your heart, but promise you will not share it, or it may not come true.'

'I promise! I promise! Come, Ceridwen. Do not keep this secret from me. Tell me before I burst!'

'Well, my miserable, little brother looks as though he might come to the fest after all,' smiled Ceridwen at his predictable change in demeanour.

'I shall, if only you will tell me the secret.'

'Very well; when I prayed to our Goddess this morning it came to my mind that you would one day be master of Gwyngariad and that you and she would be always together. Do not ask how this shall come to be, for I was not given privy to it. Tell no soul of this delight and it shall come to pass.'

'Master of Gwyngariad! That means Eithig shall not have her. How shall that be?'

'I have told you, pestling; I know not how she shall become yours. But I have seen it for sure. I have seen you riding her nobly as a man. Now make yourself a comfortable nest on Olwenna's pallet and I shall salve your wound.'

Marcus walked down from the hill fort before the appointed hour of the fest, on the pretext that he wanted to inquire after the health of Hedfan. There was some truth in that motive. He felt close to the boy, a youngling, who had yet to have his ideals and sense of justice and honour beaten out of him by the vicissitudes of life. He found himself questioning whether hope had completely gone from his own life. Several days earlier he would have said 'aye' to that, but the boy and his sister had so much energy and hope themselves that it spilled over to affect all those with whom they came into contact.

As he kicked at a moss covered stone by the side of the stream he was following, he began to admit to himself that, if he left Purple Mountain the following day, it would be with a heavy heart. Even if he were to woo this young priestess and win her longing to be his wife, how could he deprive these people of their priestess and healer? There would be no time to train another in her stead, for Old Nanw had spent many years in passing on her skills and knowledge.

He himself had fifteen years to serve before his present army contract gave him choice of career in another direction. A man who went back on his pledge was not an honourable one. Army surgeons were in short supply. Oh yes; there were plenty of willing butchers, but few with Marcus's training and medicine skills. If he abandoned the legion for a Celtic priestess he could be prosecuted; would lose all respect from his men; maybe even his own self-respect. Perhaps this love was like a fever and it would soon pass?

Tan Yr Aur itself was in a fever of preparation when he arrived. Marged and her women were carrying heavy cooking pots between them into the largest roundhouse, along with great baskets of freshly baked bannocks. Rhodri was busy basting the lamb and piglets on the central turnspit and the other children were helping the older men to roll and set up the barrels of mead at the threshold. Olwenna and Nanw, too frail to manage the heavy carrying of pots and baskets, were busy making garlands of ivy and violets to bedeck the expected visitors.

They welcomed him with a polite blessing and carried on with their preparations. Gwilym was struggling to open one of the sealed barrels and Marcus broke in to help him. He was grateful, and, wiping the sweat from his brow with his forearm, grinned a grizzled bearded acknowledgement. They shared the first ladleful of mead and agreed that it was very good indeed. Gwilym had his suspicions about the friendliness of this Roman. He could not quite put his finger on it, but he felt that it was more than a bond of protectiveness towards Hedfan, which bound them together momentarily.

The Roman asked where he might find Hedfan. Gwilym watched as he walked across the dried out mud of the clearing, past Rhodri and the roasting spit to Olwenna's threshold. Ceridwen emerged and met Marcus in the open. Gwilym watched the two young people as they engaged in polite conversation and knew then the reason for the link between himself and Marcus.

Both men loved this woman with a surge of unspoken passion: Gwilym with the proud passion of a father, who had watched a great beauty blossom and unfold before his eyes; who had played laughingly with his little girl, now this grown woman. He had nurtured her with encouragement and fondness, loyalty and stability. He felt a great pride in her, as though he and not the Gods had had a hand in her creation. And Marcus; newly enamoured by her grace, her beauty, her intelligence, no doubt had an ache in his loins, which would not be assuaged until he had bedded her. His was a different type of love.

Gwilym was conscious for a moment of a dart of jealousy; and then he remembered the madness in him when he had first courted Marged and he forgave Marcus and mentally thanked him for arousing old memories that had once given beauty to his life. It had felt so good to be young.

No time for nostalgia now. Vipsanius and his men were arriving on foot in a flurry of newly burnished helmets, their cloaks flapping around them in a chill wind, which had started from the sea. Out of courtesy they left their long swords at the gate of the enclosure, making a coronet of shining steel and colourful hilts. The forges at Deva had long since taken to fashioning a longer Celtic type of sword for general issue, rather than the usual short broadsword, which had won Caesar his victories; for the battles in these isles demanded a longer reach.

Gwilym stood in the central clearing with Marged at his side and greeted the contingent, as the children came wide-eyed and apprehensive, carrying woven trays of goblets full of hot spiced mead for their guests and armfuls of sweet smelling greenery.

Ceridwen stood apart from the main throng, observing how her kinsmen were seemingly offering hospitality to the invaders with a genuine generosity of heart. To her it did not seem like wise peace keeping. It tore at her like a betrayal. How could they forgive the wholesale slaughter of their leaders only two centuries ago? Was their race memory so short? Did it not hurt to have this so called 'super race' trample over their lands, plunder their resources and change their way of life?

The soldiers received the garlands with a great show of appreciation, responding to the giggling attentions of the children with paternal smiles; one or two of them being painfully reminded of the innocent faces of their own little ones on far off shores. Ceridwen felt herself soften a little as she recognised that these pawns in the game of the Roman military machine could also ache with human longing.

At last Gwilym requested they move to an earthwork outside the enclosure, where they would have full view of the display of horsemanship put on by the younger Celwri men.

Ceridwen felt a light tap on her shoulder.

'Are you thinking that Hedfan might be well enough to enjoy this treat? Should Dith and I help him to the audience?' Marcus queried, knowing that Ceridwen felt in charge of her brother's safeguarding. Ceridwen found herself trying to fulfil her promise to Nanw, but she was filled with a sense of confusing shame at enjoying his nearness and could not meet his gaze as she answered, 'Thank you. I shall fetch some blankets that he may sit on the bank, if you would both assist him.'

They made Hedfan as comfortable as possible. He hugged to himself the secret Ceridwen had shared with him and became determined to blot out from his mind the pain of injustice and the burning discomfort of the past two days. He would rejoice in the triumphs of his tribesmen. The spectacle disappointed no one.

It was begun by the Celwri war chant, accompanied by a warning beating of drums.

'Brave warriors,
Sons of the Sky,
Ancestors returned
Again and again
From death into life,
Champion our cause.
Claim Freedom for our race.
Redeem our land.
When enemy blood
Flows down from the hills,
Then victory is ours!'

It began as a quiet murmuring, but was repeated over and over again by the assembled tribes-people, until it became a swelling goad to action.

The two 'enemy' groups faced each other at either end of the section of straight road. Coll, heading the warriors of Lug, or Light, and Madog leading the warriors of Darkness, had borrowed the wooden ceremonial masks for the Spring Rites and sported them with great solemnity.

The challenge was heralded by a battle cry from Cullen, one of the bondsmen. It took all his strength to make the traditional blast on the ceremonial horn. Its haunting note echoed along the greenness of the valley, stirring spine-chilling memories of forgotten bloodlettings.

Vipsanius and his men shifted uncomfortably, suspecting for a moment that this might be something other than entertainment. Their doubts were soon laid to rest as Coll and Madog railed and baited each other, charging through the dust of the pummelled road, the wheels of their chariots rumbling, the beating of their horses hooves pounding in the ears of the spectators.

The two assailants skirted each other, narrowly avoiding a head on collision. They swung the horses around to face each other yet again; but, instead of dismounting in order to engage combat, competed in a breathtaking show of daring and balance, moving from chariot to horseback.

Standing precariously on the back of his moving horse, the gold of his mask and ribbons of his costume streaming behind him, Coll stirred the audience into a frenzy of cheering. He represented the coming of the Sun to the land. He must win the battle against Darkness, or the Earth was doomed and all existence void.

Marcus stole a look at the two faces beside him. The boy Hedfan was completely transfixed, oblivious to his pain, transported by the excitement of the spectacle. Ceridwen, so proud of her brother and his horsemanship, had forgotten her serene composure and was yelling encouragement with the total abandon of a child. It brought a wry smile to Marcus's face. So there was real blood in those veins after all.

'Master, how by the powers of the Gods do they do that?' Dith marvelled, bringing Marcus back to the throes of the battle. Two horsemen from the Powers of Darkness had boarded Coll's chariot whilst he was balancing on the yoke to the front.

They dodged his first attempts to slice off their heads with his newly drawn artificial wooden sword, but were simultaneously kicked to the ground when he lay on the back of the moving steed and thrust at them with his feet. This was the signal for the two sides to merge in a furore of mock fighting.

There was much clamour and shouting as men were unseated from their horses and locked together in the clash of swordsmanship; until all were playing wounded or dead, apart from Coll and Madog, who faced each other for the final struggle.

All went well with the pre-arranged fight until Madog accidentally sent Coll's sword spinning from his hand. It landed at Hedfan's feet. Both Marcus and Ceridwen helped Hedfan to stand. The task was to fall to him. He must drive away the Prince of Darkness. Although Hedfan could not move his right arm with the pain from his shoulder, his left arm was still functioning well. He raised the sword above his head in a symbol of power and started towards Madog, who was feigning the finishing of Coll.

Something on the sword held aloft caught the glimmer of the evening Sun, sinking to the West. Madog began cowering and shrinking at the shimmering of light and, when he had shrivelled to a heap of dust, the crowd claimed 'Victory!'

For some reason there seemed to be a sense of unspoken victory against the injustice, which the boy had suffered. Perhaps in the playing out of this symbolic battle, the Gods had taken the unity of feeling between Roman and Celt and woven it into a powerful prayer, which would reveal its own consequences in due course.

The sense of satisfaction at the outcome of the mock battle gave rise to a more relaxed atmosphere between Vipsanius's men and the farmsteaders. Although they engaged in rival horse races, the sharp edge of competition had already worn away. It was fun, and by the time they jostled together around the central fire in the largest roundhouse for the sealing of the contract, there was a distinct air of friendliness. It had been helped along by generous helpings of food and mead served by the children and younger people as was customary.

Gwilym and Vipsanius stood by the fire facing each other and declared their contract of sale publicly. Vipsanius took a previously prepared wax tablet, which documented the items for trade, and both men warmed their seal rings and drove them into the wax.

Although there had to be some monetary exchange in asses and denarii for the fifty horses, the farmsteaders were much happier to exchange goods in popular demand, such as wine, wax, honey, oil and fine-spun garments. These items would have to come to Tan Yr Aur with the next supply-run to the hill fort and must be taken on faith. Besides, the farmsteaders kept the legionaries at the hill fort in fresh supplies of food as a form of taxation and payment for their patrolling of the coast. If, for some reason, the trade bargain were not honoured, there was a silent understanding that the Celwri would withhold payment of taxation until renegotiations were made.

Both Gwilym and Vipsanius looked well pleased with themselves and there was much backslapping and murmurings of approval. Nanw and Ceridwen then had the task of changing the atmosphere to a more serious note as the contract was given its due weight and blessing.

Nanw threw some sweet smelling herbs into the flames and the room was transformed with the glowing from the embers and a fragrant blue mist, which filled the roundhouse up to the small central hole in the thatch. She chanted a rhyme of ancient words unintelligible to every tongue there, but plain in its meaning.

Ceridwen wound a path around the fire, making a circular trail with her pitcher of water. Then she asked Gwilym and Vipsanius to kneel and clasp right hands. Her face was composed and expressionless as she bound their wrists together with pigskin thong.

Marcus held his breath for a moment, wondering if Dith, who was standing next to him, could hear the loud beating of his heart as he beheld this young priestess doing the work of her Goddess, the Earth Mother. For the first time he heard her voice in chant. It was so ethereal that for a moment he wondered if he had entered through the portals of the next world. Its enchantment swelled and throbbed, rose and fell, like the gentle lulling of waves on a sea of light.

Ceridwen finished her drawing up of the powers of witness and, in contrast, the older huskier tones of Nanw drew the ceremony to a close, as she poured the fresh blood of the slain piglets over the clenched hands of the two men. 'Let those who have eaten meat together deal loyally, honestly, with true honour - that only the blood of the meat shall run to bind them forever.'

It was the cue for Madog to strike up on the tabor and Cullen to show the skill of his piper's enchantment, as circle dancing began around the fire in earnest, with plenty of stamping and clapping. The Romans soon learned to copy the simple stepping patterns and participated wholeheartedly. Even Dith found himself dragged into the circle by some brown toothed widow and proceeded to try his best to impress upon her that the wobbling nature of his steps had more to do with having two left feet than with being drunk. She laughed at him winningly, totally unconvinced.

Marcus, for his part seemed to have misplaced Ceridwen. He had been involved in rescuing Gwilym and Vipsanius from their bonds. By the time he had cut them loose and cleaned up his knife and sheathed it; she was nowhere to be seen.

He scanned the swaying revellers and the folk lying idly against the walls in drunken stupor. There was a young couple pawing each other shamelessly and he found himself starting for a moment thinking she might be the female under the body of the writhing youth. Then he remembered that she had not been wearing her usual homespun kirtle, but a beautifully embroidered deerskin over tunic. It could not be she.

He strode over a huddle of sleeping children to the doorway and felt the relief of the fresh evening air fill his lungs as he stepped outside. She was standing quite still, quite alone in the central clearing with her face turned up to the Moon.

He approached gently, silently, not wanting to disturb her mood. As he drew nearer, he could see tears welling in her eyes and the elegant swallow of her throat, whilst she tried to deal with them.

The wind had died by now and the silver hush of a moonlit night lay over the mountain and valley below with its huddle of huts. Had it not been so still she would not have heard him as he whispered, 'Does the Goddess hear your prayer when sadness eats at your heart?'

She froze for a moment, feeling the warmth of his breath on her neck as he stood behind her. He too stared at the waxing Moon.

'I am confident She knows my heart. I am not so sure that I know my own; for I find I hate what I do seem to love. And now that you have prised it from me, feel free to be the conqueror.'

'Perhaps if I bare my own thoughts, our minds may be naked together and there will be no need for higher or lower between us.'

'Your thoughts reveal a lower motive to lie naked, then? Am I to be the sport?'

'Is it sport to tell naked Truth? Ceridwen, for two years I have kept the memory of my dead wife and child alive. I have courted sadness and made her a home to live in, but meeting you has changed me. I had it in my mind to ask you to be my wife and honour my household, but I know that you cannot leave your people without their healer and priestess. It would be too much to ask. Only tell me that there are stirrings in your heart and that I am not imagining this urgent bond between us?'

As soon as the words were out, Marcus began regretting them; for she spat such anger at him, he imagined for a moment that she had transformed herself into a wild cat.

'Bond? Do you not mean bondage? Not only does your race invade our country, kill off the most powerful of our Druid ancestors, but you feel you have the right to bed the daughters of Mona to erase the scars, delight them in the bedchamber and fill their bellies with your offspring, so that they will not put a knife to your liver in the night.' She spat so near him that the spittle bespeckled his face. Marcus grew deadly calm and in the silence that followed he drew out his dagger and gave it to her.

'Here. If it is revenge you seek, for what happened here two hundred years ago, take it now? Here is your chance. You could say I tried to dishonour you and that you killed me in self-defence. They would not crucify you on that score.'

Ceridwen stared fixedly at the offered weapon, but it was not that that she truly saw, but the glowing aura surrounding Marcus, a glow that so attracted her towards it, yearning and pulling her into its embrace. Her own aura had the overpowering desire to melt and blend into his. The pain cleaving head and heart drove into her like a knife thrust, making her cry aloud and then crumple weakly against the wall of Marcus's chest. The dagger fell with a clatter to the ground and he cradled her pain, rocking her and stroking the silken tendrils of her hair as her sobbing rose and fell.

It seemed an age that they stood there, entwined in that soft, cradling movement, whilst her sobs gently subsided. They allowed themselves the luxury of peaceful silence; their auras blended and balanced for the first time. Neither wished to break the enchantment of it. They both knew that in a few moments the cruel light of reason must separate them.

In the event, neither had to decide to break away from the other, as a sudden yelp from the threshold of the main roundhouse made them start, then fall to laughing, as Dith emerged being chased by the brown toothed widow. Dith had never been pursued so persistently for his manly virtue and was enjoying playing a game of cat and mouse. He fully intended allowing himself to be caught, once they reached the sanctuary of the hay store.

Ceridwen's laughing eyes caught Marcus's. Their laughter silenced as desire caught at both their throats. From the noises in the hay store the widow seemed to have caught her prey. Marcus held Ceridwen's face between his hands as he had visualised, tenderly, protectively.

'I will never force you to it, Ceridwen. I will never take from you, what is not mine, freely given, for I am in bondage to your will.' His whispered pledge hung in the air to be witnessed by the Moon's light. Ceridwen dropped her eyes to the ground and stooped to return the dagger to his hand.

'Should I thank you? As priestess of my tribe it will fall to me in consultation with the elders to choose a father for my offspring. I hardly think a Roman doctor...' her voice trailed off miserably.

'And if you choose sensibly it will be some such noble warrior as Eithig, who will help your tribe to rise from the ashes of degradation?' he parried, the barb to his sarcasm striking home.

'You belittle the sense of duty we each have to our calling. If there is honour in obedience to your commandant, is there not also honour in my obedience to our tribal customs and even more so to our Goddess? At the sacred fire of Beltane, at Summer's birth, it will fall to me to give my maidenhead to the Goddess, that my people will thrive and the fertility of the land be vouchsafed.'

'And who will perform this rite with you?' Marcus attempted to say in a level voice, but he was betrayed by a tongue of green jealousy, which Ceridwen was sure she saw lashing and twisting from his mouth.

'It is not yet decided. The young men, who wish to court me, must be set a task, that I may choose between them.'

'And will you marry this bedfellow?'

'This 'bedfellow' as you name him will be the symbol of all that is male to our tribe. He will play the part of the Stag King at the rite of Beltane. He will be the strongest of our hunters; the bravest protector; the impregnator of Life. It will be a great honour to court the Virgin Goddess and, if there is offspring of the sacred union, then it will be a child of the Goddess and revered by all the tribe. There will be no need for me to marry the father unless I wish it, for the whole tribe will be responsible for any issue.'

'The Gods will me to be that father. I know it. How do I contest for you?'

'You do not. There is that in me which still wants no part of Rome. My body is weak when it is near the enchantment of your aura, but I will see that I am well protected from now on and give you no cause for further hope. It is painful for you, I know.'

'Your knowledge of my pain comes from your own. Could we not help to heal the rift between our peoples? Could we not marry and live separate lives like many of the Roman Commanders are forced to do? I could be with you at least once a year, if not more. I could pledge to be with you each Beltane. Our Gods and Goddesses are similar, our ways of worship not unaligned.'

Ceridwen had to guard against a feeling of triumph as she watched him beg for her. A Roman was begging of her, pleading with her. But she surprised herself by not tasting such victory with any sweetness. She only knew that she must put an end to this agony of spirit for them both.

'No, Marcus! Whatever this madness that has passed between us, it cannot erase what your race has inflicted upon ours. I cannot allow a surge of emotion to blind me to my duty. I want you to leave me alone. If you do love me, or have any regard for me, you will cease to torture me in this way and promise to keep away from me. Promise!'

The anguish in her voice seemed to pierce his own desires

and it was the knowledge that he was hurting her that made him finally say, 'I promise.' He raised both her hands briefly to his lips and then he was gone into the night, leaving her with an aching emptiness, yawning into the blackness of the shadows.

⌘ ⌘ ⌘

CHAPTER VI

⌘

THE FAREWELL

The Spring Rites were over; the land blessed and sprinkled with the sacrificial blood of the animals offered to the Goddess. Their meat was roasted and eaten to strengthen the tribe for the hard work of the Spring ploughing and sowing. Coll and Owain were training to perfection the last of the broken-in horses destined for Segontium. Soon they would have their reward in goods.

Ceridwen had presided over much of the ritual proceedings as her grandmother had requested, for her novice training was almost finished and Nanw was beginning to feel the constraints of old age upon her limbs and voice. Indeed she had had to be helped to the Holy Grove and had remained seated throughout the Spring Festival.

Each evening as they sat peacefully around the fire at Cae Gwynion, Nanw would repeat the tales of old until she was sure that Ceridwen knew every word by heart. They would rehearse the chants together, Nanw miming the words to save her strength and only coming in with full voice when she felt the need to correct Ceridwen.

Each morning they would check the potions in the jars, marshalled row upon row. Each clay container bore a different symbol for each herbal remedy and Ceridwen would chant the charm with which to make it most effective. She would then repeat the recipe using the ancient copper measures.

Each noon, after working in the garden, Ceridwen named

each plant, its favoured growing conditions, its uses and storage needs. And it seemed that as she grew in confidence, so Nanw grew weaker.

The old priestess had ceased to work with her plants, as the bending gave her too much pain. She concentrated on preparing food, sitting by the fire, which she tended with the sticks and logs brought in by the young ones; or given in exchange for remedies by grateful tribespeople, or even an occasional Roman from the hill fort.

It was not until Nanw made the special request that Ceridwen allowed herself to see the process of preparation, which Nanw was so painstakingly orchestrating.

An awkward young auxiliary from the hill fort had been visiting them regularly for an infection, angrily inflaming a gash in his leg. They had cleaned the wound with a lotion of betony and sanicle and to heal it had applied poultices of moss. It had healed beautifully within a few weeks and he called at Cae Gwynion to see how he might repay them for their services.

Nanw requested that he follow her to the border of the ancient burial site. Choosing a spot facing South Eastward towards the distant summit of Yr Wyddfa, she pointed to a peaceful place where she might be buried when her time came.

'You have strong limbs and friends to help you. You must dig my grave here and plant a young oak sapling to grow from my heart. As my spirit is transported to my next life, so shall my remains become part of the land and the tree and the island, the air, the sky and the sea.' She smiled at him with great assurance of her journey to come and he dared not answer for a moment, for he did not know quite what to say. Eventually he nodded and agreed to carry out her instructions.

'Are you knowing of going soon, *Nain*?' Ceridwen questioned, her voice falsely lighter than the leaden weight, which seemed to be pressing against her heart.

'Soon enough, my priestess! Why do you think I have been hurrying things along for you, making sure you have all the knowledge you need to pass on to your own daughter?'

Ceridwen swallowed, trying to assimilate all that the

passing of Nanw, her great life's anchor, would mean.

'You cannot leave us yet. It is too soon.'

Nanw tried to calm the panic she could see rising in this young mirror image of herself; this granddaughter, who seemed to embody all the good qualities that her grandparents had brought to their union. Each time Nanw stared into those deep, loving pools of Ceridwen's eyes, how memories of her own youthful days stirred and came to her again. They reminded her of how beautiful she herself had once been, how gracefully she had danced for her Goddess at the rites; just as Ceridwen was able to do now. It had been a wonderful way of serving. And, when the bloom of youth had gone, she had channelled her energies in helping others to create beauty in their lives. Now her work was almost finished.

'It is always too soon for those whom we leave behind. But for me there will be such rejoicing when freed from this ageing form. Then I shall soar in the heavens, just like those buzzards are playing on the wind. Then, O then, Ceridwen, shall I truly dance. Be happy for me.'

The auxiliary shuffled from one sandalled foot to another, aware that he was witnessing a very personal conversation between the two women. They sensed his discomfort and smiled up at him. Ceridwen felt she should ease him and said, 'When my grandmother is departed, we will appreciate your help with the preparations. Although I know my brothers would claim the honour of preparing such a grave, no doubt they will also honour Nanw's wishes and call upon your strength in the event. Meanwhile, I will endeavour to keep her with us a little longer,' Ceridwen smiled reassuringly.

'Meromic at your service! Please send for me when you have need, and thanks to you and your Gods for the healing you have done.' He bowed a brief blessing and was gone over the hilltop.

'How does it make you feel when you read admiration in a man's eyes?' queried Nanw knowingly, raising her eyebrows and allowing her granddaughter to steady her along the well-trodden route down to their hut.

Ceridwen sighed with a note of impatience, 'I think that

their adoration is somewhat misplaced and would be better spent in service to the Mother Goddess.'

'Well answered! But is that what you really know at heart, or do you tell what you ought to feel?' Nanw gazed tenderly and indulgently into the soft grey blue of Ceridwen's eyes. It was a gaze of deep knowing and Ceridwen knew she could not conceal the truth of her thoughts from Nanw's searching wisdom.

'Grandmother, you see into my soul. You hear my thoughts, so why would you have me answer?'

'Because, recognition of oneself at a conscious level is a maturing process. So often we seek to hide our weaknesses, even from ourselves; and if we do that, we cannot heal and move forwards in our lives.' They had reached the hut and busied themselves for a few moments, stirring the fire and encouraging a healthier glow at the central hearth. They felt the chill of the rising wind and welcomed the flickering flames as they began to dance into life.

Nanw sat and warmed her hands at the glowing, waiting patiently for Ceridwen to find her thoughts, to find herself. When Ceridwen stood outside herself and visualised her response to the admiring glances of the men who played a part in her daily life, she answered candidly, 'I feel a sense of pride when I feel the approval of my father and brothers. When their eyes gather round me, it seems to bring comfort and lightness to their hearts; and if I feel my own beauty, it is with the knowledge that it is only for a short time, during the bloom of my youth, that my family will enjoy casting their eyes so upon me. They must learn to appreciate other qualities than people's outward beauty. For my own part, I know that my task is to work on my own inner qualities that they may resonate and radiate as an example to our people. I know a fear to take on that task.'

Nanw looked at her granddaughter with complete confidence and whispered, 'You need not fear. You will be given the strength to do your task.' She reached up tenderly and stroked a straying strand of hair from Ceridwen's cheek.

'But for other men...I know I enjoy a sense of my power

over them. I admit I am tempted to play cat and mouse with their affections, to bend their will to mine. I know for example that the auxiliary Meromic would do anything for me. He is a willow sapling to shape any way I would make him. I see his subservience in his eyes. I have captivated him. He could be my tame wolf cub, eating from my hand.' Ceridwen felt the warm bond between Meromic and herself; someone who posed no threat; over whom she had complete control.

But a chill dart of warning rose up her spine as she said, 'There are others; the Gods protect me from them; with whom I would rather not play games and whose attentions I do not seek.' Ceridwen stared into the flames and saw again the evening of the Spring Rites. 'I speak of Eithig, arriving as he did with his entourage of young warriors, without any shame for his cruelty to Hedfan. He presided as tribal king with his subjects scurrying about him in fear of his temper.

'The only person who did not scurry was Coll. He was bent on persuading Eithig to choose a male gelding, which would obey his every command without question. I thought to help Coll when I brought Gwyngariad before Eithig. I put it in her mind to rear and buck in his presence, so that he could see she was unsuitable, but he only smiled one-sidedly and said she had a good spirit for a war horse and that now he had seen her, he was more determined than ever to have her. I knew in that instant that it was not only Gwyngariad he intended to have.'

'You mean he will have you too? Can you see the tribes-people allowing him to take our priestess against her will? They would have a new king before they would see your maidenhead dishonoured so.'

'At what price, *Nain*....war between each farmstead? It would divide our *commote* in two and set everyone at each other's throats. The tension was ill enough when Hedfan was injured. How much longer will the menfolk tolerate Eithig's highhanded manner. We get fairer at the hands of our Roman masters.'

'Your hatred of all that is Roman has not entirely clouded your vision then?'

Ceridwen knew what her grandmother was insinuating

and felt the topic of Marcus arising dangerously to the surface. She tried to bury it by ignoring the remark and running on with, 'Did you not see our king ogling me lasciviously and push into the circle-dancing to be by my side?'

'I was aware that you cringed to feel his hot breath on your neck and contrived to have your father and mother join the circle, so that you would not have to hold hands with him. He knows that if he were to couple with you, his standing within the tribe would be all the stronger. I know he stirs revulsion in you. A match between you could only bring pain. However it may suit the power seekers in our midst,' said the old priestess, taking Ceridwen's cool hands in her wizened ones sympathetically. 'But as yet you have not spoken of Marcus? Indeed you have not spoken of him since the fest which sealed the bargaining?'

Ceridwen wanted to snatch her hands away at this challenge to the inner sanctum of her most private feelings, but out of respect to her grandmother and mentor she felt she owed her some sort of explanation.

She looked down at their intertwined hands and asked, 'Why should I speak of him when it bores like an arrow through my soul? We are attracted like two animals on heat during the Full Moon. When I bond with any man it will be for life and of my choosing, not of some base instinct. I could not betray my tribe and marry a Roman.'

'Ceridwen, trust me when I say that what attracts you to Marcus is not only lust, but the knowledge that you could share trust and honour, companionship and fidelity; if only you could be prepared to put what is past behind you. You have a strong prejudice in your heart, fostered I fear by the tales of Roman terrorisation, tales perhaps omitting to tell of the inhumanity meted out from one Celtic tribe to another. Of late we have enjoyed more peace under Roman rule than we have had for many decades.'

Ceridwen made no reply, for she had no answer, but played distractedly, running her fingers along the woollen threads of the loom, where her thoughts seemed as intricately woven as the complicated patterns of the regal looking wine and gold warp and woof.

Nanw felt the pain of her granddaughter's torment and tried again to soothe, to entreat. 'I hold no love for the Roman invasion of our holy island; but think how our ancestors drove out the little people hundreds of years ago. Our tribes were the invaders then; others the victims.'

Ceridwen began to understand the course along which her grandmother's mind was taking her. 'Do you mean that now to be the victim is part of the great, just law of Cause and Effect?' Nanw nodded in response, but Ceridwen needed to know more and pressed on with, 'But when will we have played out our Karmic debt? When will our victimisation end? Do you have that foreknowledge, Grandmother? It is vital you tell me.'

It was as though the old priestess had become suddenly very weary and all she would say for the present was in the form of yet another question, 'Do you not remember the prophecy of Cadoc, your grandfather? *'When the noble bloods of Rome and Druid mingle, as the rowans intertwine; then peace and honour will come with us to dine.'* Think, Ceridwen. Think what that might mean for you and for our tribe.

'I must rest,' she continued. 'A great weariness overwhelms me. We shall talk of this again.' With that the old woman shuffled to her pallet and Ceridwen covered her affectionately with her plaid blankets. Mwg moved to his accustomed position at the feet of his mistress and Ceridwen was left to herself to ponder the true meaning of Cadoc's prophecy.

Two days later in a howling gale of wind and rain, Ceridwen found herself struggling down to the farmstead. Despite the weather, Coll and Owain were preparing to set off with the last consignment of horses for Segontium, with promises to Marged that they would wait for the gale to subside before attempting to cross the Straits to the mainland.

Nanw did not feel strong enough to attempt the rough path down the mountain to Tan Yr Aur, so had sent, instead, a farewell message with Ceridwen, along with her prayers and a special pot of salve as a gift to Marcus.

As Ceridwen handed the gift into the safekeeping of Coll she was aware that her hands seemed to linger around the clay pot. She recognised the shift in her own thinking. Here she was sending a message of well-being to a Roman and a warmth of feeling, spreading from her feet upwards, banished any remnant of guilt. Perhaps it was the beginning of a victory over her prejudice. Perhaps it was the beginning of some measure of inner peace. She prayed to the Goddess it was so.

Only Gwilym and Hedfan were to stay at Tan Yr Aur with the women and children. The other menfolk would be gone with Coll and Owain to manage the horses and help bring some goods back. Besides, with an easier feeling between the Roman army housed at the hill fort, less than half a league away, there was some confidence that the farmstead would be safeguarded against intrusion.

Those remaining behind gathered in the cutting wind to wave on the band of mounted horse-rearers and their charges. There was much hugging and leave-taking with blessings; for, although they were not travelling to the far side of the world, there was danger enough from wild animals, bandits and the sea crossing. It was going to take them two days to Segontium if they were to rest the horses before the crossing.

Ceridwen blessed the journey and smiled assurance of their safety. 'Come home to us soon. The Gods ride with you!'

With a pounding of hooves and hailing calls, the party got under way, Madog bringing up the rear with a wagon of supplies and more goods to trade.

Ceridwen was not sure if Gwyngariad whinnied at the sound of the hooves and solid wooden wagon wheels trundling along the track, or from her own leave-taking of her yearling foal.

The girl and white mare stood intertwined for a while and seemed to ease a sort of sadness in each other, but then Marged became concerned about the lashing rain and encouraged her daughter to come away in to get dry in front of the fire.

In some ways it was good to be in the family roundhouse again, sharing food with her father, mother and Hedfan, the warm lull of the fire temporarily taking away life's responsibilities; the warm glow of food in her belly making her drowsy and Marged's spinning whorl, hypnotising, tranquillising.

Her father was in nostalgic mood and recited stories of giants and fairies, stories he had not told her since she was a child. She luxuriated in the intimacy of the small family group and snuggled close to the father, who had always offered her the sort of unconditional love, which truly nurtures confidence in their offspring. With her head in his lap, she begged for her favourite tale.

It was about an ogre who was about to swallow the island of Mona whole. When she saw her beautiful island was in danger, Mistress Moon came out by day and magically transformed the island into a buzzard, which winged its way out of reach, crying and calling to the wind, 'I'm free! I'm free!'

Whereupon, the ogre drove himself to such a frenzy of frustration that he whirled himself into a furore and burst, turning into a shower of pebbles. Mona saw that if she remained in flight she would be dashed to the ground. She begged Mistress Moon to transform her back into an island. Her wish was granted; but the ogre's pebbles crashed down to become the pebbles of White Beach.

Gwilym told the tale with his gifted sense of the dramatic and the whole family tittered and grinned their way through his performance, Hedfan providing extra sound effects and appropriate mimicry.

'Do you remember, Father, I always insisted that one day it would be me who would weave the magic to save my island?' sighed Ceridwen. 'I was so sure of my powers then; so sure that *Nain* would reveal all to me and that I would be so powerful. I feel so ignorant; so unsure of myself. The more I learn, the less I seem to know.'

'Aye, its true that the older and wiser you get, the more you realise knowledge is limitless, like the waves of the sea. There's no need for fretting, though; you have all the knowledge you need for the task in hand. Trust me, little Ceri.' The squeeze of her father's hand was so reassuring. He had not called her 'Ceri' since her maidenhood, but the familiar name claimed an indissoluble bond between them.

'Your father is right. We are very proud of you. You have studied well and what you do not already know, life itself will teach you. You are well respected, Ceridwen. There's no gainsaying,' agreed Marged, who rarely dished out compliments and smiled up from her work with an uncharacteristic look of tenderness. She seemed to embarrass herself and walked to the threshold to check the weather.

'The rain is easing. Perhaps you would take Nanw some warm broth and some griddlecakes. Here, I'll wrap them in wool fleece to keep them warm in your basket,' Marged busied herself and roused Ceridwen from her comfort. 'It looks as though your fire is nigh on out - just a slivering spindle of smoke, nothing to put a cat by. Hurry on home!'

'Leave her be, Marged. She's no child now, but her own woman,' chided Gwilym, bowing in mock respect to Ceridwen, after he himself had indulged in an unadulterated show of nostalgia for the time when his youngest daughter had once sat fondly upon his knee.

It had been wonderful to go back to the cocoon of her earliest days and remember the feeling of being sheltered and protected by her parents. The feeling hung with her as she picked her way carefully along the path up the mountain, the plants and the trees so fragrant after the rain. She was conscious of delaying her return to tend her grandmother, of wanting to delay taking on the responsibilities looming ahead.

The spider webs took on their silver jewel-like magic after the rain and she stopped to appreciate their wonder before Manon's bleating called her to the evening duties at Cae Gwynion.

Nanw was so still. She had hardly stirred since Ceridwen left and had not had the strength to throw more wood on the fire. Her face was so grey that initially Ceridwen suspected she had died in her sleep, but the old priestess smiled a weak greeting when she entered and became aware of Ceridwen's frantic efforts with the worn bellows.

'Bel! Bel! Bel! Get going you stupid fire!' Ceridwen spat at the wavering timid flames, little encouraged by the half split leather bellows, used by countless priests and priestesses before her days. She stopped; suddenly aware of the rigid tension in her voice; aware that her anger, her frustration with the world was weakening the flames and creating negative energy around the hearth. Flames were just like children. They needed loving encouragement and the environment to thrive in. Ceridwen relaxed. She allowed the anger and confusion to flow down her spine, through her knees and into the underworld, to be transformed into real energy. She soothed her own heart by calling the flames with a little humming chant and as the flames grew bigger, so did the love and triumph in her humming until she gasped, 'There! There's a blaze for you!'

'You've learned so much, my *Cariad*. After you have milked Manon, bring her milk to me and when we are both strengthened by her nourishment there is much I must say to you.' There was such urgency in Nanw's voice that Ceridwen felt herself responding to a sense of occasion. Nanw must not be troubled by petty distractions. Her energy must be conserved so that she would have the strength to leave her final instructions.

Ceridwen washed her hands in some rosemary water and went to milk Manon. Manon was unusually co-operative, as if she sensed that it would be inappropriate to play games and the task was done cleanly, efficiently and the nanny goat bedded down in the hay in the half of the hut allotted to the animals.

The geese were gathered and shut in for the night with the chickens and Luce and Mwg given a platter of goat's milk to share. The wattle shutters were latched into place, the door bolt lifted across and a blanket pulled over to keep out the chill Spring wind.

Not a word was spoken as Ceridwen eased her grandmother into sitting position and fed her Marged's broth followed by warm goat's milk. The lapping of the cat and kitten, the singing of the wind in the trees, the crackle of the fire and, in the distance, the sighing of the sea was melody enough.

When the meal was done, a comforting warmth spreading through their bodies, Ceridwen held her grandmother's hand

and waited as the old lady gathered her thoughts: thoughts that would be sent down the ages by the peoples to come after them.

'Ceridwen, Cadoc has been to me. He stood on the threshold by the door, beckoning me with such a loving gaze. It is almost my time of transition. The soul of your grandfather beckons me to make my own soul journey.'

'Are you frightened, *Nain*? I think I should be.'

'How should we look forward to a journey's end, but with excitement and anticipation of reaching our destination? No, I am not frightened of the journey's end, only conscious that the final journey can be somewhat of a struggle, and in that I may need your assistance. You know what to do. You have assisted people to die before now. Use your hands and the prayers I have taught you,' Nanw exhorted weakly.

'*Nain* Nanw, you have been our priestess since you were a young mother. You have taught us all the traditions of our Druid ancestors. Why have you decided to be buried, rather than to keep with our tradition of cremation?'

'My child, tradition is the art form of our lifestyle and in itself has great importance, but it is not the same as Truth. Tradition has its place in pride and nostalgia. But I have a great yearning to be like that which grows in Nature...for the remains of my body to feed and nurture the earth. There is enough smoke in our fires of war, without spoiling the sweet smell of Spring with my funeral pyre. Let the trees grow from my body to feed the earth with their spirit. So might part of me live on in a simple way.'

'But will you not reincarnate and come to this earth in another form, to give us your wisdom and learn those life-lessons not yet finished?' was the anxious question. Ceridwen had always suspected that her grandmother was not totally convinced by the traditional Druid teachings on re-birth, but she had never thought to challenge her, not until this moment when precious time was running out.

'I have done my best to carry forward the traditions and secrets passed down to us; but there is part of me, Ceridwen, which must always re-examine and question for myself. If I am true to my own conscience, I cannot say that I believe we return here to this sphere of existence. I have no proof, but it seems illogical to me that we come here again to retrace the same lessons and make the same mistakes as previous mortals.'

'But what about those people who say they have knowledge of who they were in a previous life; surely that is proof?' Ceridwen could think of at least three clans-people who could describe in detail their life before, right down to the smallest detail, such as what they used to eat and how they dressed. She had always assumed that life continued, and that souls were recycled like the life force in the soil.

'Those people have great vision. I believe they have access to information not open to all. But once I remember two small girls who lived in separate villages. Each had knowledge of life as the same being and could describe exactly the same incidents. Unless we are to believe that two souls can live in the same body, and many of the superstitious do, I cannot believe that those girls once shared the same life. Have you not noticed people laying claim to having once been a chieftain or a priestess in ancient times? Would it not rather seem that some departed souls enjoy inter-relating with the vibration of the mortal sphere? Would it not be possible that, just as your grandfather communicates with me, so the souls of others become so intimate with their earth friend, that the mortal has the feeling of experiencing someone's previous traumas and triumphs?'

'Do you mean that we always remain this same individual even in our after-life.'

'I want to believe that. I need to know that my special individuality will not be lost, but transformed into something else equally me, but more glorious, more powerful, more good.' Nanw had put such yearning and effort into the last speech that she sank back onto the goose-down pillow and could speak no more for a while.

Ceridwen ladled more milk into a bowl and proffered it to the old woman's quivering lips. She took just enough to ease the dryness of her mouth, but refused to swallow more.

Putting the bowl to one side Ceridwen said, '*Nain*, you have travelled your journey with wisdom and honesty and will have great power in the life beyond. I feel that truly. I will need your help when you are gone from my side. I shall not be able to remember all you have taught me. You must speak to my mind and be with me in spirit.'

'I must be where my Goddess would have me be, my sweet child. I shall not always be whispering into your ear to help you make every choice and every healing remedy; for you must take responsibility for your own fulfilment and life's purpose,' whispered Nanw. 'Think of Marcus when you think of your destiny. You have turned him away this time. What of the next? If you are given another opportunity to put aside your prejudice, what will you do?'

'I must pray that I make the right choice for my kinsmen and my people,' Ceridwen replied hardly able to look Nanw in the eye, for she could not yet trust what her reactions might be, should another opportunity to couple with Marcus arise.

'Ceridwen, it is through your children that the well being of future generations will be vouchsafed. This religion of ours will be chidden into hiding for many generations, persecuted if it breathes the light of day. But there will come a time on this earth, when all religions will rejoice and with one song, will praise the Supreme Creator and Her myriad forces. People will dance the dance of unity and the place of one's birth will not bar the gate to good fortune. Reach out for your destiny. You can play your part in this great drama of life if you have a mind to, or turn your back on the opportunity. You have that choice.'

'I promise I will safeguard our religion and pass it down to my daughters. If Marcus is to help me in that task, then the times will be auspicious for our meeting and the Goddess will wipe all confusion from my eyes,' Ceridwen pledged in earnest, tears welling in her throat and making it difficult to speak. 'Let the matter rest there. I will do my level best. Now you must rest.' She patted the old lady's hand and went across to the bird basket, hanging from the roof spar.

The dove fluttered in her hand as she wound a piece of Nanw's hair to the bird's leg, opened the shutter and threw the bird into the darkening sky. It would arrive at Tan Yr Aur in minutes and the family would know that Nanw's time had come.

'Tis best you send for Marged, we don't want her scolding as well as grieving,' Nanw smiled weakly up at Ceridwen. 'Come. Let me give you blessing whilst we have our privacy.'

Ceridwen knelt obediently at the dying woman's side and felt the withered hand touch her head and her heart, then gather her two hands together. 'Go with peacefulness and confidence on your mission, my *Cariad*. Further the healing work to build peace and security in the hearts of our tribespeople. Heal the wounds of enmity and discord between races. Grow as our priestess in knowledge and understanding. Reach out for your destiny.' Although Nanw had in reality only whispered the latter, with weak, halting breath, to Ceridwen's ears it came as a beautiful chant, with an otherworldly melody of the Goddess. Then something quite unexpected began to happen.

Ceridwen was now kneeling with her eyes closed, but quietly looking with her mind into the dark of the future. She could see a beautiful light source heading straight for her forehead. She knew it would enter in the centre of her brow. She had no fear of it, only a child's sense of wonder at its beauty. It was the shape of a flame and palest gold in colour with an aura of brilliant blue. She thought at first that it was an imaginary vision and prepared for it to disappear when she opened her eyes. But it did not disappear. It kept on travelling towards her with steady purpose and she waited with bated breath for the moment of contact.

There was a cobweb of a touch as it travelled through the smooth white skin of her brow and mingled momentarily with her brain, resonating with the ease of a beautiful note. Then it left from behind her, leaving her with the knowledge that she was now truly priestess of the Celwri. Nanw's eyes were closed, but Ceridwen knew she had seen and understood.

It was time to make easy the journey, for Nanw was eager to be gone. Ceridwen untethered the door that the family may come in reverently and quietly. Then she settled herself in kneeling position, holding Nanw's head in her lap, with one hand on the crown of her head and the other resting with feather lightness on her chest bone.

She sang so sweetly, a lullaby, which Nanw had cradled her with as a babe. It seemed more fitting than a ceremonial prayer, for this was a farewell to her grandmother and not to her priestess.

Gwilym came first, with Marged and Hedfan. Marged's bustling was gone; calmed by the peacefulness Ceridwen had created. They said nothing, but each took Nanw's hand and kissed it as they would a queen's. In the flickering firelight Ceridwen wondered to find tears running down the weather beaten cheeks of her father. Her mother, she noticed, looked sad, but composed, resigned perhaps, as though she were greeting something she had well prepared for. Hedfan had fear in his eyes, and was constantly swallowing for he had only so far witnessed violent death and was not sure how this event would take him.

When the lullaby was done, Marged moved close to her mother and thanked her for the many happy years they had known together. 'Forgive me, Mother, if I have disappointed you in not taking up the priestessly duties, but I never felt comfortable with them. I hope that in giving you Ceridwen...'

'...given me...more than...mother.... deserved.' Nanw was finding it difficult to breathe and struggled now to answer Marged, but any distance that had once been between them was bridged, and Marged, who rarely showed affection towards her mother, gently gathered her face in her hands and kissed her gently and sweetly.

The peacefulness was broken then by the arrival of Olwenna, Angharad, Ness and the children, who had struggled up the path at a more leisurely pace. They had not only come to pay their last respects to Nanw, but to lighten her soul, that her journey would not be long and hard.

When the children had done with their farewells and stood wide-eyed, all but for little Rhys, whom Gwilym soothed and settled under the plaid blanket, the rest of the company washed their hands in the rosemary water, which Marged passed round in a bowl. Then, fingers together and palms upward, they all knelt around Nanw and slid their hands just under her body.

Ceridwen still managed her crown and chest bone, but the other eight adults provided a human platform of life-force energy. Ceridwen began to chant the prayer for the dying in the ancient tongue, which she knew the children would not understand fully. But she sang it with such tenderness and love; she knew they understood it as a farewell and a request for the progress of Nanw's soul.

It was not an easy passing. For several hours the waves of breath struggled to be released from Nanw's weary body, her chest rising and falling in that dance between lives. However, once, when the vigil group became weary of their task and turned away for refreshment, the lack of uplifting energy brought Nanw back so close to consciousness that she cried out for their assistance again, and after that they dared not leave their hands away.

For Nanw it was like floating out towards the glistening horizon on the sea, with a great yearning in her to join with the light beyond. She would be lifted towards it and then find herself washed up again on the shore of life. The restless tide of her breath dashed her against the pain of the world. Then the sweet call of light on the horizon would summon her again. Soon after came the knowledge that Cadoc was somehow near, as though he was part of the rhythm in the wave.

For Ceridwen it was a strange mixture of triumph and sorrow: a pain so exquisitely beautiful that it left her speechless. Like childbirth this rebirthing was a great mixture of pain and joy. She knew that Nanw was experiencing flight from the body to other-worldliness. She too sensed Cadoc's nearness, but did not see him.

Just before dawn, when the tenure of the earth's gravity is at its lowest ebb, Nanw gave her last gasp, almost as though she were surprised that at last, after the long night, her time had come.

⌘ ⌘ ⌘

CHAPTER VII

⌘

THE PARTING

Hedfan was dispatched at first light to the hill fort to request Meromic's help with the grave digging, and from thence he would visit each homestead in the tribal vicinity to call them to wake their priestess to her next life.

He was frightened to approach the fortified homestead at Din Sylwy, Eithig's seventeen-acre stronghold overlooking the coast above the bay, but he knew there was no other to carry the news. His parents had always encouraged him to step over his fears and face them head on. But with the scars on his burns barely healed, he was terrified in case they taunted or pushed him. Even the rhythmic gentle jolting of his dappled grey pony beneath him was torture enough.

The Sun was riding high by the time he drew near to the cattle enclosure at the foot of Din Silwy. He was greeted with the delighted shrieks of the children playing in the yard and the softening smile of Gwenfaen, his favourite cousin. With her round dimpled welcome, she carried on supervising the younger children and dangled a struggling babe unceremoniously from the ample shelf of her right hip.

He knew he dared not tell them the news until Eithig had heard it from his own lips, but they read his anxious face and pressed him excitedly. The women began to emerge from the other roundhouses and one of the older boys, eager to act out his role as horn blower, summoned the warriors from their duties in the neighbouring fields. Hedfan pushed past them to the threshold of the largest roundhouse, where there was a flurried scuffling as he knocked and called, 'Lord Eithig, I beg your patience!'

'You may enter,' a surly voice replied after what seemed an age.

As the door swung open and daylight spilled into the fire lit room, Hedfan focused on the hostile sullen face of his chieftain. He was florid and heavy eyed with drink from a leather flagon standing upon the table, but beyond that Hedfan could make out the terrified and tear swollen face of Eithig's younger sister, Einir. She was shaking with fear and adjusting her untidy dress. Hedfan noticed the red welts around her swollen wrists. To whatever she had been subjected was evidently against her will. She had been tied.

Her terrified face begged Hedfan to do and say nothing. He averted his gaze to the rush flooring and delivered the message he was entrusted with.

'Eithig, King of our tribe, know that Nanw our priestess and guardian of our souls is gone to the nether world and must be awakened.' Some of the women began to keen.

'When might this 'awakening' take place?' Eithig found the grace to mutter.

'As the Sun rises the morrow, Sire.'

'Tell your kindred I shall be there to support my clansmen as always. A good opportunity to ride home Gwyngariad, wouldn't you say? Word has it that her foal is gone from her now, sold to those lice your kinsmen suck up to. The white mare is ready for me now I trust?' Eithig leered into his face, his stinking breath making Hedfan heave and run, as if a pack of wolves were at his heels. The laughing scorn of Eithig rang out to the rocks, taunting Hedfan with every painful jostling tread, as he stumbled through the gathering clan's people and back along the cliff top path to where he had tethered his dappled grey.

Here was no appropriate sadness for the passing of a valued life. Here was no appreciation of the years of arduous work his grandmother had dedicated to her people. Here there was only cruel taunting and an alien emptiness of spirit. Hedfan's pain of soul and body ran with his tears, splashing onto the glistening back of the gelding that carried him along. How was it that such low beings rose to such great heights in the world of men? What made their followers vow allegiance? Was it some sort of twisted enchantment or pure terror? He could not help wondering when the Gods would listen to the prayers of the Celwri and send a noble king; someone the people could look up to; someone to give them pride in their heritage once more.

But the more immediate task in hand was to find a way to save Gwyngariad. Would he, a slip of a boy, become like the giant killer in the legends; rise up against all odds and overpower Eithig? How would things come to pass? How would he suddenly become a man and grow strong? Surely now that Ceridwen was priestess she would have the answer?

On his return to Cae Gwynion, Hedfan was not so sure. He dismounted, stopping in his tracks as he drew near Ceridwen. She stood in a numb sort of daze, watching as Gwilym, Meromic and two of his legionary friends, dug a great hole in the side of the mountain.

She had seemed fine whilst she had work to do. She had prayed over the body of Nanw until the dawn, and helped Marged to wash her, drape her in her ceremonial robes and twist fresh flowers into her hair. She had shown the men where Nanw's chosen grave was to be dug, and had accepted Marged's offer of bannock dripping with lard, eating it without interest, then suddenly giving in to a great wave of exhaustion.

Hedfan felt a great surge of protection well in his chest. He understood that, whereas Ceridwen had always been there to support him, now was the time to support her. This recognition gave him a new sense of manly energy. He consciously locked away all the confusing burning questions and stood behind her, holding her upper arms, until she relaxed, trusted and leaned on him as she did so frequently against her beloved trees.

'She was such a beautiful soul, Ceridwen. We shall all miss

her to be here with us, but we must give her a good sending. You shall do it right, I know'

'Hedfan, I have spent so long preparing for this moment, preparing to be your priestess when Nanw is gone, but I do not know if it is what I want anymore. I am so tired, so tired that I could lie down in Nanw's grave and never bother to get up again.'

'We have been up all the night in vigil. Wait until you have slept and the new day gives you fresh light. You will see things so differently. You will see how much we need you and what a beautiful burial you can make for her.'

'I must play the priestess and you must play the man,' she said flatly.

'No, you must be the priestess and I must be a man,' he protested, springing now in front of her. 'Eithig comes to the wake tomorrow and plans to take Gwyngariad home with him. How will she become mine, Ceridwen? What am I to do? Tell me.'

The weariness increased, a weariness that sapped her sensibilities and made her careless of any feeling. 'Nothing. Promise me you will do nothing. Now is not the time to battle with this viper. We shall bury our grandmother with dignity and Eithig will take Gwyngariad.'

Hedfan was incredulous. 'But you said…. You prophesied…. You promised!' He stared at his sister, whom, up until that moment, he had almost made the mistake of worshipping. Her silence now cut into him, with the sharp, stark reality of her fallibility. The next moment he was running away from her, down the mountain towards the stockade at Tan Yr Aur. He would run away with the white mare and have done with everyone.

Gwilym and Marged could not believe that Hedfan had gone and that Ceridwen had done nothing to stop him.

'He will get half way to the port at Cerrig y Gwyddyl and will come across Coll and Owain returning. They will bring him back. You'll see.' It was a desperate hope rather than a prophecy. Ceridwen threw a log carelessly to the fire and sank onto the shake down she had drawn near. 'Please, no more talk. Just let me sleep.'

Marged covered her and, after reassuring her that she and Gwilym would stay the night in the hut at Cae Gwynion, continued to worry the situation over with Gwilym in urgent whispers.

'You should have gone after him, Gwilym. He should be at the burial tomorrow, to show his respect.'

'The lad thinks only how he can save a beautiful creature from certain cruelty. He's impulsive. He'll think it over and come back. You'll see.'

'I hope you are right. I'm more in fear of what fault Eithig will find in us if he is further angered. He's not beyond setting his men to raze our fields and confiscate our stock. He will find an excuse to ruin us, Gwilym.'

'Hush now. You are tempting fate. By the Gods, he is our clansman, our king. He wishes us no harm deep down.'

'How can you say that when he has harmed Hedfan so?'

'Hedfan must have been rude or uncouth. He must have angered Eithig somehow, deserved to be punished.'

'Whenever have you known Hedfan be rude? His manners have always been exemplary. Why else would he be our messenger?'

'We were not witness.'

'The Romans were.'

'And you believe them over your own clansmen?'

'I believe them as I believe in the simple honesty of our son.'

'We must give Eithig the benefit of the doubt. We owe him some loyalty, surely?'

'We were loyal to his father, but Eithig is no noble lord. I wonder at his siring. Was he a changeling?'

'And I wonder at your flights of fancy, when your mother's body lies prepared for her burial on the stone floor of this very room. Come now. We'll face the morrow when it comes. For now we must sleep.'

Marged obeyed, marvelling at Gwilym's naivety, or was it that he was always so good at turning a blind eye to matters, rather than stirring any form of conflict. She knew deep down that the latter was the case. It was why he was successful in his trading. It was why the older boys had not taken off to seek their fortunes elsewhere. For, although their father worked them hard and expected professional standards of care for the animals, he always forgave them the impetuosities of youth. He wisely watched them learn from their mistakes, instead of telling them how foolish they often were. It was also why their own marriage worked well. It was based on candour and teamwork. They had no secrets from each other bar one and Marged saw no necessity for its ever coming to light, to harm the pride of this loving and loyal helpmate.

She shook the straw pallet on its wattle woven base and sighing settled next to her husband. It had been an exhausting day, the work of it numbing and blotting out the pain of her grief. After checking Nanw's instructions as given by Ceridwen, she had supervised the grave digging and the washing and preparing of Nanw's still, cold body. Tonight Angharad and Olwenna were keeping vigil, Ceridwen sleeping fitfully by, trying to gather her strength for the awakening.

Thankfully there was no feast to prepare, for she knew that the surrounding tribespeople would come with the customary gifts of food to sustain them for the next few days. But Hedfan must come back for his own sake and for the safety of his family. Marged used all her strength and will to call him and begged the Goddess to protect him, wherever he was that dark, chill night.

There was an urgent need to hear the comforting words of her mother. Marged stared at the rigid corpse, decked in its finery and adornment of sweet violets; flanked by the dutiful Angharad and Olwenna. The lifeless body bore no resemblance to the reality of Nanw and Marged felt surprised to find herself completely disinterested in the strange trio of women in their tranquil statuesque vigil. She would turn to her dreaming to find the comfort she needed.

Gwyngariad had carried Hedfan with all the speed she could muster away from Mynydd Llwydiarth and East towards the port of Cerrig y Gwyddyl. She had sensed the fear and urgency in the boy and his need for escape; but now she was lathered and in need of water and rest. Nightfall was fast approaching and the port not yet in sight. She slowed to a halt and sniffed the wind, searching for water. Hedfan reluctantly gave in, dismounted and followed her, grateful to find the comforting sounds of a clear brook babbling into the roadside forest.

He had galloped away unthinking with no food, water, blankets nor flint to make fire. How stupid could he have been, thinking he could run away to another tribe on the mainland, without provisions? Every farmstead knew his welcome face as the messenger boy from Cae Gwynion, the Holy Place. It was no use using their hospitality; he would be traced too easily. It looked as if a twig bed, curled close to Gwyngariad, and an empty stomach were his for the night.

The soot black of the night when it came seemed to stretch on into eternity, as Hedfan tried to shelter in the lee of a fallen tree, covering himself with his cloak. As his eyes became accustomed to the dark, he could see the vague outline of Gwyngariad's bulk, standing peacefully beside him. Thankfully the wind had dropped and an eerie stillness settled over the forest, broken only occasionally by the swoop of a bat, or the call of an owl. He must try to sleep. It would be a long journey tomorrow and he would need all his wits about him.

'Hedfan!' He heard his mother's voice in his head as clearly as if she were standing beside him. He tried to dismiss the anguish he heard in her call. It was his imagination playing tricks surely? He fought bravely to master his fear of the unknown, symbolised by the blackness before him, but his burning shoulder, his aching limbs and his very empty belly reminded him constantly of home comforts and, as he drifted in and out of an exhausted sleep, the terror of Eithig's men finding him began its torture. He tossed and turned fitfully, biting his hand that he may not cry out in fear, nor submit to womanly tears.

To soothe him Gwyngariad nuzzled him and eventually settled beside him. He huddled against her for warmth one hand on the dagger in its sheath on his belt.

Towards midnight the Moon made a shy appearance from behind the thick clouds and Gwyngariad stirred and stood, her white coat shining silver grey in the hushed magic. She whickered a welcome and Hedfan woke. He rubbed his eyes to see if he were dreaming, unsure to which world he belonged.

Between the boles of two tall firs stood Nanw, her face glowing as if lit by rush light. It was a serene face, banished of wrinkles and age but with the wise compassionate eyes of those well travelled in this world and beginning their journey into the next.

It was a look that banished all fear from Hedfan's body and mind; and as though she sensed the dissolution of his fear she drew near him, her image magnifying until she stood before him.

'Go back, Hedfan. If you love your family and your tribe, go back so that they shall not wreak the wroth of your king. Sacrifice your own desire for the good of all. Take Gwyngariad back. One day she shall be yours, but not yet. Turn back!'

Hedfan did not need to reply. Nanw saw the resolve form in Hedfan's mind and she was pleased with him. For him there was the glow of wonder, healing and soothing his fear and confusion. He felt so privileged that Nanw had come from death to speak to him; had chosen him to reveal a path of action. There was no question in his mind now. Of course he must put the safety of his family and tribe first. Gwyngariad would be protected. He would move at first light. It was as though the child in him had died at last and the man was born.

Coll, Owain and the bondsmen from Tan yr Aur had finished their business at Segontium and spent the night at the trading port of Cerrig y Gwyddyl, after a successful crossing the previous day over the Lafan sands on a succession of roped rafts. They were celebrating in the evening around a fire when the messenger from Din Silwy brought the news of Nanw's death.

The gathering became subdued for a while, each man remembering a time when Nanw had helped him through one crisis or another. Then they fell to remembering her with affection and loud anecdote, finishing their evening with a traditional lament with pipe and good voice. They would have to rise well before dawn to arrive in time for her burial rites, which would begin at sunrise; for progress would be slow with the wagons and pack horses.

As luck would have it they came upon the procession from Din Sylwy; making their way in cumbersome fashion to Tan yr Aur; laden with gifts of cooked food. Eithig lead the way in his purple finery, his golden torc gleaming at his throat and a bondsman heralding his approach, with much rude noise on a horn of ceremonial design.

Coll was dismayed that they could not, out of courtesy to their king, overtake him and pull ahead without asking his permission. He was sure that Owain and he would be needed to complete the burial preparations and then there was Ceri. What must she be feeling? Coll knew how devastated she would be at losing not only her grandmother, but her teacher and mentor. He knew how frightened she was to take on the whole responsibility of the healing and worship rites; but there was no gainsaying what the Gods had decreed. One must accept and work with the inevitable.

He reined in next to Owain and said with irritation, 'It tries my patience to crawl home at this snail's pace, Owain. Let us ride ahead and be of some service at home. I suppose I must swallow my pride and beg leave from his high and mightyship.'

'Let me be the spokesman, Coll, for you've a bite in your tongue would bate the calmest of quarries to quarrel,' soothed Owain, whose deep sadness had lent new depths to his usual quietude.

They signalled greetings to cousins and relatives as they urged their ponies to outride the slow moving trail of carts and pack horses, but, as they reached the head of the party, were unnerved by the sound of Eithig and his henchmen drawing steel. They soon realised why. In the dim light of dawning, a figure on a white horse was charging towards them, as if the mad revenge of all evils were spurring the rider to action.

As the rider kept coming, they suddenly gasped as he came into focus. It was Hedfan. They halted and waited, the shining steel of daggers and drawn swords catching the first real rays of daylight.

Hedfan galloped Gwyngariad towards what now looked like a war party, with Eithig at the spearhead. Gwyngariad put her whole trust in Hedfan. If he judged it was safe to ride at the grouping ahead, then she would find a way through. She speeded up, feeling the urging pressure of his heels and the command of his voice in her ear.

Eithig and his henchmen, splitting swiftly into two parties, created a sudden pathway between them avoiding a collision. It was only a handcart at the rear, which was unable to be moved in time. Hedfan reined in, Gwyngariad rearing and turning in one swift movement. How he kept from being thrown the Gods alone knew. He realised he was still in this world, when she tried to shake him from her mane as she stilled and snorted.

For once the strident voice of Eithig was stilled. He seemed speechless, fixing the boy with a stare of steel, as cold as the sword still drawn in his hand. The breeze blowing in from the sea dared to murmur and then became so quiet that all they were aware of was the distant sound of the waves on the shore beyond the forest, the forlorn cry of a gull, and the beating of their own hearts.

Coll swallowed hard and remembered to breathe again, ready to defend his brother if necessary, until he felt Owain's restraining fingers touch his arm.

'Sire,' rang Hedfan's voice clearly and confidently, the only breathlessness being that of his horsemanship a few moments earlier. 'I bring you proof that Gwyngariad is ready. Perhaps you have need of her on this special day to ride royally to the wake gathering? She is yours in return for your protection to our farmlands.'

There was no way that Eithig was going to show that, for a split second, both fear and anger had rattled his composure and command of the situation. He continued to fix Hedfan with his cold stare of steel.

'I shall hold her while you mount, Sire. She is biddable, I vouch,' the boy continued, whilst soothing the mare with his hands and whispering deep within her ear, 'Do not fear. One day you shall be mine.'

'If, indeed, you have trained and calmed her well then you have nothing to fear. If you lie, we can always devise an impaling doom for both yourselves and the horse, as recompense for treachery,' Eithig grimaced, his eyes sweeping the crowd to include Coll and Owain in the threat. He signalled his servant to aid him down from one horse and up on to the other.

Coll and Owain both held their breath as their chieftain made to mount the mare. Only a few days ago she had thrown Coll when he had shown impatience towards her. What by the stars was Hedfan thinking of? But to their amazement she stood obedient and still as though by some enchantment she was changed in character.

It looked a regal band, led by the chieftain on the proud high stepping white mare. Owain dare not ask permission to ride ahead, but both he and Coll agreed that, on the gentle breeze, they could smell the distinctive aroma of oil of lavender. Nanw's spirit rode with them.

⌘⌘⌘

CHAPTER VIII

⌘

THE AWAKENING

Ceridwen slept fitfully and with the first light of dawn she turned her back on the drinking vessel set by the threshold and slipped away from her now sleeping family. She went to drink by the stream. The icy coldness aroused her from the numbness, which seemed to have taken hold of her mind.

Today she would cease to be novice priestess and would gain full recognition from her tribe. There was anxiety, excitement, pride and grief beginning to play their disturbing games within her body, setting her whole being in turmoil. She must regain control.

As the light crept up behind the mountains on the mainland, painting pale gold glory to the underside of the clouds, it was as if Nanw were whispering again all those words of encouragement. 'When you fill your soul with love of the Goddess and feel your oneness with all creation, you have no room in your heart for doubt and fear. Anxiety is self-indulgence, a destructive force creating a chamber of self-imprisonment. It overflows into other people's lives and poisons the living waters of Life.

'Be strong. Take a deep breath from the wind, a rising strength from the sweep of a mountain. Wash away all that is negative in the flowing stream of the Goddess's love and make room in your soul for the Higher Power.' It had been at this very spot, where Nanw had uttered this very lesson.

The morning mist began to rise as the tentative sunlight

gained in strength and lent new energy to the day. Ceridwen prayed and she received the knowledge that all would be well that day.

She heard a rustling in the grass behind her and a 'prrp' of greeting. She turned, expecting it to be playful Luce, but to her surprise it was a purposeful Mwg, who had followed her for the first time. Ceridwen took it as an omen of trust and bent to scratch him under the chin. He rubbed himself against her legs to claim ownership.

The cortège was far from solemn. Today would see the celebration of the life of a dearly loved lady of the old wisdom and her awakening to her new sense of being. It would also mark a new era for her granddaughter as fully-fledged healer and priestess.

Eithig led his men at the front of the procession, with drawn weapons to ward off any untoward evil spirits that may lurk in wait for Nanw's soul. Next, followed her immediate family, the children strewing leaves and flowers in front of the garlanded bier, carried by the men.

'Have you the strength to walk nobly alone, Ceridwen, or do we need a bier for you?' teased Coll, confidentially.

'I will walk in the path of my grandmother with ease, for cannot you see I am floating along?' countered Ceridwen, who had donned a linen shift, let loose her copper braided hair and enveloped herself in her grandmother's voluminous mulberry dyed woollen cloak, embroidered with beaded dragons and serpents. Wrapping herself in this emblem of wisdom, used for over fifty years by Nanw, had seemed like wrapping herself in the warmth of her person. Strength and confidence seemed to have returned to Ceridwen's limbs.

Indeed she did feel as if she were floating along. She felt the blessing of prayer answered and an uplifting of spirit, which affected her bodily. The wind, billowing her garments, had been sent to help them up the steep incline to the burial spot, as did the cheerful piping and tabor playing given as ever by Cullen and Madog.

The two men held a great deal of affection and respect for their old priestess and had needed no prompting by the womenfolk to prepare the burial ground with great care.

The gorse had been axed back to provide a large clearing, the soil and stones from the grave piled in a neat mound, a woven wattle pallet straddled the hole of the grave, ready to receive the bier and two fires were set for torching.

The cortège paused at the mouth of the clearing and four torchbearers stepped forward to receive blessing from Ceridwen. They went to take up their positions; first to the North, then the South, then the East, then to the West.

Eithig and his warriors took their places at either side of the grave and, as the bier bearers approached, raised their forbidden swords in an arch through which the noble body of Nanw was guided. No evil must come near the beauty of her soul.

If there was unease about the lack of a funeral pyre from the tribespeople gathered, it was soon dispelled, as Ceridwen took her place at Nanw's head and invoked the Goddess. 'O Earth Mother, Nurture of all Nature, Conqueror of Death and Purveyor of Rebirth, grant safe passage to this our sister, Nanw our priestess, our mentor, our healer. She has served you with loyalty, obedience and integrity. She has chosen that her body become part of the Earth that she loved. Grant her spirit new life of service in the realms of glory. May she intermingle with our dreams and inspire us to all good. Grant her just destiny in the realms of Truth and Light.'

The prayer continued, the beauty of Ceridwen's voice and words touching hearts and drawing tears. For Gwilym it was such a proud moment, watching this creature he had sired lead the tribe at such an important rite. For Eithig it was an opportunity to feast his eyes and feed his obsession with this woman, whom he intended to break into his service, in the like manner of breaking in a horse such as Gwyngariad.

Ceridwen stood apart with her hands outstretched to the Earth as the warriors drove their swords into the ground around the bier and the whole company joined hands to circumambulate Nanw's stately body, chanting and stamping,

'Grant her new life in the Realms of Glory. Grant her a throne in Realms of Truth and Light.'

Beginning at a stately measure, they chanted and circumambulated Sunwise, speeding gradually into a dizzy pace, which had some of the elders stumbling and the little ones falling about giggling.

Eithig had broken away from the company and stood on a level outcrop of rock to take charge of the proceedings. He took the brief opportunity to torment himself by staring at the rise and fall of Ceridwen's breasts beneath her thin linen shift, as she summoned energy from the four quarters of the Earth. He would have her in time – when the time was ripe.

'Sit!' he barked at his disorderly subjects. His one word was reprimand enough for most and the laughter stilled as the mood sobered. Only little Rhonwen was still giggling with brothers Daf and Rhys, both hands over her mouth in an effort to stem an irrepressible tide of merriment. But it was a stern, fearfully urgent look from Ness that finally controlled it.

The chieftain motioned a young boy to step forward, prodding him into position with the point of his sword. He was a thin, gangly weakling, no more than ten years of age, with the face of a girl.

Owain found himself thinking that the warriors would find use for the wretch in the absence of available women. Hedfan, however, could not take his eyes from the hilt of Eithig's sword. He winced as his wounds began to remind him of that day of searing pain on the scorching anvil, where the sword had been wrought.

The boy was an orphaned cousin of Eithig, sent to the chieftain for care and protection. His name was Ffynan and his father had been a bard, highly respected for his poetic narrative and harp playing. People remembered his father meeting an untimely death in a bog. Was it not just before Eithig was elected as king?

The boy had some of the talents of his father: a beautiful singing voice, as yet unbroken; a talent for rhyming and story telling; but as yet halting with novice fingers on the simple hand held lyre. Today he would do his best to please and take his father's place, for he had no desire to become a warrior or farmer.

He had studied Nanw at every tribal rite during the short ten years of his life. The womenfolk at Din Sylwy had fed him with stories of her wisdom and healing powers. Hopefully he would do justice to her memory. As a hush fell upon the gathering, he stroked a repeated simple chord on his lyre and clearing his throat began to sing in a beautiful voice of rare purity:

'Lady of dignity, bowered in beauty,
Loyal to the Goddess each day of her life;
Wise as the tawny owl swooping at nightfall,
Sweeping all evil away from our door.

Fleet as the running deer was she in girlhood;
Graceful as swallows winging it home.
Fruit of her womb were her children of mystery,
Womanhood blessed by the wisdom of Crone.

Ear to all troubles and salve to the sore tried,
Hands of the Angel of Healing were hers.
Hag as she shrivelled with age overcoming,
But soulwise expanding as clouds spread the sky.

Nanw our teacher our mother, our priestess
Take hold of our dreams and our futures inspire.
Teach us to balance our daily endeavours
With justice and mercy that never will die.
Nanw, oh Nanw, remain in our memory,
Nanw, oh Nanw, never to die!

Ffynan, bathing in the warm glow of praise and loud approval, felt confident enough to approach Hedfan to offer him a turn at his lyre. The two boys went off under the trees to cement a friendship begun. It would be an opportunity for Hedfan to inspect Gwyngariad and share his hopes.

'You have a talent equal to your father's, Ffynan. I wish I

91

could stroke the lyre as you do.' Ffynan coloured with pleasure. 'Come, let us go and stroke Gwyngariad. I've a secret to share with you as long as you promise to breath no word of it to a soul.'

Doubly pleased to be praised and to be let into a secret, Ffynan allowed Hedfan to lead him over to the tethered horses. Gwyngariad whinnied her recognition of Hedfan. 'Breathe into her nostrils and show her you are a friend,' instructed Hedfan, stroking the mare's nose in greeting. 'There, she likes you because you are gentle.'

Hedfan felt instinctively that, if he could make friends with this slip of a lad from Din Sylwy, he would become a useful ally. 'This is the secret you must swear to keep locked in your heart.... the Gods wish me to be master of Gwyngariad one day. Do you swear by the wroth of Bran to tell no soul?'

'I swear,' breathed Ffynan, wide-eyed and solemn, as he put down his lyre with great care on a mossy knoll and took out his knife. Holding it point upwards before his face he kissed it and swore, 'By the wroth of Bran I will tell no one your secret.'

'How it is to come about and when I am not sure. You could keep an eye on her for me at Din Sylwy. Would you do that for me Ffynan?'

'I will always be her friend and yours,' he smiled, with his trusting blue eyes never leaving Hedfan's face. Hedfan wondered at a friendship so easily begun, not understanding what desperation for affection this lonely small soul craved.

Eithig ordered the fires to be torched. Food was to be prepared on one and the other would provide the day-long smoke for a prayer fire: for each person there, down to every small child able to speak, would approach Nanw's body to give thanks to her and make an offering into her soul fire.

Ceridwen watched, fascinated as the little ones approached the bier, Ness supervising in case they should feel fearful or trip. 'Try to think of something kind which *Nain* Nanw did for you and say 'Thank you,' to her,' Ness whispered.

' Thank you, *Nain* Nanw, for helping my cut finger to heal

better,' mumbled Rhodri shyly, as, with downcast eyes, he laid at her feet a coil pot full of mead, which he himself had helped to make.

'*Nain* Nanw, your prayers helped us to become skilled at hunting. Thank you!' chorused Daf and Rhys, who had recently become deft at catching fish with their hands in the river.

'*Nain* Nanw, thank you for making my nasty dreams go away,' breathed Rhonwen, placing her favourite straw dolly tenderly under the old woman's fingers. Only her mother, Ness, knew the sacrifice that was wrung from Rhonwen to give this gift. Ness shared the thought with Ceridwen as their eyes met. Ceridwen found it difficult to swallow, but forced an approving smile.

Soon it would be her turn to give thanks; but she had so much in her heart she wanted to say to Nanw, she would wait until the crowd had moved away and do it more privately. She was curious to know Eithig's thoughts, as she observed his solemnly bringing a gift of an unusual blanket, woven by the women of Din Silwy. It was exquisitely decorated with seaweeds and tiny strung shells. His face was masked and guarded. She would have no access to the curse, which Eithig prayed Nanw would reinforce for him - a curse against all Romans. Characteristically his mind was too preoccupied with his own boon to give thanks for the life of his priestess. Only the Goddess was witness and took note.

The men set about killing and roasting some of the food they had brought with them. The youngsters served their elders with a breakfast of honeyed oatcakes and mead. Marged, heartily glad that she need have no part in the organisation of feeding the crowd, approached Ceridwen, who was still deep in prayer.

'You spoke beautifully and with great courage, my Priestess,' she smiled.

'You call me 'Priestess' and not 'Ceridwen.' Will you find it difficult, Mother, to resist counselling me?'

'Very difficult! Am I not your mother and haven't I counselled you all your young life? And here you are our spiritual leader and I must not gainsay you.' Marged raised her eyebrows in mock wistfulness, smiled a little and then became thoughtful and sad, staring at the still body of Nanw, decked in its finery on the bier.

Ceridwen knew her thoughts and shared them silently for a few moments. She could have been caught in the trap of self-indulgent grief, for her own sense of loss yawned like a chasm before her, but she recognised Marged's need above her own. 'I must strive to be like my grandmother, for she never ordered anyone to any action, but always set out suggestions as how things might be managed.

'Let us channel our loss into action. Perhaps, as we try to emulate the qualities we loved in her, part of her will live on in us?'

'You are right, of course, and are sooner to the remedy than I. Let me not spoil this occasion. If I want to grieve, I shall do it privately. Come, let us take some refreshment, then begin our rites at the spirit fire.'

'Mother, have you brought the tea of hyssop and rosemary? For I must take nothing more until next I wake.'

'Ness has it safe for you in the small pot at her belt. Will it be a trial for you to eat no meat for nine days?'

'Only today will be a trial as the smell of the roasting has me slavering with greed. Once I am home at the peace of Cae Gwynion it will be no effort.'

As the two women left the graveside, tribespeople were beginning to bring more gifts and place them on the wattle pallet around Nanw. There were gifts of food and drink, clothing, carved wooden bowls and plates, a comb, nosegays and a pair of slippers in softest pigskin to tread lightly into the next world.

As the day wore on, everyone bar Ceridwen ate and drank their fill; gossiped and swapped news; danced and sang; or foraged for more wood to keep the fires burning as nightfall came on and it grew colder. Mercifully the wind had died to a soft stillness and the Moon, creeping from the clouds, cast her silver mantle over the grassy slopes and gleamed through the silhouetted branches of the budding trees.

They had feted Nanw royally and now needed to bury her

body along with her gifts. Eithig bent to take Nanw's circlet from her head. It was white gold, exquisitely worked with the pattern of an adder. The crowd held its breath as he transferred it to crown the brow of Ceridwen. Only she was aware that his fingers lingered overlong in her hair, sending chill shivers down her spine.

'Our Priestess!' they cried with one voice. Ceridwen did not doubt their sincerity and prayed fervently to her Goddess that she might always be deserving of their trust. She felt her girlhood slip into the shadows of fire-lit memory. Hedfan wondered if she would ever tickle and tease him again.

Only Eithig was devoid of awe at her beauty that night, cheeks made rosy by the dancing flames and serenity flowing through her, linking her with the wider starlight. His appreciation of her beauty was of baser nature. To him, this night, she had become a fruit ripened sweetly, the more to be picked and devoured. He savoured the thought.

The warriors held the bier aloft, whilst the family removed the wattle pallet and lined the grave with the blanket of respect woven at Din Silwy. Then the ash bough platform was lowered gently with its precious load. Ceridwen, Marged and little Rhonwen chanted a round, depicting Nanw's attributes of wisdom, kindness and vision. Then all got to work filling in the hole with their bare hands as a mark of love. It was soon done and the wattle pallet replaced over the grave. Marged spread a great rug of sheepskin and Ceridwen settled to sleep on top of the grave, for they believed that by so doing all Nanw's wisdom would be transferred to her granddaughter. As Nanw awoke from the sleep of the underworld in the Caves of Annwn, where all pain and misery were taken away, her spirit would be released to begin its new life elsewhere.

'Sweet dreaming,' comforted Marged, as she covered Ceridwen's aching body with thick blankets and sprigs of rosemary. Ceridwen, soon warmed by a herbal broth and comfort of her coverlets, drifted easily into an exhausted sleep; whilst the company, huddled around the fire as best they could, awaited the dawn. The waning Moon drifted peacefully across the sky, her crescent light guarding the maiden on the ground.

Disappointingly there were no mystic dreams that night, no signs that a transition of some sort had taken place. Ceridwen put it down to her sheer exhaustion. There seemed no reaching through to the mystic world, but she knew to have faith and it would be revealed in good time. Meanwhile she played along with the rite and at first light stretched languorously, putting aside the coverlets with due care.

Cullen had to be nudged into life to be on cue with his piping and began playing a wistful air. Stretching, Ceridwen announced, 'I have awakened! Nanw is awakened!'

The camp stirred and the fire was roused as Ceridwen improvised a dance, weaving in and out of her people; sometimes touching them in blessing; sometimes ducking underneath an arch made by the children's hands; or laughingly swinging on the belt of a brother. It was noticed that she gave wide berth as she skirted Eithig, using her cloak to wing and sweep around him. Some mistakenly thought it was a mark of respect.

⌘ ⌘ ⌘

CHAPTER IX

⌘

TAKEN NOT GIVEN

For several weeks, Ceridwen hid herself away at Cae Gwynion, drinking in its peace and ever hopeful of some visitation or sign from Nanw. The wind whipped up and raged outside, but inside the hut there was a stillness, that was all. Not emptiness, but stillness, silence, as though someone were waiting to speak.

Late Spring was inhospitable, gales and driving rain making it impossible to gather herbs, feed the goats and geese, or even venture to the midden toilet without being soaked to the skin.

Marged had encouraged her to go back to Tan Yr Aur with them for a while, but she had declined, wanting the peace of the hut at Cae Gwynion, needing to be near her memories of Nanw. Hedfan was sent along each day to check her needs and Gwilym had sent some bondsmen to chop logs for her fire. Hedfan was not healed well enough for such a heavy task.

She spent the days sleeping her aching need of her grandmother away, her hissing cauldron of broth, Luce and Mwg for company. But soon, the steel grey of the sky broke into silver light and birdsong beckoned her outdoors once more.

Whilst she had been sleeping and healing things had been growing. The place needed her attention. The sooner she adopted the rhythm of a daily routine the better. She washed; she tidied; she cleared; she weeded; she gathered; she boiled; she tended the animals; but above all she prayed as she worked, weaving a magic carpet of hope all around herself and Cae Gwynion. Sanctuary it had been and sanctuary it was to remain.

As the weather improved and grew warmer, she felt she could indulge herself in a walk on the mountain, up through the skirting of trees to where the young heather was putting out new springing shoots. Luce decided to accompany her. Mwg was to stay home and guard the fire.

The young kitten was growing fast, but as yet did not like to let Ceridwen out of sight, particularly on unfamiliar territory. She mewed plaintively whenever a bush or clump of bracken hid Ceridwen's sure-footed figure from view.

The climb was slow and leisurely, Ceridwen calling to Luce whenever the kitten seemed unsure of following. At last they reached a rocky outcrop bejewelled with the silver, gold and verdigris of moss and lichens. Ceridwen scooped the soft creature near to her cheek and savoured the fresh smell of wind blown fur, nuzzling and caressing her endearing muzzle.

'Is it not beautiful here as I promised, Luce? Are you not glad you had the courage to come?' The young woman laid her limbs across the warmed rock and bathed in the warmth of the sunlight, shading her eyes from the glare of the sky. A family of three buzzards was playing on the spiralling thermals of wind, wheeling in circles, the father and mother encouraging their youngster ever higher.

'They shall not get you Luce. They might think you are a young hare with your colouring, but you are safe with me. I promise.' She stroked the silken head, Luce's trusting deep blue eyes now closing with warmth and relaxation as the creature spread herself along the length of Ceridwen's breast and stomach.

She had not been aware of drifting away, but as she woke, Ceridwen felt about for the kitten. It was gone. 'Luce! Luce! Where are you?' There was no answer, only the croak of the parent buzzards as they ordered their youngster home to the roost.

'Luce!' This time Ceridwen's anguished cry echoed over the mountainside and down to the valley.

There was a rustling in the undergrowth alongside the path below and the low rumble of male laughter and banter. Then the shaft of a spear hissed past Ceridwen's shoulder and lodged half way up a silver barked birch.

There was a cheer from the male voices and Ceridwen froze in terror as she realised that they had been aiming at Luce, hanging for dear life by two front paws from a main bough of the tree.

There was no thought for her own safety, as she turned her back to whatever the danger on the path below. She scrambled urgently to the tree and, in an attempt at a gentle calm voice, encouraged Luce to let go and jump to her shoulder.

'Luce, come to me. See. I am here for you. Come to me.'

'Come to me. Come to me,' laughed and jeered the voices behind her. She paid no heed.

Terrified, Luce answered her call with a pitiful mew of anxiety, and, after some panicking, further scrabbling and more encouragement, made the leap of trust to her mistress's shoulder. Tucking the kitten safely beneath the folds of her cloak at last, Ceridwen turned to face her tormentors.

There were about eight in all, mailed men of the twentieth legion, neatly bearded and helmeted. One, who pushed between the others and stood forwards, his scarlet plume announcing him as a centurion of the Roman occupation, had been smiling more at his men amusing themselves than at the discomfiture of the she-creatures before him.

Quintus Aurelius Maximus was bored, very bored of being detailed to tiny outposts, where nothing but minor skirmishes occurred. He and his eighty men were newly barracked at the hill fort on Purple Mountain, defending the island from the sea raiders, who dared to land so rarely these days.

These Celts were a foolish rabble, rarely organised enough to give good battle, but good at husbandry, granted. They knew how to grow a good crop of wheat and keep food in everyone's belly o'er Winter. They must be kept underfoot and in line, not allowed to get too cock-sure with their masters.

Today had been tedious. Meromic, a young auxiliary from the previous posting, had volunteered to stay behind and introduce them to the local tribespeople. The farmsteaders had looked uncomfortable, if not hostile, towards their new masters. They had become too much accustomed to the sloppy management and free enterprise encouraged by his predecessor. Discipline would need tightening.

Later in the day, to give his men a measure of relaxation, he had ordered the century to split into small groups to scour the mountain for firewood and the forest for good hunting spots. The girl, now capturing his attention, did not seem to be suitably in awe of him. Indeed she was spitting and hissing at him in Brythonic like a wild she-cat. He knew little of the language and understood little of her tirade other than it was disrespectful and scathing.

'You call yourself soldiers? Have you no real work to do other than to torment an innocent creature. It is time you learnt the art of hunting for food, instead of playing child games. You desecrate sacred ground. Your feet are unwelcome here!'

The handful of troops stopped their smirking when they swore they could see Ceridwen grow taller like a great giantess in fury. Perhaps she was a witch casting a spell on their eyes. But Quintus was inured to such superstitions and only aware that his authority must remain unchallenged, his word reign supreme among his men.

'Bind her! She shall be whipped for this insult to Rome!' he seethed in his Latin tongue as yet unfamiliar to Ceridwen.

Ceridwen had little chance to escape the hands that wrested Luce from her grasp, threw the creature like a bundle of rags into the briers and bound her own hands together in front. But for one moment she gained advantage. The men, on whom she seemed able to cast a *glamour*, noticed the crescent Moon painted on her forehead. They faltered in trying to tie her to a tree and backed away fearing her curse.

She took her opportunity and ran into the nearby forest, gasping as she ran and crying a prayer for protection to the wind. With hands tied together she would not be able to outrun them, she knew. But they might be frightened to follow her into the burial ground; if only she could reach it in time.

'Idiots, all of you! Incompetent idiots! Give me that whip and I shall punish her myself. Stay back!' Quintus followed her through the trees, his appetite whetted to inflict pain. He knew he only had to keep up his huge stride and he would eventually overtake her. He would teach her a lesson she would never forget. For the men, they were heartily glad to take no part. Did Quintus truly not recognise who she was? Or was he just completely fearless?

Ceridwen found her legs, normally so strong to climb the mountain, refused to bear her quickly. They seemed to have turned to sludge beneath her. She knew she was panicking and that only a clear head could save her. She wasn't going to make it to the burial ground at this speed. To hide was her only option. Perhaps there was a badger set close by. Yes, she had her bearings. She must press on, weaving through the trees to shake them off.

If she could reach the deserted badger set, it would be just big enough to wedge herself into and cover the mouth with brushwood. They had no dogs with them. They would surely give up the chase and return to the fort if she stayed long enough.

With a flood of relief she found what she was looking for, a pile of droppings and bedding cleared from the old badger set and not far from the mouth. She grasped hold of some fallen brushwood and eased herself into the hole, her slim hips thrusting into the tunnel and her feet hoping they would not find another animal in residence.

She was just easing the final branches into place, when a stealthy, long-fingered, brown hand grasped one of her bound wrists with a grip of iron. Wordlessly he dragged her out, scraping her belly along the soiled ground. Then he stood over her and raised the whip aloft, ready to beat her senseless.

Ceridwen waited to feel the pain of his lashes, but there was a pause; a pause so full of dread that she prayed the Caves of Annwn, deep in the centre of the earth, would open beneath her and swallow her forever. He had changed his mind.

He knew his men had not followed him into the trees. It was her word against his. Who would believe this slut of a girl?

Wasn't she taunting him and begging to be taken?

With one swift movement he kicked her over onto her back against the bright yellow of the gorse, and pinned her bound wrists above her head. In another swift movement he had her tunic up over her face to reveal her writhing body, naked beneath. It was soon pinned beneath his own writhing. He had never felt so triumphant.

Initially Ceridwen did not know which torture to cry out against. She could not breathe properly because of the woollen cloth of the tunic over her face. She tried to scream out against the daggers of gorse thorns, piercing into the flesh along her arms and along her back; but the cries were muffled and she was fighting to draw her next breath. Then the cold steel metal platelets of his armour cut against her chest and belly. But it was the hot, hard weapon between her legs, thrusting and tearing, which finally jolted her body and head to one side and gave her air enough to summon a scream, which rent the air. Then there was a blow to her face and welcoming deep, red blackness; warm blackness - which enfolded her in its arms as she was enveloped in the soothing embrace of the Earth Mother.

Quintus Aurelius Maximus had dealt out what she deserved. He had no intention of letting her scream until the farmsteaders below were alerted and came running. The blow to her face seemed to quieten her and anyone thinking they heard someone screaming might be forgiven for thinking it was the noise of ravens overhead driving off the hunting buzzards with their fierce shrill cries.

In the gentle light of the afternoon Sun, he stood back to survey his handiwork. He felt satiated and strangely calm. He was surprised to note she was a virgin, for the maiden blood ran between her legs. He pulled down the tunic to cover her still body. Her face, as yet only just beginning to swell with bruising, looked strangely peaceful and beautiful. It was then that he noticed the mark on her brow, not a wound, but a painted crescent Moon. Ye Gods! What had he done?

The Sun was beginning to dip into the West when finally the kitten had the confidence to come out of hiding and scent its way to Ceridwen. Her scent was very strong, as the kitten wound its way through the trees and rough undergrowth; but it was something that smelled more like her moon blood, which drew Luce to her side. Luce nuzzled her fingers for attention and reassurance. At last her mistress stirred.

For a while the full horror of what had happened did not return to Ceridwen. She was still bathed in the semi-consciousness of that safe womb-like place, cradled in the healing arms of the Goddess. She automatically took the kitten into her arms and gave it the comfort it craved, rocking the creature to and fro; rocking herself. Then she was able to gnaw and tease the knots from the rope, which bound her and release her quivering hands.

She began to feel the wounds and see the blood. First there was a trickle of tears, then an anguish of sobbing and howling that seemed to come from somewhere outside of herself. It was as though her soul stood above a wretched creature and watched as it keened forwards and backwards in grief and agony. Pain and anger came in alternate waves, unbidden, uncontrolled.

She must try to take possession of herself. 'Oh Luce,' she wept into the soft fur, 'what deed has been done today? Where was my grandmother when I needed her most? Where was my Goddess to protect me?'

She must wash the wounds and uncleanliness away. Seawater would be best to cauterize the bleeding cuts on her back and take away the filth from between her legs. She stumbled the quarter of a league down to the shore. Luce clung grimly to her shoulder the whole way. At last she reached the beach. Was the whole of creation against her? The tide was out!

The lapping waves she longed for were well beyond her endurance on the horizon. A rock pool would have to suffice.

Normally she would have flung off her clothes and revelled in the water, caring not one jot who saw. But now there seemed shame in her body and a wish to hide it. She put Luce carefully down among the dune rushes and eased herself fully clothed into the first deep pool she came across. At first she winced as the saltwater bit into the cuts upon her back, but soon its icy coldness numbed her torn flesh and swollen thighs. She watched mesmerized as the pool turned slowly redder with her own blood.

She could not remember a time when she did not hate the Romans, who had pillaged and conquered their way across the Celtic lands. Nanw had always said the invaders could never violate the souls of the Druids, but she felt violated to the very core. It wasn't just that a young Celtic woman, standing up to the brutish behaviour of the legionaries had been raped as punishment for her sharp tongue. She was a priestess, honoured by her tribe. Respect was not only expected of her tribespeople, but of the legionaries who kept the peace and upheld the Roman law. Here was a priestess violated only weeks from her gift of maidenhead to the Goddess, robbed of the greatest gift she had to bring; violated on the sacred mountain itself.

Slowly, the implications of the deed began to sink into her brain. She saw herself telling her father and brothers. She saw their spurting anger and their hackles of hatred rise. She saw them raze the Roman hill fort and gather the tribe to do serious battle in a frenzy of revenge. She saw wave after wave of legionaries sent from Segontium and a massive funeral pyre for her people. They must not know. Her tribe must never know the humiliation she had suffered at the hands of this vile monster.

Meromic had a free duty period and felt the need to get away from the confines of the fort. He had had a busy day indeed, using all his local knowledge of the area to show the new contingent their surroundings. Tomorrow he would make a special effort to introduce his new commander to Ceridwen at Cae Gwynion. The legionaries were bound to have use for her remedies from time to time and would do well to foster good relations.

He often came down to the shoreline, especially when the sky had turned such a brilliant blue as it had done today. It reminded him, just then, of the seashore at home to the North of Rodec in Aremorica. Here he could pray to the Sea God, Mananaun and throw offerings into the waves for the safety of his sister.

He and Fiommar had been so close and had led an idyllic childhood, fishing and crabbing close to their father's estate. That was until their father had become too outspoken in his praise of the old Celtic ways. He had been arrested as a troublemaker and had killed himself on a sword at the first opportunity, before further shame could befall him. Meromic and Fiommar had been captured and sent to the slave market at Curdun in Arvernia. It did not do to dwell on the nights of terror they spent huddled together in chains.

He remembered, as though it were yesterday, when they were forced from each other; he but a boy of nine and she a year younger. They had been split into groups of male and female, to be shown off in the market square. His head had been swimming in the noonday heat, as he was picked out by a Roman legate and ordered to climb astride a mule, following the Arabian chestnut mount of his new master. All he was aware of, through the haze in his mind, was the haunting pleading in the eyes of his sister, his last link with the old life.

He never forgot those eyes. He saw them whenever he closed his own to pray, her beautiful deep blue eyes.

Meromic knew better than to be miserable around his master. Instead he learned to respect the young legate and over the years he had been able to bathe in a bond of real camaraderie. Then, when they came over to Britain with the First Cohort of the Sunici from Aachen, he had been able to prove his loyalty in battle. He had saved his master Titus's life.

Titus rewarded him with his freedom, but he did not know how to leave the side of his master, or how to set about finding Fiommar. Instead he had enlisted, travelling with the only family he now knew, the Roman army.

Sea birds were wheeling and feeding from the creatures, stranded behind with the last tide, as he dropped down to the shore. He gasped when he saw her; the copper braids and those white skinned graceful arms floating like the tendrils of a sea anemone in the rock pool. Could it be Fiommar? Or was it a *sending* of mystical nature?

His sandalled feet made no sound as he crept closer to skirt her crouching figure seaward and give himself the first real glimpse of her face. She was staring quite fixedly at the mossy rocks lining the pool in which she was lying, unseeing and in another world.

His disappointment turned to concern. It was not Fiommar, but Ceridwen. She was hurt and apparently in shock. He bent and drew closer, so that his familiar face would fall into her line of vision.

'Ceridwen, priestess, what has harmed you and how can I help?' he said softly, not wanting to alarm her.

At first she did not answer. Then she looked into his face and there seemed a moment of recognition. 'They must never know, Meromic. My family and tribespeople must never know, for it will only lead to bloodshed.'

'Know what, Ceridwen? In the presence of the Sea God, Mananaun, tell me. It shall be in confidence. You have my life on it?'

'The new centurion from the fort... He hunted me down in the forest...He forced me... He took my maidenhead. It was promised to the Goddess at Beltane.' She was beginning to shake with the shock and the chill.

Meromic knew enough of the tribespeople, whom he had lived near for the past two years, to know the true seriousness of the crime that had been committed. He held out his hand to assist her from the rock pool and wrapped his dry cloak around her shivering shoulders.

'You are right, Ceridwen. There will be thoughts of vengeance and hotheaded murder if this gets out. Who knows of this? What of Quintus's men? Were they witness?'

'They knew he came after me through the trees with his whip, and no doubt he returned triumphant. What he told them I have no idea.'

'Leave it to me. I will have a word in their ear. They may

know only that you have been whipped. They may know nothing about your violation. They will be so frightened of your curses when I have finished with them, they will not breathe a word. I guarantee.'

'What of Quintus Aur...Aur..?'

'Quintus Aurelius Maximus? He will not want to reveal that he has done something so foolish as to stir needless rebellion. His career would be finished, if he were not murdered before he was arraigned.' Meromic felt his fist tighten as he reined in the strongest desire to choke the life out of his new officer. 'I will let it be quietly known to him that his secret is safe with me. Come. Let us get you back to your fire and some dry clothes.'

Meromic's kindness did something to soothe Ceridwen's sense of dread and she gathered up Luce for the climb home. At least the exertion would stop the shivering.

It was growing dusk by the time they drew near the hut at Cae Gwynion. Ceridwen stopped in her tracks as she heard a familiar chopping sound.

'Meromic, leave me here and go back to the fort. I shall handle Hedfan with ease, telling him of the accident I had when I tried to rescue Luce from a tree,' Ceridwen urged, not wanting the added complication of explaining Meromic's part in what had befallen her. But Meromic, more than anything, wanted to be seen helping Ceridwen and insisted on escorting her to the hut.

'I will say but little and let you do the talking. That way our stories will tally,' he whispered.

Ceridwen was shocked to find not Hedfan chopping her firewood, but Coll. Of course, Hedfan was still too tender to be doing such tasks. Why had she not remembered that? Coll would be harder to fool than young Hedfan. He turned from his work with the axe, as she and Meromic skirted the hut and came into his view.

'Mother suspected something was the matter. She sent me up here to find you. What has happened to your face; to your arms?' Ceridwen knew that in replying she must act as she had never acted before. Coll was usually so close to her thoughts.

'I took Luce a walk upon the mountain. She took fright at the buzzards and ran up a tree. I climbed to rescue her and fell into a gorse and briar thicket. Meromic saw me bathing my wounds at the shore and escorted me home,' she managed a wry smile at her brother, who seemed genuinely relieved that nothing more untoward had happened.

'Come and get dry before the fire. It had gone out when I got here, so I relit it for you and got in some wood. It looks as though you hit your face upon a rock as you fell. It's beginning to bruise,' said Coll, observant and concerned for her as ever.

'Yes, I shall poultice it with comfrey tonight as I sleep,' she answered, glad of the privacy of the wattle screen, where he could not meet her eyes as she changed her clothing. They had always been able to tell when the other was lying, just by looking into the face of the other.

'Meromic brought the new contingent over from the fort today. It's good to know the coast is guarded from invaders by such seasoned legionaries,' Coll continued, in what Ceridwen recognised as his diplomatic vein for Meromic's benefit. Having stirred up the fire, he let down the cauldron on its heavy chain suspended from the roof beam and the broth she had prepared that morning began to bubble.

'Yes, I was telling Ceridwen what a professional lot they seem. They've served with the Twentieth Legion at Deva. I'm glad I volunteered to stay behind to ease them in. They've some stories to tell, mark you,' grinned Meromic wryly.

Coll gave Meromic a warning glance. He had offered the young Roman auxiliary the hospitality of food and fire. He did not want to listen to eulogies about any Roman victories. Meromic, discomfited, decided to draw his log plank bench nearer the fire and accept a wooden bowl, which Coll held out to him.

Meromic left just before dark, his cloak dry now, although besmirched with Ceridwen's blood somewhat. 'All will be well. You'll see,' he said reassuringly as he politely took his leave. Ceridwen made no answer.

She was glad to have the comfort of Coll's snoring by the fire that night. She tried to sleep, leaning on a damp pillow of bruised comfrey leaves and old, thin linen scraps. She noticed that Mwg had allowed Luce to snuggle up close for the first time. He must be missing Nanw so, but there was no peace and comfort near Ceridwen tonight.

It was hard to get comfortable, no matter which way she tried to lie down. But it was discomfiture of soul that really disturbed her. Her secret must never come out. The menfolk in particular must never know how she had been taken.

⌘ ⌘ ⌘

CHAPTER X

✤

THE COVEN

Marged had set about worrying when the new contingent of legionaries, from the twentieth legion at Deva, had arrived to relieve men from the First Cohort of the Sunici. The latter had been made up mainly of auxiliaries drafted from the Celtic regions of Aachen and Koln, men who, despite their allegiance to Rome, had Celtic backgrounds and sympathies. It had meant they were able to rub along well enough, without a great deal of misunderstanding.

However, the relief force spoke mainly Latin and needed an interpreter for Brythonic. They seemed to speak of rules and regulations, taxes and quotas and disturbing punishments, if all was not kept to schedule. Their centurion, Quintus Aurelius Maximus, seemed to have little insight into the sort of reciprocity which had grown between the fortress on the headland and the farmsteaders in the valley below. Perhaps they would learn. At least they had that sensitive young man, Meromic to show them the ropes.

She had sent Coll up to Cae Gwynion, when Ceridwen's fire had gone out. What on earth was that girl doing, allowing her fire to get so low? It would take such an age to get going again, if it were truly dead. Perhaps the kitten was lost. She thought she had heard Ceridwen's voice on the wind, shouting, 'Luce', but then the wind had changed direction and she wasn't sure. No matter. There was to be a coven in a few days, and she would leave her tasks at Tan Yr Aur in the hands of Angharad and Olwenna and climb up to the holy ground to spend time with Ceridwen.

The coven, or gathering, was to take place at Full Moon, just two weeks prior to the Beltane Festival. There would be seven women present from the surrounding settlements. Originally this would have been a gathering of the Druid Council – men and women who had studied the ancient ways and were wise in the mystic teachings. But since the coming of the Romans over two hundred years ago, such councils had been banned. Indeed, all Druids of any real influence had been slaughtered or had gone into hiding, so it was said. The women, however, were allowed to meet and plan the religious festivities. They took the opportunity to work together on a mystic level, reviving what they could remember of their Druid heritage. What they had not learned at the knee of a parent, they improvised from instinct, meditation and consultation together.

It had been agreed at last harvest festival, when the whole tribe had been together for the feast of Lugh, or God of Light, that Iowerth of Dreffos would be a suitable candidate to enact the rite of Beltane with Ceridwen. It would be doubly auspicious for the whole tribe of Celwri to have the blessing of her maidenhead, of both virgin and priestess, sacrificed to their Goddess. Iowerth of Dreffos was deemed to be worthy of the rite and if any issue were to result, then at least the child would be of good sound stock.

But Iowerth of Dreffos had proved weaker than his reputation and that Winter he had died, shortly after a fall from his horse. His only brother was too young to be mated. The group of women gathered at the coven would bring suggestions of how to solve the problem; the names of suitable men being offered from within the tribe, but without the immediate family.

Marged shook her head as she worked on some drop scones, hot from the griddle, to go with Hedfan, in a linen napkin, to Gwilym and his workers in the fields. Who would think that she had a daughter who was not only priestess to their tribe, but who would have the privilege of giving her maidenhead to the Goddess? Their lands and people would be bound to thrive, surely?

There was just one niggling thought that never ceased to plague Marged's mind whenever she became still enough to ponder. What if Eithig was determined to mate with her? Ceridwen would not want it, she knew, for she had seen Ceridwen shy away from him whenever he got too close. But Eithig had ways and means of getting his own way. Perhaps the time was now due to take Ceridwen into her confidence to protect the future.

Marged had made the excuse of visiting Nanw's grave to go early to the coven meeting. It would be an opportunity to see Ceridwen alone. They worked silently at the grave together, spreading the ashes from the deadened spirit-fire around the young sapling, which had been planted over Nanw's heart.

'You seem to be recovering well from your fall, *Cariad?*' said Marged, breaking the silence at last. 'No bones broken, thankfully?'

'Yes. I was lucky...only bruises and scratches. The comfrey and sanicle have begun to do their work already.' Ceridwen replied briefly then fell silent again. She had played down her injuries to Coll and had begged him to allay Marged's concern for her. She had needed some time alone to recover, without Marged's constant fussing. She needed to clear her head, order her thoughts and come to terms with what had happened.

But uppermost in Marged's mind was not concern for her daughter's fall. Uppermost was a desperate need to share her own secret. Marged hardly knew how to begin. They knelt at either side of the grave in quiet reverence. She saw Ceridwen's eyes look up and took it as a signal that she may speak. 'We shall have to decide who will contend for you at Beltane. It was fixed on Iowerth of Dreffos, as you well know; but he is gone. Madog was going to stage a fight with him and let him win your hand, but now something else must be arranged. I am fearful, Ceridwen, that Eithig plans to lie with you at Beltane.'

'Eithig? I would not agree to that, Mother. The man makes my flesh crawl. The thought of coupling with him brings vomit to my mouth.'

'Perhaps there is a reason for this, a natural cause...'

'The cause is plain to see. He is prisoner of the sensual - a human being without the refinement of sensibility, or manners. He is addicted to power and satiating desire. He may be strong of body and courageous in battle, but his strength is not overlaid with the wisdom of his father. He does little for his people but make noises of pomp and pride. Besides, he smells of sweat and vainglory.'

'I see you have the measure of him, but let me finish what I have begun to tell you...It's difficult for me...'

'I'm listening, Mother.'

'Once, when your father was on a mission to the mainland, Eithig's father came by to check we were safe. We offered him and his men hospitality for the night. I was lonely and very attracted to this tall creature with a mane of Sun-streaked hair. He looked so noble, his walk, his manner, his voice. When he suggested we observe the ancient rite of offering wives to the use of the chieftain, I'm ashamed to say I didn't need much persuading. We waited until the children were asleep. I enjoyed his attentions and his dalliance. I enjoyed having an excuse to lie in his arms and be unfaithful to my man. I told myself that, if I did not get with child, no purpose would be served in telling your f...Gwilym.

'For two nights we lay together secretly. Then he was gone. When Gwilym came back I was with child. But he was so happy to see me and I to see him that I could not bear to tell him what had happened. Somehow I could not bear that look of adoration to slip from his face when he looked at me; so I kept my secret and when you were born, said you had come early.'

'So Eithig and I are half brother and sister?'

'Yes, there you have it... And once your fa...Once Gwilym saw you and held you in his arms, as though there was no letting go of you, I knew I could never hurt him. I could not bear to take his pride in you away.'

'Poor Father! Poor Mother! Here am I thinking you have nothing to spoil your relationship; thinking you have no dreaded secrets from each other; envying you. Here am I thinking Gwilym is my true father... And I would have no other. Truly I would have no other!'

'Have I done wrong by not telling him, Ceridwen? Have I done wrong by him and by you?'

'There is a deep bond between Gwilym and myself. He has been a wonderful father. Is it wrong to nurture goodness in two people? Perhaps we would have loved each other even so, had we both known the truth. Who knows? But there might have been a coldness between us. I am glad you kept it from him. Your secret is safe with me. I would leave as not have everyone know I have a half brother in Eithig. There is no merit in owning his father's name. I have merit enough through your line.'

'Your real father was a wise lord indeed, and came of royal lineage. Would you not like to own to that?'

'It is my destiny and I cannot change it. It is good to know that I am descended from both priestly and royal lineage; but look at the qualities I have learned at the knee of Gwilym. In truth it is he who has been my real father, encouraging and cheering me to my goals. The Gods may do with my lineage what they will, but there is no reason to tell him.'

'We must, however, deter Eithig at all cost. Cannot you put a loathing in his heart to be near you?' suggested Marged, hopefully.

'I may find a potion or spell that would do the trick, but it would be of temporary nature. I fancy his desire is already torched and a fire well taken is harder to put out than a flame. On the other hand, perhaps we worry too much. He may only have been playing flirtatious games without earnest intentions. Let us wait until the gathering and see what the women from Din Silwy have to say.'

The five women had gathered by dusk at Tan Yr Aur, but planned to leave their male escorts and climb up to the Holy Ground at Cae Gwynion together. Betw, Eithig's ageing and bent aunt, had come from Din Sylwy with her granddaughter Elen. Tangwen of Dreffos, Iowerth's mother was there and Gwenifer, Meurig's wife, originally from Cerrig y Gwyddyl, resplendent in newly acquired copper and gold ornaments, had travelled the furthest from Dindaethwy - for the Beltane festival was to be for the whole *commote* of the Daethwy, several communities coming together. The fifth woman was Ness, now seven Moons with child, moving heavily and with as much difficulty as Old Betw.

They each donned black woollen robes, woven specially for this sort of occasion at the looms of Dreffos. For, although normally Gwenifer, being the wife of a High Lord, would outrank the others, during consultations at the coven, all would be equal.

Ceridwen was grateful of the warmth of the sacred fire, which she and Marged had lit in the clearing among the young oaks. She had thought they might have to resort to using the hut had the gales continued, but the evening turned out bright and clear, the wind playing gently, teasing the leaves playfully.

Ceridwen presided over the rites, invoking the Goddess of the mountain, who provided them continually with water from the lush springs; trees with their fruits and protection; plants for their healing and succour, and both sunshine and cloud for growth. But each individual knew exactly the part they must play. First they washed, paid homage to the four elements and then all seven held hands circling the fire. Their simple dance moved *deosil*, or Sunwise, their chant beginning with whisperings and building to a smooth crescendo, like the waves on the nearby shore, chorusing and caressing the land.

Then they sat, sharing a wooden bowl of herbal brew from the makeshift cauldron over the fire. It was a brew to sharpen the wits and give focus to their work.

Their first decisions were made easily, without disagreement; decisions about the division of labour at the festival; where hide tents and fires would be pitched for best water and shelter. They made decisions about how food would be brought; who should sing; who should play and how the rite arbour might be erected. Then, when all the small details were deliberated and fashioned, they came to the mating itself.

'Please, make your suggestions that I may respond,' said Ceridwen, not wanting to wield her influence initially.

'There is no one of age at Dreffos. Ieuan is but nine years old and the other men well wived with children. There is no one in our vicinity since Iowerth died,' said Tangwen sadly, remembering how last year Iowerth had looked so strong and manly, riding his blue-dappled grey home from the feast of Lughnasad. He had been so hopeful that the match between he and Ceridwen would turn into marriage.

'We have orders to propose Eithig and Huw the Giant from Din Silwy,' said Betw in her gruff, no nonsense way. There was an uncomfortable pause whilst the flames of the fire flickered and hissed.

'And what orders does Huw the Giant have, to make sure Eithig has it in the bag?' Marged ventured.

'Tis only the same as the game of combat we all agreed was to happen between Iowerth and Madog. Madog was to let Iowerth win, so that someone untried in dalliance could perform the rite. Huw the Giant will let Eithig win for certes,' countered Elen innocently. The other women spluttered, laughing and choking in turn.

'Untried in dalliance! Eithig? Do you not mean well worn? His trail of deflowered maidens gets longer each Samhain. He has fathered a dozen at least since he took power from his father; but not one has he loved enough to take for his wife.'

'Take care, Gwenhifer. He could have spies in hiding to bear witness to your ridiculing tongue,' warned Betw, frightening herself more than the others.

'I cannot countenance Eithig as my mate at the sacred rite. I feel unworthy of the honour myself, but feel him to be doubly so. Our teachings tell us it is such a sacred, beautiful rite; but to sacrifice my maidenhead to him would feel like violation itself,' Ceridwen swallowed in earnest. She was deadly serious now; the memory of what had occurred on the mountain still fresh and raw to her inner vision. To lie with Eithig would feel the same. She shuddered visibly and the other women took due note.

'The men from Dindaethwy and Cerrig y Gwyddyl are loath to challenge a chieftain. There are men of good combat and daring, but Eithig would not think twice to have them spirited away, if he knew there was a chance they might defeat him. There are plenty around who owe their life to him and have yet to repay their debt with a favour. I am loathe to say that, although we have young men aplenty at the port, who would feel it an honour to be coupled with Ceridwen at Beltane, there is none, who dares make move, without leave of Eithig,' said Gwenifer, her proud face softening a little in sympathy with Ceridwen.

'What say we then should be done? Ceridwen would want neither Eithig, nor Huw the Giant, for the latter is strong, but dull of wit, no match for this sacred coupling?' posed Marged, herself at a loss for an answer.

'Have you not a potion or spell which will reveal to you your true mate, Ceridwen?' suggested Elen, ever the romantic and hoping to see magic done before her very eyes.

'We should divine the future by the old means of oracle; sacrifice an animal to determine what course of action to take from its entrails,' said Betw.

'A dearly loved animal would be the best sacrifice to determine things. Mwg, perhaps?' suggested Tangwen, who felt she had already sacrificed all that was most dear and didn't see why others should not shoulder a little grief for a change.

Gwenhifer was a squeamish woman at best and had no heart in physical sacrifice and said that such offerings always made her feel ill, but it was left to Ceridwen to take the lead, after all, she was the priestess.

Initially dumbstruck at the suggestion of this last vestige of her mother being used in such a way, Marged marvelled at her daughter's level calmness. From where did she get her strength?

'No sacrifice is necessary,' said Ceridwen in the hushed smooth silken tones she had rehearsed so many times with Nanw. It was a voice that brooked no argument, yet held such love and warmth the hearer felt cocooned from discord. She found herself automatically using it to rescue the present situation. 'I know a simple herb mixture, which when combined with a chanted spell, will give us a vision of my true lover. You may all help me with prayers and with the ritual. Wait here by the fire whilst I go to the hut for my simples.'

Ceridwen prayed no one would try to accompany her. She needed time to think. Nanw had told her this spell only two

Moons previously. Why couldn't she remember it? Had what happened on the mountain completely destroyed her wits? She shuddered and shrugged away the violent memory, which could attack her afresh if she allowed it in.

The path was well trodden down to the hut and her brain was in such a whirl that it had no time to be frightened of the dark shadows cast by the trees. She was soon in the quiet of the stone and wattle building, with its thatch smelling newly renovated and a thin wisp of smoke curling into the roof opening in the centre. She began to breathe more evenly.

Mwg sat royally erect by the fire, with paws neatly placed side-by-side and eyes closed in blissful appreciation of the warmth. Ceridwen paused, her hand holding the wattle woven door by the threshold, and watched him. He opened both eyes briefly as she arrived, then promptly closed them again as if he were encouraging her to do the same; so she did.

When she opened them again she was surprised to see Nanw sitting and smiling in his place by the fire. She could hear Nanw's voice repeating the spell to her in her head; but the voice seemed strangely out of synchronization with Nanw's moving lips.

'Oil of hyssop is drunk for desire;
Feverfew thrown on a sacred fire;
Flowers of yarrow and ivy entwine
About the hands of the girl in mind.
Then bind to her breast the feather of dove,
Binding her close to her one true love,
Who shall appear when the Moon is full,
When the night is hushed and the wind is still,
In a circlet of water captured by
The Moon, as she sails in her silver sky.'

Ceridwen stood absolutely still, hardly daring to breathe for a moment, drinking in the wonder of what had happened. Nanw had come to her when needed. She was continuing her ministry to her people by inspiring Ceridwen. Then, with the next blink of an eye, Mwg was there instead, still sitting by the fire, absorbing the heat. The vision was gone. She could no longer see Nanw, but there was a lingering smell of the old priestess's lavender oil, comforting, reassuring, as though to soften the blow of the parting.

Swiftly she gathered what she needed and headed back to the waiting coven. She was disappointed that they seemed to be gossiping as she approached, and not maintaining the reverence that they had worked with initially. Their voices hushed guiltily, as she took her place in the circle and explained the simple ritual.

Marged brought fresh spring-water to wash anew the cauldron and they began invoking the Goddess of the mountain again. Having each drunk from the cauldron's hyssop brew and flung dead straws of feverfew on the fire to set it dancing, they bound Ceridwen with the dove feathers at her breast. They twisted the dried flowers of yarrow through her hair with fresh ivy and bound up her wrists with the same. Then they circumambulated the fire *deosil* or Sunwise, repeating the spell over and over until, spinning her three times around, she fell dizzily into the arms of Betw and Tangwen.

They lay her trance like body onto the mossy ground of the clearing, away from the direct firelight. On her belly they placed a bowl of clear water, then knelt around her holding hands, waiting for the Moon to appear from behind a cloud, and its reflection to silver the water.

They did not have to wait long. The breeze was scudding thin wisps across the midnight sky and it seemed as though the Moon herself rode with anticipation. Each woman stared long into the silver-reflecting circlet. If the spell worked, then each would see the same vision.

There was only the rush of the breeze in the trees and the occasional crackle from the nearby fire, to break the long silence. The night owls were hushed and waiting too.

Ceridwen was dreaming, dreaming of being held in a warm, protective embrace. It was so gentle and tender; yet so strong. She nestled against the wide chest. He smelled of leather and wood smoke. She ran her hand up his tunic towards his face, which as yet she could not see. She slid her fingers around his neck and lifted her face to press against his cheek. He was a Roman.

Ceridwen sat up abruptly, spilling the contents of the bowl, which had been balanced on her belly. The other women broke their contemplation and they looked at each other expectantly.

'Did you see him? Did you see?' squealed Elen excitedly.

'I only...I saw only the broadness of his chest. No face, nothing I could recognise.' Ceridwen was conscious that the half-truth was covering both her confusion and prejudice - the prejudice that Nanw had warned against. She felt humiliated by her own reaction, yet unable to share her real feelings with her coven sisters. She wrapped the black woollen gown defensively around her body and went to sit closer to the warmth of the fire. The questions burning in her mind whirled around incessantly and brought a great churning of fearfulness to her stomach. Why had the Goddess allowed such a terrible event to take place on the Holy Ground? Why did it seem that she was destined to be prey to a Roman mating? What purpose was this whole mess of her life to serve?

'Let us draw to the fire and each tell what we saw,' suggested Marged, conscious, more than anyone else, that Ceridwen was dazed and confused and in no fit state to handle the proceedings. The other women were happy to let Marged lead them, for wasn't she Nanw's daughter, tutored at her knee and tarred with her wisdom?

Marged continued. 'What of you Tangwen? What did you glimpse?'

'To be honest, I saw only my beautiful son, riding his dappled grey and smiling to me. Perhaps I was too much with the past and reflecting what a wonderful mate he would have been for our priestess.' Tangwen wiped at her glistening tears with the loose sleeve of the black wool robe. It had been such sweet sorrow and privilege to behold his face again. The hands of Betw and Ness encircling her for a moment acknowledged her grief, but Marged wished to press on.

'And Gwenhifer, what did you behold in the circlet of moon silver?'

'At first I found it difficult to see aught but the lurking of shadows behind the trees. When I finally found focus on the surface of the Moon water, I saw myself trysting with Meurig and a son with a crown coming out of my belly. It was Elfed my youngest; I am sure. Perhaps we should wait for our son Elfed to be fourteen. Another year, that is all, and he will be ready.'

'But Ceridwen is promised this Beltane, not the next,' said Ness, seeing the consultation twisting ever down yet a more complicated path, where they would have to choose both lady and sire for the Beltane rite. 'I saw Madog, fighting for me as he did at the Beltane of our first coupling. However, in my vision, he did not fight against one of our tribe. I could have sworn he fought with a Roman, for the man's armour glistened as he fought with my Madog. I think I was hoping that Ceridwen would experience the same joy that I had that Beltane. But with that memory did not come the knowledge of who should become her mate. Like Ceridwen I did not see his face.'

'Nor I, just the face of a long dead Lord I once knew,' said Marged wistfully. 'And Elen? What of you?'

'I saw Cullen coupling with Ceridwen,' said Elen, reddening at the memory, more with jealousy than embarrassment, for she had danced with Cullen at the awakening and had promise of a Beltane coupling with him herself. What she did not realise was that all other six women had knowledge of her attraction to him. All but Ceridwen nodded in wry understanding. Marged chose not to comment and moved focus to Betw, who, being the eldest, had the greatest experience.

Betw, knowing that the other women depended so much upon her, began falteringly. 'I beheld.... Eithig, resplendent in his best robes and with his new sword by his side, but it was not Ceridwen he was holding 'gainst the wall at Din Sylwy. It was...another.' Betw had long suspected incest at Din Sylwy, for which the Gods rained down the punishment of disease and idiocy to future generations, but she had no firm proof. The girl Einir, Eithig's young sister, had her moon blood, she was sure. There was no sign of her being with child. Perhaps there had been other torments?

Whatever was going on between Eithig and Einir, Betw felt uncomfortable about revealing to her coven sisters. However, she did feel honour bound to mention it.

'I saw him wielding his will against Einir, and she too frightened to do aught else but submit,' she finally admitted.

'Surely it was your suspicion but shown to you, Betw? I cannot believe Lord Eithig would jeopardize his family so,' Tangwen insisted, ever grateful to turn a blind eye to the unpleasant.

'That makes sense of something Hedfan told me after his last visit to Din Silwy. He said that he found Einir in tears, looking as though she had been bound and beaten in Eithig's hut. Does it not strengthen our will against him, as an unsuitable mate for the Beltane rite?' breathed Marged, even more incensed and determined that Eithig should not succeed in mating with her daughter

She trusted Old Betw's vision. She had always proved in the past to have the sight. If Eithig could be discredited to the coven sisters, without her revealing his true relationship to Ceridwen, all well and good. If the worst came to the worst then all must know that they were brother and sister. Perhaps it may not come to that. If she were clever enough, the secret might be kept between Ceridwen and herself. All six, apart from Ceridwen, who still seemed stunned and confused by her dream, nodded now in complete agreement with Marged.

Eithig has the strength, without the purity of spirit needed,' Marged continued. 'But it is apparent, by our visions, that we bring too much of ourselves to the sighting. We have reflected our personal concerns, rather than gained true knowledge of who is destined to bed our priestess,' said Marged, surprising herself at her own clarity of understanding. 'We must shed our anxieties and the thoughts we cling to, as we shed our robes onto the grass.

'Elen, bring the ewer of blessed water nearer. We shall all wash away our preconceptions and open our minds to the outpourings of The Great Wisdom.'

'Marged is quite right,' agreed Betw, taking Ceridwen's hand in hers and patting it affectionately, 'For, when the vessels of our souls are full of fears, or even petty concerns, we cannot be pure vessels for the wine of clear vision to reveal itself. We must try again to achieve an emptying of self and a unity of purpose. Then only will a course of action be revealed to us.'

Only Gwenhifer found herself clinging to a selfish shred of impatience at having to go through the process of spell working yet again. She would have to work extra hard upon her own need of warmth, for her body was slender like that of a young deer and was unused to exposure of wind and cold.

As the others put by their robes with care and stood full naked in the Spring breeze, she was shamed by their unconcern for themselves and their renewed sense of unified tranquillity. Elen poured the holy water from the ewer into the cupped hands of each sister, who splashed its biting coldness over face, then body, then feet. Gwenhifer marvelled that she was the only one physically shivering, but when they drew her into their circle and held her hands, she felt the warmth of their sisterly love flood through her veins and drive out the cold.

Ceridwen too felt herself being drawn into the ritual. As she gave herself to the moment she found all emotion gradually drain from her. As soon as she held hands with the other sisters, her qualms of fear settled and her mind became comfortingly soothed and empty. All she could think of now was that it was a simple test of trust, trust in the Creator, trust in the Goddess of the Mountain, whom she served, and trust in the love of her companions. She had let go of everything. She would not try to be in control, only go with the tide of her destiny and not try to fight it. After all, the Goddess knew more than she. The wisdom of events would become clear if she would just allow those forces to work in her life and not try to shape everything for herself. The Earth Mother knew best. What was done was done and the consequences would unfold. It was time to be. Nothing more was required of her than to be.

The sisters drew again to a mossy mound clear of the firelight and set a woollen robe on the ground where Ceridwen was to lie. The bowl of clear spring-water was made ready once more and this time they began with silence, long and beautiful, until all seven minds were clear and untroubled. Each then nodded assent and they began the circumambulating anew, chanting the spell in a chorused whisper, so as not to break the unity of thought they had created.

Now that each soul had emptied itself of the dross of its worldly cares and was one in spirit with the others and the universe, all prayer and thought was to the Higher Good, that source of all knowledge, which organises events for our advancement and spiritual education.

The chanting finished. Ceridwen was caught this time by all six pairs of hands, as they gently lowered her to the ground and placed the bowl once more on the soft rise of her white belly. This time they put their hands palms upward underneath her, so that she might be aware of their support.

This time there was no impatient hurrying and waiting for results, only an acceptance of a trust in timelessness. After all, it took nine Moons to grow a child in the womb, so what was an hour to wait for delivery of information, which would shape all their lives?

Ceridwen felt completely warm in the encircling cocoon, made by those six pairs of hands. And the women, kneeling around her, felt the glow of the Earth Mother, as she pulsed her energies up through the crust of her outer shell and through their yielding knees, feet and hands.

Then, just when Old Betw felt she might have to shift the position of her stiffening joints, the Moon came out of hiding once more and the silver light she cast upon mountain, tree and rock, bathed the waiting women in the robe of its glistening magic.

They stared into the circlet of beckoning water, as it seemed to catch the moonbeams, dancing to the rippling of the breeze. Each stilled her breath, fearful to cause more rippling. Then, in a momentary hush, the circlet smoothed and stilled; and to each, slowly but steadily clearer, appeared the same vision. It was Marcus, the Roman doctor, standing with a protective arm about Ceridwen and staring with devotion into the face of a young child, whom she held in her arms.

Ceridwen herself was dreaming the same, but gone was the hatred and bitterness, which had become the norm for her when dealing with Romans. In its place was a feeling of great belonging and love, a feeling of being truly home. There was such beauty in allowing the feeling into her soul. It had been in waiting, waiting to claim its place instead of the bitterness, as soon as she was ready.

Marcus was to be such a special person to her. Only with him in this existence would she find true happiness. All else would become secondary, for he was destined to be her lover, her helpmate and father to her children. Her heart seemed to be bursting as she acknowledged her love for him.

Then she saw the smiling face of her grandfather coming out of the ether and she heard again his prophecy, *'When the noble bloods of Rome and Druid mingle, as our rowans intertwine, then peace and honour will come with us to dine.'*

As the vision faded for each one of them, they looked at each other, speechless in wonder. Ceridwen was last to rouse. Truly she wanted to stay in that state and not return to the reality of the night.

But the cold had begun to chill the women, now that the aura of their unity was no longer a protection, and they began to shiver and reach for their robes. The fire had gone low and must be replenished and Ceridwen helped to her feet.

'I know we all saw the same,' said Betw. 'It was the Roman doctor, the man who was with you at the Spring Festival, Ceridwen.'

They all nodded, Ceridwen still speechless and spellbound, only able to nod dreamily.

'His name is Marcus,' Marged explained.

'Marcus. A good enough name for a Roman! Did they not have an Emperor of that name who was noted for his wisdom?'

The younger women looked blankly at each other, for although they had heard the name of several recent emperors, the fame of Marcus Aurelius seemed ancient history to them.

'Well now! How shall we proceed?' said Marged bringing the consultation back to its true purpose. 'I'm sure destiny will help us along, but we still have the responsibility of making sure Ceridwen has a worthy bedfellow at the Beltane rite.'

'Does he bear love toward you, Ceridwen?' queried Ness gently.

'Yes...I am sure of it. He has proclaimed it to me and I read it in his eyes. But I have rejected him on account of his being Roman.'

'Do you love him in return?' pressed Elen eagerly.

'I know him little, but I feel in thrall to him whenever he is near. There is a disturbing of my heart and a longing to be near him, to touch him, to laugh and speak with him around the home fire.'

All but Elen recognised the modesty of this understatement, for there was the light of passion in Ceridwen's soul as she spoke of him, remembering his face and his touch on that moonlit night at Tan yr Aur.

'Then we must do all we can to bring about your coupling. In your coming together there is a fulfilment of Cadoc's prophecy. Mayhap the mingling of your bloods will bring peace to our lands and prosperity to our island.' And with Betw's pronouncement the coven got to work once more.

As they completed their task, closing their circle *widdershins* or against the movement of the Sun, the dawn was beginning to break over the mountains of Eryri.

⌘ ⌘ ⌘

CHAPTER XI

⌘

THE SENDING

Marcus had been intolerably restless since his return from Mona. Life running the infirmary at Segontium was busy, but not busy enough to blot out the inner ache he felt at leaving the girl healer and priestess behind. He caught himself eyeing Vipsanius with envy as he took leave of his wife, Rhiannon, each morning. She gave her husband such adoring glances, which not only told of their nights of pleasure in each other, but more importantly of their growing relationship of trust and intimacy. What wouldn't Marcus have given for such looks from Ceridwen? Was it too much to ask the Gods?

Even though he had no injuries from warfare to contend with at present, there was always a steady stream of complaints from legionaries, auxiliaries and slaves, teeth to pull, chiropody and bone setting from accidental injury, and a stream of wounds encountered in the daily military practice sessions, upon which Vipsanius insisted. He was in the process of dressing the injured ankle of an infantryman, whose ribald talk he would normally have entertained with good humour, but his thoughts continually strayed from the task at hand.

He saw Ceridwen's long tapering fingers, stroking the silken coat of the kitten. Then she was binding Hedfan's wounds, those soothing, healing hands caressing her brother's head, cooling the heat of anger and burning. He saw her hair flying in a copper stream, as the wind caught its tumbling waves and took it playfully away from her fresh, glowing face, as she watched the races at Tan yr Aur. And he heard her voice chanting in its clear loveliness on the sacred mountain.

The infantryman winced with pain and Marcus refocused on the job in hand. He motioned Dith to bring a crutch and help the man to his feet.

'No bearing weight on your ankle for at least three weeks, and come back for a new poultice in two days. You can use the hot house bath to soak and ease it before you come.'

The patient caught Dith's eye and grimaced questioningly. Marcus was usually so gregarious and here he was dismissing him without a glimmer of camaraderie. Dith shrugged his huge shoulders. He felt that Marcus's mind had been absent without leave for a few weeks and it wasn't getting any better, rather worse.

As soon as they were alone in the treatment room, Dith felt he could no longer be kept in the dark as to what ailed his master. He had not found him so distracted from his work since the deaths of Leona and Crispian. What web of enchantment had that Celwri girl been weaving, he wondered?

'Master, What ails your spirit. Can you share it with one who would give you his life?'

'I think you know already, Dith. For you, amongst all people, have been closest to me these last nine years...I am helpless to the love of Ceridwen, yet she spurns me.' Marcus paused for a moment, washing his hands in a huge Samian bowl before reaching out his hands for the linen towel Dith had made ready. 'Even if by some miracle she were to return that love,' he continued, 'I cannot see how our life paths could meld together, for she has her calling and I mine. I know the right thing to do would be to wash all thought of her from my mind, but to tell you the truth I seem to revel in torturing myself with images of her. Can you doctor to my spirit?'

'Master, you are master of your work. You are master to slaves who respect you. You must become master of your mind. But how, I cannot tell you, for my heart has never been enslaved to a woman as yours has.'

'You are right to use the word enslaved, for this kind of mind-torture is a bondage, preventing me from functioning efficiently.' Marcus sighed with frustration and impatience with himself. 'I must clear my path and set my vision aright. Look after things here in the infirmary, Dith. I must pay a long needed visit to the Mithraeum.'

It was approaching noon when Marcus picked his way through a group of troops, burnishing their uniforms and cleaning their weapons outside the barracks at Segontium in the warm, late Spring sunshine. They smiled and hailed him. Each one of them at some time had had comfort or tending from Marcus; but he was in no mood for chatting and returned their inviting smiles with a firm one-word greeting.

He strode purposefully out of the north-east gate, with its huge stone watch tower and headed for the temple of Mithras, a small stone building set a little higher than the fort and built to last the ravages of time. It wasn't a place for massive ceremony, but befitted individual devotions, a place of quiet contemplation.

Marcus paused in the porch. Ignaus, a thin wisp of a lad, undersized and puny for his fourteen years, was busy with his temple duties, making sure that the oil lamps on each sconce were full and lit. He scurried towards the altar, climbed the altar steps and with a silent show of reverence, drew back the curtain to reveal the backdrop. It was a carved relief of Mithras slaying the bull. The bull represented all that must be sacrificed for the common good and the power of good over evil.

Marcus nodded his thanks to the boy then lay face down on a stone side bench. It was so cold to his body, but soon it would bring clarity of thought as he prayed and meditated. It was the first time he had relaxed since returning from the forage to Mona. He had prayed daily, but as a perfunctory duty, without heart in it. Now he was submitting his whole life into the hands of the Sun God, Mithras, who struggled daily with the powers of evil on man's behalf.

It was Mithras who stood by them in the times of battle, giving courage and strength. Perhaps he would also give courage and strength when self-battle was at hand. The power of Mithras was most potent at noon. Ignaus went to the porch to check the alignment of the Sun, and when satisfied, took a taper and lit the sacrificial fire upon the altar.

Marcus allowed himself to drift. The smell of incense from the altar fire seemed to be taking away all anxiety and each member of his body gradually gave up its tautness to trust. Perhaps he dozed, but he knew he was incapable of movement and incapable of thought. His mind and body were empty vessels. It was the tinkling of the bells from the processional candelabrum, set in motion by a sudden wind sweeping in through the door, which roused him.

He immediately knew what he had to do. He would take the locket from around his neck and offer it to Mithras. The symbol of his attachment to his loved ones would burn in the altar fire and with it would cease his torment of love for the unattainable.

He approached the altar calmly, devoid of attachment, empty of all emotion. Slowly he lifted the locket from around his neck. For a fleeting moment he saw the smiling faces of Leona and Crispian, but he knew that he no longer needed the locket to remind him of the happiness they had shared. He was capable of being with them in spirit whenever he chose.

He lifted the locket high above the flames and murmured a prayer of dedication, closing his eyes as he dropped it into the fire. But on hearing the soft, girlish unbroken voice of Ignaus he opened them in awe.

'There is no need to part with this gift of love. It is unwanted by Mithras. You have proved your love of the God. Now Mithras has your good in mind, trust Him. Bathe in the light of the Full Moon tonight and all will be set in motion for you,' said Ignaus, holding the locket in his cupped hands, where he had caught it over the flames. Marcus could not believe his eyes. Ignaus's hands were untouched by the flames, the locket glistening in his palms. Marcus gently took it and put it again around his own neck.

Marcus went about the rest of the day's business in a daze. He found himself unable to share his experience in the temple with Dith and set about avoiding him. He occupied himself with visiting Flavia, wife of Hortensius and one time mistress to Leona.

She was playing with her young children in the courtyard of the commandant's house. Only weeks earlier he would have found the sound of children's laughter too much to bear and he would have hurried in the opposite direction. Now it seemed to draw him irresistibly.

Flavia had grieved herself when Leona and Crispian had died in the accident. Although Leona had been her servant, in this province of male dominance, so far from their native land, she had been confidante to Flavia and a buffer against the harsh life at the fort. Together they had sought to bring comfort to their quarters and a safe haven for the children. The courtyard was full of their charming touches: a sawn off oil barrel filled with river pebbles and fresh water that attracted birds; clay pots of herbs to provide teas and balms stood in carefully arranged groups; slabs of smooth slate paved the central walkway and sloped down to a drain channel; so that even in this rainy climate, it was never awash and too wet for the small children to play in, under their careful eye.

How Flavia missed their Summer days when Crispian was suckling. They would laze in this courtyard and watch Flavia's two eldest play ball and stick along the gutter. Marcus had been a frequent visitor then and Flavia had appreciated his warm sense of humour and his ability to have her boys eating out of his hand. He had such a way with them, better than the strict formality of their tutor.

Since the accident, he had avoided her and the children. She had two more now and the eldest were out and about learning the ways of soldiers, but these two little ones would be around her skirts for a while longer.

'Marcus! How delightful to see you. Have you succumbed to my special brew of mint at last? Bernice, bring us hot steaming bowls. There's a nip in the wind today. Now, Marcus,' said Flavia, sitting him firmly beside her on the bench and drawing her woollen cloak about her to fend off the fresh wind from the sea, 'Tell me frankly, why, after all this time, do we have the bounty of a visit?'

Marcus had never really understood until that moment that Flavia had not only missed Leona, but himself. 'I am truly sorry if I have offended you by avoiding your company. As in many things, the heart and not the head rule us and I could not bear to be reminded of the happy times we spent here. It was remiss of me and selfish.

'Do you remember it was on this bench that I asked Leona to be my wife, and you were busy herding the children indoors so that we could have some privacy?'

'There was slight chance of that. Little Flavius was determined to witness every word. His excuse was that he thought it a good lesson to know how to get a wife.' Flavia chuckled, then sobered when she remembered the special happiness that was now gone.

'I have found such love again, Flavia. It is not the same love I had for Leona. Nothing can replace that, but it is very special in its own way.'

'You do not need my permission to love again, Marcus, only Leona's. I'm sure she would not hold you back from happiness. Her love for people was very special. It was unconditional.'

'I feel that...I have been to the temple. I tried to sacrifice this locket to Mithras, but young Ignaus was there and intervened. He caught the locket as it fell into the flames. His hands were untouched by the fire and he said that there was no need of sacrifice. I am sure that he meant that my love for Ceridwen would succeed. He advised me to bathe by the light of Full Moon tonight.'

'You have fallen for a daughter of the Moon, then? May you have the luck of Vipsanius. His chieftain's daughter, Rhiannon, has adapted well to our ways and fits in well here.'

'It is not quite that easy, Flavia. I am sure that Ceridwen feels the same stirrings in her heart as I. I see it in her eyes; yet she turns me away for the present. She is a priestess and healer, trained in the Druid wisdom. Like me it has taken her many years to learn her craft and it would be life ill spent were

I to woo her away from her people. I would not try to do that. It would be the same as her asking me to give up my life as a legionary surgeon. It cannot be done. But if I can have leave from time to time to visit her, then perhaps we can be married and we would be no worse off than many of the centurions who have wives in the homeland.'

'Do take heed, Marcus. It works well where there are marriages of convenience and inheritors are of import, but where there is love's true song between you, lovers need to be together. That is why I gave up living safely at my father's villa in Tarracina and took to fort life with Hortensius. We could not bear life without the other for daily comfort. It will be the same for you, mark my words.'

'To live separately may be a necessary pain, if we are to be coupled. It seems to me that, in this world, pain and happiness go side by side, like oxen in yoke.'

'You are right. The greater the happiness, the harder the leave-taking, as you have already experienced; but we must thank the Gods for both that happiness and that pain; for many do not experience its heights and depths, but rub along in the middle more comfortably,' said Flavia, leaving his side and rescuing her crawling baby from stuffing fistfuls of soil into its mouth. 'We must leave our destiny to the fates. What will be will be. Bernice has brought the hot brew. Come drink, then play with my children as you did before.'

Marcus drank with the satisfaction of a mason, who had just completed his task of building a bridge. With the Gods and Flavia on his side there was hope yet. As he allowed the hope to creep back into his soul, he realised he was beginning to relax for the first time in months. He began to play with the toddler, investigating the insect life of the courtyard. The child's laughter fed a yearning in him.

Marcus set off at twilight that evening and went down to the shore of the River Seiont, where the wharf by the warehouse was stilling. A laburnian with its double banks of oars was anchored for the night. It had brought in supplies from Deva, the main Roman stronghold to the Northeast. At last he would have a new supply of linen for bandaging and some base oils for his ointments.

He was glad he did not have the job of feeding the galley slaves, chained miserably together under a makeshift awning. He was always advising the taskmasters to take care of their investments and to feed and exercise such men with care; but there was a good deal of neglect and no doubt, in the morning, he would have the sorry task of ministering to the obviously sick amongst them. For now he must not be spotted; or they would engage him at once.

He drew into the trees skirting the path and followed the river up its course for a while. He was drawn to a part of the riverbank where he and Leona had often consummated their love. There was a tiny-pebbled cove surrounded by old oaks. It was one of the few oak groves that had survived the fellings of his predecessors. There he would have privacy and peace.

It took him a while for his eyes to grow accustomed to the dark, for he had purposely come without rush light. The damp moss smell of the earth filled his nostrils as he picked his way cautiously through the majestic trees. The silver grey light and the sound of the flowing river beckoned him. It would be a while before the Moon rose high and even then, with the mist coming in from the sea, he was not sure that Mistress Moon would appear. Would it be as Ignaus said? Would Artemis, Goddess of the Moon clear his life's path for him?

Tonight he left his outer mail tunic in his quarters and instead wore a simple dark brown tunic, which helped him blend in with the tree trunks and the riverside rocks. It was bliss to feel the ease of body, which came from comfortable clothes. The short toga like mantle around his shoulders would serve as blanket and towel as the chill of evening deepened.

He found himself impatiently longing to swim in the river, where a torrent of icy mountain water tumbled gushingly and invitingly on its way to the sea; but if he were to succumb now he would be numb with cold by moonrise. He must wait. All things in universal conscience must be sorted slowly and with due consideration. The Gods did not do their work at behest of one man, but must consider all, including the earth itself and the other creatures in balance.

For one's heart's desire to fit into the measure of destiny, one must first wait for the auspicious moment, when the ears of the Gods are receptive. He sat on a moss-clad log by the singing river and waited, mesmerised by the flowing motion of the current, the feel of the smooth pebbles in his hand. The stillness of the sleeping wood behind him seemed in sharp contrast to the sound of the rushing water.

Then there was a moment when he seemed perfectly poised between the stillness and the motion, suspended in time. His breathing had slowed and although his eyes looked at the grey and silver smoothness of the pebbles in his hands, it was Leona's lovely face he beheld. The pebbles, dropping one by one from his fingers, seemed his only response. But he was listening and seeing with his inner faculties.

Her face smiled in a glory of newfound wisdom. She seemed to have matured yet not aged. Her mouth made no movement, yet her voice whispered in his head, 'The bonds of universal love, which tie us together for eternity, are not those of bondage. You and your new love have much work to weave in the world. Be blessed together. Be blessed.' With that she turned from him and walked along a shore of dazzling turquoise light; a colour so intense that it filled him with almost as much wonder as her presence.

He found himself repeating her message over and over in his head, as though, to reach his outer consciousness, it must be rehearsed by heart.

How long the vision held him he did not know. Only that when he roused to outer reality it was full dark and the creatures of the night beginning to hunt. An owl swooped past him and landed high in a willow, pointing to where the Moon peeped shyly through the thin night cloud.

Marcus felt empowered somehow, as though by wishing the light of the Moon to intensify he could will it so. Miraculously, only moments later, She seemed to obey and shed her veils for him to see her in full light. He gazed with respect. Ceridwen would be working with such moonlight across the water in her island grove. Perhaps she would be gazing at the same sphere, maybe hoping, maybe longing.

He took off his clothes with reverence, like a lover divesting for the first time to woman's gaze. The moonbeams kissed his bare feet, which spread clawing for foothold into the shore pebbles. They caressed his thighs, thickened and taut with military discipline. Full light fell at last on his broad chest, and he felt he must throw back his head to feel the full thrust of the Moon's light strike at his cheeks, his throat, his shoulders and chest bone. He stood thus, he did not know for how long, with his palms receiving the impulses of the Moon's mystery.

There seemed no need to ask his boon. She knew of his needs by reading his soul. When they had drunk their fill of each other, he of her light and she of his essence, he felt her permission to plunge into the river and allow the urgency of his desires to flow away from him into the sea of universal knowledge, where what must be meets what is possible.

He gasped at the exquisite pain and pleasure of the icy water rushing over his body, tingling every nerve and heightening every sense. He swam downriver for a while, following the dancing silver moonbeams as they struck the water. It was so easy to be carried along. Then he turned and swam up river. For every three strokes he gained some measure, little by little. And if, by mistake, he chose a more chaotic path, where the current hurried relentlessly, then he found himself back at the same place, or even further downstream.

He knew he could choose to climb out of the river and reach his clothes along the bank, but it was as if he must prove to the Goddess, by his determination and strength, his love for Ceridwen and his worthiness to be her helpmate.

He visualised the salmon swimming upstream to spawn and felt their indomitable spirit grow inside him. If such a small creature could move against this torrent, then so could he. He paused, clinging to an outcrop of rock and gaining back some breath to continue. It was then he saw Ceridwen, standing by his neatly folded clothes with her arms outstretched in greeting. He must hurry or she might disappear.

He did not know from where came the strength to push

through the last stretch of water; for it seemed suddenly to turn into a black cauldron of evil power, mangling and contorting his efforts, dashing elbow, shoulder and knee against the jagged edges of rock like torture. Perhaps he was now too numb with cold to feel the real extent of pain. The Moon had slid behind thick cloud, but Ceridwen was still standing in the cove, casting her own light about her, encouraging him with that quiet serenity in her eyes.

At last he gained the river edge and was able to drag himself clear. He was fearful to take his eyes from her should she go; neither was he conscious of his body beginning to shiver and his teeth beginning to chatter; only was he conscious of her nearness, of her outstretched arms waiting to enfold him.

He melted into them, feeling her embrace wrap around him momentarily. It was more heavenly than he had ever dreamt; but it did not stop there. Her embrace began to pass through him, into his very core and, when it reached his heart's centre, it stilled and melded with his and they were one. He blinked and he could no longer see her, but he knew that they carried each other in the heart.

⌘ ⌘ ⌘

CHAPTER XII

⌘

PESTILENCE

Marcus was waiting, waiting for life to unfold for him and he was prepared to wait with patience; however, only nine days later, he found a path to Ceridwen that he would not have chosen.

He was summoned to the commandant's house at first light, but it was not Vipsanius he stood before but Hortensius. Flavia hovered in the background. Hortensius had not had the opportunity to dress before a messenger had arrived from Mona with urgent news and a response was needed immediately.

'Marcus. Vipsanius left very early this morning for Kanovium... a consultation re rationalising our numbers in North Cymru. He has left me temporarily in charge. There is an outbreak of bloody flux at the hill fort on Purple Mountain. We have already lost ten men in the last few days and most of the fishing family by the shore. We need you to stamp it out and try to save the lives of those now struggling with it. Vipsanius has given orders that you may take a small team of hand picked men, but leave Dith with us to see to our less pressing needs. You have dealt with such things before, I believe, and must have some immunity to them?'

Marcus nodded and caught Flavia's eye, knowing that she had encouraged Hortensius to send him.

'We have no word of the family at Tan Yr Aur. We assume they are safe at present, but such pestilence spreads like wild fire if not dealt with,' she ventured. Marcus was grateful that she had not mentioned Ceridwen in front of her husband. He was not the type to deal out sympathy for the love-lorn.

It was a mission fraught with danger, he knew. The Celwri were superstitious and hot-headed in crises. They would by now be blaming the Roman presence for the pestilence. A scapegoat must be found and sacrificed. Maybe it would be himself and he would die at the hand of Ceridwen. He chastised himself immediately for entertaining thoughts of dramatic nonsense and focused upon the task at hand. He and his men must prepare for the journey and take extra salt and tar with the packhorses.

It had been a fraught journey from Segontium to Mona. The men he brought with him were unwilling at heart. They were trained to fight battles, not epidemics. He had caught them more than once whispering uneasily. He'd waited until they had crossed the Straits of Menai and had their feet firmly planted on Mona's soil before he briefed them and tried to set their minds at rest.

'Each one of our men lost to this plague is a jewel lost to the glory of Rome and each one of the local tribespeople to die is a lost servant to Rome. We must do all in our power to understand the reason for the outbreak. We shall begin by visiting Tan Yr Aur and using their messenger system. We must gather as much information as possible.

'I want to squash any rumour of malicious poisoning. It is more likely to be something smacking of ignorance. My guess is that there is some contamination of drinking water. Perhaps they have begun sacrificing and throwing people, or animals into the lake again. I want you all to be conscious of any foul smell near watercourses or wells. I shall be splitting us into smaller groups when we get to Tan Yr Aur. You are right to fear this mission, for the enemy of disease is invisible. We must pray to our Gods for protection. May we move forward now without dissent and with courage?'

The men nodded, ashamed of their former disloyalty and encouraged by Marcus's grim determination. What they were unaware of, however, was the compulsion in Marcus to save

Ceridwen and her family at all costs.

Gwilym and Marged were heartily relieved when Marcus and his contingent arrived. There had been rumour and panic for days, but as yet no one from Tan Yr Aur had become sick. Corn, eggs and vegetables had been delivered to the hill fort, but had been left outside the gates, they assured Marcus. Hedfan had been used to visit all the farmsteads within a league of the mountain to warn people not to go up to the hill fort, nor to harbour a soldier who had deserted three days earlier.

Marcus had praised their efforts. They had done well to contain the outbreak... Marged had known the question in his eyes and had saved face for him by furnishing the answer to what was really uppermost in his mind.

'Ceridwen took herbs and charms to circumambulate the mountain two days ago. But we have it from Meromic that she physics and tends the fisher family. Only half have survived, all the old and young succumbing.'

'I must set my men about their work; then I shall seek her out, I promise you, Marged. No harm will come to her if I can prevent it.'

But, much as Marcus was inclined to rush to Ceridwen's side, he knew he must tend to the priorities at the fort, before he could possibly justify setting eyes on her.

Quintus received Marcus with a mixture of relief and suspicion. An experienced doctor in the field must have measures to contain the epidemic, surely? But what if his own leadership was found wanting? Marcus would file a report that would go straight to headquarters at Deva. All must be done to assist him in his task and sweeten his response. All must be done to save face and not allow the nightmares to take control. Since he had violated the priestess of the Celwri, Quintus Aurelius Maximus had lived in mortal fear of her curse, and not least the censure of his superiors, should they ever discover what had occurred.

Last evening his equerry had wakened him from a feverish sweat, thinking that the bloody flux had claimed his master. But it was torment of mind, not bowel, which had wracked him.

'Marcus, it is good to have you here, for I'm losing men by the day. There seems no good reason and there's rumour about that the Celwri are uneasy about my methods. There could be sabotage or worse from that she-cat they call their priestess.'

Marcus tried to disguise a quick intake of breath at mention of Ceridwen and immediately tried all in his power to turn the situation into something less dramatic, but more likely.

'I do not think you have anything to fear from the immediate tribespeople. They are usually very honourable in their dealings and their priestess possesses wisdom beyond her years. Believe me. It is more likely that your water supply is contaminated by some accidental measure. I have seen this happen on several occasions, a decomposing body upstream perhaps, or sewage in the seafood? My men shall leave no stone unturned, literally. Can you give me any of your eighty men to help with the task?'

'I have forty or so still left who are fit for work. The others are either dead or ailing, but I need to keep back at least ten to do the feeding and tending here. Then there is fire duty and lookout.

'You can have ten, I suppose. Where, by Jupiter, is that Meromic? I can never find him when he's needed.' Quintus scanned the turmoil of the hill fort without success, for Meromic had been helping Ceridwen and the fisher folk since the previous day.

It took Marcus and his team of men another two days to discover the true cause of the epidemic. They had made their own camp on the shore well away from the hill fort, which scarred into the forest above the dunes and rushes. Marcus ordered them to eat only of their own food supply, boil all water and wash frequently in the sea. Their midden was to be several hundred yards away and all excretions were to be buried immediately.

It was on a tedious visit to that midden, and not on one

of the organised search parties, that Andreus, from Marcus's escort party, became suspicious. A clay soil pipe, feeding from the hill fort latrines into the beach rushes, was dry. Nothing had drained there for days. Logic told him there must be a blockage in the pipe, or a new source for the filth to drain away. He followed the course of the pipe up through the bracken and heather to where his nose told him and his eyes confirmed there was a breakage from a rock fall.

His eyes followed the recent scar in the limestone. Someone had been quarrying, hewing great chunks of the rock away for some purpose. But the outfall of the broken sewer pipe had been completely diverted and fell towards the tiny brook running down to the fisher settlement.

Quintus paced his quarters, ignoring the steaming platter of cooked eggs and samphire brought for Marcus and himself.

'I've received word from Deva. As soon as I arrived here, I found it intolerable and contacted a friend in high places, a friend who owed his life to me on more than one occasion. My men are used to city duties. We deserve more than this outpost, forsaken by our Gods and cursed by local witchery. What is left of my century is to join the Twentieth Legion at Deva, as soon as the sick are fit to travel.' Quintus motioned Marcus to begin eating without him, but paused his pacing to slap a stylus impatiently against his left palm.

Marcus washed his hands in the bowl provided and began to eat the slippery food as delicately as he could with his fingers. Noticing his raised eyebrows Quintus continued, 'I suppose we have to leave a skeleton force here to make sure the locals do not demolish everything in sight? You will take temporary command and deal with any of the chronically sick, until a new century arrives from Segontium. Your men seem to have initiative enough.'

Although the latter remark was a compliment, it sounded more like an insult coming from a hard core of bitterness in the centurion. He had lost at least three close friends to the epidemic and many more men he respected. There was a corner deep inside him, which took responsibility for that. Had he not violated the local priestess? He could understand their Goddess visiting her night tortures upon him as punishment, but she might have spared his friends.

'My men have already scoured that part of the terrain where you say the quarrying has caused the outbreak of the disease. It was one of my first commands; yet they did not discover the fault. Their eyes were clouded, bewitched maybe?'

Marcus choked on his food and bit back a remark including 'gross incompetence.' No good would come from further antagonising Quintus. Instead he said, 'Last month, when I was here, some of the young auxiliaries were commanded to repair the footings of the hill fort wall. It was they and not your men who probably set this whole unfortunate chain of events in motion. May I suggest that an offering to Mithras, for helping us survive, would be more in keeping than disciplining your men. Have not the sickness and conditions here been torture enough?'

'You mean I should desist from roasting the culprits over a seasoned fire? Perhaps you are right. We will be gone from here soon enough and put the whole nightmare behind us. You were eager to tend the fisher family by the shore? Let me delay you no further. The sooner they are well again, the sooner we will have fresh fish for our table instead of this disgusting fare.'

Marcus did not beg to differ, but finished eating his meal appreciatively. It may be a while before he would have the opportunity to eat again. He must set his men to repairing the sewer pipe and digging out a fresh channel for pure water to make its way to the fisher settlement. Then he would find Ceridwen.

Meromic had scrambled down the hillside at nightfall to meet Ceridwen secretly. Quintus had refused to ask for her help when his men were taken so badly and had used the excuse that the contagion must not be spread to the valley people. Meromic knew the real reason why he did not want her involved. Quintus would not be able to look her in the eye.

His men, he was confident, would not believe her if she was to accuse him of rape, but he wanted no risk of confrontation.

Meromic, however, felt he owed it to the fishing family, who lived by the shore, to get help for them. Already the old people and the children had died, leaving only a young woman, her husband and brother alive. All three were sick, and not likely to pull through without medicine and practical help.

The geese at Cae Gwynion announced his coming and their cackling echoed to the rocks above. But Ceridwen seemed unsurprised to see him and welcomed him across that special threshold, where he knew the ashes of the old Druid teacher, Cadoc, were buried.

He was surprised to see that she had a bundle of supplies at the ready and small clay pots hanging from the belt at her waist. Hedfan had agreed to come up and tend to the animals whilst she was away. All that remained for her to do was douse out the fire.

'You knew I was coming for you?'

'I knew you would come and escort me, Meromic. Not all Romans are ill-natured.' He was unaware of the understatement in her comment. He had no means of knowing the truce of peace and acceptance, the great honour of love's blessing, which had passed between Marcus and she at the *sending*.

'I saw you coming this afternoon and made ready,' she continued, pouring cold water on her hearth fire. 'My family had already heard earlier of the deaths in the fisher family. They discouraged me from going to the burials for fear of spreading the contagion; but I had resolved to go to see what I could do. I needed an escort not frightened of the pestilence and I requested the Gods might send you.'

'Your thoughts must have reached me by noon. I have been trying to get away ever since, but there was much work to do at the fort. Quintus would have us burn everything belonging to the men affected. There seem to be bodies to burn each day. We have had to send a message to Eithig and his men at Din Silwy to explain the fires, in case they thought it warning of invasion. Our cook has been dead these last two days and we have had no decent food since a feasting of shellfish five days ago. They say it must be poison in the fish that started it. Those of us without symptoms have been frightened to eat anything but what we can forage for in the woods. Just collecting enough firewood seems to sap every man's strength.'

Ceridwen was reminded of her curse upon Romans and felt somehow responsible for this young man's plight. Why had it not taken Quintus? Why had the pains of the sickness not wracked him, or the retching and fluxing tormented him? He alone deserved it.

'Do your men believe our people poisoned them?' she queried, dreading the answer.

'It was rumoured at first. But then the family by the beach, who gave us the quota of their catch, proved as sick as our men, and we felt we had a common enemy. Here, let me carry some of your things and we'll set off. The night is so clear and cold, we'll be well lit.'

They skirted the mountain and made their way to the north shore, where the huts of the fisher folk could be seen nestling close to the beach. There was only one hearth fire left and an eerie stillness hung over the settlement. Instead of barking to greet them, the settlement dogs began howling.

Ceridwen set Meromic to work as soon as they arrived. She wanted all soiled linen burned on a fire, away from the huts. She wanted cauldrons bringing from the dead hearths and setting in the fire to provide boiled drinking water and herb brews to bring down the patients' fevers. She asked him to dig a deep toilet pit, so that if a patient were strong enough to be helped there, they might cease from soiling everything in sight.

She used cold seawater compresses to cool them, changed clothing with every soiling and washed it immediately in a deep rock pool of seawater. By breakfast time the heaviest jobs were completed and all three patients had settled into less fitful sleeping. She made some barley gruel for Meromic and herself, but would fast her patients for a few more days before introducing any food. She would keep them alive on boiled water and honey and, in teaching Meromic her procedures, hoped he would be able to help his comrades. He left her shortly after sunrise, taking with him a batch of her herbs and some hope for the men at the hill fort on Mynydd Llwydiarth.

'May the Gods bless you, Meromic. Thank you for your help here. I could not have managed without you.'

'I will come by every day with some fuel and anything else I can bring from Tan Yr Aur. The food from there will not be contaminated,' he promised as he set out.

'Give greetings to my family and tell them to have no fear for me. I am protected by their prayers and mine. I shall be home soon, I am sure of it.'

He was out of sight before she could take in her next breath. She was suddenly engulfed in a desolate sense of isolation. She alone was responsible for the lives of all three people, lying weakly on their pallets. The work seemed unrelenting and endless without Meromic's support, for he did not return the next day, as he had promised, nor the next; and, although her patients were improving, she was feeling the lack of sleep. It seemed to disorient her mind and tasks, which normally took her a few minutes, seemed to stretch out unendingly as her efficiency ground to a halt.

She was bathing the torso of the girl's sweating brother when she felt a presence behind her. Yes, she remembered the dogs' howling a few minutes ago, but for some reason her mind needed to focus on every movement of her task, such was the effort to keep going. She had ignored the warning. If he were enemy, she was past caring. She only wanted to sleep. Forever would be fine.

She turned. It was Marcus – Marcus with a soft expression of compassion and a smile of greeting. Marcus with his arms ready to catch her and pass her some strength. Marcus with his strength like a tree trunk...Was it a *sending* once more?

Marcus saw a moment of delighted recognition on her face, but, as she tried to stand and greet him, he rushed to catch her as she finally gave in to utter exhaustion. She collapsed and lay unconscious in his arms. He cradled her, rocking her back and forth with his face buried tearfully in her hair. He had not come all this way to witness the death of his second love, surely? The Gods would not be so cruel, would they?

'Ceridwen, do not go from me! We need each other to make sense of life now! *Cariad, Cariad.* Be with me.' Somehow his pleading was getting through to her. She was struggling to open her eyes. Then by some miracle she seemed to gain the strength to turn and nuzzle close to his chest like a sleepy infant.

'Marcus, let me sleep. Let me...Let me...' she murmured, sighing and drifting off into the slumber she had been fighting against.

Marcus began to cling to the hope that she was free of disease. Perhaps she had just reached the end of her physical strength to cope with all the nursing alone. He carried her outside the fisherman's hut into the fresh late Spring sunshine. The Sun was warm and the sea breeze gentle for once. He took her to a sheltered hollow in the springy beach grasses, where he would soon make a bed for her. But just for now he must hold her and let her sleep in the security of his nearness.

He had longed to hold her in his arms, not like this perhaps, but here was a moment to savour, a precious memory to keep for always – the memory of her serene, beautiful face, lying with such trust against his swelling heart. He studied her face, framed by tendrils of copper gold, which had escaped her recent attempts at hair plaiting.

The crescent Moon claimed its place in her life in the centre of her forehead, the dye from the berries it was etched in now faded and due for renewal before her next ceremony. Her skin, so usually rosy with her outdoor life, was pale beneath a speckle of freckles to her nose and cheekbones. Dark shadows had begun to master the framing of her haunting eyes. She looked so child-like, so vulnerable.

His fingers caressingly traced the outline of her brow, her cheek, her lips. He brushed his against hers, so lightly that she would not wake. Her sweet breath whispered a sigh against his throat. The moment etched itself into his mind with its backdrop of incredibly blue sea and sky. The call of the gulls and the rhythm of the waves on the shore were her lullaby.

How long he sat holding her he could not tell, but when the first signs of stirring within the hut called him back to tending duties, he found his arms stiff and unyielding, as he gently lay Ceridwen down and wrapped his cloak around her sleeping form.

Thankfully, late in the afternoon, she recovered from the fainting fit brought on by exhaustion. She and Marcus spoke little as they worked together in quiet harmony. The fever seemed broken for two of their patients. Only the young wife was still sweating and shivering dramatically. Marcus left to inspect the beach nets and discover if there was fresh fish for supper.

'Roderic, lie close and warm your wife when she shivers. Call me when she sweats again and I shall bathe her. I need to make food for Marcus and myself. Gared! Stay close to the fire. Let Marcus and I tend it. You are too weak yet to help.'

Ceridwen pulled back the wattle door of the hut and stepped outside into a shaft of evening sunlight. The strong sea breeze felt good as it filled her lungs. A flight of wild geese was making its way home across the scarlet streaked sky. They had taken their fill of the offerings at the seashore and were making for their breeding grounds at the lake, far across the island. They hooted and cackled like a quarrelsome gang of youths returning from a carousel; yet their flight path was purposeful and straight as an arrow, with urgency to feed their young.

Soon it would be Beltane, the festival heralding Summer. Already the blossom from the hawthorn scented the evening breeze. If Marcus was to be her willing mate at the festival, she must prepare the ground. Her stomach churned and she felt suddenly nauseous with the thought that he may refuse her. It would be impossible to lie with him as a virgin. He would guess at something for certes. She must tell him the truth.

Her eyes scanned the deep blue of the horizon. The sea was now way out and the fish caught flapping in the beach nets way up the shore would be good to eat. Marcus was returning with a basket of fresh catch. She would know his stride anywhere, but she had never seen him run and leap along like a boy before. Not the army, nor duty, nor the scourge of disease was going to take away this moment from him; the moment when the woman he loved waited with smiling eagerness for his return.

He reached her, breathless and stinking of fish, with a broad boyish grin. He hesitated one moment, before dropping the basket and holding out his arms to her. There was no holding back in her kisses, no coyness; only a deep longing in them both to be entwined in the safe haven of each other's arms.

Like the twin trunks of rowan intertwined, they stood in the waves of sea-combed sand and swayed gently together as the Sun began to set. Marcus pulled her closer. She winced in pain, but did not pull away, explaining, 'Scratches from the gorse when I fell. They have not yet healed.' Now was not the time to tell him…not yet.

'Marcus! Ceridwen!' It was a sweating and dirt-streaked Meromic come to make his amends, bringing food and fresh clothes on the back of a pony from Tan Yr Aur. They refused to listen to any of his excuses, until he was drinking watered-down hot mead and sitting by the outside fire next to Marcus, who was roasting fresh fish on skewers of hazel.

'Forgive me. I have let you down, Ceridwen. I was waylaid so many times; first by the lookout sentries, who were ill and had to be got back to fort; then, when I tried to make my way by short cut through the burial ground, I found it impregnable with new nettles and thorns. I had to spend the night in an old badger set, not the most comfortable of places I can tell you. Then in the morning mist I missed my way and came upon a pig in a trap. You will not believe this, but I swear it spoke to me and asked to be set free.'

'That would be Hen Hygar's piglet. It has been roaming free since Imbolc, since the first frost-melt. I hope you did as he asked and treated him well?' said Ceridwen attempting a smile through a pool of panic, which she was desperately trying to quell. Try as she may, it began to flow upwards from her solar plexus. There was only one old badger set that she knew of in the vicinity of the burial ground. The wounds on her back and between her legs throbbed and smarted anew. A tight knot, suppressing her hysteria, wound itself about her stomach.

'Do you mean I'm not going mad, listening to a talking pig? I wondered if the disease was catching up with me and taking my brain,' Meromic sighed in relief.

'He is a piglet we set free to roam the Holy Ground and fatten up until the feast of Beltane. My grandmother put a charm upon him so that he would not be killed before his time. You were but his saviour as it was meant to be. At one time it would have been a great stag, which we would hunt, and sacrifice to the Celtic Sun God, Bel. Now, since the cutting down of the great forest, deer is scarce and not easily hunted.' Ceridwen surprised herself, noting that her remark held only a deep sadness and was devoid now of anger. Even so, both Marcus and Meromic hung their heads in momentary discomfort.

'He's fattened up for you for sure. He'll make a good feast. You won't have to feed the garrison from the hill fort at any rate. Quintus has permission to pull back to Deva, only leaving a skeleton manning.'

Ceridwen's eyes widened at the mention of the figure in her most recent nightmares. 'He's going? Quintus is leaving?'

Meromic nodded. The news brought immediate relief to her anxious face, but then a new worry dawned.

'Does this mean you are both leaving also?'

'Yes.'

'No,' both began simultaneously.

'I have requested that I join what is left of Quintus's century to go to Deva. There may be news of Fiommar, my sister, in a city so much a port to the world. She is nowhere in Cymru for certes,' Meromic explained.

'You deserve to find her, Meromic. You must come to Cae Gwynion for blessing before your leave taking.'

With so much unsaid between them, Meromic nodded assent and then looked with growing understanding at Marcus, who now took Ceridwen's slender fingers in his.

'I must stay for a while to nurse the weak and keep order at the fort. But soon there will be a new contingent from Deva and I will be recalled to Segontium. Meromic, I shall stay tonight by

Ceridwen. Tell Andreus that he is in charge at the beach camp and inform Quintus that I shall be back to my duties at the fort in the morning.'

At Din Silwy, Einir served her brother's evening meal with her usual sense of terror, for, if the meal displeased Eithig, then it was she who would suffer and not the cooks. She was amazed to find her brother in high good humour and laughing with his comrades. They had already emptied a flagon of mead before the meal and were swapping ribald tales. She attempted to shut out their laughter as though it was of no consequence to her.

She placed the shallow wooden bowl before him and he sniffed appreciatively at the steaming stew.

'Young lamb freshly slaughtered, kept on the boil for a long time, tender, yielding to the tongue.' He caught her hand as it left the dish and held her stare, his tongue licking lasciviously around his lips.

A picture of her brother, indulging in his usually private explorations of her body in front of his men, immediately leapt before her, but he had other things in mind.

'In three days time I shall have a wife of the Beltane fires, a great beauty and priestess to boot. She shall take my sword to her sheath as many times as I am able to draw it stiffly out. She shall be milked and poked and tamed to do my bidding, like unto my darling little sister. Since I am to wife, however, you must fall from your brother's high favour and become useful to my men. Here take the slut. She is slight, but will no doubt widen with usage.'

Any tenuous blood bond, which had given Einir any loyalty to her brother, was finally broken as he pushed her into the seething mass of warriors. The pawing and prodding, their laughter at her expense, as they passed her from knee to knee, was nothing to the hurt Eithig had just inflicted upon her. She would see his downfall, she swore.

She finally landed upon Huw the Giant's knee and as he sought with his huge rough hand to play between her thighs, she gave a great tug upon his beard that set him shouting theatrically, as the men roared and fell about with laughter.

She seized the opportunity to run for the open door, whilst their mood was still jocular and escaped to Old Betw's hut to lay plans.

⌘ ⌘ ⌘

CHAPTER XIII

⌘

TOGETHER

Marcus and Ceridwen had finished making their three patients comfortable. The task had seemed to take all evening. All three should recover well. The fever, sickness and fluxing had almost disappeared. The worst thing to witness was the sobbing and keening of the young woman, in despair at the loss of her child. Ceridwen held and soothed her until she fell into an exhausted sleep. Then Marcus held out his hand.

'Come. We'll take a breath of air together before we bar the door.'

They did not wander far from the bothy, for they must be in earshot in case they were needed. The Sun shot his final rays of blue and pink into the sky, but the air was chill and blustery. Gusts of wind caught at their garments. Marcus enveloped them both in his huge oiled woollen cloak and they smiled into each other's eyes.

'Marry with me, Ceridwen. I need to know that you and I have tasted of each other's soul. Whatever peril lies ahead of me, I know that it is your love alone will give me courage.'

'We have already tasted of each other's soul. Did you not witness the miracle by moonlight, last Full Moon? The *sending* was no trick of the light, Marcus, nor flight of fancy on your part. It was a pathworking from our coven, a search into destiny to discover my soul mate. It was where I first met you, without the trappings of prejudice bound about my soul.'

'Do you love as I love, so that it seems to consume you?'

breathed Marcus into her ear as he held her close to his chest.

'I feel bewitched by you – as if some sorcery had dealt me an everlasting love potion. Yet somehow it is not blind love. I appreciate you as a human being and I accept your faults…Sh!' she silenced him with her finger against his lips and continued, 'It is not your fault you were born a Roman.'

'It has been very hard for you to come to terms with that, I see. Is the rancour gone from your heart?'

'All rancour against you is swept aside, for it is displaced by such a warm rush of love, that I would blush to admit it. But for Rome and our invaders the flames of hatred still burn deeply in my heart.'

Ceridwen knew that she must seize this moment to tell him her dreaded secret. He must know all; share all, if he were to be her true soul mate. It would be a test of their bonding. For a moment she was overcome by a rush of fear; fear that he would reject her once he knew. But she trusted her Goddess and pressed on, stepping over the darts of anxiety, as though they were merely sparks from the fire.

'There is that taken from us, which can never be replaced… And there is that taken from me, which can never be returned,' she ventured.

'I understand the first. We conquered and made orderly your homeland. It was a painful process.'

'Painful! Do you call thousands dead and maimed, our isle scorched and torched and brought under your laws this last two hun…'

'Ceridwen, *Cariad*, we must not quarrel about what is irretrievable, but look to the future. I understated the past because I did not wish to replough the furrow of your pain; that is all. But I do not understand what has been taken from you, personally. Your calling, your family, your farmstead; they are all still here for you.'

'You may not wish to talk of marriage if I tell you…but you must swear by Mithras, whom I know you believe holds your future, that it will remain your secret and mine for as long as we both shall live. Swear it Marcus!'

Marcus took hold of the locket hanging from his neck and

squeezed it between his palms. 'I swear by my life and all I hold dear that your secret will remain locked in here.'

As Ceridwen recounted the terror of her violation on the holy ground, the fact began to sink to the bottom of Marcus's cauldron of incredulity and he began to shake with rage. He paced back and forth across the valley of the sand dune, his face contorted by feeling the depth of her pain. Then he was gripped by such searing talons of outrage that, had Quintus presented himself, there would have been no preventing his tearing him limb from limb. It was crime enough that a centurion in good standing had dishonoured his legion and Rome itself, but for Marcus it had destroyed a personal dream. He had seen himself awakening her to the art of love, tenderly arousing her passions to ease her loss of virginity. For both of them it should have been something sacred, dedicated to their Gods. He slashed again and again at the fine dune sand with the cut of his hands, scattering it to the wind.

'Remember your oath, Marcus,' Ceridwen now whispered in an effort to calm them both.

'Sweetness – so spoiled!' Marcus murmured, aching all the more now he was beginning to master his anger.

'It is done and cannot be undone, and you well know that no one witnessed the deed. If this got out, your court would have me for sorcery and my family would die in the resultant bloodletting. 'Tis best the secret lies dead. Do not let it come alive in your head or you are doomed. I know. I wrestle with the torture of it each night.'

'Your family? Have they not guessed? Do they have no scent of what was done to you?'

'They think I had a bad fall into the gorse, trying to rescue Luce from a tree. That is all. Meromic alone is party to the secret; for he found me washing after it was done.' Ceridwen looked down, seeing in her mind's eye once more the salt water pool, sullied with her own blood. 'He loves me for his sister and would not let out my secret. He will be loyal, for certes. But the Beltane rite is so sacred, so beautiful. Nothing must spoil that festival for my *commote*!'

By now what had begun as a proud, defiant speech

disintegrated with a tearful cry of distress. Ceridwen was overtaken, by sobbing in such uncontrollable waves, that it seared into Marcus like a dirk into flesh. His mind was in turmoil, at one moment carrying the guilt of Rome and the next plunging him in to a deep well of pity.

He did not try to speak, nor reason. He held her until the convulsions subsided and she was able to wash her face in a rock pool and dry herself on the hem of her under tunic. Only then did he say, 'It will still be beautiful, the Beltane rite. It will still be beautiful and you will be beautiful. I shall seek your father's permission to lie with you at Beltane and we shall be joined together by your rites. Later, when I have gained permission from my general, we shall marry by Roman law.'

'I cannot believe that you would still want me thus spoiled. I...I thought...'

'You thought I would abandon you? Neither am I a virgin bridegroom. It is three Springs since my first wife and child were killed by falling masonry at Segontium. It is you alone who is able to wipe away my grief and give me hope again.' Marcus brushed her forehead and cheek with his gentle fingers and the chasm of despair began to close a little in her heart.

'You see how the Gods contrive to throw us together for healing and comfort? They will open the path for us; you will see,' he said earnestly, drawing her closer to his chest.

'Beltane is but seven days hence...'

'That is time enough. Quintus will be gone with the best of his men by then. I can leave mine to cope at the fort and can take a few hours to be with you, I am sure.'

'It is not so simple, Marcus.' she sighed, dropping onto a nearby tussock as though it would comfort and support her. 'It is not only my father and kinsmen whom we must convince of this suit. The whole tribe must know the justification for it. The elders must see the wisdom in their choice of sire to their future. Already the women are convinced that you are my destiny and fulfilment of my grandfather's prophecy. They will work upon their menfolk and Gwilym will make a pronouncement at the rite. But Eithig will contest it all the way. The combat for my hand will be no ritual. It will be real. I have the knowledge that he is determined to have me; not only at the Beltane rite, but as his wife!'

'It would considerably improve his standing in the tribe,' Marcus replied, beginning to understand the awesome dimensions of the situation he found himself in. 'We have already clashed wills and he sees me as an enemy. This fight at Beltane, is it to the death?'

'In ages gone by it was, but with a shortage of young strong men, our elders gainsaid the tradition. All contenders for my honour must race from the foot of the mountain to the Holy Ground. The first two contenders to the top must then join in combat to decide who is the stronger. Like the great stags of the forest they must prove who is superior to engender the tribe.

'Thus far we have Huw the Giant and Eithig our chieftain. They are no doubt already rehearsing a highly theatrical display of Eithig's skills in vanquishing Huw. However, Huw may withdraw when he knows you aim to contend, for they will see you as easy meat for Eithig in combat.'

'I am strong and skilled in combat, Ceridwen, but I confess I am no real contender against Eithig. His reputation of strength, speed and wiles has carried even as far as Segontium.'

'Marcus, the prophecy, given to us by my Druid grandfather ere he died, goes thus.... *'When the noble bloods of Rome and Druid mingle, as our rowans intertwine, then peace and honour will come with us to dine.'* My women and my family believe that prophecy to mean a bonding between us. You are the key to our future peace and prosperity. They will support our auguries done at Full Moon and will expect you to beat Eithig at whatever trial the coven sets you. The Gods are with us in this, I know, but it would help if you would do two things.'

'Whatever.'

'Firstly, you must make an offering to our Goddess as well as your own God and believe utterly in their power to create a future for us. I shall make you an amulet, for you must be protected from this plague at the hill fort and from Eithig's machinations.'

Marcus nodded in agreement. 'I see no impediment to

asking help from your Goddess. We worship different sources of power; yet it is like all rivers; they eventually flow into the one sea and that sea sends forth its clouds to recreate again the different rivers. So it is with our faiths. I will gladly pray to your Goddess, if you in turn will pray to my God.'

'Think it done. Now...to the second request! Where stand you strongest? Tell me at what you excel, besides your ability to make me weak at the knees.'

'Let me remember. At spear and swordplay I am but mediocre. With sling and bow I am truly poor. My shoulders and back are particularly strong and I am excellent at parrying blows with a shield.'

'I know that Eithig would relish combat with you. I am sure that Huw will be left behind in the race and it will then be Eithig and yourself face to face. The combat you engage in will not be with any conventional weapons. You will wear deerskin and a helmet of stag's horn. Your weapons will be what you can find to hand in the natural world, nothing fashioned by man.'

'Then the God's protect us both, Ceridwen. I will do my utmost against Eithig, because, without you, my life would become empty. Enough of thinking about the danger ahead! For now let us be together in this moment and treasure what precious time we have.' He drew her up from her tussock seat and they walked in the waning light of the evening among the abandoned fishing coracles, drawn up along the shore.

⌘ ⌘ ⌘

CHAPTER XIV

⌘

PLANS AFOOT

'A Roman! Marged, I cannot believe I gave my consent to the coupling. I know I have dealt with them and owe my good livelihood to them, but to hand over my dearest daughter to be coupled with such. What have I come to?' Gwilym wrestled with a leather bridle he was paring down, bit away the excess and spat it on the floor in contempt of himself.

'I told you, it is destined and there is nothing you can do to alter the situation. Besides, you melted with sentiment when you saw them together. Their faces were so aglow with each other. Would you rather have Eithig as son-in-law?' Marged retorted as she handed him a bowl of meadowsweet brew for his aching joints.

'Hmm, Eithig, there's the rub.' Gwilym sipped at the brew in the wooden bowl and sat by the centre fire, wiping the drips from his greying moustache with the back of his hand. 'He's not going to let a mere Roman surgeon beat him at Beltane. There is too much at stake; the prize too precious.'

'It will be a knock to his cock-pride, more than anything. He will recover. But you must not see Marcus as a 'mere Roman doctor.' Did you not hear his men say he is a blood relative to some famous emperor?'

'We should not rely upon gossip,' counselled Gwilym. 'We should take Marcus at face value. Oh, he seems sincere enough and Roman blood aside, a good match for Ceridwen, but that is not my main fear. This marriage could well be the undoing of Ceridwen and Marcus, for I am certain that Eithig will not permit it. If we go ahead there could be reprisals upon the whole family. You know Eithig's temper when he is roused. We may all live to regret this.'

'We women have ways and means of getting what we want, Gwilym. Between our Goddess and our ruses, we shall have prophecy fulfilled. Mark my words. Off!' When Marged was in this determined mood Gwilym knew better than to cross her. He obeyed, stripping off his woollen tunic, so that she could torture him by massaging his aching neck muscles with a liniment used for horse as well as human. He grimaced silently at both the smell of the oil and her kneading, as she punished him for his incredulity, working it into his shoulders as though she worked her dough.

'Marcus earns enough denarii to keep any future offspring in comfort, and his physic is complementary to Ceridwen's healing arts. They will learn each other's skills,' she argued.

'As a husband he will not be at home long enough to make any real contribution. We must have the care of Ceridwen on a day-to-day basis,' he countered.

'And that would pain you for sure.... your favourite daughter and her offspring to hand? Horseplay with grandsons and pretty granddaughters to dote over you?' Marged paused, becoming quite breathless from her task and then continued, 'It cannot be helped. It is the way of the world for many women. They must live apart from their men and see them seldom. Fair play, their love is too strong to gainsay and life too short to miss its bounties. The prophecy will come true, Gwilym. Have faith.'

'I need your prayers, Marged, for I must ride to Din Silwy this afternoon to wrestle with Eithig's tongue. When he knows our plans he will try to encourage the rest of the tribe to oppose us in this.'

'The rest of the tribe pay a great deal of lip service to him. Believe me. The women will have done their job well. Marcus will be the favourite in the combat.'

Gwilym was unconvinced. Life was so complex these days. It was impossible to please everybody.

Huw the Giant paused for breath and leaned upon the stave with which he had been baiting Eithig. The man was speed itself and although Huw's height and strength gave him advantage, Eithig's speed was like a whiplash.

'We'll give them a good show, eh Huw? This will be a Beltane to remember, comrade,' said Eithig, slapping Huw triumphantly on the back. 'I shall not only ride my white mare, but my copper haired, blue-eyed beauty. There's a prize for the taking. And what of you Huw? Which mare can bear your weight atop her this Beltane?'

'I'll organise something, never you fear. I'm a little spoiled for the choice at present. Maybe I should keep several wenches happy at the same time.'

A horn from the watchtower at Din Silwy, heralding visitors, interrupted their banter and they strode through the hut circles scattering hens, young goats and children alike, to stand in the centre clearing and greet the guests.

Gwilym, Coll and Owain rode their ponies through the gates and dismounted before Eithig, Huw and an excited crowd, which had gathered. They bowed awkwardly, touching their foreheads in submissive greeting and were handed bowls of water to quench their thirst 'ere they spoke their business.

Gwilym was relieved to see Old Betw and her women standing close and met her eyes knowingly. 'I need to seek private audience with you Lord Eithig, on a matter of sensitive issue,' he requested at last.

'About arrangements for Beltane no doubt? There is nothing secret about that, Gwilym. My comrades and relatives all know the lie of the land. They know I am up for Ceridwen against Huw. Does that trouble you?' Eithig chuckled salaciously, enjoying Gwilym's obvious discomfort and the angry stares from both Coll and Owain.

Gwilym swallowed. Diplomacy sat with him uncomfortably when he was so urgent to speak his mind. But he knew he was treading on dangerous ground. 'I felt I ought to warn you that there is a serious contender for Ceridwen at the Beltane Rites, a contender who is bent on wedding her should he win.'

'As I am bent on wedding her when I win. Did you know

that, Gwilym; that I intend to wed your daughter? Are you not flattered? Or does that look mean you are out of temper because I did not ask your permission, or hers, as is custom? I beg your pardon, but I did not think to request permission in the match, for, as your chieftain, you know I have the best interest of the tribe at heart and would not be gainsaid at any rate.'

Gwilym at last found his tongue and replied as best he could, feigning pleasure. 'My Lord, that you wish to contend for and marry my daughter is honour enough for any man, but Ceridwen....'

'Lord Eithig, let Gwilym tell us who this young man is, that we may put charms against his winning,' Old Betw wisely interrupted before Gwilym was able to let the whole cat out of the bag. 'But what am I saying? Would not the Gods themselves and Ceridwen wish you, our chieftain, to win? What need you of our charms and spells?'

'Indeed. Indeed. There is no cause for alarm, for the contest is foregone, as you say, Betw,' followed Gwilym, wisely changing tack. 'And you, my Lord, shall win for certes. Perhaps, my Lord you will be kind to the contender?'

Eithig noted that Gwilym shuffled from one foot to the other. The man was procrastinating for some reason. 'For the sake of Bel, tell us his name man and put these clan's people out of their tittle-tattling misery.'

'It is Marcus, the Roman doctor, who so ably contained and found the source of pestilence at the fortress on Mynydd Llwydiarth. He is encouraged to contest for the honour of Ceridwen. He thinks it a fulfilment of Great Cadoc's prophecy, foretelling a time of peace when the bloods of Roman and Druid intertwine,' proffered Gwilym, searching the faces of the crowd to find where there was hostility or support.

The women and some of the menfolk were silent, well primed by old Betw, but Eithig's warriors had not been forewarned. Their allegiance to Eithig was always without question and there had been no point in her trying to persuade them from their master. They railed or scoffed, at one minute angry, at another incredulous of Marcus's daring. But it was

Eithig's grim faced silence that sent a chill through Gwilym and his sons, standing like two threshold posts to support their father.

The crowd stilled and silenced at a slight hand gesture from Eithig and the stony set of his cruel mouth began to work and release.

'I thank you for your warning, Gwilym. You have served me well this day. For although we leave it to the Gods to seal our fate, there is no harm done in giving them a helping hand. Have no fear. This Roman scum will not escape to wreak his havoc on our clan, nor taint your daughter with his seed.

'Women, see that these men are well fed and rested before they journey home,' and thus dismissing them, Eithig turned on his heels and stalked into his fire hall to lay plans with his men. That he had no trust in Gwilym and his sons was evident. They were not to be privy to his plot. In some ways, however, they were relieved, for it gave them opportunity to discover what the women had in mind.

⌘ ⌘ ⌘

CHAPTER XV

⌘

THE RACE

Ceridwen had begged to be left alone the evening prior to the Beltane rite. Traditionally she should have been with the other maidens in her mother's house preparing herself, but she needed above all else to be alone, to conjure thoughts of Nanw and take comfort from her advice.

She lifted the heavy lid of the oak chest and drew out the crimson and gold gown, worn by her grandmother at great ceremonies. It smelled of sweet applewood smoke and lavender oil and was soiled a little along the bottom, where it had trailed the ground. No matter, it would only remind her more poignantly that she would be treading in the footsteps of such a wise soul. She fingered the swirling patterns of embroidery lovingly. 'Be with me, *Nain*. I cannot do this alone. It should be you leading the ceremony and I giving my maidenhead to the Goddess. Neither is possible. There it is. There is no help for it, but that I should play both parts and hope that the Goddess will accept the purity of my heart, in exchange for our fertility and well-being this coming season.'

'Have no fear my sweet grandchild. You serve your people and your Goddess well. She knows your plight and approves your actions. The maids of Heaven will assist you,' Ceridwen fancied she heard, in Nanw's whispering, insistent voice. She was unsurprised, however, that there was a sudden stirring of breeze through the open threshold door and that Mwg was instantly there, weaving and brushing against the door posts as if in greeting.

'You are missing her too, Mwg. You love it when her thoughts visit you. There then. I shall rub you as Nanw used to. You must make do with me for mistress now. You like it better when Luce is not at home. You are king of your fortress for a little while longer, for Rhonwen took her to care for her, whilst I nursed the sick fisher folk. She will stay at Tan Yr Aur until after the Bel fire.

'Soon you must teach her to hunt for herself and not keep bringing her mice to play with.' In response, Mwg nuzzled her with his wet nose and allowed her to sit him upon her lap and pet him. 'I pray protection for Marcus this day and hold that he is subject to no cat and mouse games by Eithig.

'See this amulet I have made for my man with every dram of my love energy?' said Ceridwen, teasing Mwg by dangling the necklet from its plaited thong.

She had spent much time the previous evening preparing three amulets, one each for the racing suitors, to show her goodwill towards them. To the untrained eye they looked identical; an unusually striped pebble caught round by a mesh of hair and red thread and hung on a plaited viper skin thong. But, instead of a pebble from the beach, for Marcus she had chosen a piece of polished agate from an ancient ring of Cadoc's. Her grandfather had always worn the ring to give him strength and courage in difficult situations.

She had bound it around with threads of her own copper tresses, a pull from the crimson ceremonial robe, and whiskers and hair from the tails of Luce and Mwg. It was backed by a fan of buzzards' feathers and all the while she worked she had thought only of Marcus as strong, agile and victorious. As she prayed, she had held it briefly in the fire, washed it in the running stream and hung it to dry on a nearby rowan in the new Summer breeze.

She had allowed no qualms of fear to disturb her as she worked, for she had killed each niggling doubt just as it had been newly born in her stomach. Eventually the anxiety had given up its efforts to take hold of her and she had gone to sleep.

Ceridwen had found herself floating on a sea of calm certitude. As she moved she had been aware of the slight sensation of being uplifted from the ground, assisted on all sides by the love of her ancestors. She had made sure that the amulet, she had made for Marcus, caught the moonlight as it hung from the tree. All that night it would have been blessed and energised.

Meanwhile Ceridwen had worked on the two fake amulets, striped pebbles, bound in linen thread and fine red-dyed wool, with a weaving of mouse hair and a fantail of chicken feathers. She had imagined Huw and Eithig stumbling clumsily, out of breath and confused as their bodies refused to do their exact bidding. If their performance at Beltane were as ineffective as her visualization, then the morrow would bring only good to Marcus.

It had been warm enough to sleep outdoors and she had fetched out her pallet from the bothy, stretching out beneath the rowans. The scent of blossom from hawthorn and blackthorn had been heady and sweet. The amulet made for Marcus had swayed gently above her in the night breeze.

As she had drifted to sleep beneath the Moon and stars, she had felt Marcus twining his arms about her as the rowan twines its twin trunks about itself, and she had known he was thinking of her with a great swell of love in his heart to match that in hers. Would that the Earth Mother and all Her nature spirits might protect Marcus from all danger...Protect him... Protect.

Einir had promised her favours to Edwyn, a young warrior companion of Eithig's, who did not seem to mind her being second hand and who assured her that he would play gently with her at the Beltane rite. She had no intention of being anyone's mate that evening, but the promise was made to extract information from him, so she spent a good half hour with him behind the meat tower at Din Silwy.

Old Betw and some of the other women at Din Silwy had

been primed to interrupt their dalliance on a signal from Einir. She was to throw her apron into their clear view as they washed undergarments in a nearby trough.

Edwyn was proving not quite so unpleasant a lover as she had anticipated. At least there was an attempt to woo her.

'Sweet Einir! How long you have tempted me, as you brushed past my thighs and served the mead to the men. You have such a luscious mouth, and those eyes, so proud, so secret. I cannot believe that you are willing to lie with me this eve. So often you have spurned my smiles,' murmured Edwyn as he moved her back against the stone of the tower wall and leaned his thighs against hers, so that she could feel the hardness of his member against her.

'I dared show no interest in another man until my brother gave me leave. You are handsome enough to sire my children, Edwyn the Shield. Have you not done great service to my brother in combat and saved his life on more than one occasion?' Einir encouraged him, moving against him slowly, rhythmically, arching her back to thrust her budding breasts into his groping hands.

'Indeed I have deserved you. The scar down my back, where I took a blow for your brother, proves my worth. You shall see it tonight. I promise.'

'Are you loyal enough to my brother to do his bidding this eve? The plans against Marcus...Is all prepared? Eithig must win. Our chieftain must not lose face.'

'Have no fear. We have already dug out and spiked the pig-pit near the pathway up the mountain. We shall cheer Marcus all the way to his death and it shall seem by way of accident that straying animals will force him into the trap.'

'You are so loyal, Edwyn' she murmured, nuzzling and kissing his struggling new moustache. 'You will come to no harm, I trust? You know well where the pit is dug and will not fall into it yourself?'

'Never fear, *Cariad*. Your trysting mate is safe. It is clear where the pit is dug, for we have cut off the lower branches of the nearby ashes to make the spikes.' Edwyn's ardour was beginning to gain urgency and Einir was anxious that he should not gain entry. She had already unfastened the ties to her rough spun apron and drew it away from between them with pretence at encouraging him.

The women responded to her signal and came by with their laundry, chattering noisily. The young couple sprang guiltily apart.

'Einir we need your help with your brother's clothes. Time enough for coupling at the Belfire,' scolded Old Betw, the younger women giggling, nudging each other and casting knowing glances at Edwyn's dwindling manhood.

They ushered Einir busily away, leaving a pink faced Edwyn burning with embarrassment and with their teasing rhyme ringing in his ears.

'Maidens like their lot untouched
By other hands unsullied...
Fair in love
And fair in war
To be a lover bullied.

May your spindle dwindle so,
Ere thrust in lust you wander.
Your passion slain
For causing pain
To one, so true a lover.'

Edwyn was fixed in the hostile stare of Bethan, the girl he had lain with last Beltane. He had promised faithfulness, but had soon tired of her possessiveness. She had found solace elsewhere, but she was not beyond bearing a grudge forever. Her spittle landed at his feet and, as he adjusted his attire, he felt the knives of her glances cutting into his privates. At that he ran, like a proverbial gust of gale-force wind, to the top of the lookout tower at Din Silwy, where he might feel king of the castle for a few moments at least.

He needed to clear his head, only then could he anticipate once more possession of Einir that very night. She must be experienced in the art of pleasuring a man, surely, if her brother had used her as often as was intimated. It would be a change from boring into a novice maiden. His loins stirred once more, and he was relieved to know that the curse of the women seemed to have had little effect after all.

When Einir slipped away at noon, she remained unnoticed by the majority of the population at Din Silwy. They were too preoccupied with their preparations for the Beltane Eve; for, although the journey to the Holy Ground at Cae Gwynion was but a league away, there was food, bedding, animals and personal attire to be prepared for the great feast.

As the cacophony of human and animal voices grew fainter, Einir found herself by the track to Tan Yr Aur and was relieved to find Hedfan waiting in the thicket with a grey dappled pony.

'Einir!' he greeted her, dismounting and leading the pony towards her. 'You seem anxious. Have you discovered the plans afoot?'

It was a few moments before she regained her breath and was able to tell him her news. 'They plan to kill Marcus during the race to the knoll. They have built a spiked pig-pit to one side of the forest path. They will allow Marcus to run ahead; then drive animals and such-like onto the path, making him divert into the pit. It will look like an accident. Then Eithig will fight Huw the Giant and be allowed to win as fore planned.'

'We will ride to Tan Yr Aur, where our menfolk await Marcus, and then to the Holy Ground to warn Ceridwen. Marcus must win the day at all cost. Jump up. This little one can take the two of us without difficulty.' So saying, Hedfan pushed Einir unceremoniously onto the back of the pony and soon broke into what was for her a terrifying gallop.

Ceridwen was all but ready. She stood by the need fire, burning brightly next to the sacrificial altar on the Holy Ground. She steadied her breathing and took time to make contact with her Goddess, calming herself for the ceremonies to come. She looked beautiful and radiant in the long, crimson ceremonial

robe, which had once adorned Nanw's regal figure. Her copper
tresses hung free about her shoulders and her grandfather's
torc glistened at her throat. Her cheeks and eyes were bright
with the rush of preparation, belying the turmoil and sadness,
which from time to time visited her solemn prayers.

'*Nain* Nanw! Be with me! Help me through this day. Goddess
of my mountain and forest give me courage, and dignity. Most
of all give me your power to turn the darts of hatred into
good...to serve my tribe with all honour.'

This was precious time. Soon the maidens, to be lain with at
Beltane, would be arriving for blessing. Soon the horn would
sound from the foot of the forest and the race between her
three suitors would begin, and she would wait to see which
two out of the three would fight together for her 'virgin' blood.

She held Marcus's amulet between her hands and prayed
as she had never prayed before. Nothing must be left to chance
that could not be humanly done to protect him. Hopefully,
every contingency for his success had been prepared. Marged
had personally promised that she would rehearse with Marcus
every detail of the contest, every word of the ceremony,
and especially the instructions regarding the victory cup.
Ceridwen knew her mother. At times her attention to detail
was exasperating. On this occasion Ceridwen was happy to
trust that trait to see them through. All would be well!

Marcus had had little sleep the night prior to Beltane by the
fire at Tan Yr Aur. He was touched by the family's concern for
him. His every need was anticipated and Ceridwen's brothers
washed and massaged him with oils prepared by Nanw for
menfolk going into war. They were clever strategists. He
would give them that. These Celtic farmers were survivors,
not stupid pawns to be played with by the Roman army. It
rankled a little, as he realised that the Roman propaganda was
not altogether truthful. The truth was that these Celtic people
were clever and powerful when they united. But they spent so
much energy on inter-tribal squabbling that it dissipated the
thrust of their endeavours.

Eithig lacked the wisdom of his forebears, but carried the cruelty of powerlust. It seemed strange that he, a Roman army surgeon, would perhaps play an important part in his downfall. He was beginning to feel that he must conquer Eithig at all cost, not only for the sake of his love for Ceridwen, but for her people. That Eithig meant to kill him he had understood from his first encounter at the scorching of her young brother.

Dishonourable traps had been set for him, but he was forewarned. If he were to die on the morrow it would happen surrounded by a family, who had quickly come to love and respect him. At least he had come to know another form of love. The journey of his life had not been totally in vain.

He recognised that he had never really known the love of a family before. The memory of playing at his mother's knee was faint and without real substance. He desperately tried to tease out the childhood memories before they were gone forever. Hope in the effectiveness of his prayers did not rule out the possibility that this might be the last night of his life.

He stared at the dancing flames, and an enigmatic picture began to form in his mind. He could see the smooth curve of his mother's bronze chair and hear the soulful sound of the notes she picked out on her cithar; but, when he plucked at the folds of her white tunic to attract her attention, there was no voice to scold, no smile to recognise him, only the brush of her hand as she brooked no interruption and continued her mournful playing.

She had died bearing her next child, who had been stillborn. His father had returned from the campaigns in Thracia to put his household in order. It was then that little Marcus had been given into the hands of a trusted Greek slave, to be educated as a doctor and surgeon. For it was his father's firm belief that his mother and sister would have survived, had they had access to proper medical attention. To give his son to be educated thus, would both atone in some way for their death and be of wonderful service to Rome.

Marcus had grown up in a household where he felt a stranger. It did not seem to matter that there was a rumour he had a famous ancestor, Marcus Aurelius, once the greatly loved and respected Emperor of the Roman Empire.

The story went that his great-grandmother was married to a member of the Praetorian Guard, the only men at arms allowed into the City of Rome and guardians of the Emperor. She had had a brief affair with the Emperor and Marcus's grandmother had been the result. It was hushed up, but somehow the rumours took hold. As a young boy Marcus remembered using the information whenever he craved some attention.

Troilus the Greek had taken his tutoring seriously and spent much time in study and instruction; so much so, that his wife and family grew jealous of the attention Troilus lavished upon Marcus and actively sought to ignore him as much as possible during day-to-day intercourse. The atmosphere in the house was always strained and any show of affection towards Marcus only acted out during his father's brief periods of leave, when he returned home to the villa to pay his servants and pat his only offspring dutifully on the head, before setting out on another mission for his general.

It was strange how at home he felt, here, leagues away from his birthplace, where the faces of a Celtic family shone at him with unaffected affection and admiration. Here there was trust. Here there was fierce loyalty, which had a different ring about it, compared to the comradeship he had always found so supportive in his legion. Would the warmth of that affection burn away his life this coming day? Would he be a sacrifice, or a lord? He had prayed and performed the rites as Ceridwen had directed. Now it was the turn of the Gods to aid him. The fates had brought Ceridwen and him together; the paths of their lives intertwining until this Beltane, when their future would be dramatically decided once and for all.

In the valley below Cae Gwynion it was a surprisingly sweet, mild afternoon without the usual cutting wind from the sea. All was ready for the race to the Holy Ground. Old Betw presided as senior member of the coven, her wizened hand reaching into the bowl of salt water with which she was to anoint the three competitors. All three were naked, their muscles rippling under a glisten of aromatic oils and red ochre, which their menfolk had rubbed into their skins with great ceremony until their bodies were the colour of the forest deer.

Marcus felt uneasy about his nakedness. He felt small and insignificant standing in this circle of Celts, who were both taller and better endowed in the privates than he. He was grateful that he had insisted his men stay at their posts and even more grateful when, around his waist, someone tied a small but discreet deerskin apron. Coll and Owain had been his attendants, but now they stood back, not wanting to seem to favour Marcus.

Huw the Giant reminded him of some great elephant he had come across in one of the Alexandrian campaigns. His privates were painted a brighter colour than the rest of his body. Even as his member hung between his legs, it was grotesquely huge. Marcus was relieved that there would not be the possibility of Ceridwen's having to accommodate it. The real threat was Eithig.

As both Eithig and Huw were adorned by their attendants with their deerskins, Eithig eyed Marcus with a smile of contempt, totally sure of his forthcoming victory, already visualising the satisfaction of witnessing the spiked and bleeding body of his rival. The thought of Marcus's oozing entrails and screaming in his death throes was something he particularly relished.

Old Betw paused before anointing them and handed the salt-water bowl to another old crone. She insisted on inspecting the stag's horn headdresses. The oldest trick was to embed thorns in the headband to the detriment of a rival. She would make sure that all three were of good, comfortable standard.

She nodded her approval and the three men donned the headgear, which was to endow them with the spirit energy of the forest. The ancient ritual commanded respect and the three stood proud as their attendants tied the headgear in place with leather thongs. Old Betw found that she must be getting cynical in her old age, for as the crowd sent up the shout of 'Hail Kings of the Forest!' she found herself disassociating, witnessing the whole as from afar. She would have found the spectacle comical, had she not noted how tense the two main enemies were becoming. She took the bowl and muttered the blessing.

If it had not been for Old Betw's serene smile, Marcus would have sworn she flicked the purification water over Eithig with more of a spitting curse than a blessing. But Eithig's eyes were fixed in mental combat upon Marcus. He noticed nothing; not even the extra few moments Betw took in her blessing and protection of Marcus. And all the while, Huw the Giant stood ridiculously between them like some oversized, over-ripe gourd.

Marcus had competed in games before, but never were the stakes this high. He estimated that Huw the Giant's long stride would easily outdistance both he and Eithig to begin with. But, when the valley sides became steep and the terrain more difficult to negotiate, Huw's body weight would be against him. Marcus was not slight, nor was he nimble like a goat to leap the mountainside. Would both he and Eithig have similar chances of being first up the mountain?

It was essential at this stage that Huw be eliminated, for in the forthcoming hand-to-hand battle between the first two up the mountain, he knew he would have slim chance in combat against Huw.

He tensed in readiness for the run of his life. Someone blew the horn over and over again. He could hear the throb of the warrior drums, used for sending their men into battle. No one was to move a muscle until the shaft of a spear, hurled by Edwyn, reached the ground in front of all three men.

'Wait!' It was Marged, dismounting from Hedfan's pony. 'Your priestess has sent amulets to aid her three suitors. All three are identical, but it will be the Goddess who shall choose who best to father our best.' She gave two of the thonged objects to Betw, but personally tied the third about Marcus's neck. It lay over a locket he wore. Perhaps he would be doubly protected. She hoped so. She smiled a brave smile at him and he returned the slightest of acknowledgements. But they could both smell the fear in each other. By this Beltane Eve he would either be related to her or dead.

Edwyn spat into the wind to get an accurate sense of its direction and poised his spear a second time. He suspected that Eithig would have him spear Marcus by 'accident,' just to wound him slightly and put him at disadvantage. But, although his bond of loyalty to his master was strong, he had no intention of his people's blaming him for inaccuracy. He prided himself on his throw. It landed quivering in a patch of grass just two body lengths ahead of the contestants and they were off to great cheering, piping, drumming and stamping of feet.

At first Marcus had great difficulty in getting power to his legs. The fear in him seemed to have weakened him from the waist down. Huw was striding ahead, familiar with every patch of ground where he placed his feet in this stretch of marshland below the mountain.

Marcus caught a glimpse of Eithig as he passed him, moving with the fluid ease of a well-oiled catapult, more a rhythmic machine than a man. His own feet kept sinking and slowing his progress, as panic in him clouded his judgment in the choice of each new step. There was no hope of victory if he continued thus.

Suddenly he heard Ceridwen's voice in his head urgently pleading, 'Save us, Marcus. Save us!' Then there seemed to be a rush of strange energy flowing up from the ground and coursing through his body. It was like a cleansing, cooling stream. As it reached his head, it seemed to flush away the fear and give him heightened clarity of vision. He felt strangely weightless and no longer sucked into the ground beneath him. The burden of his strange headgear no longer overbalanced him. Time, too, seemed suspended, as everything moved in slow motion. He had the sensation of swooping over the valley as effortlessly as a bird of prey.

As they began the muscle wracking run up through the forest, the feeling stayed with him until he drew neck and neck with Eithig. They could both see Huw beginning to slow ahead of them, the sweat pouring from his face and onto his shoulders. He was breathing heavily now. Carrying his weight uphill was causing him problems.

Marcus marvelled a moment how Eithig's breathing seemed so normal, so regular. His own breathing was beginning to labour and his calf muscles already ached. The tribespeople followed behind more leisurely, making the din of hunters trying to flush deer from the forest. The path up the mountain, through the arching forest, seemed well trodden. Soon they would come across the trap, which lay in wait for him. He hoped he would remember what to do.

Suddenly Marcus was surprised by a squeal to his left. A young pig was running alongside him, squealing in the terror of being hunted. Perhaps the plan had changed and he was to die in a 'hunting accident.' For what seemed an age, the pig and he ran side-by-side, the trees whizzing past and the shouting of the hunters bearing down on them growing closer. Marcus kept imagining the point of a spear carving a gaping chasm in his back, but somehow he kept going, faster and faster.

The pig made a dart into the undergrowth ahead of them, but Edwyn's spear was too fast and brought it down. Marcus slowed and watched as Edwyn and two of his companions netted it and tied it, squealing, to a pole in order to carry it up the hill for sacrifice. Then he heard Coll's voice behind him. 'Go! Get going! You're losing ground.'

Marcus glanced behind him. The young men hunting had caught up with him, but Huw had now fallen behind. Only Eithig was ahead of him now. The trap would be coming soon.

As he suspected, Eithig made a show of becoming breathless and allowed Marcus to draw level with him. Overhead the silver birches waved in agitation. The wind was getting up. Marcus noticed the stumps of newly sawn ash poles to the side of the track. To their right was more than wind movement. There was bellowing and snorting as a herd of cattle pushed through the undergrowth and then stubbornly stopped, blocking the track ahead. Eithig made a show of trying to get past them to the right and failed. He expected Marcus to take the only route open to him, skirting into a clearing on the left and into the spiked pig trap.

'Psst! Marcus!'

Marcus looked above him in the direction of the voice. It was Hedfan, throwing down a rope ladder attached securely to a huge branch of an overhanging ash. Hedfan seemed to be sitting precariously in a hurriedly erected tree house. If the Gods could provide a convenient herd of cattle, they could just as easily provide a child's hideout.

Marcus seized his chance with the rope ladder and, swinging it first to gain momentum, leapt onto it to clear the herd of cattle, now four deep. He landed safely on the other side of them and with a grateful glance up to Hedfan, sped on his way to the Holy Ground.

Eithig, enraged that his plan had gone so awry, was shouting and cursing at his men to clear the cattle. He had no intention of using Hedfan's proffered rope ladder. It may well conveniently break under his weight. At last his cries frightened two heifers enough to move, so that he could risk edging past them and on to follow Marcus. Huw would arrive he had no doubt by the time the cattle were cleared.

Ceridwen could hear the hunting cries below. She killed all fear as it began in her. She turned towards the sacred need fire on the altar and prayed with all her concentration and strength to Grainné, Goddess of Beltane. At this stage it mattered only that Marcus was safe.

The virgins, gathered for her blessing, became restless and, giggling amongst themselves, exchanged ribald comments about the competing suitors. She ignored the desire to turn and censure them. She must stay focused upon Marcus's safety. She paused in her breathing and in the stillness came the reassurance that all would be well with Marcus.

She turned, now serene, towards her companions and was rewarded by their gradually and guiltily coming to silence. Ceridwen smiled and its radiance spread around the semi-circle of young women as they waited for the men to reach them.

Marcus was well ahead of Eithig as he sped away from the cattle, but Eithig's lifetime of running the hills was to his advantage and he closed the gap between them just as they entered the sacred circle of trees surrounding the Holy Ground. It was hard to tell which man reached Ceridwen first.

Marcus prostrated himself before her, as was the custom, grateful to have a few moments to ease his bursting lungs. But Eithig seemed only slightly breathless and had no intention of observing the indignity of prostration. Instead he gave a little half bow and taking her hand, kissed it, smiling into her eyes with a practised air of gallantry. 'I shall do better for you next, my priestess. A little matter of escaped cattle put matters awry. I shall not disappoint you.'

The tribespeople, including Lord Meurig and his entourage from Dindaethwy, had all gathered by now and they witnessed how Ceridwen drew each suitor to her side; Eithig to her left and, as he rose, Marcus to her right. Two virgins stepped forwards with a cloak each to wrap around their sweating bodies, and as he arrived Huw was surrounded by his warrior friends and served with drink.

'You have done well my suitors and pay me honour to compete thus. And I must thank Huw, who did well notwithstanding and is no less of a man that he climbed the mountain last. After all there were only three of you, so to come last is no shame. But, for the first two, a victory cup of mead, blessed at the altar.' Ceridwen turned and took a small amphora from the altar. Einir, dressed as a virgin in a tunic of white and a chaplet of flowers around her head, stepped forwards with a tray carrying two goblets, the victory goblets, kept especially for this occasion each year.

Ceridwen poured the mead herself, noting with satisfaction that the goblet without the slight crack in the rim, already contained a strong brew of valerian.

'Here. Receive Grainné's blessing and grant that the combat between you will be fair and pleasing to her,' chanted Ceridwen before personally passing the cracked goblet to Eithig and then the perfect one to Marcus.

Einir was at once by her brother's side and held his arm before he could put the drink to his mouth. 'See how your goblet has a crack, brother. That augur's not well,' she murmured.

'You serve me well sister,' he whispered, then in full voice to Marcus he challenged, 'As a token of respect for each other, let us exchange drinks; for the Gods decree that the better man shall win and there should be no bitterness between us.'

'You are right, Lord Eithig.' Marcus agreed, having just pretended to take a long swig at his drink. 'It is the Gods who will decide the winner of the next task and there should be no bitterness between us.'

As they drank thirstily from each other's cup, the gathered crowd cheered. Ceridwen wondered how many could detect the true depth of enmity between them.

⌘ ⌘ ⌘

CHAPTER XVI

⌘

BELTANE

The pig was killed with all due respect. Ceridwen blessed and tried to calm the creature, but its cries terrified some of the children, until Edwyn hit it sharply over the head with a huge club and it was stunned into silence. He awaited the honour of slitting its throat, revelling in the crowd's attention upon him.

Ceridwen blessed the bronze and golden sickle, honed and worn, worn and honed for hundreds of such ceremonies. She purified it by passing it through the smoke of the need fire, then kissed the blade reverently.

She handed it to Edwyn and stood back, glad that she did not have to kill; for that was the prerogative of the men. Besides she did not want to soil Nanw's ceremonial robe, nor the thin flowing virgin's tunic beneath.

With great relish and one dramatic swoop of his arm, Edwyn sliced beneath the pig's throat. Its blood spurted, then spilled into the waiting bowl, its twitching body soon released of life. The adults cheered and whooped. Several little ones stared, or cried out in terror, but were admonished by their parents for being squeamish. Wait until the pig was cooked. It had fed upon the fruits of the forest, provided by the Goddess of plenty and, when cooked, it would taste wonderful and provide everyone with its spirit of tenacity and courage. Was it not an honour for a pig to die in such a way, rather than being slaughtered behind the huts?

The children were soon involved with the roasting

procedures and once the smell of the cooking meat had them slavering, there was little thought given to the protests of the pig, which had so alarmed them.

The sound of cattle driven towards the Holy Ground was becoming deafening. The bondsmen had herded them into the field below to await Ceridwen's blessing. Marcus was relieved to learn that, before combat with Eithig could commence, the local cattle would be purified and driven between the Beltane fires. It came as welcome respite and a chance to take in the sheer beauty of the afternoon from such an amazing vantage point.

Marcus drew away from the shade of the sacred grove, passing people guarded in their smiles of encouragement to him. How he missed Dith at his back to protect him. Dith, whose loyalty he never questioned, who had never left his side since Marcus had nursed him back to health after a fall from a horse nine years ago. The thought of never seeing Dith again hung heavily in his heart, as he gazed towards Segontium. He could not actually see the outline of the fort, but he could see the drifting of the legion's cooking fires in the red gold of the Sun to the Southwest. He wanted to say so much to Dith whilst there was time; to thank him for all the times he had worked so tirelessly by his side; for the times, when in action, Dith had prevented lethal blows from assailing his master. Strong thoughts for the *sending* must suffice. What did Ceridwen say you must do for a *sending*? He could not remember the detail. But he would centre his message on the shafts of sunlight, bathing that stretch of mainland near Segontium at Porth Arfon.

There was a rustling in the foliage behind him and he jumped instinctively to defend himself, but it was only Coll, hiding in the undergrowth, keeping a secret guard upon his person. They exchanged a smile of camaraderie and then Coll was hidden once more from view. It was good to know someone cared for his safe keeping. He relaxed a little and took time to gaze at the crimson, pink and gold, painting the blue of the late afternoon sky as the Sun began its journey into the West. At one time, loyalty to Rome would be enough to swell his heart with pride, but he realised that there had been a great shift in his perspective. He had not only begun to love Ceridwen, but her people and her land were becoming part of him. On the one hand they had enchanted him, but on the other, it was he who had allowed himself to be willingly captivated.

Lady Tangwen knew she must act swiftly and approach Eithig before his mood became altered. He was drinking warm broth from a wooden bowl, surrounded by his usual warriors. The valerian had begun to do its gentle work and calm him into an unusual form of benevolence, relaxing his taut muscles and even the usual grim set of his face. But how long it would last, especially diluted by the broth, was hard to gauge.

Eithig threw her an approving smile as she approached. 'My Lady Tangwen, you look radiant. I see you have put away your mourning and are bedecked with flowers to suit the gaiety of the eve. Take your pick from my warriors to suit your whim.'

'I come bedecked thus to celebrate the begetting of Iowerth my eldest. Eighteen years this Beltane did I first couple here with my husband. But they are both gone from me now. I do not wish to substitute the love of my husband, nor my son by lying with another. We have handsome men indeed, but let them find young women to beget them heirs, not a widow like myself.'

'A rich widow with lands and bondsmen and good looking to boot.... What more could a man desire? Are you not mellowed by loneliness my lady? Do you not desire a bedfellow who will protect you?'

'I have protection enough from my bondsmen, who are loyal indeed, but I do need a companion, I admit. I was hoping to persuade you to part with your sister to be my personal maid. It would be such an honour to have her grace our household. She would have to be maid in deed, you understand...no children to run about my feet. I have no patience for that at present.'

'Your husband was such a brave lord; perhaps your second

son inherits his father's fighting skills. You should send him to us for instruction. He looks of ripe age for it.'

Lady Tangwen glanced across the festival clearing to where Ieuan was struggling to help young Rhodri turn the spit for the roasting pig.

'He will be man soon enough, true. But you will understand that I need him to help about the farm at present. There is much to do in the stead of his father. Perhaps in the Winter, after the cattle killing, he can be spared to be schooled by you.'

'I look forward to that. Meanwhile take Einir. I mean to have Ceridwen as my wife and it is irksome to have such a doting sister around me. Take her. Take her now!'

Edwyn was incredulous. How could his Lord so soon forget his hopes for this eve? Eithig knew that Einir was promised him. At any rate, should he not have the pick of the virgins for his prowess at killing the festival pig? 'My Lord, have you forgotten that Einir is promised to me this Beltane? I wish to honour her with marriage, if she will have me and with your permission.' His voice shook with suppressed rage.

"Tis no matter! She is unpromised. 'Twill do your killing instincts the power of good to be thus frustrated. You have proved your prowess at hunting animals. Now you shall be my prize hunter of man. I must keep you keen, not coddle you with home comforts.' Eithig grinned and slapped Edwyn heartily upon his back, but Edwyn knew it was no slap of camaraderie. It was a threat to hold his tongue.

'Be not discomfited, my Lady Tangwen. We shall find some dalliance for young Edwyn here. He shall not go home unsatiated. Take Einir and keep guard of her, that she remain a maiden this most powerful of nights,' Eithig continued, the thought of denying his sister the opportunity of marriage, adding an edge of pure pleasure to his magnanimity.

Tangwen took her leave and pushed through the crowds to find Einir; the triumph of rescuing her from her brother's clutches sullied by extreme anxiety about Edwyn's future plans for revenge, which she had read in no uncertain terms in his eyes. And how would this contest between Marcus and Eithig end? Very messily, no doubt! Pray the Gods would sort it all out, for no human could address such a conundrum.

Ffynan had gone down to the shore below Din Silwy that morning. He was worried about his performance at the Beltane rite. His father had taught him the special song; but it was so long ago, at least a year before his strange death. Betw had taken him to one side and rehearsed it with him, but she had no patience for him this morning. She had been busy whispering instructions to the womenfolk. He needed to clear his head after a night of tossing and turning in his hut.

He was disappointed to find the sea far out and the sands of the bay stretching almost to the horizon. But he was glad that the usual busy activity on the shoreline was abandoned on this special day and that he was quite alone. He would hide himself in the deep valley of a sand dune, out of the wind and practise his verses. His lyre he stroked lovingly for several minutes, but, finding the comfort of the music soothing him towards a dream-state, he finally gave in to his overwhelming need and slept soundly.

It was the sound of the horn that awoke him, coming way over from the foot of Mynydd Llywidiarth. The race had begun and he should be there. He had missed his ride on Aunt Betw's cart. She would assume he had gone ahead with the other lads to shout and tease the competitors. He must set out on foot and run, for he would be expected at the festival clearing for the Great Rite.

He found it hard to run uphill carrying his lyre, so he stopped to catch his breath and tied it to his back with his belt. His thin spindly shanks were not meant for hill running. They ached already and he had only covered a quarter of the distance. How he envied Hedfan his strength and speed. At this rate it would be twilight before he reached the Holy Ground.

At last he reached the run up to Mynydd Llwydiarth through the forest; but everyone was well ahead of him and, from the cheering at the breast of the mountain, he concluded that the race was now won by one of the three contestants. He must push ahead quickly, for, as evening drew in, he would be summoned to sing the Great Rite.

Anxiety weakened his knees, but Ffynan prayed to the spirit of his father to give him speed. With renewed urgency, he put all his remaining strength into getting up the well-worn path, as quickly as his panicking feet would take him. Not to be there at the most important of rites would be such shame, not only for him, but would shame the memory of his bardic ancestors.

It was no use. He could hear the cattle bellowing as they were driven between the fires. He would be late for certes, missing the final combat between the contestants for Ceridwen's maidenhood. He had no choice; he would have to rest. His chest was bursting with the effort of the climb and his legs would carry him no further. Through the beads of perspiration and tears, welling in his eyes, he could just make out a mound of newly scythed grass. He flung himself down with gratitude, only to find the ground giving beneath him and the spiked pig-pit opening up to receive him.

Time slowed and for a brief moment he was conscious of the face of his father, smiling at him through the gloom. Invisible hands seemed to suspend him for a moment. Then, just as the first pike approached his eyes, he was caught and jerked backwards by something. His lyre had caught on a strong tree root behind him. He was suspended above the spikes, now swinging, now stilling, terrified to move or yell in case the strings of the lyre gave way. His feeble shouting would be ignored. Until his people came this way home the next morning there would be no hope of rescue.

Hedfan was restless. He felt too old to join the children in their games, but neither was he old enough to fully participate in the rite. He would seek out Twm from Cerrig y Gwyddyl. It would be good to hear his stories again.

He found Twm looking after the horses in a rough meadow beneath, on the breast of the mountain. Twm was delighted to see him.

'Greetings, o fleet footed messenger,' teased Twm, patting the fat flank of a dappled grey tied to a tree. 'I see you are well healed. You show no sign of your injury.'

'The sign is still there, I assure you,' smiled Hedfan, pulling down the corner of his tunic and proudly revealing his long pink scar as though it were a hero's battle wound. 'It does not hurt now unless you press upon it. Ceridwen, my sister, saw to the healing.'

'Was it not the quick action of Marcus, the Roman doctor, who helped you at the time?'

'You speak truly. He is a good man for a Roman and I wish him well in combat with Eithig. It seems strange to hate your own and respect an enemy, but that is the way it is and I do not pretend to understand it. I would sooner Marcus couple with my sister than that grizzly monster.'

The two boys laughed and went about an inspection of the horses, showing off their knowledge to each other, like veritable old horse veterans. They turned a corner by a thick hawthorn bush. Gwyngariad stood gently grazing, tethered to a bush.

'Twm, what say you to a ride like a king? No one will notice. Everyone is too busy with the cattle drive. You take Ieuan's dappled grey and I shall take Gwyngariad. We shall ride like chieftains down through the forest and maybe along the beach before nightfall.'

Twm needed little encouragement. All the other horses were safely tethered and, besides, he resented being left with the lonely task of horse keeper. He was entitled to some fun surely, especially on this most sacred of festivals. The Gods would surely protect the horses.

With a whoop of pure joy they steered their mounts away from the meadow and down the path between the trees. They were not stupid enough to race the horses here. Going downhill with a horse was trickier than going up. They would wait until they could gallop out towards the shore. Their joy for the moment was to have well trained horseflesh between their thighs and to prance proudly along, playing their roles as chieftains.

So thrilled was Gwyngariad to have Hedfan once more on her back, that she responded to his every command. Her obedience was total, her response to his touch and voice instantaneous. But, as she reached the part of the path near to where Hedfan and his brothers had built the rough tree house, she stopped short and refused to press on.

'It is that rope ladder hanging from the tree. It moves in the breeze and spooks her,' suggested Twm, reining in behind him. Hedfan now stood upon the mare's back and threw the ladder right up onto the wooden platform of the tree house. She still refused to move on and side stepped, backing away, grunting and tossing her head towards the pig-pit.

The boys dismounted and crept towards the gaping hole, sickening as they saw the body of Ffynan suspended above the spikes.

'He's dead for sure' whispered Hedfan, noting the stillness of Ffynan's limp body.

'No, he lives. See how his breath stirs this bird feather when I hold it near. I think he is uninjured by the spikes. Look. See how the strings of his lyre hold him against this root!'

'But they could give way at any moment and then he is done for,' Hedfan replied, already urgently moving Gwyngariad back beneath the rope ladder. 'Help me make this into a sort of cradle to put under him. We shall tie it to Gwyngariad's neck and she will pull him clear.'

'I'm with you,' Twm agreed, noting how the sides of the pit had begun to collapse and shift under his weight, near where he had been kneeling by Ffynan.

Every turn of their rescue task seemed to bring them new problems; knotting the rope ladder into a cradle until it was strong enough to bear Ffynan; securing it around his body, without slithering from the crumbling sides of the pit themselves; persuading Gwyngariad to accommodate the end of the rope ladder and to pull gently back, so that they could unbuckle Ffynan from the security of his lyre.

It seemed an age and both boys were sweating with both effort and anxiety, by the time they were able to lay Ffynan safely by the pathway under a huge ash tree.

'Ceridwen would do this,' motioned Hedfan, showing Twm how his sister would use her hands to summon energy back into the seemingly lifeless boy. Hedfan had seen her bring a dead hare back to life and he was sure that by using the same method he would be able to rouse Ffynan. 'Help me Twm. Put your hands gently on the other side of his chest. Ask the spirits of the forest to help us. It will work, I know it!'

'It is not working,' Twm despaired after a few moments.

'Be patient Twm. It takes time for the energy to build. We have been ages getting Ffynan out of danger. Now we must spend time helping him to come back to us.'

'But we are no healers. We do not have the power to make him well again. We should get him to Ceridwen quickly,' Twm objected.

'My sister always taught me that, after an accident, it is better to keep the injured person still and quiet and to do what healing work we can before moving them. Besides, we all have healing in our hands. It grows stronger with usage. There is no time like the present to start. Try with me, Twm. Two pairs of hands are stronger than one.' There was a strange confidence now in Hedfan, as he repeated Ceridwen's teachings almost word for word, just as she had schooled him.

It was a full half hour before Ffynan began to stir; for he had been to the womb of the Earth, where the pleasant deep-red warmth of his parents love had cradled and protected him. He had heard their voices and had felt their arms about him. He had no wish to return to the harsh reality of the woodland. But it was not so hostile as he expected. There were two friendly faces awaiting him. Gradually he left his spiritual cocoon and risked opening his eyes.

'Hedfan! It is you!'

'Ie, and Twm is here too. We rescued you from a pig-pit. It had not been pennoned as is the law. Someone should be hung for the crime.'

'I thank you both. I remember thinking that I was falling to my death when I was jerked upwards.'

'It was your lyre. You had strapped it to your back and it saved you when it caught some roots. You have it to thank for your life,' Twm explained. 'Here. It still hangs on your belt. It has only one string broken.'

'The Great Rite! I must hasten to the Holy Ground,' gasped Ffynan, full memory now returning as he grasped the lyre, tested its twang and stood up and sat down dizzily, all at once.

'You are in no state to do anything quickly,' laughed Hedfan. 'Come let me help you astride Gwyngariad and we shall walk you to the festival.'

The walk up through the forest, thought Hedfan, would give him time to rehearse what he was going to say to Eithig.

Edwyn was in foul mood. He had not even had access to Einir, to test her reactions to the deal Eithig had struck with Lady Tangwen. Tangwen seemed to be keeping her amongst a group of mature womenfolk, who were busy laughing and gossiping, instead of getting on with the food preparations. Edwyn would rather face a brawl with a wild boar than entanglement with a brood of females in full spate.

He tried to catch her eye, but without success. She was either distracted or deliberately ignoring him and his vanity tried to deny the latter. He would look elsewhere for his Beltane prize. Hand in hand with a real virgin... she was bound to notice him then. His gaze scanned the whole scene; the men putting the finishing touches to the fire stacks, the women handing out refreshments; the children playing tag games; Eithig resting with his back against a huge oak, his warriors about him, and the virgins putting their finishing touches to the bridal bower for the King and Queen of the festival.

He had never really noticed Elen before. She had been a child last time he had taken a good look at her, someone to cuff around the ears when she got in the way. Now here she was with the other young maidens, a chaplet of woodland flowers and ivy nestling in her long waving hair and her limbs moving gracefully under her white flowing tunic. Betw's granddaughter...perhaps some of the wisdom had rubbed off on her? If she were to grow into a crone like her grandmother, then all well and good. Influence with his chieftain was most desirable. What matter that her face was plain and her teeth a little crooked, she seemed as well endowed with creamy white flesh and sparkling eyes as Einir.

'Elen, I beg to take you a moment from your task...' She stopped weaving ivy through the willow archway of the bower and allowed him to draw her to one side, through the trees and into the privacy of the woodland canopy.

'I have left it late to choose a partner for this eve. I wished to compare the loveliness of each before making my choice. I would choose you, if you are not bespoke?' he said, using his eyes to captivate her. They had never failed to melt the resolve of a maiden yet.

'How strange, Edwyn. I could have sworn Einir told me she was promised to you. Oh, but time moves swiftly...I remember only a few moments ago, overhearing her say she is to become maid to the Lady Tangwen. That will be why you are at a loose end.' Elen's eyes wide with innocence were something to behold. Such beauty in dissembling was, no doubt, every man's downfall. Edwyn lost a little of his composure, but pressed on.

'Be mine tonight, Elen and we shall determine if we are good together for true marriage. You would like that would you not, to be wife to Eithig's favourite warrior.'

'You honour me indeed, Edwyn, but I'm afraid my heart is to another given, secretly of course, to give edge to the occasion this eve.'

'Then it is ungiven. I killed the festival pig. It is my right to choose a mate! You will lie with me!' he seethed, grabbing hold of both her wrists to terrorize her into submission.

'Let go of her!' It was Cullen the bondsman, axe in hand from the fire building. Then followed more – Owain and the other bondsmen from Tan Yr Aur, encircling the scene and closing in.

'A maid taken unwillingly is a curse upon our tribe. It is *geas*. You know that Edwyn. Let go of her, before you are shamed in front of all your people,' whispered Owain persuasively.

'Take us before Eithig. He as good as promised me my choice!' Edwyn demanded. But, by this time, Owain had prized his hands from Elen and Cullen had moved behind him to pin and tie his hands. The next moment he found himself gagged and being prodded along and down a path.

'I doubt Eithig will be pleased to entertain you right now. He has other things upon his mind,' breathed Owain ominously into his ear. 'I'm sure you will not mind waiting at Nanw's hut. Tie him to the doorpost, Cullen. The remains of my grandfather may wish to speak to his conscience.'

Edwyn's skill was in the use of weapons. But, lighter of body weight, there was no way he was match for the sturdy muscular frames of both Cullen and Owain. He knew it was hopeless to struggle and squirm. Outweighing his fear of ridicule was a terror, now growing in his mind...that of being left alone at the threshold of Nanw's hut in complete darkness. All home fires and lamps had been extinguished in the anticipation of being re-lit from the blessedness of the Belfire. Cullen and Owain sped back through the trees to the festival, ignoring his gagged grunts, begging for freedom.

As twilight gave way to darkness, so he grew in fear. The nightmares he could summon from his brief life were legion, once his conscience began to replay some of his warrior history. His Beltane was then to be self-torture at the most gruesome, reliving the pain of his victims, both animal and human. Tied here above the remains of their former priest, Cadoc, there seemed no escape from his own vivid memory. His desensitisation to the pain of others, so useful in gaining respect from Eithig, was now reversed, so that he felt all with full empathy.

Elen threw Owain and Cullen a grateful smile, as they returned from dealing with Edwyn. Owain noticed how her eyes lingered upon Cullen and he muttered some excuse to busy himself elsewhere. She must ask Cullen now, for, as a bondsman, he would never approach her.

'He'll not bother you the rest of this evening, lady,' said Cullen, his eyes encouraging her to speak further.

'Will you dance with me at the rites, as you promised, Cullen?'

'Do I have leave from your family?'

'The only close family I have left is my grandmother, Betw.

She is not too old to remember her first love. She leaves me to choose as my heart dictates.'

'She is wise, but did she not warn you against being wooed by a bondsman? I have little to offer you Elen.'

'Your treasure is in your voice when you sing, in your vigour when you play the horn, in the humour of your pipe. Your music gives us great pleasure, Cullen. In my eyes you are like a great bard, for there is poetry in everything you do.'

'What magic was in the morning dew you rolled amongst this morning?' he laughed. 'It has bewitched your eyes.' He paused to appreciate them fully for the first time and held her gaze. 'How long does this enchantment last I wonder?'

'For some it lasts but 'til the morrow, for others augurs trials and sorrow, but for the truest brings the song of love's eternal, deepest bond,' teased Elen walking shyly around him like a cat scenting its owner.

'I shall certainly dance with you, if I can find some other to play the music. I am for certes in great need of the 'deepest bond."' Cullen left her good-humouredly with the slightest touch of his fingers sending sweet thrills to Elen's novice heart.

With a nod from Ceridwen, the virgins brought vessels of water from the nearby stream for her to bless with her hands and pass over the sacred fire. And, just before the last glimpse of the Sun's red orb disappeared behind the trees, she motioned two warriors to take torches from the sacred need fire and set alight the two great piles of brushwood which had been several days in the building. It caught quickly and with a great crackling. The crowd cheered and there were excited cries of, 'Belfire! Belfire!'

Then the children came forwards for their blessing and took the water. First they drank some; then carried it carefully away to perform the purifying ritual upon the cattle.

The little ones loved this part of the proceedings, for it made them feel so special. As soon as they were strong enough to carry water pots or wooden buckets, they could join in fully. Now, even the toddlers took part with their sisters and brothers helping, by carrying little bowls of the precious water up onto the carts, standing at either side of the passage to the fires. They aimed to sprinkle the holy water on the cattle, as they were driven forwards between the carts. There was much laughter, spilling, overbalancing and flicking of water in the wrong places, as they chanted in an attempt of unison, *'The blessings of Grainné make you fertile and strong.'*

Ness held Rhonwen's hand as she climbed precariously onto the jostling boards of the ox cart, swinging and slopping a miniature pail. Ceridwen cast a wistful eye towards her burgeoning sister and little niece. There seemed such a warm bond between the mother and child, as they laughingly shared a precious moment of simple delight.

'You shall have a child soon enough,' whispered Old Betw, casting a knowing look at Ceridwen. 'Motherhood will suit you well.' In that instant the suspicion, which had plagued Ceridwen for the last few days, became a certainty. The queasiness each time she saw the geese fly home in the evening; the gradual browning of the sweet pink of her nipples; the sparseness of her last moon blood – all became clear to her. She was with child, the child of a Roman. She had longed to get with child by Marcus and had held on to the hope that the terrifying act in the gorse would produce naught. The Goddess had decreed otherwise. There was no help but to accept it.

The realisation made Ceridwen feel suddenly faint and she swayed and clung to Old Betw's hand. She was in danger of being sucked into the terror pit of full remembrance. She could feel her panic rise, as the memory of Quintus's foul-smelling hand, covering her mouth and pressing her down among the thorns, came vividly back to her. But Old Betw called her back from the brink of it.

'Ceridwen, my priestess, look at me,' she commanded. Ceridwen responded, breathed deeply and brought her eyes to meet Betw's, leaving the vision behind and returning to the present. It seemed to her that as soon as she began to heal and recover from one life blow, the next followed stronger and harder, like the pains of birth travail itself.

Betw's hands, aware of her needing, passed her some

strength. 'Have courage, Ceridwen. Yours will not be an easy life, but an important one to us all. Your sons and their sons shall become kings of the Cymry and your daughter, your sweetest child...to her you will pass your healing secrets and your spiritual knowledge to be safeguarded for all time. It will be passed from one generation of daughters to the next, for as long as there is humanity. Take heart and be strong.'

Ceridwen swallowed hard, as though making some attempt at digesting the import of the last few moments. At last she was able to look Betw fully in the eyes and say with conviction, 'I only have to reach out and is not the aid of my ancestors to hand and my Goddess walking with me?'

Old Betw nodded and smiled, 'Cadoc, your grandfather, and Nanw your grandmother are formidable guardians of your safety, but I see the grace of the Goddess is with you today. She walks within you and by your side at the same time, to smooth each perilous step you take.'

'I thank you, Betw. You have cheered my heart. But I neglect my duties. The cattle must be driven between the purifying fires, for the Sun is now set and the day of Beltane truly begun.'

'Wait! There is something you should know about Eithig. There is an old terror in him of fire. As a child there was an accident with his bedstraw. Just in time his mother pulled him from the burning mass. You will know what to do with this information, for certes.'

Ceridwen nodded, 'It will come to me. My Goddess shall provide me with inspiration. I thank you, Betw. Your prayers, I know, are with Marcus and myself. Cullen, the horn! Madog, the drum, if you please!'

At the signal of horn and tabor, the children were lifted from the carts and the carts drawn together to seal the exit to the enclosure. There was now only one way out for the cattle and that was between the two fires. They could be driven through in panic, but the safer way was to take their leader through and they would try to follow, despite their instinctive fear of fire.

Dunos was a black cow, whose trust of humanity came from being hand reared as a calf. She was a natural leader and where she went the herd would always follow, trusting her wisdom. For this reason she had been spared slaughter and had been allowed to grow old.

She came to Owain, as he held some treat in his hand for her and in that instant he expertly slipped a hood over her eyes. She would not like the smell of the fires, but she would trust him now to take her between them into the lush field waiting beyond.

A hush fell among the crowd, as she allowed Owain to lead her through, only giving the slightest sign of a suspicious snort when she got wind of the smoke.

Ceridwen was helped to her place on the ox cart and held out her hands in silent blessing. The bondsmen followed by encroaching upon the herd with brushwood to protect themselves. The cattle were reluctant at first to brave the passage, but with the encouragement of Dunos, now de-hooded and grazing on the lush land beyond, they started to move and gather momentum. The clamour of people and children shouting and banging, whatever utensil was to hand, added to the cattle's desire to follow the black cow and once the first few were through the fires unharmed, the rest quickly followed.

It was time now for Ceridwen to announce the form of combat the trial between Eithig and Marcus would take. For the last few years this had been a good-natured piece of pantomime, where everyone really knew what the outcome would be between the contestants. Most couplings were pre-agreed and the winner pre-arranged, tradition only demanding contest. But there was more than a special edge to this one. The majority of the people there viewed Marcus as the hero, who had saved the tribe from further succumbing to the pestilence. There were rumours of his love for Ceridwen, with some suspicion of her regard for him.

The people also knew their chieftain. He had ways of getting what he wanted and there was no doubt in everyone's mind that he wanted Ceridwen, not only as his Beltane queen but as his bride. This would be serious combat, perhaps to the death. There fell an unusual hush as Ceridwen, still above her people on the staging of the ox cart, raised her hands. Her grandmother's crimson robe billowed from her shoulders in the soft evening breeze, her face lit by the flickering of the Belfire and her burnished hair flowing loose about her.

'The uniting of Grainné, Queen of the Land and of Bel, the King of the Sun, shall be preceded by a contest of strength. Stand forth my suitors, who claim me for the Great Rite,' she proclaimed in the strongest of voices, which belied the weakening she felt in her knees.

Marcus moved forwards into the blessing of her gaze. This might be the last time he would behold her. He drank in every beautiful feature of her face, the arch of her brows, the tilt of her nose, the soft play of her lips as she smiled now, only for him.

Then she shifted her gaze and held the smile upon Eithig, playing her part, noting that the usual hostility, read in his demeanour, was now lacking. Instead, he seemed calmly confident. The valerian had done its trick, but the effect would not last long. She must hurry proceedings.

'Our women have consulted and here be our decision. It is our tradition that no man-made weapon may be used in this combat. There is a long bole of pine, which has been lopped to feed our Belfire. You shall each take hold of either end and, positioning yourselves across the fire, you shall tug between you. The first to be pulled into the flames, or to leave go the bole, is lost.'

Marcus found himself feeling suddenly sick at the thought of the injuries that might be incurred. What had possessed Ceridwen to set such a task? It would be justice indeed for Eithig if he were pulled into the fire, after what he had done to Hedfan, but could he countenance maiming anyone thus? He would as soon go for a clean kill.

As though reading his mind Marged now approached him, whispering urgently, 'Do not let go that bole out of compassion. Your rival has no compunction about injuring you. He must not win, Marcus. Our whole tribe, apart from a few of his warriors, wish to see him shamed. We are depending on you.'

'I shall harden my resolve, Marged. There is too much at

stake for me to lose. Trust me and weave some of your magic for me. I need the help of the Gods in this.'

'You shall have it. For your destiny is not to die here today. There is yet much of your life to unfold.'

'Thank you! I hope you are right,' grimaced Marcus, suddenly surprised by its weight, as one end of the pine bole was thrust at him by a warrior.

The pine bole had been roughly trimmed, the notches, where the branches had been pared away, leaving good handholds. He recognised the importance of choosing a strong branchlet and a piece of worn, rough ground to dig his heels into. He could see that Eithig had already chosen his patch and someone was pounding the ground with a mattock to make footholds at varying distances from the fire. Owain had begun to do the same for him and cast him a nervous glance. Madog had begun an ominous beat upon his drum.

Marcus fingered the amulet about his neck and felt in the same instant the hardness of the metal locket hanging next to it. It seemed as though he were taken out of the moment and away from reality. The scene at the Belfire seemed to be totally surreal.

'Suitors take hold and upon my instruction begin to pull. May the Gods choose the best to father our tribe,' commanded Gwilym, his face already reddening from his umpire's place besides the fire between them.

'Pull!'

Marcus knew that if he looked into the fire he was done for. Eithig's sudden jerking of the bole wrenched him suddenly down onto his next foothold, four feet in distance from the fire. If only he could hold there. Although the flames were hot, they were bearable, like the hot noonday Sun in his hometown of Ostia, the seaport at the mouth of the Tiber. If only he could hold there, as if bathing in the Sun's rays. Mithras! Make him strong, strong enough to ignore the agony now tearing at his arms and shoulders, then deeper into his back.

The wrenching of his muscles was making breathing difficult. He opened his eyes momentarily and flung a glance towards Ceridwen. He could see her willing all her strength to him. He remembered to take a deep breath and pulled anew, rocking on his feet to give himself momentum. He could not even see his adversary across the flames – only feel the dreaded tugging ever nearer to the hot inferno.

Betw stood not far from Eithig, feigning encouragement. Instead she was willing his strength to sap and his heart to fill with his childhood fear. Already Eithig was aware that his usual superior strength seemed lacking. His muscles seemed more tired than usual and did not respond quickly to his efforts. The usual rush of excitement, giving an edge to his performance in combat, seemed lacking. Despite that, he did not give up hope yet. Had he not run the race with barely a trace of real breathlessness? Marcus had been truly winded. It was obvious he himself was the fitter man, both in body and nobility, to win Ceridwen.

'Take care Eithig! Leave behind your childhood fear of fire!' shouted Betw above the noise of the cheering. 'Do not let memories of your burning bedstraw come to haunt you!'

Curse the hag for reminding him of his terrifying childhood experience. True, it had been Betw who had roused the family, when she had sensed he was in danger. Why could she not have kept it to herself? The terror of it was already taking hold of his body and mind, even as she spoke. He could smell the smouldering of his child's woollen tunic and feel the searing lick of a flame to his leg from his bedstraw. He remembered how he froze in terror and could do nothing to move; then the smothering blanket, which engulfed him, as his parents put out the fire around him. He remembered gasping for air, the fear of being smothered sharper than the fear of being burned. He remembered his mother's screams and his father shouting something to her and the servants.

Then something had burst over him...The will to survive had given him sudden strength to move his arms, to fling away the blanket from his head and take great gasping breaths of smoke-laden air.

Eithig came back with a jolt to the present. With a tortuous yell he flung his end of the bole into the fire and fell backwards onto the mossy earth. He was safe from the fire, but had lost his goal. People were muttering something about the will of the Gods, but to Eithig there came the suspicion that he had been bewitched. He was confused and dazed and was helped to his feet by his warriors; but by the time his sight cleared and focused, Marcus was standing somewhat incredulously victorious, King of the Beltane festival. He was holding aloft the stag's headdress in one hand and the hand of Ceridwen in the other.

Could jealousy burn like a searing fire? Despite the valerian, Eithig's feelings against Marcus reached new depths, ignited anew in the core of his being, as he witnessed the lovers' soul-bond shining from their eyes. The crowd cheered their king and queen and began the celebratory dancing and singing. But Eithig, smarting with hatred and wounded pride, withdrew with his warriors into the forest to recover and to plan his next course of action.

⌘ ⌘ ⌘

CHAPTER XVII

⌘

THE BOWER

Before the Great Rite itself there was great feasting and drinking. The pig was succulent and, to satiate grumbling bellies, new bread soaked in its juices was passed around in baskets by the children.

Betw was searching for Ffynan to remind him of his coming role, but he was nowhere to be found. He was not serving food with the children. He was not trying to impress any young virgins with his skill upon the lyre. He was not helping the young lads from Dreffos to erect the great, carved bole, a symbol of male fertility, to the South of the clearing. Nor was he practising his drinking skills with the men. Perhaps he was with Hedfan? The two boys always had a good rapport. Where was Hedfan? Betw's mounting anxiety and guilt, about not thoroughly checking Ffynan's whereabouts that morning, cut her away from any knowledge of where to find them.

She could not bear to spoil the precious time between Ceridwen and Marcus. They were so enjoying being open about their relationship, laughing and dancing together. No, she must not ask Ceridwen. There were plenty of others who might know where the boys were to be found.

By the time she had questioned each member of the family from Tan Yr Aur and equally conjured their anxiety with a frantic search amongst the throng, the question answered itself.

The crowd parted and music stalled, as Hedfan, leading

Gwyngariad, approached the fire clearing. Behind him followed Twm leading the dappled grey. As Ffynan now rose from lying about the neck of the white mare, the crowd was uncertain. Perhaps it was a new form of ritual, parading the bard upon the chieftain's horse? A boy's cheeky prank perhaps? The procession halted and Ffynan slid shakily into the arms of the waiting crowd.

Hedfan approached Ceridwen and Marcus, who now stood on a rise above the fires. 'Hail King and Queen of Beltane,' he began uncomfortably. 'By the design of the Gods, we have rescued your bard from a cruel fate; for he hung above the spiked pig-pit waiting to die!'

'It was unpennoned and a great danger to life. The builders of it should be hung from the trees and gored with spears!' cried Twm, bloodthirsting for justice.

'Gwyngariad pulled Ffynan clear with my rope ladder about her,' said Hedfan, somehow hoping to be exonerated from his taking of the chieftain's mare.

Ceridwen was more concerned about Ffynan. 'Ffynan, you stand a little shakily I see,' she said, tenderly taking his delicate musician's fingers in her hands. 'Did it fright you much, this experience?'

'I was frighted, but was comforted by my parents coming from the spirit world,' he whispered. 'I am not frighted at all now I hold your hands and, if Cullen will help me mend the string from my broken lyre, I shall sing the Great Rite for you both.'

'You were saved with sweet purpose, Ffynan. You shall grow to be a famous bard. Mark my words,' soothed Ceridwen, pulling him towards her and enveloping him in her cloak. With her arms wrapped around him, he peered at the gathering before them, like a chick peeking from its nest. 'Hedfan, Twm, thanks be to you both. There may be time for you to return the horses, before Eithig knows you have them,' he chirruped.

'Go now. You shall not be discovered,' Ceridwen reassured them.

The boys could not believe their luck.... no admonishment... no punishment. They led the horses away, back to the pasture.

How did Ceridwen know that there might be time to return them before Eithig and his men searched them out? Where were Eithig and his warriors? Sulking somewhere, no doubt, because of lost pride. They could be hiding in the forest to the side of the track.

For Twm and Hedfan it was a journey fraught with tension and the blackest of shadows, cast by the undergrowth, made them jumpy. They had not dared to bring flaring torches to light their way, but the path through the woodland was well worn and they knew, from the horses' reactions, that there was no one about. They reached the safety of the moonlit, silver pasture without incident; the only noise, the soft nickering of the tethered horses as they recognised Gwyngariad and the dappled grey.

'It is time, my people, you knew about the treachery of your chieftain,' Marcus announced to the gathering. 'It was Eithig who ordered the digging of the pit for my downfall. My death was planned this day.' There was a chorus of disbelief from those who were in ignorance and gloom from those who had known about Eithig's plan.

'But we were remiss not to pennon the pig-pit, once we knew of its existence,' Gwilym admitted. 'For that we are responsible and beg your forgiveness Ffynan. We did not wish Eithig and his men to know that we had tumbled to his plans. With hindsight we can judge what best course of action should have been taken.'

''Tis time we had true elections and put in power a man of wisdom to rule our territory,' Coll voiced, seething with rage. 'It goes against all that is noble and true for us to be puppets of a leader so viperous.'

'Hush, Coll. Do you think Eithig has no ears for what you say? Do you want to return home to our huts burned, our crops razed and our animals confiscated?' warned Marged.

'I am tired of pretending loyalty to him,' Coll protested. 'I can hide no longer behind diplomacy. Perhaps Eithig needs to be brought to a Roman court and his deeds dealt with there.' There were true gasps of horror. To admit to their Roman rulers that they were incapable of maintaining simple discipline within their tribe was tantamount to treason.

'Leave matters be Coll. Do not stir up the vengeance of war within our tribe,' pleaded Owain, pressing upon the arm of his brother.

'Best leave matters to the true election time of Lugnasad at harvest,' Lord Meurig advised. 'Even then I cannot imagine Eithig willingly yielding a smattering of his power to any other. He has suffered indignity to his pride this day. He will not let matters be, mark my words. It is best not to cross him further.'

'It would be easy for me to send for my men from the hill fort and have him arrested. If that is what you think is best for you people? We have good case here for attempted murder,' Marcus suggested uneasily, unsure of how he should proceed.

'I have known Eithig since he was a boy. There is no one shrewder at wriggling away from responsibility in matters of right and wrong. He is as slippery as the eels in our waters. He would have no scruples against using one of his warriors as a scapegoat,' warned Old Betw. 'You would be unable to prove the case against him and he would turn the situation on its head and say that you had tampered with our traditions and deserved the wroth of our Gods.' The tribespeople found themselves nodding in agreement. They all had reasons to vote for Eithig at election time. Many of them owed him favours, or he had some hold of fear over them.

Somehow Ceridwen was given the tongue to ease the moment. 'My people, my family, my friends, my children! Tomorrow we shall come together and consult about this weighty matter. But, for now, we have a much more important task to hand.'

From somewhere deep inside her, below her and above her, she summoned great love and power. She enveloped the whole gathering in the love of the Earth Mother.

'Be still and smell the scent of pine upon the wind. Our Goddess bids us be calm. It is time to celebrate the Great Rite and we argue about leadership of our tribe? Look. The Sun has sunk beneath the coverlet of the hills and it is time; time to honour the great source of our well-being. Yet we allow the treachery of one so ignoble to deter us from our task? Leave the Gods to punish the wayward. Focus your mind and hearts upon the regeneration of our tribe. Resolve that from the sacred unions of this night might flow a stream of wisdom, courage and loyalty. Ffynan make ready. Madog, Cullen, we have need of magical music!'

Ceridwen moved into the centre of the clearing, opposite the decorated bole to the South and between the flickering fires. She stood quite still, until the hushed silence wrapped its calm about the whole throng. She could feel the earth energy between her feet, feeding her with its magical, tingling stream. She felt the heat from the flames of the fires; symbols of the Sun God come down to Earth, play upon her outstretched palms. She could smell the scent of the May blossom wafted on the evening sea breeze and could feel the strength of the maybole, the tree of life, course through her loins and up through her spine.

Then the throb from Madog's low, expectant beating was joined with a fluid melody from Ffynan's lyre. The cadences reached into the soul of each one present and, by the time Cullen joined to it his pipe, the sounds had gained the sweet piquancy of both nostalgia and future promise. The swell of the music rose and fell with such intensity, conjuring the times when Nanw had stood thus.

Ceridwen felt the power of Nanw join her, bringing with it all the old priestess had taught her about reverence to the Earth Mother and the Sun Father. She began to move with such grace, that all who beheld her wanted to gasp in witness to her ethereality. Marcus could only marvel how a new surge of desire for her throbbed in every vein, a desire to be at one with her spirit. His longing for her was much more than for a momentary coupling. He knew he wanted to be with her into eternity. How it was to be achieved he did not know, nor whether he deserved to be her soul mate.

For Ceridwen, there was such a welter of emotion to contend with. The presence of Nanw had initially brought tears to her eyes. To conjure the idea of spirits was easy for

Ceridwen's fertile imagination, but she had never expected to feel such awe at Nanw's presence, newly empowered with its goodness, after leaving the dross of its humanity behind. She felt so honoured and undeserving of the precious gift of those few moments. Yet she knew she must become open to working with the empowerment that coursed through her.

The moment of incredulity passed as her sense of wonder increased. She allowed Nanw's spirit to inspire every movement of her body. It was Nanw who was choreographing the ancient dance, causing the earth energy to flow through her limbs, the wind and flames to call forth the shapes and steps. It was a dance witnessing the great beauty of the Earth and all creation.

Then the virgins gathered one by one in reverent circle about her. They began to copy her flowing and weaving gestures. A gust of wind seemed to signal a change in mood as the sweeping tide of music suddenly held its breath. Now only the constant rhythms of Madog's tabor could be heard.

The young women began to change their dance to one of shy enticement, casting glances towards their men. The mood changed yet again, becoming passionate and insistent. Ceridwen spun around, her robe creating more firelight of red and gold, as it flared with her circular movements. It was time for the spectators to gather and holding hands step *deosil* to arouse the powers of fertility.

A sharp drum beat brought them to a halt, as Ceridwen took her wand of hazel and began to open the pathways of magic to the East, the South, the West and the North. Only then did the men move solemnly through the pathways towards their virgins. Betw noted with satisfaction that Cullen requested the hand of Elen and Elen nodded her consent. Other maidens, not yet foresworn, had suitors simply offer their hand.

Despite several shakes of the head from some unwillingly suited, all present were eventually paired to someone they accepted. There were three virgins missing. No one had thought to admonish them when they saw them slipping away to find their warriors.

Marcus and Ceridwen repaired to a carved love seat, which

had been brought especially by Tangwen from Dreffos. It had been a favoured place for courting, handed down from one generation to the next. It was said to be magical and impart oneness of soul to couples who swore their love in its vicinity.

But Ceridwen needed no magic now to join her in soul to Marcus. Whatever dangers lay ahead, the certainty that they would go together into the future was strong and the bonds that tied them of an eternal nature. She had had the feeling of it that night of the *sending* and at this moment, as he gently pressed her hand between his, she came to know it for sure.

There was much feasting and dancing, even Old Betw and Madog's mother, Olwenna joined in the circle dancing. The couples snatched kisses between dances and to arouse friendly rivalry flirted outrageously with those other than their partners.

Einir, no longer looking over her shoulder for her brother, nor Edwyn, played safe and danced with the little ones who had not fallen asleep in the hay cart. It felt so good to be free of men's demands...She imagined her new life at Dreffos? It was no splendid villa, but a large stone and wattle farmstead, defended by moat and high wall. It sported many more home comforts than the sparse fortress at Din Silwy. To think that she would eat the same food and share the same home with the Lady Tangwen. Perhaps she would wear her lady's cast-off clothing. She might yet look like the princess of her birthright. Eithig had seen no need to waste money in dressing his sister in fine clothes. Warmth was paramount in the sharp, coastal winds.

She could see herself now, dressed in long, flowing robes, instead of her rough woollen tunic; collecting herbs in the walled garden; fending off her suitors with coy smiles. Being maid would suit her fine; for the time being, at least.

Betw thrust Ffynan forwards, nodding her huge, wrinkled smiles of encouragement. It was time to sing the Great Rite. The fires were dying to a comforting glow. They had danced and sung, feasted and drank and, above all, honoured the great spirits of progeny, the Earth Mother and the Sun Father. Couples held each other close. It was almost time.

Ffynan stroked his lyre shakily at first; then, as he began to relax and grow in confidence, he allowed the great love and respect he always bore his instrument to shine through his music. Now it was more special to him than ever. Not only had it belonged to generations of bards before him, but had, this day, saved his life.

Competing only with the firelight's hiss and glow, he began to sing with his clear, sweet unbroken voice, as couples old and young leaned against each other in equally sweet expectation.

'Bel, our Lord of fire and heat,
Lord of Earth's fertility,
Warm our hearts and sear our land
With power and might and progeny.

Come Grainné, Queen of Earth and Night!
Join with your Lord of Day,
That soon the swell of belly show
The fruits of His fecundity.

The land to prosper, stock to breed,
Our seed to sow in virgin soil
And children sent like arrows true
Into our future's journeying.

Join now in marriage of Great Rite,
Begetting and becoming one;
That male and female all renew
The weaving of Eternity.'

Gwilym motioned Marcus to lay his stag's horn headdress aside. Then, both he and Ceridwen were divested of their cloaks. During the sacred song, they received simple crowns of willow, dressed around with woodland flowers and blessings from Lord Meurig and Lady Gwenifer.

They stood scantily clad, Marcus in his deerskin loincloth and Ceridwen in the white flowing tunic of a virgin, Cadoc's golden torc, glowing in the firelight, at her throat. Marcus thought he had never beheld Ceridwen so beautiful. There was a mixture of such pain and love within her soft, grey-blue eyes. He hoped to erase that pain and to replace it with joy.

'It is time to jump the Beltane fire together.' Gwilym announced, striking his staff on the ground. 'Marcus and Ceridwen, you have agreed to play the sacred roles of King and Queen of Beltane, but do you desire also to accept each other as true helpmates, pledging lifelong loyalty one to the other?' he queried noting Ceridwen's moment of hesitation as Marcus held out his hand.

Ceridwen moved against him, outwardly to kiss his shaven cheek, but in reality to forewarn him of her suspicion. Jumping the fire together was a serious declaration that they wished to be bonded for life. It would be his last opportunity to reject her as his wife.

'I am with child, for certes, Marcus,' she murmured urgently against his ear. Do you wish to claim the babe as your own? If so, we shall marry by these rites and jump the fire of life together.'

'Do you not think I have already considered that possibility? Nothing will deter me now, after I have been through such tests to gain you? You may have need of my name to the child, but we have need of each other more.' He held her face now, gently between his hands. 'Ceridwen, this is forever. From this moment in time, I am always by your side. How could you doubt me?'

'Forgive me,' whispered Ceridwen 'but I thought the news might give you second thoughts. I could not bear it if I felt I had trapped you to this somehow.'

'Are you going to jump the fire together or not?' Betw queried, with wry impatience. 'We are all waiting, for we cannot proceed before a signal from you both.'

They nodded simultaneously in answer to Gwilym.

'We are ready, Betw. Please chant the challenge,' Ceridwen reassured her with a gentle grasp to her wizened hand. Ceridwen as priestess should have performed this rite herself, but as she was Queen of the occasion she knew that Betw would enjoy the privilege in her stead. The old woman's voice tremored with age, but only Rhodri smirked in his innocence. There was great respect for Betw. She had been close friends with Nanw and had assisted with priestess duties for many years. Ness, who was leaning her bulk against a tree trunk close to Rhodri, gave him a sharp kick to the shin and a withering look. He was to listen with respect, as Old Betw bound the King and Queen's hands together with a bejewelled thong.

'Those who come before the sacred fire
Witness this coupling of heavenly desire.
May the Gods of good fortune
Keep strong and safe
Your lives, entwined in the memory of fate.

To the pathway of good keep you close and true.
Both friend and lover discover anew
The treasure lain hidden,
Without and within
The soul of each other, layed bare of its sin.

And cursed be the man or woman to break
The bond of loving so wedded this day.
Life's journey to teach, for Heaven's sake,
Great wisdom and courage,
Where destiny takes.

Be warm for each other in Winter's cold grasp.
Take each to your bosom,
Your hearts to enclasp.
May your home be a haven for all who call there;
Your welcome embracing the dark and the fair.

When children surround you,
When age bends your limbs,
May your lives hear the music eternity brings.
Jump now together the glow of the fire,
Burning with life and with wedded desire!'

A carpet of green leaves had been strewn around the glowing embers, to make the jump less hazardous and a springing board to give added height to their leaping. Marcus was faintly aware that Marged and Gwilym were cheering them on. It was good that they approved. It augured well.

A great cheer went up as with bound hands he and Ceridwen ran the short distance to the embers and in perfect unison sprang from the board to land laughing and safely in the carpet of leaves on the opposite side. Other betrothed couples followed suit. There was a great deal of clamour and hilarity as couples fell about each other in untidy collision as they landed. But none dare consummate the rite until the King and Queen of Beltane were bedded. The anticipation was more aphrodisiac than any love potion, as couples old and young planned to sneak into the privacy of the trees, once Ceridwen and Marcus had been bowered.

Ffynan, Madog and Cullen kept the music flowing. The music had shed its solemnity and was now true celebration. Marged led the couple to the bower, constructed of willow canes, woven about with the most scented foliage and flowers to be found. She parted the reed curtain, revealing a bed of fresh hay covered with a white sheet. There was the delicious smell of May blossom from the flowers strewn around it, and sweet smoke from the oil lamps and candles, shining in the crevices of the rock, against which the bower had been constructed. All was in readiness. She kissed Ceridwen tenderly upon her cheek and, with a look towards Marcus saying, 'Be gentle with her!' she was gone to Gwilym.

The light in the bower glowed and cast a soft pink and golden radiance all about them. The heat from the lamps and candles teased more perfume from the flowers. The scent became heady. They drank of each other's eyes, incredulous, adoring. For a moment time seemed suspended.

'Hold me, Marcus,' Ceridwen said in hushed tones. 'Pretend that you will never let go of me. Let us imagine that this, our night, will last forever.'

Complying and with his face in her soft burnished hair he breathed, 'I have so longed for this moment. Not only are you my wife by your laws, but your family would have it so. We have their blessing. You have put aside so much in coming to love me. I know what it has cost you,' he murmured, cradling her head against his shoulder.

'What cost it has been to me?' She drew away far enough to look into the dark pools of his eyes and placed both her hands into the curling hairs upon his chest. Her fingers made contact with the amulet, then the locket. 'You have risked your very life for me this day. You know that. But you have wived a Druid priestess, who cannot leave her homeland to travel in the wake of her husband. You know that my place is here with my people. My task is to tend to their needs...'

'Sh! No talk of our parting, tonight at least,' he begged, putting his forefinger to her lips, then tracing his fingertips from her brow, down her cheek to her chin, as though he were trying to etch every feature upon his memory.

But she continued, 'Besides, I am of conquered tribe and bound to cause you problems. Our present chieftain has murder in his eyes every time he meets with you. I am no virgin and am with child by another man, to boot...And you say, 'What cost it has been to me?' Marcus, I had only to step over my prejudice to see your worth. Coming to love of you has been a salutary lesson, a very necessary spiritual one on my path to wisdom. I want you to know that, whatever befalls us, I love you for who you are and not which race begat you. I will always love you. Always.' She swallowed hard but could not stop tears welling into her eyes to concern him.

He brushed them tenderly away with his well-manicured fingers. 'Must we...? With your wounds and the babe?'

'Yes, we must consummate the Great Rite. If this were only our marriage we could perhaps wait a little while, until I was healed and might prove more willing. But there is no help for it, Marcus. The magic of our coupling is the key to our tribal prosperity. It must be done this night. That it might hurt me, is neither here nor there.'

'Last night, when I could not sleep, I walked by the shore. I cast my seed into the sea, a gift to the Gods. I did not want to rush at you, overwhelm you. Leona...Forgive my mentioning her name. Leona taught me to pleasure a woman, to take things slowly and teasingly. I shall try my best not to hurt you.'

She nodded shyly, handing him a goblet of warmed mead and vervain. They sipped silently sharing the same cup. Slowly he put it aside onto a cleft in the rock and began to unpin the shoulder of her tunic. It fell to her waist revealing the now yellowed weals of bruising to her breasts and arms and the deep gorse scars to her back.

'Allow me...? Let me...?' He turned her about. Tenderly he stood behind her, kissing each wound, stroking down each scar. Eventually he cupped his fingers about each breast, discovering the silken skin, playing teasing circles around each nipple, which now stood proud in response, despite her fear. She felt arousal deep within her and gasped. Her breasts unaccountably arched for more into his hands.

He continued to stroke her, playing his hands down the hill of her hips and along her thighs between the slits of the thin tunic. Ceridwen found she did not want to hold back. The pain of the scars seemed miraculously dimmed and the throbbing in the valley between her thighs seemed to promise both pleasure and pain. She writhed urgently against him, and he found it took all his control not to rush her.

She was conscious that his hands shook as they undid the enamelled gold clasp of her girdle. The tunic fell to her feet. Still behind her, he kissed and nuzzled at her neck. With one hand he undid the tie to his deerskin apron. He held her close to him for a moment, folded into him. Then his hands slid down over the gentle rise of her belly. It surprised her that her body begged him to go further, further down, to the curling nest of her privates.

He turned her gently to face him and he could see the desire playing around her parted lips. Her eyes were half closed, still remembering the ripples of sensation he had caused.

'Ceridwen!' he whispered.

She opened her eyes and smiled into his. They stood apart to appreciate each other's nakedness. She began by taking in the dark, sweeping waves of his hair; his sun bronzed face with its aquiline nose and generous mouth; and those dark, deep, laughing eyes. It was like the first course of a banquet to her. She seemed to be savouring every flicker of light upon him.

His shoulders were still gleaming from the oils with which the menfolk had anointed him. He was broad and strong without being thickset, the muscles of his military training filling out his torso. He was not covered in hair like her father. It grew a little upon his chest and down his well developed thighs. But it was the weapon between his legs, which suddenly frightened her. She was used to seeing her father and brothers naked, but without an erection.

True she had heard tales of how big the male member could grow once excited, but she never imagined...

Marcus immediately read the fear in her face and he knew he could not proceed. The Gods give him control, for he had never been so aroused. Despite the scarring and bruising, her beauty and vulnerability fired such passion that he felt he must scream for relief. From somewhere, somehow, control came from the compassion she conjured in him.

'Sweetheart. *Cariad.* I would not harm you. Come. I shall lie down and be your plaything. You shall taunt me and molest me at your will.'

At his smiling invitation she pushed away the fear and began her shy journey of exploration.

Outside the music played on and on. The bedded couple were being tiresomely long in coming up with the goods. By now the shout, signalling the breech of her virginity, should have been heard and the soiled sheet with her virgin blood thrown out of the bower. This was to be paraded by the young boys around the fires, rubbed against the bole and dragged through the nearby fields to spread the blessing of fertility. No one else might consummate the evening until the King and Queen of Beltane were mated.

Eithig had been blind with rage as he led his warriors from the blazing scene. What hocus-pocus had been levelled at him? He should have won the day without a doubt. He was the stronger. Physical strength was everything to him. He could not abide weakness, even in himself. He was never ill and despised all those who succumbed to sickness or any part of infirmity.

This fuzziness in his brain was quite unnatural. Perhaps it had been something to do with the celebratory cup. Perhaps one of his entourage had meant it for Marcus. It was no doing of Ceridwen's he was sure, for she was obviously besotted with Marcus. He had not realised it until the moment they had stood together as King and Queen of Beltane.

He could not tolerate seeing them together. For as long as he could remember, he had fantasized about possessing Ceridwen. Many times he had called by the hut at Cae Gwynion and been physicked by the old woman, just so that he could set his eyes upon the girl. She had always made some excuse to avoid him. He had flattered himself that it was shyness. Now he knew different and resentment against her began to smoulder.

He needed time to think, time to sleep off this overwhelming tiredness, time to eradicate the confusion in his brain and come up with a plan of action. He was striding along the path to the paddock where the mounts were tethered when a strange sound came to his ears. It was muffled screaming from the throat of a man being disembowelled for sure.

His sense of curiosity was heightened and he must discover the owner of the cries. His men had heard it too and they veered off urgently down a track, which brought them crashing through the young bracken to the hut at Cae Gwynion. The geese let out their anxious cackling and the gander made an unfortunate play for Eithig's leg. With one swing of the ceremonial sword, it lay decapitated and bleeding amongst its terror stricken wives.

Eithig gave a wry smile as their torches lit up the horror stricken face of Edwyn, tied like a sacrificial lamb to the threshold post. He let out a great anguished cry, as they cut away the gag, and dissolved into tears at his master's feet when he was unbound, the madness of his visions ebbing further away with each sob.

'What have we here? Have you been letching after someone else's maid, perhaps? What pranks have you been playing behind my back you treacherous slug?' sneered Eithig, wiping the bloody sword across Edwyn's back to clean it. 'Did I not tell you I would find you suit this night? I have other work for you at present, which will teach you to tremble! Light the fire and hang this bird, dripping above the cauldron. I need its blood for broth. We shall eat it at Ceridwen's hearth and she shall never find peace here.'

Eithig looked around the hut. It had been well maintained, despite the lack of a man to tend it. No doubt the men from Tan Yr Aur had kept the stone foundations, the wattle and daub walls in good repair and the thatch well sealed from the rain. But for some reason the cleanliness and tidiness, displayed by Ceridwen's housekeeping, irritated him beyond belief.

Perhaps in the morning he would repent, but for now he had the burning desire to smash every pot of tincture and ointment she had made. With no more than three swipes of his soiled sword, he swept all her clay pots smashing to the ground. That two of his warriors begged him to cease he paid not the slightest heed. He had destroyed several years' work in a few moments. It would take her many seasons of growing, gathering and brewing to build up the medicinal stocks to the same level.

He paused and gazed at the shattered remains, then calmly bade his men sweep the mess outside. 'If anyone queries this deed, you did it, Edwyn. You were understandably so incensed to have been tied here. Do we understand each other,' Eithig glared menacingly at the still trembling wretch, who had paused in disbelief at his master's behaviour, whilst shakily attempting to tie the gander above the cauldron over the fire he had just made.

Edwyn had always acknowledged that his master was cruel. Eithig kept his tight rein on things by inducing fear. Edwyn had known no other form of leadership, but his master's voice had always held a quality of endearment when it addressed him. He had never before been the subject of his master's despite. He had never before fell victim, until this day. To see his loyalty so flung in his face destroyed any bond that had previously tied them. To survive, Edwyn dissembled compliance, but he would wait his opportunity. The Gods would provide him with one, no doubt.

Eithig sank wearily upon Ceridwen's pallet, pulling her coverlet about him and smelling her smell. His men had brought bread and mead with them. He would satiate his belly; drink his fill of the broth and dream.

The men were cowed by his outburst, but once their Lord drifted into sleep, began to murmur their disaffection at their lack of women. They were delighted when three maids appeared, grinning coyly at the threshold. They were led to warm themselves by the fire and take refreshment. They had come to claim their warriors. They did not realise that they would service the whole contingent, crowded into the priestess's hut and the outbuildings. Their muffled cries of pain and terror would go unnoticed against the louder celebration higher up the hill. Only Mwg, perched in hiding on the branch of a hawthorn tree above the hut, lashed his tail in anger and registered the abomination.

Ceridwen ran her fingers over Marcus's body, slowly and lingeringly. She wanted to etch the shape of his every curve into her memory, but he could wait no longer

'Ceridwen! *Cariad.* Quickly. Sit astride me as you do the ponies at Tan Yr Aur. Move against me as though you were riding.'

She needed no instruction to master the rhythm, for it was a dance she knew by instinct. The pain in her bruised body shifted to make room for the overwhelming desire to take him into her. She leaned lower over him, writhing against him, brushing her lips against his face and then their mouths sought each other. His tongue flickered around hers, lighting darts of delicious longing throughout her whole being. The desire in her throat became thick and aching, the need in her loins becoming even more urgent. She writhed once more, the hard rise of her nipples tantalising, promising. They both groaned with the effort of holding back. Then he thrust upwards, hard against her belly and with a gasp his seed spilled between them like a sacred offering, a warm, delicious honeyed wetness.

They lay for a moment quite still. Ceridwen enjoyed her powers as priestess, but she had never before experienced the heady power of satisfying a man. With Marcus it felt good and wholesome and seemed nothing to do with the terror she had experienced by the badger set.

'*Cariad*, you must take my member inside you before it becomes too small, quickly, whilst the seed is still fresh. We shall be able to say our marriage is consummate then.'

Ceridwen knew him to be right and reverently stroking the now dwindling phallus, did her best to slide it between the swollen lips of her vulva. She gasped with pain at the penetration and cried out, but once inside her she wanted to hold onto him forever. It felt as though they were joined in one body, part of each other. It was destiny. It was home. It was where they both belonged. Their hearts had known it from their first glance.

They smiled into each other's eyes, not wanting to speak, not wanting to move away from each other. Then the clamour of voices from outside the wattle curtain grew.

'Throw out the sheet! We have waited too long!'

Their chant of 'Virgin blood! Virgin blood!' pressed against Ceridwen's brain and she at last drew away from Marcus, anointed with his seed, blessed by the Sun God. She took a sharp golden sickle from a shelf in the rock. The light from the candles flickered. There was a glint of gold as she made a swift slash to her inner arm.

'Now it is your turn,' she whispered as she handed him the sickle. He obeyed her with only the slightest questioning glance and when the bright slashes of fresh blood appeared on both their arms, she threaded her fingers into his and pressed both wounds together.

'*When the noble bloods of Rome and Druid mingle, as our rowans intertwine, then peace and honour will come with us to dine!* That was a prophecy of my grandfather, Cadoc, arch druid. It is fulfilled this day...I know it. From now on our tribe will go on to nobler things.' She stared into his face, willing it to be true, their mingled blood dripping onto the white sheet at their feet.

'Would that you are right,' Marcus replied. 'May the Gods protect us all!'

They both cleansed themselves with the sheet and then she kissed it and passed it beneath the reed curtain into the waiting crowd. A great cheer went up and Hedfan tied two ends of it to a pole. He was determined to lead the boys in their torchlight procession around the Holy Place and on into the fields. They would need to be fleet to keep up with him.

Marcus was feeling the cold all of a sudden, but he did not want to join the throng outside, around the fires. He wanted to maintain what little privacy they had. He picked up two plaid woollen rugs from a neat pile made ready for them and wrapped them around both their shoulders, but Ceridwen broke free, suddenly ravenous and reached outside to retrieve an offering.

It was a huge bronze platter, filled with freshly roasted meats and warm bannocks. 'Come and share with me these offerings my people have made to the King and Queen of Beltane. This night we are the earthly symbols of our Gods. Come. Eat,' she commanded.

Later they slept in each other's arms, warmed by the naked heat of each other's body and enveloped in the plaid blankets. The revelry outside soon died, as couples fell about their mating and others dozed. Only Old Betw woke frequently to prod a bondsman and make sure that the Beltane fires were kept burning.

⌘ ⌘ ⌘

CHAPTER XVIII

⌘

DAWN

The camp around the Holy Ground stirred late and the sky had already burst into golden light in the East, by the time Marged rose from Gwilym's side and organised pots of barley gruel to be heated over the cooking fires. Each family would make and serve its own breakfast this morn and then it would be time to take leave, throwing old belongings into the flames of the Belfires to symbolise the cleansing of the soul and a death to bad habits. Each family would take home with them torches lit from the blessed fires to kindle their own hearths and to make blessing fires for the cattle which could not all be driven such distance to Mynydd Llwydiarth.

Marged should have been feeling a sense of satisfaction. Marcus had won his bride and she approved of the suit. But there was unease on the warm breeze, which belied the beauty of nature's carpet spread before her. The dawn chorus, usually so thrilling to the ears at this time of year, was subdued and only the call of a brave lone blackbird shrilled in the clear dew-laden air. She felt eyes watching her every movement and the feeling intensified as she brought Marcus and Ceridwen their bowls of steaming gruel.

Her eyes told her all she wanted to know, as she parted the reed curtain. They were still sleeping; Marcus curled protectively around Ceridwen and she clasping his hand to hers. Their faces looked so young, so smooth and innocent as they slept. No one would dream that their minds held so much knowledge, so much wisdom upon which their peoples depended.

She touched them both. 'It is time to stir and dress. We must take counsel to decide about Eithig and his men. Then each family will want to speak to you both before they leave. Watch out. There are hot bowls at your feet.' There was sadness for her daughter in her voice. For, having known the happiness of the sacred night, Marcus must be gone to his duties again and Ceridwen must learn to live without her new husband. She turned and left them swiftly to some precious moments of privacy.

Marcus handed Ceridwen her tunic. She held it for a moment against her naked body and stared wistfully into his eyes. 'Maybe the rest of my life will be fraught with tests and difficulties, but to know that the Gods were willing to give me such moments of happiness...The memory of it will stay with me forever. Marcus I thank you.'

'You speak as though we shall have no more life together. I shall visit you whenever I have leave. This will not be the only time we can be together, I promise you. There may be a month or so before the relief contingent arrive and I am called back to Segontium.' He paused to buckle on his belt over a purple tunic someone had thought to provide for him. 'You could come to the hill fort? You may heal well in the next month. I have still to pleasure you. You shall know what lovemaking can truly be. I promise.'

'Marcus, no! It is impossible for me to come there. You see how it is with me? I have accepted you. I love all that is you, but to come to the fort...It would be to accept the Roman army and all it stands for. I cannot love Rome! You expect too much.'

'I am sorry. I beg your pardon. I was not thinking. I thought only to hold you in my arms again. I want to be near you, to share your life whenever it is possible. That was my only motive. I do not expect you to love Rome.' His eyes pleaded with her and she repented her outburst, drawing close to him and holding out her hands.

'Marcus,' she pressed, 'was it like this with Leona? Were you close yet far?'

He smiled. Ceridwen was so wise in many ways, but she was novice in the ways of men and women. In seeing her as a woman he had forgotten that she had had no lovers before him. He must be patient and kind. The truth was that he had found very little discomfort with Leona. Was it his imagination or had they never quarrelled? With Leona there were cultural things about each other's lives they found interesting, but she had been content to live every day philosophically. They saw so much death that living for the moment had become a way of life. They had dedicated themselves to sweetening the life of the other. There was no pull of loyalties, no barriers between them that had mattered. Having access to each other most days had matured their relationship. To be realistic this could not happen between Ceridwen and himself. They would have to be content with time snatched from their calling.

'We must not compare our lives to the daily rub that Leona and I had together. You and Leona are two very different people and the challenge our marriage gives to us will be very different. But there is closeness and distance in every relationship. Sometimes we shall be able to read each other's thoughts and at others we shall be way off mark...just as I was, a few moments ago. It takes practice to be at one with the other and we shall be short on that, so must make allowances.'

'I have spoiled this precious time. I shall take care not to do so again,' she murmured miserably.

'You have spoiled nothing. Never be frighted to speak your heart and be honest with me. A good marriage is built on trust. We must trust the other.' He tilted her chin with his hand and smiled, his eyes dancing with hers. They kissed long and hard and sadly.

'Our subjects await us,' Marcus attempted to joke, at last pulling away and toying clownishly with the now bedraggled chaplets of flowers. His he set rakishly at a drunken angle upon his head and pulled the most idiotic face he could muster. Hers he set playfully, dipping upon her nose. It was good to see her laugh as she set them both straight and then they stepped out into the fresh sunshine, smiling upon the world.

Gwilym poked Cullen in the ribs and he was suddenly roused

from the fog of his night of mead and love. He staggered and blinked against the morning light, then attempted to muster the tribespeople together upon his horn. Elen lingered by him, not wanting to be separated from him and irritating him by trying to rearrange his very tousled hair. His horn blowing left a great deal to be desired and was so horrendously novice that, at one point, the whole company broke into fits of laughter.

'You've been all blowed-out from the night before!'

'Your kisses have taken all the wind from him, Elen.'

'Can you not make him rise again to the occasion?' were some of the ribald comments bandied about. He grinned tolerantly and grimaced once more at Elen's attempts to tidy him.

Marged brought Nanw's cloak of crimson and gold, from where it hung outside the bower and draped it over her daughter's shoulders.

'We have had an eventful Beltane. The blessings of Bel and Grainné go with us all and issue from this night,' she murmured, as she caught the clasp at Ceridwen's throat. Ceridwen noted her mother's worried frown and shaking fingers and suddenly found herself watchful, her eyes scanning the gathering and beyond to the fringe ring of the oaks.

The children were helping the bondsmen to stoke the fires, but Coll, Owain and her father were lowering the bole. It would be chopped into logs, one for each household, to symbolise the begetting of offspring.

It was the duty of Marcus and Ceridwen, as the King and Queen, in their moment of Mother and Father of the tribe, to bless each family and kiss all the children in turn. For Marcus it was a warm, glowing, welcoming feeling; taking tiny trusting hands into his once more; smelling the freshness of their young skin against his cheek. Here, on the sacred mountain, the feeling of trust from the little ones felt like the greatest of honours.

A fleeting memory of Crispian's rounded cheeks and huge eyes brought a lump to his throat, then a tear to his eye. Little Rhonwen noticed and leaned towards him, where he sat on the love seat next to Ceridwen. A delightfully chubby, grubby forefinger brushed the tear away and she said very seriously,

'Mam says you are my uncle now, as well as our King of Beltane.'

''Tis true, Rhonwen, and you are now my niece. I am blessed this day by your God, Bel. I belong to a family for the first time in my life.'

Her eyes widened in disbelief. 'You had no mother, nor father, no brothers nor sisters, no *Nain*, no *Taid*?'

'My mother died in childbirth, and my father was away on campaigns with the army. I never knew my grandparents. I was brought up by my tutor.'

'Will my mother die in childbirth?'

He winced at his own careless slip of the tongue. 'No your mother will not die birthing her babe, for has she not you and my Ceridwen to tend her? She is safe for sure.' Marcus sensed the child had more awkward questions, but was saved by Cullen blowing the horn for assembly.

Lord Meurig presided and motioned all to form a circle.

You have shown dissatisfaction with your chieftain. You must decide how he is to be dealt with. Do you wish him arrested and brought before our great assemblage of chieftains at the feast of Lugnasad, or do you want to hand him over to the Romans to be tried by their law? Keep in mind that witnesses must be called in both cases.'

'It is better if we call him before an assemblage of our chieftains, who will decide what is to be done with him,' argued Betw. 'Not only has he broken the laws of Rome, he has broken our taboos. Only our chieftains can understand the gravity of his actions at the sacred Beltane Rites.'

The crowd agreed wholeheartedly. But Ceridwen and Marcus observed grimly and silently. Marged too was silent, too deep in thought to respond. Perhaps if she had been honest with Eithig in the first place, none of this rivalry would have got so out of hand. If Eithig knew he was brother to Ceridwen, he could not have challenged for Ceridwen in the first place. That was not to say he would not have attempted to kill Marcus. Nor was it to say he would not have abused Ceridwen in the same way she suspected he had abused Einir; but it would have put a very different slant upon things.

'If he is proven guilty, it will be the death penalty for him, whoever presides at the trial,' said Lord Meurig, trying to impress upon them the consequences of what they were about to do. 'In my opinion he should be tried by his fellow chieftains and, if to die, should be sacrificed at their hands; not crucified by Rome.' The crowd was heating up with indignation and Ceridwen could sense the unhealthiness of mob feeling aroused. She could read revenge in Coll's eyes. But it was Marcus who broke into their building hysteria.

'Peace! You forget that I am chief witness to his crimes and that I am honour bound to bring him before a Roman magistrate, who may well then turn him over to you for punishment,' Marcus bellowed, trying to get them to focus more reasonably. They quieted and he continued in more measured tone, 'That would be correct procedure.' There was stunned silence. No one could argue against him.

'You are right, Marcus. That would be correct procedure. I have influence with the magistrates in certain quarters. We should see things go that way, so that there is no reprisal from Rome,' Lord Meurig ceded with a sigh of defeat.

'Who shall come forward to witness?' Betw queried, casting her eyes around the whole company. There was much shuffling of feet and murmuring under the breath. Marged's heart sank as Gwilym stepped forward.

'My lads would witness, but they are full of hot anger, which is not always the best way to represent a case at whatever the court. I shall stand for the tribe and for Marcus.'

'It was I who discovered the plot from Edwyn.' Einir's voice rang out, as she stepped forwards. 'Without me to witness, Eithig could blame it all on misadventure and turn the blame upon his own men.'

'You are right, my sister!'

The whole assemblage froze. Eithig's voice cut through the air like ice, calculating, casting a menacing cloud over the proceedings. They all turned in response to the south pathway, where he stood in full battle paint; his hair splayed about his head, stiffened with white lime, radiating like a grotesque crown. Ceridwen and Betw were not the only ones to witness the shafts of yellow-green light, which sprang, from his eyes and the unhealthy aura, twisting and writhing about him.

Marcus could see the whole vista of the Holy Ground from where he was standing on the knoll. Eithig's warriors surrounded them, all painted as for war and carrying swords and spears. Lord Meurig and his men felt vulnerable. No one was allowed arms, especially not so near to the Holy Ground. The only tools they all carried were knives and axes. If they fought they would have no chance against the swords and spears. The men silently drew their knives, but Meurig shook his head and they sheathed them again. Before Marcus could cry out, there was a sack thrown over his head and he was bound up like a pig for the slaughter. Einir was pushed towards Eithig at spear point and then tied by her wrists. If she were to die, he would make sure it would not be a quick, sweet release. He pulled her against him by the hair. The point of his knife teased her throat and a red scar appeared where he pricked at her skin. No one dared to breathe, or move.

'Good. You recognise that I am in control. I do not advise any of you to move. I want no little messenger sneaking away to tell tales at the hill fort.' Eithig cast his eyes around the circle. They narrowed and focused upon Ffynan, who began to tremble with fright.

'There is a rite of this Beltane yet unfinished. *'When the noble bloods of Rome and Druid mingle, as our rowans intertwine, then peace and honour will come with us to dine.'* That is the prophecy of our forebears. Is it not?' Eithig's voice sliced the air like a sickle, sending shivers down the least sensitive of spines.

'The soft whimpers of our women would have us believe it means a marriage between our priestess and this so-called descendent of Marcus Aurelius. But I have a better interpretation. It means none other than ritual sacrifice. Their blood shall flow and mingle on our sacred altar. We shall drink it and be empowered to rise against Rome and rid this isle of their rule. Hold them now. Ffynan, you shall compose a fitting verse for their end. Huw, find the sacred golden sickle. We must take care to observe the rites correctly!'

'No!' screamed Marged, held back by Gwilym from flying

at Eithig and thus on to his followers' swords. Marcus's muffled voice came from the pig sack where he lay trussed and writhing upon the ground. He could hardly breathe and his speech came forth like nonsense. He must pray with all his might. Surely his men from the hill fort would somehow know of his dilemma? With despair he remembered giving strict orders that no one was to approach the Holy Ground during the sacred time of Beltane.

With spears prickling between their shoulder blades, Ceridwen's family dared not move, but the young warriors, who had made to tie up Ceridwen, were suddenly surprised by the red and gold swirling of her cloak. They found it awesome and impregnable, the energy, emitting from the patterns of gold, played with their fears and kept them at a distance.

Ceridwen was tempted to focus on Marcus's discomfort, but she knew she must control the outrage rising in her and think clearly. There must be no room for fear. It was not only her own life and his at stake. The forces of good must conquer. *Hatred never ceases by hatred. Hatred is only conquered by love.* She could see the faces of Nanw and Cadoc smiling from the other world, filling her with confidence. If it was her time to die, it was no matter to her; she and Marcus would be together. But the message was clear. The voices in her head told her it was not time. She and Marcus had an important part to play in the unfolding destiny of their peoples.

She felt a surge of energy from the ground beneath her and, as a buzzard's call rang out over the mountain, she felt as though she was flying high above the congregation. Her eyes filled with power and love, love for Marcus, love for her family and love for her homeland.

She swirled around, the colours from her ceremonial cloak catching the golden glory light of the morning, as it filtered through the budding trees. She stilled and faced Eithig, her hands outstretched to receive blessing and strength. She held every eye transfixed.

Miraculously she spoke without fear and to her audience it seemed her young girlish voice was displaced by the deeper tones of a mature Nanw.

'My brother! For that is who you have always been to me...a brother. Your eyes are veiled with misconceptions. Your heart you have allowed to rule your head, without thought to your subjects, without love for your people. Our ancient traditions have always stood in our best interest and the counsel of Druid priest or priestess taken priority over the wishes of our chieftains. When our chieftains have disobeyed that counsel, we have had disunity and become weakened as a result.' Lord Meurig was seen to nod in agreement and several warriors hung their heads as she pressed on.

'It is over two hundred years ago since we last sacrificed our best nobles to our Gods, hoping that our gifts would so please Heaven that our Roman invaders would be vanquished. Those sacrifices brought no fruit but the wroth of the Gods upon our heads and the annihilation of our Druid power base here upon Mona. It was decided by what remained of our secret Council that human sacrifice would be no more; that only felons would be treated thus. Your demand for our sacrifice is utterly erroneous and shows but a meanness of spirit and an unworthiness to lead your people!'

'You deign to call yourself priestess, when you are not even old enough to have finished your priestly schooling,' spat Eithig. 'What kind of healer and Druidess are you? Can you magic this knife from my hand?' His spittle erupted onto her cheek, his eyes bulging with fury and his knuckles white as they clutched both knife and victim.

'Brother, I cannot; but you can,' Ceridwen whispered close to his face. Her voice was totally measured, her eyes full of all the love she could muster. It must not be feigned. Her love of Eithig must conquer her loathing for him, even if it were only for a moment. 'It is only fear and pride which keeps it at Einir's throat. If you did none of the evil deeds you are accused of, you have nothing to fear. You will be exonerated. You will have no need to kill your sisters and burn in the fires below the earth for eternity. Take care that your fear does not prove your guilt to all assembled. Show us your innocence that we may have you as our Lord once more.'

There was a hushed silence for a few moments, whilst

all hung in the balance. Eithig felt the calm of Ceridwen's enchantment easing his confusion and suddenly he saw her logic. 'You are right, my sister, for that is who you shall be to me from this day. You counsel well and I must prove to all here, that Edwyn it was, who set the plot against Marcus.' He cut the ties binding Einir and she fell to the ground, crawling and whimpering into the arms of Lady Tangwen and her bondswomen.

'Where is Edwyn? Stand forward you lunatic!'

'He is gone, My Lord. Does it not prove his guilt?' suggested Huw the Giant, whose eyes had been dissembling searching the crowds for his whereabouts since their arrival.

'The truth will out with our auguries, if it is truly he whom we should blame,' countered Betw, knowing that it would put fear into Eithig again and throw him off balance. 'You have chosen well to retract your interpretation of the prophecy. How could we function without our priestess and healer? She must live to instruct the next generation, or our knowledge will be lost. She must beget a daughter, who will take our skills into the future.

'She may be young, but she has studied with her grandmother since she was a small child, and the spirit of Nanw instructs her still. Allow me to cut free her husband.' Betw held out the palm of her hand to take his knife and he was suddenly aware that he thought he was dreaming, confused about what was reality and what was a fabrication of his own mind.

As Marcus was freed and stood up once more besides Ceridwen, Eithig saw Edwyn drift into focus. Edwyn was no longer the weak, shaking mass of jelly he had sent up to the hill fort to filch armour. It had been Bethan's murder that had galvanised Edwyn's resolve to pay back the cursed chieftain. He stood before his lord in the heady triumph of revenge.

Eithig had been furious when he had wakened at the hut at Cae Gwynion. There were three sobbing girls, who had been abused all night long and who were about to be released to heap their families' revenge upon his men. He had not been able to believe his men's stupidity. He had ordered the girls' murder immediately. It was over and done with in moments. But it must look as though the Romans from the hill fort had had a hand in things. One or two items of Roman uniform should be enough evidence. It would be a plausible story... Marcus's men being jealous of their Beltane Rites and taking their pleasure with the three virgins. He had sent Edwyn alone on the mission for false evidence, as he had not seemed capable of fighting.

However, he had misjudged the tie of Edwyn's loyalty and now here he was in full fury, accompanied, it seemed, by almost the whole of the Roman contingent from the hill fort on the other side of the mountain.

Eithig was still unfocused and all seemed to whirr about him in slow motion. He saw his men drop their arms and Marcus take control. He heard Edwyn accuse him and spit upon him. The scene of the murders at Cae Gwynion was described and the women screamed. Little Rhonwen vomited and babes cried. Lord Meurig and his men, along with the bondsmen, helped the Roman soldiers to take prisoners. There was scuffling and confusion. Only Huw the Giant was fleet and strong enough to escape, crushing his two opponents against the trunk of a mature oak and, before they could recover, speeding away upon Gwyngariad. For a while no one noticed he was missing.

Marcus was leaving nothing to chance. If Edwyn's testimony was right, then Eithig and his men were rapists and murderers and must be brought to justice. There was a court at Cerrig y Gwyddyl in three weeks. Until then, Eithig and his men must be imprisoned and kept under strict guard. It would tax his manpower and the accommodation. His men would have to sleep in tents and lock the prisoners in the hill fort. It was a bad business.

Huw the Giant must be hunted and captured. Hedfan had caught a glimpse of him, riding towards the East on the white flash that was Gwyngariad. The boy begged Marcus to allow him to go with Lord Meurig's arresting party and in the end he gave in, knowing that Hedfan knew every pathway and short cut through the forest. If they moved quickly, they might draw ahead of him, enough to warn the guards at Cerrig y Gwyddyl.

Ceridwen knew she should be comforting the families of the girls, but this fresh tyranny had hit her hard and she was unable to summon the energy needed. She had used all her reserves when she had stood up to Eithig. Now her knees turned to jelly and she sank onto the knoll, viewing the chaos around her. Thank the Gods that Betw was strong enough to take control. She had already ordered the bodies of the three girls to be brought up to the Holy Ground. The families were already being consulted as to their wishes and it was agreed that a joint cremation would be the best, the remains being buried in the freshly dug earth about Nanw's body. She would have little time to recover before the evening's ceremony. Marged came to her side.

'If only...' Ceridwen tried to swallow the tears, which had begun to well, but it was no use. She heard a strange wailing noise and found it was her own keening. Her mother rocked her back and forth, but was sobbing herself. The noise spiralled then fell, leaving them quivering.

'I...If only I had told Eithig you were his sister, long, long ago,' sighed Marged. 'Perhaps this would never have happened?'

Ceridwen shook her head. 'The rivalry against Marcus would have been just as intense. Marcus told me of their first meeting, when Hedfan was injured at Eithig's hand. Their lives were to be at odds from that moment. You must not punish yourself, Mother.'

'Perhaps I should be blaming myself for falling in love with a Roman. Could this be the result of disloyalty to my race? Are the Gods angry with me for this? Is this my punishment for my arrogance in thinking I could unite our peoples? I was so sure of everything at the *sending*.'

Ceridwen's heart felt as though it would break with pain. She could see Marcus now, giving orders to his men, already a world away from her, and Betw counselling the grieving families. Marged could offer her no words of comfort. She was too distraught and guilt ridden herself. What if they had been mistaken about the prophecy and it was meant for future people and times? Oh ye Gods what a travesty!

CHAPTER XIX

⌘

STRIFE

Despite Edwyn's cries of protestation, he was arrested with the other warriors, although kept separately from them. If he was to be witness to the murders at Cae Gwynion, then he must remain alive to tell the tale. Marcus did not trust him. If released, he might conveniently disappear.

He jabbered continuously about the girl Bethan, who, by all accounts, had despised him for his rejection of her. He had tried to wake Eithig from his stupor, when the girls had been subject to the rape; but Eithig's sleep had been deep and, even when shaken, he had refused to stir. Edwyn had been terrified of Bethan's curses.

She had cried out to him for help and he had tried to stop the men from their pursuit, but to no avail. Her curses had rung in his ears to torment him and followed him at every turn. He knew Ceridwen could help him from his mind torture, but the hostility he read in her face told him he dare not ask it. Besides, something in him begged for punishment. Being tied to a post at the hill fort was of little consequence, compared to the traumas being replayed in his mind. Those were his just deserts.

It was Old Betw who performed the cremation rites. Ceridwen had been there initially, but was taken sick and had to rush away. Gwilym was not surprised. The bodies of the girls were badly mutilated and even with the ministrations of their families, they looked grotesque as they lay on their funeral pyre. They all felt sickened at the sight. Only Betw suspected the true reason for Ceridwen's sickness, and she was quite content to think it the result of a premature liaison with Marcus.

Marcus was on edge and taut. He was used to handling emergencies, but he felt uncomfortable being in sole charge of this situation. His men had been responsive and professional in executing their duties. He had no complaint with them. They did not quibble about any of his decisions, but he felt the loneliness of the leader, who must make the final decisions and carry the responsibility. The sooner the trial was over and he was called back to his normal duties at Segontium the better. It was a feeling he felt he could not share with Ceridwen, but he knew she sensed it. A rift was widening between them that neither seemed to be able to talk about, a distancing that confused them both.

When they met they talked sadly of practicalities. The carnage of the three girls hung like a cloud between them. Each felt responsible, yet logically knew they should not.

'Nanw would say we must press on and take no responsibility for the evil of another. The initiator must bear the weight of the crime. Yet I feel the whole tribe is being punished in some way. I have nothing to say that will bring them comfort. I thought I was their priestess and would always have ways and means to do my work, but I find I cannot even pray.' Ceridwen bit her lip and sighed wearily, 'I cannot even summon my grandmother to my side. I have no strength left to fight this spiritual battle.'

'Then you must rest. Stay with your family here at Tan Yr Aur. Let them look after you and you will regain what you have lost.' Marcus brushed her hand with his. It was a tentative intimacy, asking if it dared go further, but it was as though she ignored his desire to protect her. There was no response as he had hoped; no throwing herself into his arms; only a dull numbness, which detached her from him.

'You are right. I must stay with my family. They have need of me and I of them. I cannot go back to Cae Gwynion.

My father has forbidden it. Only he, my brothers and a few chosen bondsmen have been there to set things aright, to note evidence and to clean up the mess. The animals have been brought down to Tan Yr Aur. The men tried to catch Mwg, but he has gone into hiding. He will not starve at this time of year. He is good at hunting and he will guard Cae Gwynion in his own way.'

'Do you know what has happened to your remedies?'

Ceridwen nodded despairingly. 'I dare not think of the hours and days it took Nanw and I to build up the stocks of tinctures and ointments. The destruction at the hut seems to be the last straw upon the mule's back for me. If I allow my anger to take its course, I feel it will destroy me. We shall have to rely on freshly brewed herbs. Thank goodness it is the growing season and many plants rear their heads again. If it had happened in Winter, I do not know what we would have done.'

'I can spare you two men who can help with the collecting and preparation of your herbs. They have worked with me many a time. They know the difference between the leaves of new foxgloves and comfrey. They will not let you down. When I get back to Segontium...' Marcus paused for a moment. He thought he saw a look of yearning in her eyes, but then she shut it away and it became cold between them again. 'When I return to Segontium I shall have ointments and medicines sent to you. I shall send mostly things with which you are familiar.'

'When are you to go?'

'Soon. I am not really a commandant. I am needed back at my fort as its surgeon and the new contingent will guard the headland here. It would be sensible to leave when we take Eithig and his men to the court at Cerrig y Gwyddyl. That is in eighteen days' time.'

She was silent, not knowing how to digest the news. It felt as though part of her had already died, but she truly wondered if the flickering of a will to live would be extinguished when he had gone.

'I must organise the building of our hut here at Tan Yr Aur. I will send money and goods. Your father has already given permission.'

'I do not know if I can live in the enclosure. I am well used to the freedom of the mountain and being near to the Holy Ground. Would it not be more sensible to build me a new hut there?'

'But you are with child and you will need help with the babe if you are to continue your work as healer. Besides you have need of more protection than a black cat and a gaggle of geese.'

'It is strange. I always felt safe on the mountain, until that day I found Luce in the stream. Nothing very much had happened to disturb the rhythm of my life with my grandmother until then. But, from the moment I saw the glint of a soldier's helmet in the sunshine, I became uneasy, wary of the future. And now, it would seem, with just cause. I have not ceased to love you Marcus, only to question whether I should?'

'The blood Eithig has spilled splashes upon all our lives. Because it splashes upon us does not mean that we spilled it. We must create such a tide of good in our lives that it will wash away all the evil that has been wrought,' said Marcus resolutely.

'I remember Nanw speaking similar words when she talked about the lives of our forebears. I think you talk great sense, Marcus. Would that my heart could know it so.'

'Begin by believing it and you will heal. It is strange. My own hope was rekindled when I began to know you. Now it is my turn to try to give hope to you in some measure.' Marcus stroked the crescent Moon upon her brow and kissed it gently with reverence, willing the clarity to come back to her mind and give her some ease. 'I must go now. There are many duties waiting for me at the hill fort.'

She nodded. He held her hand for a moment and then he was gone. She looked down at her hand, trying to remember the feeling of his grasp around it, but she could not. There was only numbness. Then she ran to the midden outside the enclosure to be sick.

Huw was not long exultant at his escape. Gwyngariad seemed

uneasy to carry him, for she was unused to such a heavy weight atop her. She complained and tossed her head, but carried him nevertheless. He feigned riding towards Cerrig y Gwyddyl, for he guessed someone might spot his dust trail upon the road. He dismounted once over the horizon and veered North towards Din Silwy, walking in the course of a stream, so that his trail would not be noticed. There would be a few lookout guards at home, who would be only too willing to help him, as long as he told only half the story. There would be provisions, more weapons and horses.

By the time Marcus arrived back at the hill fort, it was almost sunset. His prisoners were still rowdy and complained of their quarters and their cramped conditions, as though to be a prisoner was to be a guest. They were certainly making it uncomfortable for his men. If they continued this racket, then his men would get no sleep. It was an organised campaign of curses, intended to unsettle the camp, but Marcus was in no mood to put up with it. They were told that if they did not observe silence, Eithig would be taken out and tortured. It soon quieted them, but they continued the cursing by mouthing and gesture, the wild whites of their eyes showing at the window slits of the wooden barracks. Marcus turned his back on them and gathered his men around the campfires to consult about manoeuvres and eat supper together.

With Huw on the loose there was no telling what might happen. If he could get to another town before Lord Meurig could spread warning, he could whip up a frenzy and return to do battle. Innocent people might be taken hostage in exchange for Eithig. Marcus shivered. He did not want to imagine what might ensue. He had already sent a messenger to Segontium informing Vipsanius of the situation and asking for back up; as it was he felt under-manned. The round the clock supervision of the prisoners was enough for them to cope with, but they still had to have lookout troops all around the camp. They were short on fetters and chains and had to rope many prisoners together. They had only to sneak in a sharp implement or stone from somewhere, and there was the possibility that they would break free. Eithig, and those of his men who had struck down the girls at his order, were chained. Marcus alone knew where the key to their fetters was kept. They must not escape, but must be brought to trial and executed.

A profound weariness seemed to take hold of him. He usually enjoyed the feeling of being in charge. Now it sat uncomfortably upon him like an ill-fitting yoke. To escape it he would doze by his campfire covered with his cloak and ready for action when necessary.

At first the sleep was dreamless, as his exhaustion took hold, but then he became aware of a dread spreading throughout his body, a dread that froze him and made him unable to move. He could see Ceridwen clutching at the bars of a huge wicker construction. It was a cage made in the image of a man, constructed completely of withies. Young women and babes were crammed into the massive construction and it was being set alight. Ceridwen's screams for mercy tore at his soul, but he was impotent to do anything but watch. He was mesmerised by her hands. Her scorching fingers gripped the bars of the cage turning redder and blacker.

He awoke with a sickening start, his heart pounding in his chest like the beating of hooves. Was it a *sending*...or a warning? He had not detailed any men to guard the farming enclosure at Tan Yr Aur. He had not enough men to do that. Surely Gwilym would be on guard, knowing that Huw was on the loose? He went to check the prisoners personally. He wanted nothing left to chance. Andreus he sent to Tan Yr Aur to make sure they had it defended. He need not have fretted.

Gwilym had given orders for all the horses to be driven into the enclosure at the east end. He did not want Huw and any allies helping themselves to his livelihood. He ordered the bondsmen to lift the triangular block of the chicken hut. The children stood in awe, as the men dug beneath it and brought out a great oak chest. Coll lifted the lid and wordlessly handed out the swords and spears. Arms might be illegal, but to be caught without any real defences would be stupid. The arms had been well oiled, wrapped in skins and buried, to be dug up for such contingencies.

Ceridwen wandered listlessly about the enclosure, attempting to smile reassurance at the women, but feeling less and less like their priestess, as the morning wore on. She had never encountered such strong self-doubt before. Nanw had been such a wonderful teacher, her criticism always constructive; unlike Marged, whose directness was not always diplomatic.

It had been good to be nurtured on the mountain, away from the busyness of the farm in the valley. The softness of the surrounding trees had protected her and Nanw from the sea winds. The sense of peace and quiet at Cae Gwynion had provided her mind with the concentration she needed, to learn her lessons well from the tireless patience of her grandmother. If only she could be like Nanw, untouched by life's vicissitudes, riding the waves of life's challenges instead of letting them drown her.

Nanw would have been working hard by now, praying, visualizing, weaving such a tumult about Huw and such protection about themselves, that he would be impotent to cause them harm. Ceridwen knew how to do it, but felt so overwhelmed that she could not even begin to draw power to her. Her anger at the rape and murder of the girls shook her body, making her clumsy. She had been trying to help the women prepare vegetables for the cooking pots; but her fingers had seemed to disobey her and with a frustrated cry she had flung the knife and the scallions on her apron to the ground.

Olwenna had stared at her uncomprehending. They needed all the help they could get and all their priestess could do was throw a tantrum. So much for inherited wisdom! Nanw would have counselled and reassured them and spent time praying with them, blessing the food they prepared to make them strong. Olwenna shook her head. The girl was far too young to have all these priestess duties on her shoulders. She should be bearing children and tending her husband.

Ceridwen drew away from the women to the far side of the enclosure. She needed to get away from people; their demands; their expectations of her. She strode purposefully towards the southeastern wall of the horse pen. Some of the horses recognised her and came trotting up. She stroked and petted them, allowing their movements to soothe her.

Her anger at her Goddess for failing to protect her people was even stronger than her anger against Eithig and his men. How could She have allowed such abomination? Why had the Spirits Of The Forest not banded together and prevented it? Why had Cadoc, her grandfather and Nanw, her grandmother, not protected the Holy Place?

She leaned her crescent painted brow against the white star on the nose of one of the ponies and closed her eyes. She knew the answer. Somewhere deep in her mind she knew, but whenever she tried to grasp at it and put it into words it escaped her again...something about allowing the forces of destiny to work and weave the good and evil that men do together, in order to forge good for all. The prayers and desires of each individual had to fit into a wider pattern. But what was destined and what could be altered? She wished she could summon the future to her, but the peace of mind to do it would not come.

Something white and speckled brown was trotting urgently towards her. It was Luce, her tail held high like a sail. Her greeting was ecstatic and she fussed and rubbed against Ceridwen until she was safe in her mistress's arms, nuzzling against her face, her silken fur and wet nose delightful. Ceridwen was taken momentarily out of her own misery and guiltily fondled the kitten, which she had not so much as spared a thought for these last few days. She expected it to relax and snuggle against her breast, but it did not happen. It jumped to the ground and looked alarmed, its nose tilting to sniff the wind. Ceridwen was not fool enough to ignore the signal. The horses too had begun wheeling restlessly, snorting and flaring their nostrils. At what had they become alarmed?

She scoured the landscape, her eyes coming to rest on the mountain of Mynydd Llwydiarth above the valley, its budding trees gleaming golden-green in the noonday Sun. It was not her imagination. The thatch at Cae Gwynion was on fire. The spindle of smoke soon became a pall. Then she saw the darting flash of fire. Her eyes travelled Eastwards. Another spindle of smoke was taking hold in the forest, then another, and yet another. This was no natural bush fire. It must be Huw seeking to draw attention away from the prisoners.

By the time she had breathlessly reached the vicinity of the huts, the men on lookout had already noted the fire. With swords at their belts and wooden flails to help beat out the fire, the men of Tan Yr Aur surged towards the mountain. They left the women and children to douse down the thatch on their own huts and animal pens. Marged's organising voice could be heard shouting instructions, but really there was no need. Fire drill was well practised. Fire was the most common threat to enclosures like this, made almost entirely of wood, mud and thatch, with only their footings and ovens made of stone. All were well rehearsed in their responsibilities. The young children dammed up the stream that flowed through the enclosure and lines of women and children got busy with buckets, bowls and barrels. Anything that held water was used to douse the thatch, so that if the woodland fire were to creep nearer, sparks would not catch to their homes.

Rhodri, Daf and Rhys had shed their tunics and were each atop a roof, waiting for the buckets and bowls to arrive. Only Rhodri complained. He had wanted to go with the men and see Huw the Giant cut down like a great tree. Madog had done a great deal of threatening and boasting about what he would do to Huw and Rhodri had believed every word.

'Why cannot I wield a sword like my father? Why do I have to do the work of little boys like this?' he grumbled.

'I wish we had had a young man like you to protect us, when the raiders came from the sea and fired our farm,' Anghared retorted. 'There might have been more of us left alive, more livestock and something to salvage from the fire. We need you here, Rhodri. Can you see my old bones scrambling up the roof like you? You are like a young deer. You are so sure footed. Now, take this heavy bucket from me, before all is spilled.'

He quieted and did her bidding. He would slosh twice the number of buckets as his younger brothers; prepare twice the number of hut roofs. The containers began to arrive with great speed now and he found it took all his strength to cope, as arms and hands passed him more and more water. He thought no more of complaining. He must save the farmstead so that the men had something to come home to.

Huw had only two men with him, but it was surprising how much devastation and diversion they could cause if they set their minds to it. The winds were southwesterly today. Lighting the fires in the forest where he did, between the valley and the fortress, would at first threaten the Holy Ground, then the hill fort. As evening drew on, the sea wind would gain dominance and blow in from the North, threatening Tan Yr Aur and its crops. The homesteaders would be kept busy and hopefully the scarce manpower would be drawn away from the fort, enough to gain access and free Eithig and his men.

The horses, he had brought with him, were a nuisance in that they would scare when they smelled the fire and start hurtling around and snorting; but, by that time, so would the horses at the hill fort. With any luck, that might cancel out any warning of their arrival. He had tethered them in some brushwood near the shore. Although he had walked them here quietly, under the cover of the forest, when they made their get-away it would be by a different route along the beach to Din Silwy. The tide was about to turn. If he timed it right and drew off the horses from the hill fort, Marcus and his men would not be able to follow once the tide was high. It would give a precious hour's head start to himself and any escapees.

Marcus sickened when he realised Huw's intentions. The hill fort was set high, like a wart upon a chin and was not very likely to catch fire from the forest below, but the forest was sacred. It was food. It was shelter to wild animals to be hunted and full of precious plants and berries on the forest floor. It was timber for homes and kindling for fires. Its devastation would threaten the livelihood of all around.

He thought for a moment and then saw that, in the long term, the survival of the forest was more important than the capture and execution of Eithig and his men. He made the decision to leave the prisoners with a skeleton force and send the rest of his men to try to contain the fire. He wished he had Andreus by his side. How he valued his quick reactions to danger. He should have left him here in charge of the prisoners instead of sending him to Gwilym. He scanned the faces of his men. They were loyal enough, he knew, but not the brightest.

'These prisoners must not escape. Huw the Giant will be here shortly to effect it. He must be caught and made prisoner with the rest. You might find fishing nets useful. It will take at least four of you to hold him down. Swear on your lives to honour this task.'

'By our lives, commander! By our lives!' they chorused in reply.

With a sinking feeling Marcus left them. He knew he must take care of the operation to save the forest. He had already sent beaters ahead with blankets and men with axes to try and cut an avenue between the banks of trees; but it had been a warm, fine Spring and the forest floor was strewn with dry bracken and dead tinder, ready to catch alight at the slightest provocation. O ye Gods, send rain, now!

Huw watched quietly with his comrades, hiding in the forest undergrowth to the Northwest. It would not do for them to cough with smoke and reveal their whereabouts. They must steer clear of the fire. Their plan was working. He estimated that most of Marcus's men were out fighting the fire, leaving only the men in the lookout towers and the prisoners' guards to be dealt with. The lower part of the hill fort was made of stone, surrounded by a series of deep ditches, but the upper ramparts were made of timber. The majority of the roofing was tiling, making it difficult to torch. He would have to think of another distraction.

An opportunity presented itself at last. Two guards left the north gate of the fort and headed stealthily down to the beach. They seemed uneasy; as if they suspected they were being watched; but eventually gathered in a great, heavy fishing net, which had been lying on the beach. It was empty of fish, awaiting mending, perhaps? The gentle sound of the incoming high tide lulled the shallow shelf of the sands.

'Aled! Gwyndaf!' Huw whispered urgently. 'Climb the trees above the path from the beach to the fort. Once those two auxiliaries have reached the path under the trees, they will be screened from the lookouts for just a few moments. We must take our only chance then. They must be killed silently and you must take their places. Then you will pretend to capture me in the net and get us into the fort. Go!'

Huw's comrades needed no second encouragement. The life of their chieftain and their warrior band depended on split second timing. Everything must be executed so swiftly, that the lookout guards would not grow suspicious.

Aled and Gwyndaf were skilled hunters. Neither made a sound as they shinned up the trees and hid against stout branches. The two guards, hauling the net, were breathless by the time they reached the cover of the trees and paused to their peril. There was little sound as Aled jumped first upon one, a hand jerking back the auxiliary's head and the other slicing his throat simultaneously. The other guard had only time to turn and gasp, before he too was held and his throat slit. Their bodies slumped and fell like heavy sacks. It was inconvenient that there was so much blood; but if they feigned a struggle to capture Huw, then a wounding would explain blood upon the uniforms they were now about to don.

Marcus darted between each group of men working on the fire, encouraging them and giving further instructions as to where they should move next. With relief, he noted that, as his men worked from the North, so Gwilym's men worked from the South, sandwiching the fire between them. The smoke was the worst for Marcus's men now. Every so often they were compelled to give up their task and run for fresh air to fill their bursting lungs. Creatures scurried to safety. Their squeals and cries were enough to make the hardiest of soldiers wince and all the while they expected to be pounced upon from behind.

He drew near the devastation at Cae Gwynion. The acrid stench of burnt-out dwelling attacked his nostrils. The thatch on the hut was almost burnt through, and the oak timbers blackened, scorched and smouldering, but amazingly the door posterns had survived, with their carved greetings. For a moment Marcus thought he saw a black cat weave about the doorway, but when he looked inside there was no sign of Mwg. Perhaps it was a trick of the light.

He turned his attention to the herb garden. With relief he noted that it seemed intact, despite the protecting hedge of gorse and hawthorn being scorched. At least Ceridwen would be able to salvage something.

Huw and his men did not know the password to get into the fort, but they staged a scuffle in front of the gates, as though Huw were trying to escape them, shouting, 'Help us!' in the few words of Latin that they knew. Two more guards opened the gate and made to help them, but Huw was, by now, out from under the net and it was easy for the three of them to overcome the two.

By the time a guard had rung the alarum from the north watchtower, they were already through the gates and breaking down the barrack door, which held the murderers. The watchtower guards came down from their posts to attack them, but by then, several roped prisoners had been freed and armed themselves with axes and other tools they could find to hand.

Huw did not waste time trying to find the key to his master's shackles. With several great blows from a forester's axe, he smashed through the chain attaching Eithig to his henchmen and then the chain spanning Eithig's feet. What he did not manage to do was cut the iron manacles from his wrists. That would be a patient task once they had escaped.

'There is no time to free you others. The alarum has sounded!' gasped Huw, pushing Eithig before him towards the horses.

'At least free us from misery,' came a shrill cry from within the barracks.

'Huw, go back and kill them, for the sake of the Gods. I would do it myself but I can wield nothing!' Eithig commanded.

Huw paused only a moment then turned inside. He could not look his comrades in the face. Instead, he focused on each of their hearts, piercing each with precision, so that they might die quickly, sending them to their great hall of warriors in Hel, where the Goddess Ceridwen supervised the cauldron of inspiration and rebirth.

By the time Eithig had positioned himself near a horse and tried several times to mount, he realised this was not going to work. The horses were terrified by the smell of the fire and even more suspicious of him because he was manacled.

Aled and Gwyndaf, along with his freed men, had dealt swiftly with the lookout guards and Edwyn. Now they flung wide the north gates.

'Gwyngariad.... she waits for you near the beach. Follow me, my Lord!' yelled Aled above the squeals of fear from the hill fort horses.

He caught a fleeing horse by the bridle and managed to mount it, dragging Eithig up behind him. Huw followed, running and shrieking, waving a long blood-soaked sword in the air, so that the horses would shy away from him; but they were too bent on their own escape to turn aside for him. He was huge, but no match for a stampede of terrified war horses. He fell at the gate with a great thud, the sword flying from his hand. The horses kept coming, trampling him underfoot as though he were a rag.

Eithig glanced behind him, as Aled fled downwards towards the beach. He ordered Gwyndaf to ride back and see if anything could be done for Huw. Gwyndaf felt it unwise, but, as always, obeyed. He instantly recognised the bejewelled sword lying a few feet from Huw's lifeless body. Huw, loyal to the end, had retrieved it from the enemy. Now it would be returned to its rightful master and it would become the symbol of their efforts to overturn the power of the Romans.

Eithig and his men reached their own horses, sweating and panting for breath, but in moments they were mounted and galloping along the beach to Din Silwy, with the riderless Roman war horses following close behind. As Gwyngariad carried him away from his imprisonment, Eithig kissed the hilt of the retrieved sword and held it aloft in an act of defiance. The whooping victory cries of his comrades rang out to the mountain.

By the time Marcus had gathered his men and responded to the alarum, the hill fort was empty of live prisoners and horses and all the guards dead or fatally wounded. Edwyn, still tied to a post, was breathing his last, his eyes rolling up into his head, the life-blood pumping rapidly from his severed genitals. The chief witness to Eithig's atrocities was no more. Marcus's anger rent the air with a great yell of frustration, but at the same time his resolve hardened into a pledge. He ran towards the north gate in time to see the trail of Eithig, his men and the majority of their own horses disappear through the shallows of the bay, Eastwards towards Din Silwy.

'I shall kill you, you fiend!' Marcus swore under his breath. 'The Gods have only to give me opportunity. There is no bringing you to just court now!'

One casualty he was not sad to see. The huge body of Huw the Giant was unmistakeable. He lay face down in the dust at the north gate. His head had been beaten to pulp.

Marcus himself sprang up to the watchtower. He could see the Celwri warriors already a mile down the beach and the tide closing in. By the time his own men had brought fresh horses from Tan Yr Aur and given chase, it would be hopeless. What was Eithig going to do next? If only he knew. Perhaps an augury would tell. Ceridwen would surely be able to help. The fire was coming under control. Only a small patch to the Southeast was still blazing and he could see Gwilym's men making their way towards it now.

Andreus was back. Thank the Gods that he could leave him in charge to bury the dead and he would personally be able to go down to Tan Yr Aur to get augury.

'I will be gone but a short time, Andreus. I must get fresh horses and find out what is going to happen. I shall send messengers to Cerrig y Gwyddyl and Dindaethwy to warn that the prisoners have escaped. They may try to get over to the mainland and away into the mountains. I cannot foresee them holding the fort at Din Silwy when so many of their tribe is against them. Oh no! The women and children! Surely he will not hurt his own kith and kin?'

'He was going to sacrifice the woman he loved most in the world. Nothing is sacred to him. He is capable of anything,' Andreus reminded him gravely.

Marcus ran almost all the way down the mountain path to Tan yr Aur, taking a small group of men with him. Someone sniggered that he would not be running so fast if it were not towards his woman, but he pretended not to hear. He was in no mind to discipline them. This was not a social call, but one crucial to the next step.

The women on gate duty recognised Marcus through the small window hole in the gates. Thanking him and greeting him, they swung them wide, glad that the Romans had helped extinguish the fire. The men walked breathless and coughing into the compound. Marged came to offer refreshment to them all and to greet Marcus. Marcus took the drink and a wet cloth to wipe the smoke and sweat from his face, but he had no stomach for food.

'I think your enclosure is safe from the fire, but Eithig and his men have escaped. Only Huw the Huge is dead. May I talk urgently with Ceridwen?'

'She is with Olwenna and Angharad working on the looms. They are busy weaving a spell of protection about our farmstead.'

Marcus left his men taking their refreshment and made his way alone towards the weaving hut belonging to Olwenna and Angharad. He passed the children dancing in a circle and chanting. Rhonwen gave him a shy heart-melting smile of greeting, but did not break out of the circle. They were all taking their task quite seriously. They were praying for rain, to finish off the work the men had accomplished and make safe their crops and homes.

Ceridwen resented the break to her concentration, but when she found it was Marcus her heart leapt momentarily. The old women had been doing their best to encourage her, reminding her of old spells they had become accustomed to in their childhood. She had pretended at first to be enthusiastic, but now she did not need the pretence, for she found that her own rhyming and memory were returning. She was weaving a beautiful cloth of mixed blue-dyed wools as she chanted, when she became aware that Marcus was standing at the threshold of the loom shed.

'No thought of fear when danger is near...only the clear... Marcus! What is it?'

'It is Eithig and his warriors. They have escaped with our horses to Din Silwy. But I do not think they will stay. They will load up and move on, going into hiding. You must perform the rite of augury as a priestess? You must be able to tell me where they are headed!'

'I...I am uncertain whether I can summon the knowledge, Marcus. I have done it frequently, but always at the altar on the Holy Ground. It seems strange for me to try it here, for my mind is uneasy. I cannot settle to peacefulness.'

'We shall leave you and Marcus alone, then,' said Angharad knowingly, dropping the shuttle she was using on her wooden framed loom as she rose. 'Your grandmother would use the flames of the fire when she visited us to tell us our future. We know you can do the same, Ceridwen. You have been observing her since you were a child.'

Ceridwen nodded her appreciation to Olwenna and Angharad as they left, then turned her attention to Marcus. 'I had Nanw's coelbreni, her oracle sticks, brought down from Cae Gwynion. Here they are in this drawstring pouch at my waist.' Her slender white fingers shook as she drew them out of the pouch. 'They remind me of my calling whenever fear taunts me.' She raised her eyes to Marcus. He read some sort of torture there and felt himself tempted to hold her, to gather her to him, but there was urgent business. Time enough to examine their own feelings, when Eithig was recaptured.

The moment passed and she spoke of the augury. 'The symbols carved in them will suggest a line of thought as they fall. When we ask a question and throw them upon the ground, it will be as though they speak to me. Ask now. Ask your first question.'

'The bondsmen...the women and children at Din Silwy, are they safe?'

She blew a blessing of life force into the sticks and let them fall before the firelight. 'Look, the symbols for the rowan and oak trees fall atop the pile. That means they are safeguarded for the moment. I shall look into the flames and see how that comes about.'

Marcus became conscious that he was holding his breath in an effort to control his anxiety and give her the stillness she required for her visualizations. It was hard at first for Ceridwen to focus. Marcus was standing so close to her. She could feel the sleeve of his tunic brushing her arm. She sighed in an effort to release all her own thoughts and feelings. She must focus; not with an iron will, for the tension of that would not allow the visions to come through; but with a wise steadiness and calm. Her mind must be like a clean and empty cup, awaiting its fill.

The firelight from the centre of the hut flickered. She found herself floundering and struggling at first. There were so many thoughts and feelings competing in her head. She thought of a cool flowing spring and allowed it to cleanse her mind and body. She began to sigh and relax. Her gaze steadied and once she caught a glimpse of Nanw's encouraging smile, she knew she was on the right track. It was several agonising minutes before she spoke.

'The search party you sent with Lord Meurig and Hedfan... they approach Cerrig y Gwyddyl. They meet a crowd at the gates and the crowd shakes its head. They have seen no sign of Eithig and his men. They turn back, making their way West, but then take the route to the Northwest. They are heading for Din Silwy. The women, the children and the bondsmen greet them with relief. They enter and set about making the fortress a stronghold. Eithig and his men arrive expecting to gain entry. I can see Eithig now, his face like thunder, astride Gwyngariad. But he and his men are forced to ride single file towards the gates, as the pathway narrows.

She paused for a moment, but Marcus did not interrupt. He could see, by her concentration upon the flames and the widening of her eyes that her vision was strengthening. He was conscious that her voice became hard, like weapons of steel.

'Lord Meurig and his men launch their spears upon them. Then the catapult is fired, with burning pitch blazing, as its missile falls upon them. My brother Hedfan is helping to fire it. There are screams as men are injured and killed, but Eithig is unharmed and escapes with at least thirty men. They are going now into the sea...the sea of the future. I am losing the pictures. I see the mainland, the mountains. I see them swallowed up by the mists of Eryri.' Ceridwen paused. The final vision faded and she turned to Marcus. 'They will journey by night's cover across the Straits and take cover in the mountains, but I am not sure where. I shall ask the coelbreni once more.'

Ceridwen gathered the augury sticks from the hardened earth floor and again blew upon them before casting them down. She could see no place suggested, only the symbol of blackthorn, ominous with its warning of a cleansing conflict.

'I'm sorry. I seem to be clear about what has already happened, but the future is uncertain and its path is yet to be cleared and chosen by the Gods. One thing is for certes; our part in it will be of great importance. The knowledge of that is given strong to me, as I gaze at the sticks.'

'You have done well. I shall not send men to Din Silwy, save a messenger to ask their help. I shall make certain that all the lookout stations along the coast are forewarned and wary. We might apprehend them yet, before they disappear into the mists of the mountains as you foretell. I take my leave of you now. The new contingent from Deva will be arriving soon. I shall endeavour to meet them as they arrive on the island and then make my way back to Segontium. There is urgent need of me there, I know. And if Eithig goes into hiding in the mountains as you say, I shall be better placed to help capture him. Your father and brothers will soon be returning from their fire fighting. Thank them on my behalf.'

He took her hands in his and studied them for several moments, as though he were trying to imprint their image on his memory. 'We have worked well as a team...you and I...my men and your family. May the Gods protect you, Ceridwen, my wife, my priestess, my love.' With that he kissed her palms and was gone, not daring to look back at her for a sudden weakness had overcome him.

She watched him go, her body longing to be held once more in his arms. Her mind was too locked in its pride, its sadness and confusion, to ask it. His name fell without sound from her lips and there began an ache in her heart that no amount of prayer and herbal medicine could remedy.

⌘ ⌘ ⌘

CHAPTER XX

⌘

BEREFT

The days following Eithig's escape and the scorching of Cae Gwynion at the Holy Ground passed in a haze of frenzied activity. Bodies were hurriedly buried with little ceremony. The hill fort at Mynydd Llwydiarth was temporarily abandoned, apart from a small look-out detail, as all Marcus's men frantically searched for signs of Eithig and his band. But no trace was found. They must have crossed the Straits by dark, walking their horses silently over the sands to Aber on the mainland. By daylight the tides had swept away all trace of any crossing and the rain, prayed for so fervently by the children at Tan Yr Aur, had brought with it mists that all but obliterated the mountains.

Marcus and his troop scoured the forests and the beaches, but the shingle washed by the recent high tide revealed little. They rode from Cerrig y Gwyddyl to Dindaethwy without finding a scrap of evidence. There they encountered the new century from Deva on its way to man the fort at Mynydd Llwydiarth and exchanged information. Messengers were sent to the Roman forts on the mainland, to Kanovium above the Conwy River and to Bryn Gefeiliau, the tribal stronghold deep in the mountains.

There were several outlaw bands in the mountains, living in caves deep underground. If Eithig were to join forces with another outlawed chieftain, he could play havoc with the trading routes. He must be captured at all cost. It was out of

Marcus's hands now. Technically he was not responsible for Eithig's recapture, but he knew that when Vipsanius heard the whole story from his own lips, no stone would be left unturned until the fugitive was found.

Marcus hoped and prayed that the opportunity to finish the job he had started would come his way. For now, he and his men must return to Segontium. Perhaps the daily hustle and bustle of the fort and port below would help him to shut out the newly stirred longings within him; the longing to be part of a family and to look up and see his wife across the home fire. His pony swayed beneath him. Listlessly he stroked its mane, but it felt more like Ceridwen's Sun-bronzed tresses he had tangled between his fingers, and deep pain played its aching melody across his heart strings.

Gwilym, Coll and Owain kept their bondsmen busy, salvaging what they could at the Holy Ground. Luckily most of the older oaks had survived, but the young saplings had been burnt beyond help. They did what they could to cut back burnt branches and clear the pathways through to the central clearing. The stone altar survived unscathed and although a few mounds in the burial ground showed signs of scorched stones, little harm was done. By next Spring there would be a coating of new moss and lichen to hide the scars.

Sadly the hut at Cae Gwynion was almost a total ruin. It was decided to rebuild it slowly as a sanctuary. No one was to live there at present, so the work was not pressing, but help with the garden was. Two of Marcus's men were already on site, tidying the beds of precious herbs and digging up others to begin a new planting site at Tan Yr Aur. They were going to fence off part of the corral and make a raised bed for convenience. The garden at Cae Gwynion would remain their plant stock, but, for day-to-day use, it would be better if Tan Yr Aur had its own supplies in more abundance.

It niggled Gwilym that he would have to give up precious horse space for the project, but he could see the sense in it.

'As long as we are not forever trying to keep the horses out of the hyssop and the mint. I don't want to be forever mending fences,' he grumbled.

'We will plant good blackthorn to deter them. It will be the mice from the grain store which will do more damage,' one of the Roman legionaries advised.

'There's a black cat keeps slinking around. I would swear it was watching our every move,' said the other Roman, uncomfortably superstitious.

'Bag it and bring it down to Tan yr Aur. It will enjoy being with my daughter and will earn its keep controlling the mice,' Gwilym said carelessly, as though it were an easy task. He, Coll and Owain would enjoy the light-hearted escapade of watching a slip of a cat defy the utmost efforts of two Roman legionaries. They exchanged knowing winks. They might be the underdogs when it came to being ruled by Rome, but Romans did not have the monopoly on skills.

It would be a tale to be exaggerated and told around the home fires with relish; how the inscrutable Mwg had hoodwinked two Roman legionaries into spending the entire afternoon chasing, cajoling and enticing him.

In the end he had to be coaxed down from a tree with a singed dead harvest mouse, dangled from a piece of thin string. The fight he put up in the sacking was vicious. He clawed and spat, but eventually became calm. It took a great deal of self-control on behalf of the Celwri men. Coll had to run behind a tree and grip a branch between his teeth, so as not to guffaw and offend Marcus's friends. Nevertheless it was burst one way or another. In the end he pissed himself and glad the day was warm enough to dispense with his breeches.

Gwilym was heartened to see some camaraderie between the men. It was a great release from the awful tension of the past few days. They returned laughing and joking to the homestead, as the evening Sun began to supplant the day's warm drizzle and paint the backdrop of the mountains with moods of orange and pink.

Ceridwen felt disorientated. It was one thing to be visiting her family, knowing that she could escape back to the peacefulness at Cae Gwynion, but it was quite another to live with them in the daily hubbub of their farming community.

At Cae Gwynion she had known her identity; had been in control of every minute of her working day. Here at Tan Yr Aur, her mother organized relentlessly. Marged took her task very seriously. Sometimes she felt as though it were she alone, who cared enough to make sure the community had enough food stored for the Winter. She kept everyone on their toes. Even the small children had little tasks to do, such as collecting eggs, or fetching fresh water. It seemed strange then to Ceridwen that Marged never asked her to do any task. Her mother was trying to respect her role as priestess and defer to her, but it made their relationship awkward.

They had both coped well with the role delineation before. At Cae Gwynion Marged always treated Ceridwen as her priestess, but when she had come to Tan Yr Aur she had treated her as a daughter. It was a simple demarcation. Now Ceridwen was to live at Tan Yr Aur, it was more complex. Ceridwen was in charge of the planting at the new herb garden, but she must negotiate with Marged all the way. Manpower, timing, tools, planting area; all had to be discussed. How much easier it had been, when a work detail had arrived at Cae Gwynion and had taken all instruction from Nanw or Ceridwen.

It was as though a taskmaster was there in place of her mother, and, oh, how she needed real mothering. If only Nanw were alive. Last night Ceridwen had thought she heard her grandmother whisper to her, but the voice had been indistinct and was soon drowned out by the sound of Gwilym's snoring. Priestesses were not supposed to feel this vulnerable, lost, bereft. The whole point of coming down to the enclosure had been to remove her loneliness and ensure her safety, but here she felt more isolated than living alone at Cae Gwynion.

There never seemed a moment of true peacefulness when she could get to grips with her prayers. The makeshift shrine they had set up, just outside the enclosure, was a dismal attempt at a sacred space. Perhaps it was her own attitude at consecrating it which had been at fault, for she was constantly comparing the flat, uninteresting landscape of the valley floor, with the uplifting feel of the mountain.

Atop Mynydd Llwydiarth you could feel so alive; as if you could swoop over the hills like the buzzards winging on the breeze. Here she felt trapped.

'Mother, I must speak with you,' Ceridwen at last broached.

'Certainly. I will send Ness's children on some errand then we can have the hut to ourselves. Rhodri! Daf! Leave the fire to me now and go and gather some fresh straw to make the sleeping pallets more comfortable. Mind you find it dry...from the storeroom, away from the threshold, not where the rain gets at it.'

'Right you are, *Nain*,' said Rhodri grinning in anticipation of a fight in the straw with his brother. They ran with faces beaming. Marged knew that they would take their time. Her two grandsons could never resist tumbling in the hay and throwing it around until they were utterly exhausted.

'I feel like a lyre with broken strings. There is no melody in me. My home is gone. My man is gone. My Holy Place is scarred. I am so weary, Mother, but I have this great need to be upon my mountain.'

'You have not yet found a way of being here with us, that is all. But time will give you a new song to sing and you will adapt. Think about it. Look ahead to the Winter. Heaven knows you may be with child by Marcus. The Winter will be warm here and food constant. You shall not have to tend your own fire, nor your animals. Whenever you need to go to the Holy Ground, Coll or Owain will go with you to see you safe. Soon you shall have your own hut, which will give you more privacy, and besides, it is nearly Ness's time. She will need you near.' Marged's argument sounded so sensible, but did little to ease her discomfort with her situation.

'I have always loved to come here as a visitor,' said Ceridwen, grasping her knees and rocking to and fro in a child-like fashion upon the bench before the central fire. 'But it is your way of life and not mine. I have found it so hard to conjure visions since I came, these last six days. My mind cannot grasp what is happening. I feel cut off from my Goddess and my true self.'

'It is only temporary; believe me. There is nothing that can change the skills you have, nor your inner identity. You will always be you, wherever you are,' countered Marged, picking up a spindle and soothing her nerves with the busyness of the spinning. She could always think for the best when her hands were occupied.

'I need to go home,' said Ceridwen, moving to the threshold of the hut, where she leaned her arms and forehead against the postern to catch a glimpse of the scarred mountain breast, caught in the glow of the late afternoon Sun. 'The Holy Place needs me. It needs to heal after the burning...the murders. I must pray and cleanse it with the breezes of the four winds. And I need to heal...I need to heal my heart; for Marcus has taken part of it with him.' She paused, trying to control the trembling of her lips and the sobs, which lay beneath the surface of her resolve to stay calm.

'Lying with him at Beltane...We became part of each other. Now, being apart is torture; but the worst is to have been the cause of all this bloodshed and to see the rift between us ever widening.'

'Keep faith, my *Cariad*.' Marged put down the spindle and crossed to the light of the threshold. She gently lifted her daughter's chin, so that they looked into each other's eyes. Marged knew that Ceridwen had little time for her; that their personalities always worked at cross-purposes.

Nanw had been Ceridwen's spiritual mother and mentor. Marged had never tried to compete with that, but she had never stopped loving Ceridwen with that aching longing for closeness all natural mothers crave. Perhaps the time was ripe for them to grow closer? The depth of love and compassion in Marged's eyes brought all Ceridwen's emotions to the surface and she unashamedly allowed her mother to cradle her as she wept.

'The Gods did not bring you together to dash you against the rocks of the world. You have been brought together to create a family, to create a future for our tribe. Do you not know it?' Marged murmured into her soft copper tresses. The tenderness between them was something they had not experienced before. It hung between them like a small miracle and they both wondered at it for a moment. Then Marged felt the need to return to normality. 'No despairing now,' she said brusquely. 'There is much for the Gods to take care of. Time will unravel the mystery of your lives together. Wait. Have patience.'

'I question everything. I question my marriage to Marcus. I question the motives of the Gods. I question my calling. I am uncomfortable with being here; with who I am; with living in this time. It is the first time in my whole life when I do not know what to do for the best. I am trapped and imprisoned.'

'The only real prison is the prison of self.' It was Marged speaking the old wisdom, but it was the voice of Nanw that echoed in Ceridwen's ears.

The sound of men's laughter reached them. Both women looked up towards the path down the mountain. Gwilym, Coll, Owain and the bondsmen were coming home for supper. Their joking voices echoed incongruously across the valley. The stones covering Nanw's grave and that of the three young women glinted in the evening sunshine; death and life rubbing easy shoulders together.

Reading Ceridwen's thoughts, her mother said, 'We are fortunate to have such beautiful spirits to inspire us. Their power on leaving their bodies was sweet and heady.'

'It will not seem so to their families. They will blame Marcus and I for our coupling and setting Eithig and his men against all...But you are right, Mother. Even when my own thoughts are touched with despair, I am tempted to feel the ether and the knowledge comes to me that the girls are well guided in the next realm. They are content to know that the actions of Eithig and his men come back to them threefold; for that is the law of the worlds!'

Hedfan was heading home, helping Coll and the men to drive back some of the escaped horses, which they had found grazing around Din Silwy. He hung his head as he rode, his misery evident to all. He was riddled with guilt and had been called 'stupid' by Twm and Lord Meurig's men, who had fended Eithig from the fortress. Fynan and Old Betw were the only folk to have spoken to him over the last few days, as he helped put things to rights at Din Silwy and gather the horses. Everywhere he went he was cold shouldered, or stared at with hostility. Even old Betw had sighed sadly and shaken her head at him.

He had been helping to man the catapult. He was proud of being allowed this manly job. He was to help the team of men to set fire to the burning, pitched missiles, before they found their target on the heads of the enemy. They were all silently hiding behind the wooden ramparts, when they received the signal from the lookout tower that Eithig and his men were approaching. The last thing Eithig expected was his own people to have turned against him, so the beguiling welcoming wave of women, atop the lookout tower, drew him on.

The west entrance to the fort was by way of a narrow passage, bridging the series of enclosing ditches; just wide enough for a cart, and certainly not wide enough for two horses comfortably abreast. Eithig led his men in single file, expecting the doors to be flung open. Instead there was a rain of missiles, from spears, to stones, to balls of excrement, thrown by men, women and children.

Somehow, in the chaos, Eithig and his followers managed to fend off most missiles with their huge, round, bronze, leather-embossed shields. Gwyngariad stood her ground for a few minutes, but then started to rear and panic as she could not retreat against the fallen men and horses behind her.

Lord Meurig's men, manning the catapult, had Gwyngariad as their target. If they could fell her, she would throw Eithig to the ground and he would be more vulnerable. Hedfan acted instinctively. His love for Gwyngariad had never wavered. She must not fall. With a great scream, he pretended to be hit by a flying object and hurled himself at the burning missile, knocking it, with his club, from the catapult to the deck of the rampart, where it immediately took hold with fire.

Someone had put it out by smothering it with a sheepskin. The pungent smell accompanied the men's railing fury at

Hedfan's stupidity.

'By the fire of Bel, we have missed our golden opportunity to capture him! We had him in our sights! He was ours for the taking!'

'You idiot! Could you not have fallen in the opposite direction? There was plenty of room for you to break your neck elsewhere. You've ruined all!' The men were unable to refocus on their task, their anger burned so hot. In the few seconds it took to reload and fire the catapult, Eithig had managed to turn Gwyngariad and jump her over the injured in his path. In retreat he took two thirds of his men and horses. The dying and injured he left to the mercy of the inhabitants at Din Silwy.

They needed a scapegoat for failing to capture Eithig. Hedfan would do very well. It was made to seem that the escape was entirely his fault. He would never regain the respect of his kinsmen.

The tears of his own shame and compassion for Gwyngariad burned hotter, the nearer to home at Tan Yr Aur he came. He tried to examine what he had done. If faced with the same situation all over again, he knew that he would be unable to act any differently.

'An honourable man would have put his tribe and family first, not love of a horse,' Coll had snapped derisively when he found out. Hedfan had to admit that he was right, but his own anger against Ceridwen grew. If she had not promised him Gwyngariad in the first instance, then perhaps he would never have done what he had done.

As he dismounted in the compound at Tan Yr Aur, she waited for him, her arms outstretched in greeting. She smiled with relief to see him safe and knowledge that her oracular vision had come true. But it was not in brotherly greeting that he ran to her. His torment raged as he grabbed at her braided hair with both fists.

'You lied!' he shrieked at her, tugging with all his might and enjoying the moment when she screamed out in pain. Now he was punching indiscriminately at her and she was trying to fend off his blows with all her strength.

'You told me Gwyngariad would be mine! I could not see her harmed! They were going to fell her with the cannon!' he raged. But it was Ceridwen who fell now to her knees, Hedfan's blow to her belly knocking her sick. Coll came running to drag him off, but, by that time, Hedfan was also on his knees, sobbing some kind of explanation into Ceridwen's shocked and stricken face. 'Now they blame me! They blame me for Eithig's escape.' His unrecognizable face crumpled in grief.

For a moment Ceridwen thought she was going to lose consciousness, but something in her brother's torment held her there in the moment and her compassion won out. She motioned Coll to stay back and cradled the boy wordlessly until his weeping was done. The crowd that drew round she sent away. Marged stood her ground momentarily, but challenged by Ceridwen's pleading eyes, withdrew and made pretence at some business.

'Come with me to the shrine. We shall have some peace there and be able to talk,' she said gently. He shook his head and refused to move.

'It is no good, Sister. I cannot mend what I have done. The Gods would not be interested in me. The only interest will be a story, by every fireside this night, of how the messenger boy, Hedfan, betrayed his tribe for love of a horse.'

'When things are daunting and the tide of fortune against us, we must live in hope and visualize the best of outcomes. The Gods know what is afoot and deal with us as best befits our actions. Perhaps it was not time for Eithig to be caught. Perhaps you were a tool of the Gods. Maybe he will bring together more evil men, who will be vanquished in the long run. Like is attracted unto like.'

'You say words to comfort me, but how can I believe you? Nothing you have promised has come to pass so far?'

'Hedfan, you are not yet thirteen years of age. Time is young for you. I did not promise you Gwyngariad immediately, only within the fullness of time. Besides, if you have displeased the Gods as well as your tribe, you shall have to work harder to serve them and make atonement, before your reward is given.'

'Does your Goddess want my life? If she does she can have it. It stinks!' He drew his knife from its sheath and carved a great gash into the trunk of a nearby young birch. Ceridwen winced with the pain of the tree. He still clutched at the hilt, the blade gouging deeply into the sap.

'Anger at your mistake is making you do more wounding things. Look, this birch pours out its life sap at your hand, for no good reason. You must turn the energy of your anger into helping situations, not despoiling them.' She held his hands gently, until she felt his regret release the tension in his hold on the knife. He allowed her to sheath it.

'These hands have much work to do in their life. Your Goddess needs no sacrifice but your patience and allowing time to work for her.' She kissed and blessed his hands and was aware that her family and bondsmen witnessed it from afar. If their priestess had forgiven him, then so must they. They hung their heads in uneasy conscience. They had been so eager to lay all the blame for Eithig's escape at Hedfan's door. In reality he had averted one shot to save a beautiful horse. He was not entirely to blame and they must stand by him in that. They murmured together and came to Hedfan to apologize.

'There will be other chances to capture Eithig, my son,' said Gwilym approaching him and slapping him cordially on the back. 'You did well to help hold Din Silwy. Who knows what would have happened to the women and children if he had gained entry. They would have all been living in mortal fear.' His brothers and the bondsmen nodded in agreement and the younger men invited him to share their meal. There, he would have opportunity to recount the whole adventure in a completely different light.

'If only I could take my own advice,' muttered Ceridwen. She did not realise that Marged was directly behind her.

'You will in time. All in good time...Your foot! Look, it is bleeding.'

'No Mother, it drips between my thighs. I must rest. Hedfan's punch has set me bleeding after the Beltane Rites.'

Marged gaped in horror. 'He punched you so hard, that maybe you will lose a babe you have conceived, even before it is set in the womb? I'll flail him! I will have him beg me for mercy.'

'No Mother!' commanded Ceridwen catching at her mother's hand. 'There shall be an end to violence. Hedfan was not himself and saw me an easy target rather than to begin a spat with his brothers. He had a need to spend his anger. He was confused and it is hard when he is so young – barely a man.'

'That was no excuse to harm his sister. I shall have strong words then.'

'Leave it be, please,' begged Ceridwen. 'Just help mc to my pallet by a warm fire. Bring a brew of bistort to aid my healing and some of your warm broth. That is all that is necessary.'

As Marged helped her to bed by the fire in the main hut and screened her round to change and wash her, Ceridwen prayed with all her will. She utterly surprised herself. She had expected to examine her thoughts and find she would be grateful to lose the child begot of Quintus's abuse. But she could not find it in her to blame the child for its method of coming to the world. She felt stirrings of compassion for the tiny creature, moulding its life inside her. She felt wonder at the whole process of birth and rebirth.

The Goddess worked such miracles, despite the wrongdoings of her creatures, and the greatest of miracles was new life. Ceridwen's healing hands sought her belly and she held their power and her love above the tiny growing foetus, willing it to hold on to its life in her womb. Marcus would claim the babe as his own and it would be honoured and respected. He might even come to love the child. She sensed he had it in him to be a wonderful father.

Cleansed, fed and drowsy, she sighed and leaned back gratefully against the cushions Marged had brought. She did not understand why she felt so fiercely protective of this child stirring in her womb. Perhaps his future was important to her family and tribe? 'His?' How did she know that it was a boy? The knowledge was so strong in her and would not be denied.

She did not even feel disappointed when the certainty that it was a boy came to her conscious mind.

Women were always saying that a sort of serenity came to those bearing life in the womb. It had definitely come to her, for her anxiety was beginning to wane and sure confidence supplant it. Or perhaps Marged had put something to calm her in the brew she had drunk? Whatever...She must sleep. It was but a slight bleed. There had been no violent cramping to suggest the babe would abort as yet. She must rest to give it the best of chances.

For once Ceridwen did not resent her mother's fussing about her. She was so weary and grateful to take respite. She would be needed soon enough. She snuggled down on the pallet beneath the plaid blankets and both Luce and Mwg, giving up their natural hostilities, came to nestle quietly beside her. She had given them nurture, now it was their turn to repay her with their care.

Soon, she escaped to the comfort of her dreams and found herself soaring above the mountain as a buzzard. The hut at Cae Gwynion seemed to glow golden and its energy called her, so she spiralled above it, sensing Nanw's presence. She flew down and alighted by the door postern. The light of love radiating from Nanw's eyes glowed from the hearth within. She drew closer, feeling the hypnotic effect of love across time and space. When, for a moment, they embraced each other in spirit, it did not seem like a physical embrace, where bodies wrap about each other, rather a gradual entering of one spirit into the other, a fusion and a temporary melding of soul. Courage and strength seemed to dance between them in soft waves of violet iridescent light. Ceridwen longed for it to go on and on, but gradually she found the dream energy fading and she stirred with a jump.

'I thought you would never wake, you seemed so deep asleep,' said Coll. 'How are you now? Will you come a walk into the sunset?'

'No, Coll! I must rest for a few days. It has all been such a shock. I shiver, yet the evening is warm, I'll vouch.'

'You are right. I had hoped to take your advice about

something, but I see it is not meet.'

'Coll, resting my body does not mean that my mind must cease to function. Come. Let me put my head upon your lap for a change. Then you can tell me your heart.'

'I cannot. I am not your husband, Sister. You are wed now, and no other man has the right to touch you.'

'Does it mean we must cease to be brother and sister, now that I am wed? I have no man to console me. 'Tis best a brother comes to love me, for family's sake; do you not think?'

'I suppose...but I should not like it if my wife were to be so close to her brother.'

'How do you know, Coll? You have not yet chosen a wife. How do you know if she should be jealous?'

'Because I did not like the way Marcus was able to bring a great brightness to your eyes. I should have preferred to be so empowered.'

'You shall be, Coll. One day you shall desire to bring the light to another woman's face. Until that time, comb my hair and listen to the voice of your sister. We have comfort in our togetherness and, until there comes a time when other men and women supplant our time together, there is no harm in it. Come. Do not be afraid of conversation. I am not being unfaithful to my husband to crave the company of my brother. It is a camaraderie we can prolong with Marcus being away.'

'You are right. I strive to be too sensitive. I should have known your need of me. What would you have me do with Hedfan?'

'Nothing. His loss of Gwyngariad and the knowledge that he has hurt me is punishment enough.'

'He rails at himself now. I do not know how to console him, but I have suggested that he helps to rebuild Cae Gwynion. I know that the hut for you here is almost ready, but you will have need of Cae Gwynion to bring you peace.'

'How did you perceive that, Coll? It is my dearest wish to have my sanctuary again, even if my day-to-day living must be here with the family.'

'We always knew each other's thoughts. We always shall.'

'I know that something eats at you - a restlessness that will not be stilled.'

'I shall never have peace of mind whilst Eithig lives. The outrage of his recent reign of terror has set me against him, and I see it now as my personal task to vanquish him. Everything in me wants to seek him out in the mountains and make sure he can harm no one again, but my tribe, my family demands me here to protect them. I cannot do both.'

'When you were at Din Silwy, did they murmur about who they wanted to take the place of their chieftain?'

'Why do you ask?'

'Because I look at you and see a princely torc around your throat and a plaid of purple about your shoulders.'

'I do not know how you do that...just look at someone and know something about their future...I can never...Do you not think you could be wrong?'

'Do you want me to be?'

'No...I admit that, when the people at Din Silwy started to hint about electing their next warrior king and eyed me up and down to get the measure of me, I found it flattering. That they should be thinking I would be good enough to take on that role makes me glow with pride and honour. So far my skills with horse and weapons have been confined to training and small skirmish, but I must admit to feeling ready to take more upon my shoulders...The thought of leaving Tan Yr Aur, though...It makes me feel so guilt ridden. Father and Owain rely so heavily upon me to help with the horse rearing.'

'Life surges and changes like the waves of the sea. Perhaps it is time for Owain to come into his own and take on more responsibility here. You know he lives in your shadow. Perhaps it is his turn now to be the tall tree? Hedfan too can be trained to rear the horses just as you have done, and Rhodri will soon be old enough to take Hedfan's place as messenger. You should do as your heart dictates. Life is short and quick to pass.'

'I knew you would counsel me well. In any event, they might not choose me. They were thinking I might take temporary charge, after I have settled things here with Father. The proper elections will take place at Samhain in Autumn. I shall have the whole Summer to prove my worth.'

'I see your eyes shining with the prospect of challenge. May the Gods go with you, Coll, but do not forget to visit your little sister from time to time to tell her your heart.' They hugged and parted. Marged, above all, would miss Coll's humour and liveliness about the place. She might be another soul for Ceridwen to console.

In any event, the respite at Tan Yr Aur was short lived. The blood show stopped and she felt much better after a few days of Marged's nurture. She was soon keen to be supervising the planting again and enjoyed being out all day in the warm sunshine. There was something about working with the plants that energised and relaxed her at the same time, so that she was able to keep going for long periods, as long as she did not have to do the hard digging. That was no problem, as Tergmud, the white ox, had helped plough the whole area, both down and across. Then, once hand weeded and de-stoned by the bondswomen, the fertile ground could be planted up with ease.

Ceridwen found that if she drank mint tea and took a cleft of bread before supper, the evening nausea did not come. How strange that other women felt queasy of a morning, yet with her it was always at sundown. Perhaps it was a sign that her child would be special. Time would tell.

Ness was still vomiting the contents of her stomach each morning and it was nearly her time. She had become heavy and slow, tiring with the slightest activity. Fortunately, she had plenty of clothing left from her previous children. She did not have to sew mercilessly by firelight. Only a little mending was necessary to have the new babe's clothes prepared.

Ceridwen had taken to spending a little time each evening in Madog and Ness's hut. She sat by their fire and cradled Ness's weary head. Madog was grateful, in a way. Ceridwen had a calming effect on the children and told them grand tales of magic, giants and princesses, in a hushed whisper, whilst her healing hands stroked and caressed his wife.

However, he did feel a pang of jealousy that someone else

could make her feel so comforted. It was his special time of day with Ness, when they would chat over the day's affairs, retell the children's escapades and nuzzle close. He felt redundant and useless. At first he hovered about in the hut, in case the children were unruly and would not settle, or the two women might need refreshment. In the end he had taken to excusing himself and drinking mead with the bondsmen.

'Why has the Goddess given me another babe, when other women crave but one and cannot beget? Could She not see that I have enough mouths to feed?' breathed Ness, kneading the straw in her pallet until it proved more comfortable and easing herself down.

'You will feel differently when I place the babe in your arms,' whispered Ceridwen, folding the newly washed and mended baby clothes into a wicker basket. 'Besides, where safer could the Goddess place a young soul than in your care? You are a wonderful mother, Ness. I shall look to you for instruction, when I have babes of my own.'

'You will need no instruction from me. I see how you are with my little ones. They adore you.'

'Ah, but being an aunt is not being a mother. I fear I shall be too soft with the discipline. I do not wish to order my children about like a general his army,' said Ceridwen, arching her brows by way of explanation.

Ness smiled conspiratorially. They both knew she was referring to Marged's manner of keeping order. Both sisters were more like Gwilym. They had always preferred to imitate his cajoling, negotiating good humour than bark instructions. He had never needed to beat his children. His stern, silent look of disapproval had always been enough to keep them in line.

Both sisters reflected for a moment, staring into the flames, enjoying memories of Gwilym in his role as their father. Ceridwen felt such a rush of love and respect for him. It really did not matter that they were not blood related, and it would be the same for Marcus and this child growing within her, she felt sure; if only Marcus would be able to see enough of the child to bond with him.

Ness interrupted her reverie. 'Ceridwen, if this child of

273

mine is a girl?'

'She is. I told you so three Moons gone by.'

'Would the Goddess accept her? Could she come to you to be trained in the secrets?'

'If I have no daughters of my own, then I shall gladly take her to pass on my knowledge. Shall we wait to see how the future unfolds? I have only access to limited foresight. There are as yet many things undetermined.'

'You are right. It is foolish to plan too far ahead.'

For the first time in nine months, Ness woke refreshed and without the cursed nausea that had dogged her whole pregnancy. The dawn was sweet and the first birds beginning to sing their chorus to the world. She lifted the door batten and let in the first morning light. Madog and the children were still asleep, breathing rhythmically under their thin Summer blankets.

She was propelled by the urge to be alone, to taste the sweet pleasure of peace and tranquillity. She must get away, before the whole farmstead began to hum with activity. A dog ran submissively to her ankles, but thankfully he made no sound as she fussed and greeted him. She slipped through the farmstead gates and headed along the path that bordered the river. The Braint fell gently, from a spring in the mountain, half a league to the Northeast of the farmstead.

If she followed the river it would lead her to the delightful hanging valley, forested either side, with the delicious pool of clear water, where she had learnt to swim as a child. There she would float and the burden of the child would seem to disappear. The anticipation gave her the energy to push on and upwards. It would be well worth the climb.

Rhonwen turned and reached out for her mother. She had taken to sleeping next to Ness ever since she had heard the story from Marcus of his mother's death. She was just in time to see Ness disappear through the gates. It would be wonderful to be with her mother, just the two of them alone together. The morning dew teased her bare feet, but she dare not go back for sandals, she must catch up. She too slipped soundlessly through the gates, remembering to close them behind her so that the animals would not wander.

Ness was breathing hard by the time she reached the pool on the breast of the mountain. She had had to pause for rest several times and fancied she heard deer on the winding path behind her, but she had arrived without sight of whatever might be following her.

The pool was disappointing, for it was not so clear and sparkling as she remembered, but it would be cool and hold her up whilst she swam. She found the stone jetty where people used to come to throw offerings to the Goddess of the river source, but where they now came to wash their best clothes. For a moment she sat and dangled her feet in the water, then she pulled her shift above her head and slid into the cool depths. She swam out a little and turned on her back facing the rising Sun, drinking in the peace, the quiet, the release of heavy burden.

'Mam!' It was Rhonwen yelling in fright. Was there no peace for more than a moment? 'Mam, you will drown. Mam you will die!'

Ness repented her irritation. She had never spent the time with Rhonwen to teach her to swim. She had always been too preoccupied to think of it as important. Guiltily she remembered that, in her own childhood, it was Marged, who had made the time to teach her. She swam to the jetty.

'Look, Rhonwen. We call this 'swimming'. I shall not drown if I paddle like a dog, or reach out like a cat clawing the water. Come. Take off your tunic and slide into the water. I shall hold you.'

'I cannot, Mam. I am frightened. Father said the Spirit of the pool would come up and swallow me if I went near to the water.'

'Listen. Reach out carefully and pull the blossom from that hawthorn. Good. Now throw the blossom into the water as an offering to the Goddess of the pool.'

'Like that?'

'Yes. Like that. If She is hungry, She will come and swallow the blossom; if not, then it is safe to come into the water.'

Rhonwen obeyed and watched fascinated as the sweet-scented white blossom moved dreamily along the surface of the water.

'It did not get swallowed,' she wondered in bright-eyed innocence.

'Then the Goddess of the pool does not want you to drown. Come now. Step into the water and I shall show you how to float like the blossom.'

They enjoyed the closeness of mother and daughter, drinking in the sparkling sunlight together, their laughter bubbling like the nearby brook, as it echoed down the valley in the stillness of the morning air.

When Ness was suddenly wracked with the cramp of labour, she almost left hold of Rhonwen to grab at her belly. She tried to stem the shriek that left her lips, but instead it rent the air with its pain, terrifying Rhonwen, who panicked and went under the water.

Ness had the presence of mind to push Rhonwen, spluttering and gasping, onto the jetty, as soon as the cramping in her own body began to subside.

'Come...out...of...the water, Mam! The Goddess...is trying to kill us!' wailed Rhonwen. She gave way to a wave of shivering and sobbing, shakily pulling on her tunic over her dripping body; her tears competing with her dripping hair and running nose.

Breathing heavily, Ness dragged herself onto the jetty and lay gasping until the last of the pain had gone. She knew it would return again soon. Her last two labours had progressed so quickly. She would never make it back to the farmstead. It would be best to send Rhonwen for help.

'Rhonwen, look at me. Hold my hand and know I tell you the truth. There is nothing to fear. There is no Goddess trying to swallow us. It is my birthing pains. I feel another one beginning already. The babe will be born here. It is important that you go back to the farmstead and tell *Nain* Marged and

Ceridwen.'

Rhonwen was trying hard to pull herself together. She knew she had an important task before her. She needed to listen to what her mother had to say. She rubbed her eyes and wiped her nose with her free arm. Although her lips still quivered, she dug her chin into her chest and nodded assent. As yet she was unable to form words from the tangle of her emotions. She pulled her hand away from Ness, offered her mother her dry tunic and then began to run home as though wild boar had given chase.

As Lug would have it, half way along the river path she came upon Madog, escorting Ceridwen to the Holy Place. They each led a pony, sporting back sacks to take precious seedlings on up to Cae Gwynion. They returned to the farmstead, Rhonwen riding behind Ceridwen and clinging to her for dear life. It would take but a few minutes to collect some brewing herbs and bowls Ceridwen had ready, some old blankets and some new. Marged was nowhere to be seen. Perhaps she was out searching for Ness. Ceridwen decided to leave a message with Olwenna, so that Marged could follow on as soon as she could.

Ceridwen was thankful that Angharad volunteered to help with the birthing. *Nain* Olwenna had already taken charge of Rhonwen, enveloping her in her cloak with grandmotherly kisses, promises of a honey cake feast, followed by a special patterning on the loom.

'Madog, you will need to come with us to light fires and keep guard. The wild animals will be attracted by the blood and we must guard Ness and her baby vigilantly,' Ceridwen ordered gently.

'I've already a shovel, sword and spears on my pony. I'll take dry tinder and flint.' Madog was so pleased to have a role and to be nearby Ness. He would pray by Ness's guard fires and make an offering to the Goddess.

They found Ness exhausted and lying limp and whimpering on the jetty. She had not managed to pull her tunic back on, but she had wrapped it about her shoulders. Angharad helped her to redress and gave her some sips of spring-water with precious honey to keep up her strength.

Ceridwen chose a mossy bank nearby, where a willow reached out a horizontal arm towards the water. It would make a good birthing aid. It was low enough to lean upon and high enough to pull against.

'Madog, dig a hole deep enough to receive the babe, just here in the shade of this branch. Then we need a comfortable log to sit upon, just beneath the arm of the tree. I will fetch fresh grasses and herbs to line the hole. When you have done that, we need three guard fires, one with a pot for brewing herbs, one...'

'Aaaagh! Aaaagh! Aaaagh!' Ness was on all fours now, yelling her protest to the Goddess of creation. Angharad rubbed her back and spoke soothingly, but it did not really reach across the pain. Ness focused on a duck with her ducklings, streaking across the silver light at the far side of the pool. By the time the birds reached the end of the rough stone jetty, the pain would be manageable. She could stop screaming and begin to pant like a sweating dog. She was glad it was early morning, for the Sun seemed welcoming and relaxing. By midday perhaps her child would be bathed in the Sun's strong light, but it would be too hot for her. She would be glad of the shady place Ceridwen and Madog were preparing.

'Do not move against me, Angharad. I cannot bear to be rubbed. Just let your hand rest upon my back and drink the pain away from me. Let your thigh be my pillow. I am so weary between the pains. I need to sleep.'

'You are welcome to my ample thigh. Use me how you will. Ceridwen will soon have her helping brew ready for you, and Madog your prayer fire.'

'Aaagh! It begins again...so soon. Sing a song with a story that I might listen beyond the pain.'

Angharad told the story of a giant vanquished by a little man, who had a magic sword and the Gods upon his side. The height of the contraction came at a particularly bloodthirsty part and Ness and Angharad yelled in unison. When the contraction began to ease they smiled at their joke and Ceridwen brought a brew of thyme and mint, raspberry leaves and powdered bistort root. It was thought the first three helped to ease birth and the bistort helped prevent haemorrhage. Despite the warm Sun on her body and the warm brew to drink, Ness began to shiver uncontrollably. They all knew that the babe would soon come. It would be born well before noon.

Between contractions, all three managed to support Ness to the birthing area, where she was soon to squat and pull against the branch to deliver her precious burden. Meanwhile Madog would keep the fires burning around them, to ward away hungry animals. They would be particularly interested in the afterbirth as soon as the scent of it was on the wind.

Ness lay with her back against the log and pulled up her knees so that the women could see how she was progressing. It was not the crown of the baby's head that was presenting, but a chin or even a knee.

'Your babe is lying awkwardly, Ness. Ceridwen has fine slim, healing hands. We shall use goose grease in an effort to ease her out.'

Ceridwen waited for the next birth pang to begin its course and, as it grew stronger, greased the opening around the babe. With the next of Ness's cries, she managed to secure her fingers around the baby's head. It was trying to come chin first. She must push it back in a little and try to tilt the head. For a moment Ceridwen panicked. What if she lost her grip and made the whole process much slower than necessary? Ness was already swollen and sore with the child's chin catching against her. This was going to be more painful than usual. She prayed and saw blue light all around her. It would go smoothly from now on, she was sure.

Ceridwen sighed with relief. 'The head is properly crowned now. Drink more of this brew and when your next pains come try to ease her out. Push slowly so that I may catch her as she falls.'

Ness was feeling disorientated with the pain and the tiredness which engulfed her was overwhelming. 'Madog, please come and lean against my back. Pass me your strength as I squat here. Prevent me from falling.'

Madog stirred the fires, left his prayers and oblations and came to do his wife's bidding.

'Madog. Remember not to look at the child until Ceridwen has presented her to the Gods, ere they be jealous of a man's first seeing. It does not augur well for a child, if men set eyes on it, before the Gods see the beauty of their handiwork,' Angharad instructed.

'I will do my best, but I must keep my eyes on the forest for danger at any rate.'

'Push, Ness! Do not give up. The head will be out with your next push and then your hardest work is done,' Ceridwen encouraged.

It was all soon over. A girl-child lay upon Ness's belly, awaiting the throbbing of the blue and white of the umbilicus to cease. But the baby herself seemed strangely motionless. She soon turned from pink to blue. Angharad checked that she was not choking, nor was she strangled, but she would not breathe. Ceridwen used her healing hands and prayed as she had never prayed.

'Slap her! Shock her into taking her first breath!' shouted Madog. 'Here. Give her to me!'

They each tried in turn to revive the child, but it was in vain. In the end they wrapped her tenderly in a blanket and put her into Ness's arms. Ness was dumbstruck for a few moments. They had cleaned up the babe's face. She looked so beautifully formed. It seemed incredible and so unjust that such beauty should be reclaimed so soon. Ness traced her finger over the tiny brow, her nose, and the sweet curve of her plump cheek. She kissed the silken skin and smelled the newness of the damp curls. The tiny nails looked so perfect on the dimpled hands, which Ness held so reverently. She noticed a callous blister upon her tiny thumb.

'Look. She sucked her thumb whilst in my womb. O Sweetness! Taken from me, even before you tasted this fine milk I have made for you. Did you hear me say I wondered why you had come to me? Why did the Goddess give me another child, when I had enough already? Did you hear me say that and decide to wing your flight to some other body, some other time? Is it my fault you have fled this life so soon. Is the Goddess so displeased with me?'

'Come now. Do not blame yourself, Ness. You said that, if it were a girl, you would like to give her into training as a priestess and healer. Perhaps the Goddess has called her early to serve in the next realm?' Ceridwen said soothingly, laying her hands upon Ness's belly to encourage the afterbirth to come.

'Perhaps it was me? I looked upon her when she did not breathe. Maybe it was my looking which prevented her from taking her first breath!' Madog cried guiltily.

'Nonsense, Madog!' countered Angharad. You did not look until the child was out. She had lain upon Ness's belly quite long enough for the Gods to see her. The Goddess did not want to give her life here. It is that simple.'

By the time Marged arrived with two bondswomen and a litter, she knew something was wrong. Madog was standing stock still, looking out over the water. His back measured defeat and sadness. Ceridwen was sending sweet smoke on the prayer fire, and making an offering of the umbilicus. Just as it joined life to life in the womb, so it would join life to life in the spirit. Angharad was washing her hands over and over in the pool, as though she could wash away what had just happened. And Ness, poor Ness, sat against a log under the willow, tears streaming from her crumpled uncomprehending face and the dead-white cheek of her infant pressed against the swollen blue veins of her left breast.

Marged approached slowly and said with great compassion, 'Ness, I am so sorry. May I hold the child?'

'No!' whimpered Ness, suddenly alarmed and clutching the babe as though someone were going to steal her away. 'No, she must be kept warm. I must always...keep her warm.'

⌘ ⌘ ⌘

CHAPTER XXI

⌘

DRAGON'S BREATH

It was almost four years since Ness's loss of her child. She had been a difficult patient for Ceridwen to help. Sometimes, being close sisters got in the way of the healing process. It had taken Ness three days to part with her child's body. Only when it had begun to stink, did it lose its appeal and seem really dead to her. Even then, it had to be prised away from her. It was cremated and then buried at Nanw's feet, so that she could show it the pathways through the nether world and into the light.

Ness could often be found crooning to a swaddle of empty blankets. For several months she ignored her other children and would not even look at Madog. Some said he had taken up with a woman from Din Silwy, but Ceridwen knew he had not been unfaithful. He just needed to get away from his wife's rejection and bathe in the attention of an audience at Din Silwy, who appreciated his music and applauded him as a man. Besides he needed to see Coll. Their friendship had been very close since their youth. Their camaraderie was special and Coll kept such a jolly band, since he had become chieftain. They trained hard, but they laughed hard too.

Madog loved nothing better than to spend a whole evening around their hall fire. He bathed in the glow of Coll's power. Coll did not have to try too hard to be popular. He soon won the hearts of the people, whose lives he protected. There were no contenders at election time and he became the first tribal chief to be loved, as well as admired, for many a decade. Madog often invited Ness to travel with him to visit her brother, but the answer was always a firm 'No'.

Madog knew she was frightened of getting with child again. She was so fertile. Ceridwen could advise on herbs and phases of the Moon, but Ness's desire always soared when she was most fertile. It was just easier to keep Madog at arm's length. In the end, Ceridwen had been able to help her with the grief and depression. Once Ness had recognised that something ailed her, she began to take the herbs that Ceridwen administered. Slowly she began to function again, cook for her family and care about their whereabouts, but the old, warm, carefree Ness would not return.

The boys did not seem to mind her carelessness of them. They spent a great deal of time with Madog, Owain and Gwilym, doing men's things, but Rhonwen did not know which way to turn. She tried so hard to please Ness. She longed to hear the warmth of her mother's voice, delighting in some activity they did together, or praising her for a job well done.

Ceridwen tried to take her sister gently to task about it, but it was too early, Ness was still wallowing in self-pity, guilt and anguish. When Madog was about in the hut, there was always unspoken tension and, when he was away, it was Rhonwen, who was the nearest at hand to punish with bad temper.

'Go back to the river and rewash these bowls. There is still grease all over them. You did not clean them with wood ash first. You are so stupid you make me want to scream!'

'I cannot give you back the little babe who died. But I do not deserve your tongue-lashing. I shall go and live with *Nain* Marged. I shall be appreciated there.' Puberty was making Rhonwen more assertive of her own needs and she was tired of taking Ness's verbal abuse.

'Go then you ungrateful slattern. I can manage better without you!'

In the end it was forthright Marged who turned the tide.

Rhonwen arrived on her threshold with her belongings,

tied up ironically in a baby blanket. Marged had tried to hold her tongue to give Ness time to grieve and sort through her emotions, but this was the last straw upon the mule's back.

'*Taid*! Look after your granddaughter. She has dire need of some comfort. I am away to sort out that daughter of mine, once and for all!' With a determined swish of a cloak, swung about her shoulders against the evening squall, Marged left Gwilym by the fire, with Rhonwen clinging about his neck and marched over to Ness and Madog's hut.

She could see Ness was repenting her harsh tongue and weeping into the stew she was stirring over the fire. 'Ness. Things have come to a pretty pass when you drive your own daughter away from your home fire. Look what devastation you have wreaked in the lives of others with this interminable grief. Do you intend to lose all your children and Madog as well?'

'There is no help for it, Mam. I do not seem to be in control of my tongue,' Ness replied miserably. 'There is an emptiness inside me and it is as though another speaks for me. I am absent so much of the time.'

'And where do you go, might I ask, when your children have need of their mother?'

'I...I go somewhere safe in my head, where I cannot be struck by the responsibility of pity for anyone else, or plagued with other people's sympathy. I know it is not a good place to go. Ceridwen has tried to help me to meditate and pathwork my way to a safer, healthier place in my thoughts, but whenever I try to follow her there, my fear stops me in my tracks.'

'Then you must try harder, and Ceridwen will give you a charm for your fear, if only you will trust her. We still have love for you Ness, but you must see that you are making all our lives intolerable.'

'I shall take my own life then and you shall all be the better for it.'

'O no, my daughter! You dare to lay more anguish on your family by escaping to the next world. If you go in torture, you will only return to relive your lessons. You must learn your lesson now, here with us, your loving family, who wish to support you.'

'The Goddess took away my reason for living when she took my child!'

'She took one child and you have four! Four who still need their mother and Madog, who still needs his wife!'

'Madog must satiate his needs elsewhere. I cannot bear to get with child again.'

'You could satiate each other. How do you think your father and I have managed to be childless all these years, when my moon blood is only now drying up? It is possible to make love without full consummation, to ease the tension and make the other feel valued.'

'I know that, but I fear our desire would cast caution to the wind.'

'And what is this behaviour of yours doing, but digging a well for your own misery and all those about you. You were a wonderful mother before the death of your babe. You had patience and tenderness in abundance. Now your children are made to feel responsible in some way for your misery. The Goddess gave them life and it is you who cheat them of their happiness, not Her!'

'I know...I know that you are right. O ye Gods help me! Help me to turn this pain about and ride upon it, instead of its riding me!'

'Good. You are in courage to fight for your children. I shall go and take care of little Llew and send Ceridwen to you. Your task of taking yourself in hand begins tonight!'

Rhonwen stayed for a little while with her grandparents, but by the time the women had spent several evenings in Mam's hut, chanting and pathworking, she began to notice a difference in her mother. It seemed that wanting to move on from her grief, instead of wallowing in it, was half the battle.

They took her up to the Holy Ground at Full Moon and she came back a little different, more mild-mannered and responsive to smiles. A month later, she was approaching her children and touching them again. Within three months, she was hugging them without reservation and she began to allow love to flow from her heart again.

They even caught her kissing Madog in the grove of apple trees at harvest time and laughter rang once more in her voice. Madog did not care if they never had consummate sex again; he was so relieved that she allowed him to hold her again. In some ways it was even more arousing, for they knew that they must not go all the way. He must be satisfied that he had four healthy children to prove his manhood and the wife he once knew had returned to him. The coming Beltane would be celebration indeed.

As Ceridwen trod the heather above Cae Gwynion, the gentle breeze released the scent of the hawthorn blossom all around her. She decided to cease collecting kindling in her apron and to take a well earned rest from the climbing and collecting.

In two days it would be Beltane and Marcus would come to her, as he had promised. Ness's response to grief had made Ceridwen examine her own and now that she had a child to nurture, nothing was going to get in the way of a happy childhood for Llew. She could see him now, riding piggyback on Owain's shoulders, whilst they checked the horses grazing on the pasture below.

Marcus had been to her nine times in the four years since their marriage. Sometimes he came as a surprise, when he was called to the hill fort for some case of sickness. But always at Beltane he had promised to take leave, leaving Dith in charge of his patients at Segontium. She hoped that no urgent crisis would prevent his coming. They had grown closer his last visit. He had brought little gifts for her and Llew; a fine worked brooch of Etruscan gold with blue enamel to pin up her tunic and a little belt with a lion's head buckle for Llew, because his name meant 'lion'.

The slaughter at the terrible Beltane seemed years ago, although it was but four. It was hard to imagine there had once been a life without Llew. He had been born with comparative ease for a firstborn and had slept and wakened with a cooing contentment, which endeared him to all. He was even tempered and adored his mother. How could she not adore him, he was so delightful? The problem was finding time alone with him, for Rhonwen wanted to play mother with him each day and every meal and rest time he was handed from one admirer to another.

Ceridwen felt a pang of guilt occasionally, when people remarked how like Marcus he was, with his deep brown eyes and dark curls. But she had found herself almost believing the lie, when Marcus first returned home to their hut and fell in love with Llew as passionately as he had fallen for Ceridwen.

She remembered the first day Llew and he had toddled together to the river, Llew's deliciously plump hand in Marcus's. They had spotted a fish and Llew had cried, 'Father! Look'. It was the first time Marcus had heard himself addressed thus, for Crispian had died before his first words. Marcus was amazed at this toddling child, who could hold a conversation and called him 'Father'. What he did not realise was that he had become something of a hero, renowned equally for his handling of the pestilence and for his courage in contest against Eithig.

Gwilym, Marged, and even the bondspeople, kept Marcus's name on their lips, so that Llew would not forget him. Owain was frightened that Llew would mistake him for his father, so taken was he with the child. That is why, whenever they played together, he compensated by telling Llew exaggerated tales of Marcus's exploits. Llew heard how his father had escaped the pig-pit in the race up the mountain and how he had almost tugged Eithig into the flames of the Belfire in order to win his mother's hand. As a consequence, Llew thought of Marcus as a huge good giant, who would always be there to protect them.

Ceridwen herself was guilty of building the myth surrounding Marcus. There were times when she would climb the mountain before dark and take Llew with her, half walking with him, half carrying him. Sometimes she was reverent and did and said things he did not understand at the altar at the Holy Ground; but at others, she would scan the landscape and, with a tremor in her voice, would point far into the distance towards Segontium and say, 'Your father is with the soldiers away into the Sun. Let us pray for his safe return.'

Last time, she remembered, in their own beautifully thatched roundhouse, they had all three huddled together on the family pallet before the fire and told stories to make each other laugh. Llew had fallen asleep between them, and when they had laid him to one side, she had encouraged Marcus to lie with her, hoping she would fall pregnant with a girl child. She prayed and prayed that she might conceive. A girl child, to whom she could pass all her skills, would be wonderful. It had been a poignant love tryst, for Marcus could only spare one day with them and he too was finding it hard to leave and return to his work.

'I must leave for Segontium first thing in the morning. The men at the hill fort will nurse the injured auxiliary as I've instructed,' Marcus had sighed, sadly stroking the silken roundness of her flushed cheek in the firelight.

Ceridwen had nuzzled close to his bare chest with a groan. 'Why so soon, Marcus? You have eaten but one meal with us. Llew will expect you to spoil him and play with him tomorrow.'

'There is much quarrying of stone, near Segontium. We are trying to strengthen our buildings and ramparts. I know, from past experience, that men will become careless as they try to hurry the job before Winter. There will be accidents and consequences.'

'You are expecting to be attacked?' she had whispered with alarm.

'There is rumour that the Ordovican tribes to the East and South are gathering strength. We suspect Eithig of instigating a rising. So far, he and his men have contented themselves with sabotaging trade routes through the mountains with small ambushes, where they steal, kill and run. But last month they completely wrecked the grain ferry, bound for Segontium from Dindaethwy. You must have heard about that?'

'Indeed we heard tall stories of your starving at Segontium. But we knew the tales to be an exaggeration. All you have to do is increase the quotas of grain, which come from other areas, intensify your fishing and you have no problems. But it is high time Eithig was caught. He has done so much damage. It is more than forty moons now, since he ran into hiding in the mountains.'

'He is like a Will o' the Wisp, never staying long enough in one place for us to trap him. If we take hostages of his men, he pays no heed and lets them perish,' Marcus had said, ashamed that the sophistication of his own army had failed to track down Eithig.

'The Gods will punish him, Marcus! Last time I made augury, I was given the knowledge that his reign of terror will soon come to an end...How it is to come about was not given to me.'

'Would you not like to see Segontium besieged and Rome pull out of the area?'

'That Rome rules now seems the lesser of two evils to me. Can you imagine our lives, if Eithig worked his way to being High King? At least your armies protect us from inter-tribal warfare and raiders from the sea. There is enough peace for us to farm our lands and rear our stock.'

'Am I the lesser of two evils then?'

'You have invaded my reason and for that I forgive you. I am sensible that your love for me, like mine, is neither rational nor timely. We are tools used by the Gods to intermingle the bloods of our peoples. We must come together to raise sons and daughters for future generations, who will champion the cause of peace and justice. For that is not the prerogative of one race over another, but a marriage of equals.'

'You would do well as an orator in the forum at Deva. There is such power in your eyes and voice when you speak with conviction.' Marcus had laughed, kissing her playfully on the lips. 'For now might we concentrate on the conceiving of sons and daughters?'

They had aroused each other again and made love less urgently this time, pleasuring each other with tender, lingering strokes, both keen to hold the fire-lit scene in the vision of their memory, to be replayed when they were no longer together.

It had been a gradual process for Ceridwen to let down all barriers against Marcus. Each time he had come to her, he had managed to bridge the awkwardness between them more successfully. Little by little she came to trust and appreciate him. How easy it was now to melt into his arms and become one soul temporarily. It was like losing herself into the light of the Sun, like dying to the incompleteness of self and resurrecting more whole. Their union at their first Beltane had been symbolically sacred, but it had taken them these four years to experience its depths.

Ceridwen rose now from her rest on the mountain and languorously meandered down through the Sacred Grove. She lingered by one of the oaks, stroking the grey-ridged bark, remembering their last conversation here. Marcus had surprised her by admitting that his allegiance to Rome was not all it had been.

'In the past I've listened to speeches from generals, so stirring that I would gladly have lain down my life for Rome. Rome was my mother; my sister; my mistress. But since we have become man and wife, I no longer feel married to all the ideals of her culture. Your family has given me a sense of belonging and it is you who have given me a broader vision. It is hard to be narrow again.'

'How can you work for your 'former mistress', then? Do you not feel uneasy that you continue in her pay?' she had teased.

'Phew! You challenge, boldly there, Ceridwen...' Marcus had paused and had had to think, for several moments, how to justify his actions. 'To begin with, it was Italia gave me my education and schooled me in surgery and medicine. I have much to repay her. I have made a binding contract, which swears allegiance to the welfare of the Roman army. I could not foreswear my word. I could not shame my own ancestors and family name by shirking my task. I must endure what I have set in motion.'

'Even if you no longer believe it to be right?' She had not sought to make him uncomfortable, but she had a need to know.

'The Pax Romana is evident in many places we have conquered. We have brought law and order out of chaos. We have brought trading routes and prosperity to many, culture and skills from the world over. It is good to feel Roman, but it is also good to feel part of your tribe. I feel I have two homelands, that of my ancestors and that of my wife. I sit astride two horses. They have both served me well.'

'By the will of the Gods, I hope you never have to choose between us.'

'I hope I never shall. Let us hope that my work at Segontium will go on and that I shall retire in my old age to spend my days with you.'

'Do you never have the urge to return to your homeland, to your father's house, which one day will be yours by Roman law?'

'Hmmm. When the ice winds of Winter blow through my tunic to shiver my bones...Yes, I dream of a sun drenched courtyard in Ostia, overlooking the sea; and the hanging terraces of vines behind the villa on the hillside call to me.'

'That is called '*hiraeth*' in our language. Even when I am at Tan Yr Aur I have a great longing to go home, a *hiraeth* for Cae Gwynion. I am drawn to it whenever I am restless. It always calms me here. I come alone to pray and be with my ancestors.'

'It is good to have a special place. Once when I was captured in Gaul, we were chained together in an old cesspit. We were there for days. I lost count. But I found I could escape in my mind to the vine terraces above our old house. It kept me from madness and gave me hope.'

'It must have been a terrifying ordeal. How did you escape?'

'Dith had not been captured in the skirmish. He sought out an old friend of my father's, whom he knew was holding Gallic prisoners. I was exchanged in a rather tricky deal. I shall always owe my life to him. He gets cross when I am away to you. He sees my absence as a great indulgence on his part.'

'Then I shall always be in his debt, for not only has he given me your life, but the time which you spend with me.'

They had paused and held each other close for a moment by the threshold of Nanw's hut, now lovingly repaired and kept like a shrine to her memory.

'From this time onwards,' Marcus had breathed into the copper tendrils on her brow, 'I shall have a new special place to go to in times of distress. Here at this threshold, I shall be

with you…. whenever you have need.'
    'And I with you.'

There was mounting unease at Segontium. The work of replacing wooden ramparts with stone was going too slowly for Vipsanius's liking, and work on replacing the partially wooden barracks and infirmary was not even begun. He found himself being unusually sharp tongued with his men and he felt their resentment at being pushed to their limit. A contingent of slaves had been recalled to Deva, just as the quarrying had begun to gather momentum and his skilled stonemasons had grumbled all Winter about the sharp frosts affecting their work. At least the frosts were well over now and early Summer about to breathe its honeyed warmth into the year.

One good thing had been the completion of the southwest tower, guarding the gateway to the road through the mountains. The new ballista it housed had been tried and tested these last few days. It was a formidable weapon, capable of firing arrows a distance of three hundred yards. Perhaps the coming of the warm weather signalled a turning point.

Vipsanius needed to consult Marcus about the new design for the infirmary, before he took leave for Mona. He seemed to use a lot more local herbs in his medications these days. The pharmacy room would have to be made larger, as well as the barracks where the sick men were tended.

He knew where to find Marcus at this time of day. He would be supping with Hortensius and Flavia, playing with their children with a look of strange yearning in his eyes. At least it was better than the grief that had haunted him after the deaths of Leona and Crispian.

Hortensius was the only centurion of six to have his family with him. It made sense to house him and his family close to himself and Rhiannon, in the commandant's quarters. Flavia had been invaluable to Rhiannon, teaching her how to become a commandant's wife, how to instruct the slaves and welcome visitors. Rhiannon in her turn was able to teach Flavia many of her customs. It was a comfortable life to have one's wife and children near; to see them each evening and know they were safely within the walls of the fortress.

As Vipsanius surveyed the fort in the orange glow of the evening Sun, he allowed himself a sigh of satisfaction. For today, at least, the building work had made some headway and the mason soldiers could be heard revelling in the bathhouse, easing their bones before slipping down to the whorehouses at the port. They would be given passes and expected to be back in barracks by midnight. It kept them sweet and in mood for hard work the next day.

He was thankful that he had Rhiannon's arms to lie in each night. Initially, it had been a marriage of diplomacy, convenient to Lord Geraint, the grey-bearded Ordovican chieftain at Porth Arfon below. But Vipsanius fancied that their marriage had blossomed into love; if he were to believe the affection Rhiannon showered upon him. She had borne him two babes already, but the boy had died soon after birth. Flavia had been a handmaid of the Gods in the way she had nursed and coaxed Rhiannon. Rhiannon had been brave and was hopeful that the babe she carried now would be strong and healthy.

He listened to the courtyard noises as he stood in his own gateway. No one was aware of his arrival, so absorbed were they in their tasks or play. It gave him great satisfaction to hear the children's laughter as they played their games. His own little Corellia was peeping deliciously from behind the fig tree, that grew in the middle of the courtyard, her auburn curls bouncing as she giggled, unable to hide silently. Hortensius's boy Clarus was pretending he could not find her and was darting about in a frenzy of make-believe frustration. Marcus, Flavia and Hortensius joined in suggesting ridiculous places where he might find the two year old.

'She's in the gutter!'

'Under the cushions!'

'Up in the clouds!'

It was warm enough now for the evening meal to be taken under the verandah, skirting the inner rectangle of the buildings. Bernice was arranging their cushions upon the floor around a low table, so that the two families could dine together.

Rhiannon was seated in a shaft of sunlight, her golden-red Celtic braids falling about the shoulders of a generous Roman dalmatica, hiding the fullness of her pregnancy. Vipsanius smiled fondly. She was struggling to write her letters with a stilus, into the wax tablet Dracus had made for her. He was the children's tutor, but had undertaken to teach Rhiannon to read and write in Latin. Vipsanius's eyes filled with warmth. She really did try to please him and she was determined to learn.

Eventually she felt his gaze and looked up, crying out a welcome. All homecomings should be thus, thought Vipsanius, as his companions and family enfolded him in the embrace of their laughter.

Dith was feeling decidedly grouchy. He pretended to Marcus that he did not mind his leave taking, but he always became on edge when Marcus was away. Marcus's surgical assistant Demeter was young and inexperienced, but not always willing to give credence to Dith's sound advice. Things never ran smoothly when he was away. Packing Marcus's saddlebags always gave him this incredible knot of fear in his stomach: fear that Marcus would encounter danger and that he would not be there to protect him; fear that he would have to undertake some delicate surgery his ample fists were unsuited to, because Demeter had not yet learned how to do it; fear that he might administer the wrong medication and kill someone in his ignorance. For, no matter how hard he tried to remember the exact measurements of the remedies, if it was something not already made up by Marcus, he found his memory playing tricks on him.

He had been unable to master reading, no matter how hard Marcus had tried to teach him. The squiggles of writing seemed to play games with him and hopped around in his head, when he tried to make sense of them. Luckily Marcus had devised a simple colour and shape code to help him identify the medicines.

To Dith, Marcus was the focus of his life; his only family, the one person he looked up to. He made no pretence at being religious. He worshipped Marcus, tolerating all his shortcomings and that sufficed him. His prayers and desires had never been answered, with the exception of Marcus's miraculous survival on several occasions. So, whenever Marcus performed ablutions and prayed, Dith would hover sceptically as though indulging some naive child.

On this occasion Dith found himself more than ever uneasy. Much as he respected Ceridwen and appreciated her loveliness, his fear that she would steal his master completely away from him, was becoming stronger. The jealousy squirmed uncomfortably up from his belly and, much as he tried to talk sense to himself as he packed the last of Marcus's clean underclothing, the pain of their parting this time seemed unusually intense. Why could Marcus not have fallen for a local girl? There were plenty of pretty Cymric lasses who would have warmed his bed for little more than a smile. But no! These Gods of Marcus had to complicate matters and bind him to someone a day's ride away. What stupid Gods!

He could hear Demeter calling for his assistance already and Marcus had only stepped out to dine. Demeter would just have to wait until he had finished packing the saddlebags. Dith picked up the damp towel his master had just brought back from the bathhouse and something fell from it. It was Marcus's locket; entwined with the talisman Ceridwen had given him three Beltanes ago. Marcus must have removed them whilst bathing and forgotten to put them back on. Dith decided to strap them inside the saddlebags in case there was a light-fingered patient about. Nothing was safe from pilfering hands these days. He would lock the saddlebags in the pharmacy for the night.

Marcus was in excellent mood. It was not only the sumptuous supper and wine, which Hortensius and Flavia had provided that relaxed him. When he had given his last instructions to Demeter and Dith that evening, it was as though a great weight had been lifted from his shoulders. His work at the infirmary had finished for a whole seven days and he could relax in anticipation of his sojourn on Mona.

What was Ceridwen doing now? Perhaps she was unbraiding her hair to wash it for the morrow and little Llew clinging to her skirts, marvelling at the waving tresses falling about her shoulders? Or perhaps she supped with Marged, Gwilym and Owain, singing a tale of Celtic magic to soothe Llew to sleep? Soon he would be with them and the feeling of being a family would be his again. It must soon be time to conceive the girl child Ceridwen was so sure they would have. He glanced enviously at Rhiannon and Vipsanius, who had retreated behind an ivied pillar on the verandah and were already engaged in tender intimacies.

'You are already on the Druid island, Marcus. You have left us before you even mount your horse,' teased Flavia, as she motioned Bernice to gather the children together and put them to their beds. 'Here. Take a last cup of wine, Marcus. It may be the last you see for a while.'

'Enough, Flavia,' smiled Marcus, holding his hand above his cup. 'I thank you for the hospitality, but I am comfortable. I must have a clear head for the ride tomorrow. Besides, the Celtic mead is not something to be scorned. It is very good.'

'You will be growing a long Celtic moustache next!' laughed Hortensius, slapping his friend upon the back. 'They will make a Cymro of you yet!'

The sound of urgent beating at the courtyard door suddenly interrupted their frivolity.

'Commandant, Sir! An urgent message from Porth Arfon! The slave insists on delivering the message personally.'

'Come!' ordered Vipsanius, passing his fingers through his hair and straightening up to his full height. He motioned the slave to join him under the tree in the centre of the courtyard. The man could hardly get his breath.

'Breathe deeply; then speak freely,' snapped Vipsanius impatiently.

'A cup?' queried Rhiannon, passing the heaving messenger some water in deference to her own custom. The slave shook his head.

'No thanking you,' he gasped. 'It is a message for you Lady, as much as for your husband, who must grant permission. Your mother is direly sick, my Lady and sends to see you and her grandchild, before taking leave of this world!'

'No! It cannot be! I saw her but three days since and she was in good health. She cannot be dying. O, Vipsanius, I must go immediately!'

'It could be a trick, Rhiannon. There may be someone who wishes to capture you. Is there any way you can be sure the message is genuine?'

'Did my mother say any words to prove your source?' queried Rhiannon tremulously.

'Ie, my lady! She said to tell you, *'Crossed by the ribbons tangled in your red, red hair'.*

"'Tis truly from my mother! She was always laughing at me when I was a child. I would always have a tantrum whilst she was braiding ribbons in my hair.'

'I shall order you an escort immediately. Hortensius! Choose me ten of your best men to escort Lady Rhiannon to her father's house. Make sure they use a litter to carry little Corellia,' Vipsanius ordered anxiously. 'Her mother is too heavy with child to carry another. Make sure the men post themselves outside the house and are vigilant. I do not want any kidnappings and holding to ransoms. Is that clear?' Vipsanius added, breathing confidentially into Hortensius's ear.

'It is done, commandant!' Hortensius replied, casting a worried look at Flavia. She knew what he meant when he looked at her like that. She was to barricade the quarters and keep the children and the servants quiet.

'Maybe I can be of some use, my Lady. I do not know what ails your mother. But there may be something I can do to ease her,' offered Marcus honourably, hoping, in all heart of hearts, that he could spend just an hour with Rhiannon's family, leave his advice and quit.

'Marcus, you are on leave as from this evening. I cannot expect you to treat my mother,' Rhiannon objected, more from the knowledge that her mother was likely to reject treatment from anyone other than the town's wise woman, than for any regard for Marcus's feelings.

'Your mother must let Marcus look at her. He is an excellent doctor. Tell her I insist that he treat her and I will personally provide any medicines necessary. You never know. The Gods may be smiling upon her by my sending Marcus to heal her.'

Rhiannon nodded her assent. Vipsanius never ceased trying to please her mother. He did not believe, as Rhiannon did, that her mother would always be as hostile towards him. Perhaps this would be the very last time he would try.

Rhiannon always felt comfortable in Marcus's company. At least he would be her buffer against the escort of legionaries, who were bound to be aloof. She felt like howling with anxiety and misery, but instead she play-acted with dignity. Was she not, above all, a chieftain's daughter, far greater in rank, by view of her kinsmen, than a commandant's wife? Then she must act as such.

Her limbs shook as she gathered a cloak about her against the evening breeze. To contemplate her mother being so ill... why had she not known? They had always been so close. Perhaps her head was too full of Vipsanius and little Corellia and the happiness she shared with them. A knot of guilt mixed with her anxiety began to make her feel physically sick. 'O ye Gods, not now!' she screamed in her head. She must get to her mother's side.

Marcus seemed to understand her state. Wordlessly he took her arm and steadied her through the northwest gate. The sentries saluted and pulled their pila across to allow them through. Rhiannon refused a mount or a litter for herself. She did not wish to tolerate being joggled along. She felt safer descending the hill to the town on foot, but little Corellia, still sleeping, swung contentedly in a hammock-like bed, carried between the shoulders of two infantrymen.

It was a strange procession as they passed down the highway, Rhiannon heavy with child, preceded and followed by the helmeted legionaries and Marcus taking her arm. Tradesmen and their wives, sitting outside their makeshift shelters became silent as they passed and made the sign of Celtic blessing. Perhaps they thought the child to be sick, or maybe they knew, before Rhiannon did, that her mother was dying.

They approached the flatter, sprawling conglomeration of circular huts and tiny streets. The smell of rotting fish, unwashed bodies and excrement seemed overwhelming today, especially to Rhiannon's highly sensitive nose. She would have a word to her father about it. Standards must be kept even though they had their private grief. They passed a long wooden hut. Legionaries on leave-pass sat on trestle benches outside, drinking local mead, whilst waiting their turn in the whorehouse. Rhiannon hated what the women did to earn a living, but without husbands they would be a drain on the chieftain's resources, if they could not ply a trade of their own. She knew her father relied on one whore in particular to feed him with regular information about life at the fort.

Raucous, bawdy laughter reached her ears. It seemed so distasteful when she was about to meet with her mother for the last time. She would demand respect.

'Albinus! Tell that rabble to do what they have to do in silence, or, by Bel, I shall whip them myself. Do they not know their Queen is sick?' Albinus nodded and bowed. He would have his work cut out keeping the rabble quiet, but shortly Rhiannon would be out of earshot and who knows, he might be able to avail himself of an ample Brythonnic girl.

The procession halted at a large stone-built roundhouse, overlooking the sea.

'Stand guard outside and by no means leave. I shall check inside,' Marcus ordered the legionaries. 'I shall take hold of the child now and enter with my Lady.' Gently he picked up the sleepy Corellia in his arms and she smiled dreamily up at him, totally trusting. 'Time to see your Nain and Taid,' he whispered into her ear.

'I must wake up then,' she yawned, rubbing her eyes, but still quite content for him to carry her. He had been her playmate on numerous occasions and she liked how he smelled.

'Father, O Father! Why did you not send for me before?'

complained Rhiannon anxiously, as she greeted Lord Geraint in the outer chamber. 'Was there no warning that Mother was so sick? I have brought Marcus with me to physic her.'

'Hush, my child. Come through to the inner fire. Your mother is there,' replied Geraint of Arfon, strangely resplendent in his best robes.

Marcus followed, carrying Corellia. Lady Branwen sat before the fire on what Marcus could only describe as a throne. It was a carved wooden seat, set about with burnished bronze. The chieftain and his lady rarely stood on ceremony. They must think of this as an occasion of great import. She looked flushed and red-cheeked. Perhaps she had a fever?

'Do not fret yourselves on my account,' whispered Lady Branwen. 'I am very well indeed, as you can see. But we are all in grave danger and I had to have you near me, *Cariad*. You will forgive me for that? Will you not?'

'What do you mean, Mother? What grave danger? I must warn Vipsanius!'

'You must do no such thing at present,' said Geraint gravely, holding his daughter gently by the shoulders. 'You must stay here with us. Eithig and his band have pulled together three Ordovican tribes, including the dreaded Ceiri from the South. They are ready to strike at Segontium. They have a plan to get themselves inside the fort, but at this moment in time the children from the whorehouse are captive in the slaughterhouse. They are to be burned alive unless the whores go along with the plan.'

'What plan? What is happening? They will kill Vipsanius. I know it, Mother. I could not bear it!'

'Calm yourself, Rhiannon. Do you want all to know that we suspect something?' said her mother, Branwen, icily. 'If we raise the alarm, the children will be set afire. It is as simple as that.'

'How could our kinsmen treat their own with such treachery?' Rhiannon agonized, her face crumpling and tears welling as she reached for Corellia. 'Those children could be their own offspring for all they know. The whorehouse is frequented by Celt and Roman alike.'

'They tell themselves it is for the greater good. Thus men excuse great crimes,' answered Geraint. 'My fellow Ordovicans see me as a traitor; that my daughter is wed to a Roman commandant; that we trade peaceably with the garrison. I have but a handful of men at my disposal whom I can trust to be loyal to me. I suspect that most traders here will sit things out and take to the winning side, but I am done for and expect to be slain, captured or executed. I shall meet my fate honourably, but I ask you now, Marcus, to take a boat on the next tide and convey my family safe to the shores of Mona.'

'I have a plan you may prefer. I have nine legionaries with me. If we can release the children and get them to safety, the women will fight their way out of the whorehouse, by fair means or foul, and we can get a message to the fort to forewarn Vipsanius. I have fisher friends at the port. They will brave the tides and take all the children and your family to safety, in pretence at putting out to fish. But I must stay to fight with my friends. I cannot abandon them.'

'I understand, Marcus, and I am with you,' said Geraint rubbing his chin thoughtfully.' If you have men enough, then we must risk all to save all. No one knows that I am privy to the plan. Nesta smuggled one of the children into an empty wine barrel, then had it taken outside the whorehouse to create more space. The child ran here with the whole tale. Nineteen children are being held in the slaughterhouse tower, strung and gagged with the dripping meat awaiting to be smoked, if the whores raise the alarm.

'The whores are to engage the last twenty legionaries in an orgy. Stripped of their clothes and weapons left by the door, they are to bind their customers and offer their services. The Ordovican warriors will enter and kill all legionaries, taking their clothes and returning to barracks at Segontium in their places, as if drunk and disorderly. Once past the gatehouse, they will begin burning and killing, leaving the gates wide for their fellow warriors to swarm in.'

'We cannot do nothing! Vipsanius and Flavia's family... We must warn them. We must at least give them a chance to defend themselves,' argued Rhiannon.

'We can warn them when we have the children to safety. All we can do is our best, *Cariad*,' soothed Geraint stroking her hand. 'It is the Gods will decide our fate.'

Lady Branwen and Rhiannon silently set about packing the necessary items for the sea journey; whilst the boy from the whorehouse played a game of catch the pouch with Corellia, pretending he was not terrified. If the children were going to be rescued from the slaughterhouse, they would need warm cloaks to brave the chill night wind as they sailed across the Straits. They did not want to alarm the servants and thus risk a leak of information.

'Come now, Corellia, and you boy. You must come with us. We are going on an adventure. You must help us carry these blankets to the boat,' whispered Lady Branwen. 'We must be as quiet as mice, trying to escape a cat.'

'*Nain*, if we are going on an adventure, may I take Clarus with me?'

'He is her friend at Segontium, Mother,' said Rhiannon, a note of warning in her voice. 'Corellia, we must play hide and be very quiet on our adventure. Marcus will go to find Clarus when he has helped us. Quickly now! We must sneak quietly down to the harbour and make ready to sail.'

When they were ready, Marcus took them by moonlight to the harbour, where he found Sunico, the fisherman, hauling his newly mended nets aboard his boat. Marcus allowed himself a glance towards Mona, but it was too dark to see the summit of Purple Mountain. How he yearned to be with Ceridwen. The sweet-scented, evening breeze was created by the Goddess for lovers, not for arson and murder.

'Sunico, Greetings! You are well again and that arm of yours is strong?'

'As strong as ever, doctor. Thanks to you.'

'Sunico. I have a special request, which may save many lives. Could you manage to take some women and children across to Mona? The port and fort could be under attack in the next hour.'

'We have small fishing boats which can take up to ten people. You are lucky. We were going to take the boats out fishing on the next turn tide. They are ready to sail as we speak.'

'Take Lord Geraint's family and your own this instant, but let your friends be ready to take more women and children from the town, as I direct them down to the harbour. Do all as silently and normally as possible.'

'I shall do my very best as you did for me, Doctor Marcus.'

Marcus left them without more ado, knowing he could trust Sunico to fulfil his task at all cost, but now he must help Lord Geraint to free the hostages.

He caught up with him, as he was about to approach the guard to the slaughterhouse. The morrow would be Beltane Eve. What could be more natural than for Lord Geraint to inspect the best meat for the great feast? Marcus knew when they drew near the meat store by the stench of blood, soaked into the earth. There were four men to guard the round tower, where the carcasses of slain animals were hung from great pulley racks and bled, salted or smoked.

Lord Geraint recognised one of them, the usual butcher man, his eyes bulging from his florid face in silent terror, as three others he did not recognise, no doubt held a blade to his back to silence him.

'The blessings of the Moon Goddess be with you. I see you have the meat well guarded for the morrow. We do not want Eithig's men stealing our feast fare, now do we, Iolo?'

'No...No indeed, my Lord! Nothing must harm the meat for the great feast. It is locked up s...s...safely, I assure you!' Iolo the butcher dissembled, pointing to the keys dangling at his belt.'

'Iolo, you know how important it is to keep your hands clean when handling the meat? Approach and let me inspect them. Your torch man, hold it over his hands that I may see the clearer,' ordered Geraint imperiously.

The warriors were uneasy, Marcus could see. For a moment he wondered whether they would attack or carry on with the pretence that nothing was wrong. The warrior with the flaming torch in his hand pushed Iolo forward. Iolo staggered; terrified that one false move would end with a thrust through his spine. Perhaps they had already beaten his legs. He stood shaking before his chieftain, holding out his hands for inspection.

'What do you say, Doctor? Does he have old blood down his nails?'

Marcus bent over the butcher's hands, but instead of replying brought his hand up swiftly to snatch the torch and thrust it into the face of the warrior. As the man screamed in pain, the other warriors made to attack; but were immediately set upon by the Roman legionaries in hiding. Geraint dragged Iolo free of the fighting melee and unbuckled the man's belt of keys. He personally unlocked the round tower, cutting the bonds of the terrified children. They had all been gagged. Several had wet themselves or worse; they were so terror stricken. But there was no time for sobbing and wailing. They had to be got to safety before warrior reinforcements arrived.

The warrior sentries were quickly outnumbered and their throats slit with legionary hands gagging their cries. No one knew if a spy messenger had been lurking, but the scream that had rent the night had certainly brought townspeople running.

Geraint took the torch from Marcus's grasp, thankful it did not achieve its night's purpose. 'Men who wish to stand fast with me, gather your weapons if you want to save your homes from the Ordovican warriors. Women and children to the fishing boats, all! Leave all slaves manacled. They will create havoc if let loose in this situation. Go now, with the blessing of Bel!' Lord Geraint drew three great circles in the air with the torch he had taken from Marcus and it let out great tongues of fire in blessing.

Marcus, with Lord Geraint and the legionaries, left the townswomen to get the children down to the boats and commandeered tethered ponies to take them through the streets to the whorehouse. Several townsmen followed them, running with makeshift weapons.

The street outside the whorehouse was eerily empty. No one sat outside as usual, drinking leisurely under the rush light. As they approached, they could hear muffled cries and sobbing coming from inside.

The smell of fresh blood was overwhelming as Marcus held the door for Geraint. Several women were gagged and tied to the central roof support, in various stages of undress. At their feet were strewn the naked bodies of at least two dozen legionaries and at least six of the young whores. All had had their throats cut and the rushes on the floor squelched with their blood as they trod. Marcus inspected the bodies for any sign of life, but there was none and he shook his head.

'Nesta! The children are being sailed to Mona on the fishing vessels. Get you and your women to the harbour and sail over for now. Quickly!' Geraint ordered as he cut her bonds.

Most of the women went about salvaging some clothing for their journey and covering their nakedness, but one young girl sat hunched and quivering against the bole of the roof support. She stared wide-eyed at the body of her best friend, still entwined in an embrace, joined in deadly coitus with Albinus, one of their favourite clients.

Marcus shook her. 'Come on! You can do nothing for her. Up you get and save yourself. This place could be torched in no time.' He pulled her to her feet, and she responded, reaching for a soiled tunic. He headed for the door, following Geraint, but noticed that the girl lingered and stroked her friend's blood soaked hair before she fled.

Marcus mounted the pony again and followed Geraint and his small band of followers up the highway towards the fort. They were too late to give warning. Somehow the seemingly drunken play-acting of the disguised Ordovicans had fooled the guards, for flames were already billowing from the guardhouse at the northwest gate. They could hear war horns sounding the Ordovican advance. The stealth party had succeeded in opening the gates to the fortress and hundreds of warriors from Eryri and the Lleyn were roaring and ululating their way in, some on foot, most on mountain ponies. It would be a blood bath they were honour bound to fight out.

Vipsanius smelled the smoke from the northeast guardhouse fire, before he heard the trumpet warning from the southeast watchtower. Hortensius he dispatched to rouse the troops in their barrack bunks. 'Any women and children secreted in barracks are to be sent to my house. Flavia knows what to do!'

Hortensius nodded compliance guiltily. He had not realised Vipsanius knew about the irregularities in the sleeping arrangements, to which he himself had been turning a blind eye. But now was not the time to discuss the matter. He ran to his duties, not daring to waste another second.

Vipsanius ordered the house slaves to be given weapons to guard the civilians in their care. He trusted them implicitly, their loyalty to his family and friends unquestioned. They would give their lives. As he left the courtyard of the house to take command, he heard Flavia's voice chivvying them, her courage momentarily outstripping her sinking confidence. He hoped that, when he next returned, she and her children would still be alive. Then he thought of Rhiannon and little Correlia down at the port and knew that if he gave in to where his thoughts might lead, he would be useless to the men relying upon him. He uttered a desperate prayer as he strapped on his sword and made his way out into the main thoroughfare.

He gave strict instructions to the house guards to bar the gate once he had left and to let no one enter, except for women and children, until next they heard his voice.

Chaos already reigned. Half naked Ordovican warriors in their strange, blue-woad war paint and spiked, limed hair, rode their mountain ponies in great circular sweeps, torching all wooden buildings in sight, the flaring light catching burnished and polished weapons, shield bosses, golden necklets and armlets in its glare. A great sea of colour and sound rushed at Vipsanius's senses. The orange and gold of the torchlight and flames; the reds, purples and greens of the warriors' cloaks and multicoloured breeches; the red of spurting blood, as the legionaries braved the doorway of their barracks and were driven back again and again; the ugly sound of death throes and tortured injury; injury mingled with cries of triumph and yells of combat.

His head reeling, he reached the relative safety of the stone headquarters building, or *principia* next to his own house,

307

where his five centurions, with their junior officers in various stages of breathless dressing and arming themselves, awaited his orders. Only Hortensius was absent, not yet back from his mission.

'Our well-rehearsed plans for siege are useless to us now we are so breached. Januarius! Let your men take care of the headquarters. Blockade the surrounding streets so that this rabble cannot career through on horseback. Victor! Round up the largest group of auxiliaries you can find. Get them outside the gates somehow and attacking the enemy from the rear, creating as many diversions as possible. The signal posts may be sabotaged. Use four of your men to take different routes to Kanovium. It is imperative we get help. Take these tablets of authorization.' Both Januarius and Victor were gone before he could draw his next breath.

'Timerius! Gather as many of your men as you can find and head for the southwest gate. That is our strongest defence. Get food, water and medical supplies up there, as well as arms! We shall need them if we are to hold out. Gaius, take back the northwest gate and the route to the port. Cerialis, as usual, concentrate on the southeast gate, but save a rescue detail to get any injured men to the safety of the bathhouse. Abandon the area to the Northeast. We have no hope of saving the buildings. The Gods are in our favour, as long as the winds do not change. Go! For the Glory of Rome and our Emperor Severus Alexander!'

The Ordovicans had already discovered the barn of animal fodder near the northeast gate and had set it ablaze. The smoke was choking and filled the air, mingling with the screams of legionaries in their blazing quarters. Vipsanius could see there was only one rampart which was holding and that was the southwesterly gate, with its constantly manned ballista, catapulting a rain of arrows at both man and beast. He must concentrate his manpower in that area until he had won back the fortress for the Glory of Rome.

Dith and Demeter had worked hard to settle all their patients for the night. There was only one legionary with a fever, and another who had undergone surgery, who would have to be tended during the hours of dark; and they would take turns of four hourly shifts with that. They were settled cosily in the sanctuary of the pharmacy, chewing on some stewed mutton and sipping the last of their wine quota from their regulation wooden cups, when they heard the first signs of invasion. They had already barred the door, but would it hold?

The infirmary had been designed to be light and airy - wooden shutters at four-foot intervals down the length of the building. Dith unbolted one and peered out to see the matter. It did not take him long to understand that they were in grave danger. Ordovican warriors were already whooping their way towards the building, carrying flaming torches. They would try to torch the roof, but its recent slates, replacing the old tiles, would hold good, he hoped. The next thing they would try would be torching the window shutters. Once those took hold, the whole building would go up.

'Demeter, the best chance we have is to carry our patients through the pharmacy and out to the back alley. If we smear enough blood upon them and ask them to play dead, we can lay them against the opposite wall, out of harms way, until this thing is finished one way or another.'

'Shouldn't we stay and fight? That would be more honourable, surely?'

'And die for certes, all our patients too? Demeter, I can already smell the singeing of the shutters. Come quickly. There are several who could manage to walk it themselves. Here's blood from that amputation we did this afternoon. Make it look horrendous.'

In the end, they only had to carry two patients between them. It was amazing how fear of death by fire could move the immobile. They hobbled and dragged themselves to safety, smearing fresh red blood near their hearts, as though they had been stabbed. Only the amputee and the man with the fever did not understand what was happening and had to be manhandled outside the rear door.

They were just in time. No sooner had they deposited the second man upon the ground, against the back wall of a barracks building in the alley, than the sound of pounding hooves drew close.

A hoard of half naked Ordovicans, riding of necessity single file, raced past them, towering above them, their spears ready to take any life they could find. Dith could have screamed in pain as a hoof kicked his knee bone, but he gritted his teeth and screamed out in mind only. The man with fever lay at the end of the line shivering and vomiting. Dith lay on his face, not daring to move a muscle, despite the stench making him want to heave. Demeter had poured blood over his back. He hoped he looked a convincing corpse. A moment later he knew from the cries and death throes that some Ordovican warrior had thought to put the man with the fever out of his misery. He probably would have died anyway.

The fire in the infirmary had now taken good hold and when it reached full ferocity, the roof timbers could hold no longer. There was a tremendous crashing, with dust and mortar flying, as the new slates slithered to their smashing doom. By some miracle most slates slid to the front of the building, otherwise they would have been buried alive in the rubble.

The sick men tried not to move as the earth shook beneath them. They were frightened they would take the same fate as their colleague.

Two grim hours later, Dith passed the whispered instruction down the line to move against the shell of the infirmary wall. It would be warm against the stones in the chill of dawn. He suspected the amputee would die soon in any case, but he might as well die without the added discomfort of cold. Demeter helped Dith to carry the man across the alleyway in the gloom of early light. The man's breath came in rasps. 'My savings...I have no family...Give them to Nesta...for the children. You never know, one of them may be mine.'

'There are a few who have a look of you, Renatus. We shall do all we can,' whispered Demeter gently. 'Dith, have you any valerian with you? His pain is becoming unbearable. I am afraid he will start to cry out soon and we shall be noticed.'

Dith had a tiny metal flask, cast in Celtic scrollwork on a thong about his neck. He tipped some of the contents onto Renatus's tongue and within minutes they felt him relax more and begin to breathe more evenly.

For a moment Dith envied him his peace. Who knew what tortures lay ahead for the rest of them? The outcome had not yet been decided. The din of battle had not ceased. But there was an occasional lull. Thank goodness the wind was blowing from the Southwest, taking the majority of the smoke away from them. Otherwise fits of coughing might have betrayed them.

The southwest tower nearby still held, but manpower was becoming increasingly stretched, as the Ordovicans retreated, rested and then re-attacked, wave upon ceaseless wave. There were barely three hundred legionaries left now, against what seemed like a thousand warriors still harrying the fort. Had Vipsanius not sent for reinforcements from Kanovium? Did he not realise they were done for unless help arrived?

Vipsanius ensured all fit and fighting men, along with weapons and some food and water supplies, were directed towards the southwest tower. There was a chance they might be able to hold out until back-up troops came from Kanovium, the Roman fortress in the mountains to the East. The signalling posts on the hills linking the fortress of Segontium with that of Kanovium had been sabotaged. No reply was had from the first link station when they raised the flaming signals. Help must be had, by sending messengers. Of the four envoys he had sent with the same message by different routes, two, he knew, were already dead, cut down before they even reached the gates, but the other two he hoped to the Gods had got through.

He now left the fighting to his centurions and their very able infantrymen. The Ordovicans would have prepared well for this battle, invoking their Gods, singing hymns of praise, sounding their war horns and drumming up their courage with oratory. He too must urgently beseech Minerva at the Sacellum shrine, asking for some miracle.

He took several trusted legionaries with him. They must guard the headquarters and all it stood for. Here was the regimental shrine with its statue of Minerva, Goddess of warriors, with her owl perched upon her shoulder, ready to see into the dangers of the night. She held a spear in her hand, ready to pierce the hearts of all enemies. Why had they been taken by surprise? Had they all become too complacent about vigilance? Was Minerva displeased with their work? She had not protected her worshippers. Was she angry? Had she felt neglected?

Vipsanius knelt and kissed the hem of the statue's tunic.

'We have been negligent in our duties, O sweet Goddess of preservation. We must redress what negligence there has been. Show sweet mercy. Accept the blood of the dead which lie all around you, as sacrifice enough, and turn around our fortunes, that we may hold the fortress of Segontium for the Glory of Rome!'

He gazed up into the eyes of the statue, but he could detect no answer, only a thought in his head that he should shift his gaze to the left. It was then to his horror he realised the standard was still there; the great standard with its great eagle atop, its wings swooping over the enemy to claim victory for Rome, carrying in its talons the power of Jupiter, Father of the Gods. It stood proud and unmoved by the chaos outside. Its gold emblazoned victory wreaths, twined their way to the base, set in its stone trestle, awaiting Leontes.

Leontes was the *aquilifer* or standard-bearer, who, bedecked in lion skin over his chained mail, rode with the standard into all battles. The men looked to the standard for comfort and guidance. It symbolised strength and courage. It symbolised, on the one hand, the indomitable power of the Roman Empire and, on the other, the paternal care of its law and order. The standard's commands were those of the deified emperor and its signals in battle obeyed implicitly. Leontes always stayed close to Vipsanius in times of trouble to take orders, as did Vitellius his apprentice. Neither was to be seen. Vipsanius assumed they were dead or held captive, otherwise the standard would be out there, leading the men, awaiting his commands.

He hurriedly finished his prayers and went through to the office at the rear of the headquarters, where Antoninus, the chief actarius and scribe, sat with his head in his hands.

Vipsanius pulled him up sharply. 'We are not lost yet, Antoninus. Have more faith in your Goddess. I am leaving you with a small band of armed men. You must protect the regimental shrine, here in the headquarters, with your lives. Is that understood?' Antoninus nodded ashamedly in response, but dared not speak. He could feel a trembling starting in his body and this was shame enough, without a trembling voice to boot.

'Pull a rug and move the altar over the trap to the underground strong room. The Ordovicans will be after booty, as well as severed heads to boast about. Draw water from the well in the courtyard and douse the timbers. I do not want this building destroyed.' Vipsanius strode purposefully out towards the Saccellum. 'I must get the standard to our men and give them courage to hold out.'

He took the standard in his hands and kissed it reverently, then ordered his men to cluster round him with their shields. This was going to take some doing, but he was determined to get to his men at all costs.

Llew was curious about the preparations for Beltane, and his excited chatter mingled a pitch higher than that of the older children. They were gathering wood for the Beltane fires the following evening and singing the pathways alive as they worked. Grandfather Gwilym was supervising the bondsmen and Owain, as they erected a huge bole to the South of the festival clearing. There was much tugging on ropes and orders to heave. Llew ran under the ropes, as quick as a mountain cat.

'Llew! You menace!' Uncle Owain complained. 'You will get yourself strangled yet. Go down to *Nain* Nanw's hut and see your Mam. She'll be working some magic and might be able to calm you down.'

'Will she turn you into a toad if I ask her nicely, Uncle

Owain?' grinned Llew, repeating a joke he had heard Owain himself use.

'Na! More likely she will turn this chill wind around and give us a dry warm evening. Now! Go!'

Llew scuttled away, dodging Owain's pretended spanking. He would go down the path to the breast of the headland, where Mam would be chanting her spells on the threshold of the hut, with its squiggly pictures on the doorframe; but first he would climb right to the top of the knoll, so that he could pretend to be King of Prydain.

He scrambled through the rocky, lichened outcrops and greening heather, grazing his knees, but he did not care. In a moment he would be King of the whole world. By the time he reached the summit of the knoll, his breathing was laboured and his little limbs ached and ached. He heard a mewed greeting behind him and saw that Luce had followed him. She was more like a dog than a cat, always following him if he left the enclosure, as though to check on him.

'Look, Luce! I am King of all Prydain. I can see for leagues and leagues! I can see the whale-shaped headland to the East, and the top of Eryri, still crowned with snow. I can see down the dragon's tail of Lleyn to the West.' He had heard this rehearsed many times as his cousins played the same game, so he made a clumsy attempt at sweeping imperious arm movements, which nearly cost him his balance. But he had never felt like this before. He really did feel Prince of all his kingdom, and he felt his connection with it, as sure as a babe knows how to find its mother's breast. This land was so beautiful, and one day it would fall into his care. He did not know how, but it would. He was too young to stop and examine the thought, but he was old enough to enjoy its certainty, as it took root in his mind.

He sat and watched as the Sun set on the eve before Beltane and bathed the mainland in its glorious light, casting its orange glow across the mountains. Then, relaxed, lulled by the evening birdsong, he lay back upon the springy turf and looked into the deep-blue sky overhead. Luce climbed upon his chest and nuzzled close to his face, making him chuckle delightedly at her tickling devotion.

'I will be the King and you shall be the Queen and there will be no sorrow in our kingdom. My people will be kind to cats and I shall pass a law that you may not be drowned, nor stuck on a spear for sport.' Luce purred her approval and they dozed together for a little while, as the last warm rays of the Sun warmed the mountain.

The shrill cry of a buzzard overhead made Llew jump. The evening had turned chill, but very clear. He sprang to his feet and Luce jumped from him, disgruntled. He must get back to Ceridwen before she sent a search party for him. Prince or no prince of Prydain, Mam would be cross that he had not returned home before dark. It was then that he noticed a pall of smoke coming from the direction of Segontium, at the head of the 'dragon's mouth'. There was an orange glow beginning to light up the darkening sky. His father and the soldiers he lived with must be celebrating their Beltane a day early. It must be a big fire! Perhaps his father had to have two Beltanes, one at his fort and another one here with Mam.

He scrambled down the rugged pathway, through the trees that protected the hut at Cae Gwynion. There was smoke coming from the centre of the thatch. He knew that his mother was still there, for on leaving she always doused her fire.

Ceridwen felt strangely tired, her limbs felt heavy with the mere walk up the mountain, but her heart did occasional leaps with the thought of seeing Marcus early on the morrow. How she loved that man. Just to behold his face, smiling at her, was enough to send joy speeding through her veins. She would see him soon and he would hold her in his arms like that first Beltane. She marvelled how, once she had allowed his love into her heart, the resentment that he was Roman seemed to fade into insignificance.

A family of swallows had decided to take up residence in Nanw's deserted hut, so that when Ceridwen arrived to clean and bless it, it was soiled everywhere. The parent birds were flying freely in and out of the door, left open wide by some careless pilgrim.

She stood upon a trestle and could just reach into the mud nest, clinging precariously to the shelf of a rafter. She probed gently with her fingers. If there were eggs, she would have to wait for the brood to hatch and fledge before she could lock the door again. She was shocked and thrilled to find five tiny silken nestlings, which suddenly woke and began cheeping and reaching for food. She would have to do her work here intermittently, so that the parents would feel safe to return with food to the nest.

The first time they ventured in she was washing down the trestle seats. They screeched with alarm and would not go near their nest, for fear of betraying their young ones' whereabouts. First they beat their wings against the mud and wattle walls of the circular building in blind panic. Then they tried to distract her away and to follow them through the doorway into the bright sunshine outside. She sat very still and used her hands in blessing to soothe away their fear.

Gradually they began to trust her, so that now, when they flew in, she retired to the opposite wall and stayed there quietly until they had finished their work and left.

It was a necessary irritation, which slowed down her own day's work, but she felt so blessed by their trust that it melted her frustration away. There was just a niggling thought that began to worm its way to her full consciousness. Where was Mwg? Apart from times of frost, when he came down to Tan Yr Aur to be warmed and fed, he kept guard here. He would not have allowed the swallows to take up residence.

She left her work and prayed to know his whereabouts. Instinctively she was drawn towards Nanw's resting place, still crowned with its mound of stones, each one placed with reverence by someone with regard for her.

The stench of Mwg's body soon gave notice of where he lay, in the underhedge of the hawthorn flowers. Carrion had already made good meal of him, but she knew it was he. No other cat had such a smudging of grey whiskers about the neck. He had tried to get to Nanw's grave, but had collapsed before quite reaching it. She knew it was unseemly to howl with grief so. After all, he was only a cat, but, whilst he had lived, there seemed a vestige of Nanw's life still with them.

She fetched a shovel from the awning of the hut and buried him with fresh herbs and dignity at Nanw's feet. She could hear the men working in the neighbouring festival clearing, but she hoped her work would go unnoticed. She wanted no one to witness her snivelling sadness. Nothing must spoil tomorrow's Beltane.

She need not have worried. No one came to the hut to help her. They were all too busy preparing the clearing with its two great fires and bole. She was grateful of the privacy and, as she washed her hair in the stream, the cool waters washed away her tears. She would stay quietly in the hut and prepare herself an evening meal, then go down into the fields to greet Coll and the neighbours from Din Silwy, where they were to make camp for the night.

She was stirring her broth over the fire, when she heard Llew's excited voice. 'Mam! Mam! Come and see the dragon's breath. Father must have his Beltane a day early!'

'Llew! What do you mean, 'dragon's breath'?'

Llew tugged at her and she followed him in the growing twilight to a spot above the tree line overlooking the festival clearing.

There was no mistaking it now. Segontium was ablaze. How the lookouts, on the rise above, had missed it, she could not fathom. She was seized by panic and dragged Llew roughly down towards the festival clearing, where she could hear the men still at work. As she passed Nanw's hut, she caught a fleeting glimpse of someone by the threshold. Marcus! It was Marcus and no mistaking him, standing in the doorway with the firelight glowing behind him, giving him a sort of halo.

The joy of knowing he was safe was such an immense relief. She paused and stared, expecting him to smile and greet her.

'Mam,' Llew bleated, pulling at her sleeve. 'Mam, why are you staring?'

In the next blink Marcus was gone and she knew she had witnessed his *sending*. Then she remembered his parting words, *'From this time onwards, I shall have a new special place to go to in times of trouble. Here at this threshold I shall be with*

317

you...whenever I have need.'

Ceridwen froze momentarily, then wordlessly, relentlessly dragged Llew the remaining short distance to the festival clearing. Uncomprehending and thinking he had done something terrible, Llew ran to the safety of his grandfather's arms.

'Where is Madog?' Ceridwen found herself screeching. 'Find him, Owain, and tell him to sound urgent council upon his horn! Father...Segontium is attacked. Eithig has arisen at last!'

It was not to be the gentle loving reunion that Coll was anticipating with his sister. He had never found her so hysterical and lacking in control. Once she had understood what was happening at Segontium, her vision sharpened and she was able to see, in her minds eye, each horror as it unfolded. She felt the pain of burning upon her flesh and the shafts of spears through her breast. But worst of all, came the dread that Marcus may be harmed and the fear of it clouded her vision to knowledge of him. She screamed and writhed tortuously and fell at Coll's feet as he approached.

He lifted her and tried to soothe her. Gently he held her head between his hands and raised her eyes to his. 'Ceridwen! Sweet sister! Stop partaking in the atrocities you see and come back to us here. Now! We need you to help the Council. You need to be calm and tell plainly what you see.'

For a few moments she continued to shake with terror and then, swaying slightly, she called herself back to the mountain and composed herself, standing still before Coll and the crowd which had gathered around her. There was dread silence whilst they awaited her revelations.

The words fell from her lips like leaden weights...'Eithig has raised tribe upon tribe to fall upon Segontium. The women and children are not being spared. It is an attack of great cowardice and deceit. Not only the fortress is ablaze, but the port is invaded and its inhabitants are being slaughtered!'

For four years, Coll had been waiting for the opportunity to face Eithig. He must not escape justice this time.

'Now is our chance to seize Eithig. If the battle still rages as

Ceridwen advises, then we must join the fray and search him out. What say we men go tonight and lose no time?'

'Ie!' was the inflamed response, for all there remembered the murderings of four Beltanes gone and the deceit of their so-called Lord.

'But which side do we fight for? Are we for or against the Romans?' queried Owain.

'Father what say you?' said Coll uncomfortably, for he was a man of action and felt a novice in the art of diplomacy.

'I think we should go, but not fight with either side unless we are attacked. Remember our purpose in going. It is primarily to capture Eithig and bring him to justice.'

'But we shall be taken for Ordovicans and the Romans will slay us!' objected Owain.

'The warriors will be painted. We go as we are in our work clothes,' countered Coll. 'We must do all we can to defend the civilians in the port below Segontium, for they are Ordovicans too, remember.'

"Tis best we go down to Tan Yr Aur and take horses and weapons,' Gwilym advised. He stared at the position of the rising Moon. 'The tide will be low across the Straits. We can cross over at Dindaethwy if we are lucky and take the men of Daethwy with us.'

All nodded in agreement. Then Coll became decisive.

'Yes, we shall cross this night and rest near Heli, before coming on Segontium at dawn. Hedfan, ride to Cerrig y Gwyddyl and bring men from there to meet us at Dindaethwy. Ceridwen, take charge here and perform rites with the women and children, which will appease the Gods and aid us in our endeavour.'

'Forgive me Coll, but you must see that it is impossible for me to stay here!' whispered Ceridwen in consternation. 'I must find Marcus. There are many injured and our healing skills are required. We shall need a field hospital, if the survivors are to stand a chance of becoming well again. Let me take some young women with me and we can leave the older women to care for the children and perform the rites. Old Betw can take charge of proceedings here. She has powers.'

'You are right. Best take materials with you for litters and bandages. Now, to Tan yr Aur.'

Marged knew something was amiss when she heard the shouts from the mountain. The knot in her stomach refused to go away. She and the women greeted the men, as they barged into the enclosure and immediately set about digging up the weapons of war.

'Gwilym! Will someone tell me what is happening? All I can make sense of is that you plan to kill Eithig.'

'It is time for his come-uppance. He has roused the mainland tribes to rise against Segontium. We must take him before he disappears into the mountains again.'

'But all the menfolk are going. Are you going to leave us defenceless here?'

'There will be Romans left behind at the hill fort who will look after you. They are not stupid enough to leave the area unmanned. Tomorrow morning, I want you to visit with some food as usual and tell the commandant why we have gone.'

'But what about the rites...the rites of Beltane? They ensure our future.'

'You must manage best you can with the children and Old Betw. Ceridwen comes with us. We need her to minister to the harmed.'

'No Gwilym! No! Not all my family, for Bel's sake! You could all be killed, every one of you. I could be left here alone to become bitter and twisted in my old age. Do not go. I beg of you.'

'I could not sleep at night if I did not do this, Marged. A man is no man if he has no honour. Besides, you shall need me to watch out for those three precious sons of yours.'

'Three! It is unbelievable. You mean to take Hedfan with you?'

'He is sixteen. He will soon be a man. It would be *geas* not to take him with us. He will father a child soon. What man is he if he does not fight for his own?'

Marged crumpled defeated upon the bench by the threshold

of their hut. She knew Gwilym to be right, but maternal protective instinct for her family took precedence. She could see only sorrow coming from this. She already felt robbed of her family, even though nothing had harmed them so far.

Gwilym was impatient to be gone, but he paused a moment, reading Marged's despair. 'Keep the hearth warm for our homecoming,' he said, a sudden rush of tenderness welling in his throat and betraying itself in his voice. 'I shall do my best and the Gods will do the rest. Will you bless me Marged?'

'Ie. I will bless you and be with you in mind. I shall boss you and admonish you, until you come safe home to me with my children!'

Silently, a smile of age-long love broke through her anxiety and she blessed and embraced him. She hung onto the moment and cherished it, marking it to memory, in case this was the last time she would ever see him alive.

Coll and Owain had assembled, with the other menfolk and the horses, by the gate to the enclosure. Ceridwen was busily packing the last of her supplies in a saddlebag and giving instructions to Non, a very capable maiden from Din Silwy, who had been the only volunteer to agree to help her run the field hospital. It was not for her compassion that Non would be most useful, but for her sturdiness and ability to fetch and carry. She chattered excitedly, seeing all as an adventure. Ceridwen knew that was all about to change, but felt it unkind to belabour the horrors they were about to face. Instead she smiled encouragingly, belying her own anxiety. Her constant prayers under her breath would have to do. There was no time to perform holy rites.

She now had the flood of fear in her under control. Doing something was her major aid and the busyness kept a good deal of the visions at bay. She crossed to the hut that she had cleaned and prepared for Marcus's arrival. Nanw's ceremonial robe hung from a rafter, freshly prepared on a rope through the sleeves. She cut it down and held it achingly to her body. This was to have been her Beltane robe with which she would bless the proceedings. Its golden threads called to her in the firelight and she held the faded red cloth to her cheek, inhaling the familiar smell of lavender oil and mint.

On sudden impulse she rolled it and squashed it into her saddlebag. There was no parting from it. It would have to go with her, practicality aside. She was ready now; ready to face what the Gods had prepared for her as her lot; ready to do her duty by her kith and kin, whatever the cost to herself. The hardest part would be to leave little Llew. He had finished suckling long ago, but still crept close to her of nights. Marged would find him a comfort, no doubt, and keep a special eye on him.

Marged glanced towards the flurry of preparations by the gate. Simultaneously, as though with one mind, her brood responded to her need and came to bid her farewell. Coll and Owain wordlessly embraced her in turn. Ceridwen held both her mother's hands and focused upon their work-worn beauty. 'It will not be long, Mam. We shall be with you again before another Moon. All shall be well.'

'Lift your eyes to mine and say that with conviction, Ceridwen. You cannot. You see some tragedy unfolding, as I do, and yet you go to play your part.'

'We must all play our parts and Eithig must be routed out and vanquished. Only then shall we have a measure of peace,' Coll interjected.

'Peace will come, Mam,' added Owain.

'At what price, my dear ones? At what price?'

⌘ ⌘ ⌘

CHAPTER XXII

✠

THE RECKONING

Marcus beat off an Ordovican warrior, who was attempting to cleave open his head with a huge axe. He was quick enough to dodge the blow and come up under the man's shield to thrust his sword into his chest. It would not be a quick death. Marcus's aim at the heart had misfired, but the wound under the ribs would be fatal, he saw, as he threw off the man and withdrew his sword. The bay pony, which had taken him up towards the fort had reared and whinnied once they drew close to the fighting, unused to the clashing sounds and the cries in the smoke laden air.

Lord Geraint and his comrades decided to circle the fort and seize any opportunity to gain entry. Geraint was still mounted on what seemed a fearless black hunter, as thickset and sturdy as its rider. His cloak, the colour of ruby-red wine, flashed with its golden, swirling markings in the glare of the fires and torches, as Marcus tried his best to keep up with him to no avail. There was no way his mount would brave it into the fray.

Giving up, Marcus dismounted by a hazel copse and tethered the pony within, in case he had need of him again. He soothed the pony, thinking what best to do next. The sound of sobbing reached him just a few yards away. Suspicious, in case he was being led into a trap, he crept forwards in the gloom to hear better the sounds.

'Damianus! O Minerva! Let him not die! Damianus! Do not

leave me here all alone. Do not go. I beg you!'

A sudden shift of the Moon from behind a cloud illuminated a young woman, leaning over a Roman legionary. He was unconscious or dead by the way she lifted his unresponsive head in her hands. A darkening pool of blood was still gushing from his hacked thigh.

'Pax, my lady! What is amiss here? I am the surgeon from the fort. Allow me to see if I can help him?'

The woman drew up proudly to full height, her tunic soaked with the man's blood.

'He is my man. He was sent to Kanovium to fetch help, but called by my father's house to take me with him on the back of his horse. My father cleaved him with his butcher's axe. We escaped, but we had to dismount when Damianus lost consciousness.'

'The orders? Do you have the orders from Vipsanius?'

'Look under his breastplate,' she suggested, defiantly wiping the tears from her face with the back of her hand.

Marcus slid his hand between the tightly fitting breastplate and the legionary's chain mail until his fingers made contact with the parchment. Tentatively he drew it out, wrapped in its large pigskin wallet.

'I am sorry. There is nothing I can do for him. He has lost too much blood. He is dead.' Marcus challenged her anguished cry of response and caught her wrists before she was able to fling herself upon the corpse.

'Listen! You cannot help your man, but you can make sure that many others like him do not die. Take my horse and ride five leagues along this road by coast and mountain, until you arrive at Kanovium. Do not stop until you give the commandant there this pouch personally.' For a moment Marcus did not know whether she would do his bidding. She stared fixedly at the lifeless form upon the ground. Then she raised her gaze to his and said, 'I will go. I will go for Damianus and his friends. Please, take his body into the copse and cover it with branches. I shall bury him when I return.'

The woman mounted the pony. It was a better size for her than the legionary mount and Marcus was hoping the larger legionary horse would prove better for his own needs. She grimly gritted her teeth to fend off another flood of tears and kicked flank, setting a fleeing pace for her steed and was gone like a bolt of lightening.

It was pointless to try and gain entry to the fort. The fighting was thickest around each of the four gateways. Geraint's ploy was to pick off warriors from the rear as they charged forwards. Marcus decided to use his new mount to join him and seize opportunity to gain entry whenever the opportunity presented itself. He mounted and noted the horse was completely obedient to his touch.

For a moment he stared into the nightmare confusion of shouting and flames, uncertain where to head for the best. A few yards in front of him, a woman appeared. He did not recognise her immediately. Her face was twisted in terror, but, as her arms reached out to him, her expression softened and a vision of Ceridwen rose up towards him. A second later he felt a breath pass over him, brushing him like a cobweb and she was gone, leaving behind her need of him, her yearning for him carving a chasm into his heart.

Whether the horse sensed something too, or was responding to Marcus's tension, he did not know, but the horse shifted in fear, as though assailed from some quarter. Marcus pulled himself together as he steadied the horse, but his purpose was resolved. He would come through this battle, no matter what, for Ceridwen had need of him. His hand searched automatically for her amulet about his neck, entwined with Leona's precious locket, but it was not there.

The band from Mynydd Llwydiarth picked up more strength upon the way; Lord Meurig being as determined as Coll that Eithig would meet justice, once and for all. And, by the time the Daethwy had armed themselves and collected provisions, Hedfan rode in from Cerrig y Gwyddyl to say that a band of fifty or so were on their way to join them.

It took almost an hour to cross the Straits to the mainland from Dindaethwy. It was done by ferry, by swimming the horses and by little fishing coracles owned by the Daethwy. A huge net traversed the expanse across and prevented vessels and horses being swept away by several dangerous eddying currents. It was useful, but disentangling horses' legs became a problem and inevitably slowed down proceedings.

Once across, the band swelled with men from the small trading settlement on the mainland side. And again, towards midnight, when they reached Heli, a small fishing village half way along the shoreline to their goal, the fishermen were adamant about joining them; for they were heartily sick of Eithig's forages to plunder their catch.

Coll decided they should stop and rest. The horses were in need of a rub down and refreshment and they were all weary. They would rest for an hour. Soon it would be Beltane and time to light the ritual fires. Ceridwen drew alongside the old priestess of Heli, bent and gnarled as a twisted hawthorn and watched her as she blessed their preparations. The ancient's voice tremoured with age and failed to project across the festival clearing. Ceridwen heard her own voice, strong and commanding, belying her bodily weakness and underlying fear.

'May Bel look down upon us and give us strength to deliver this region from the terror of Eithig. May we take strength from our forefathers and wisdom from our mothers. We sacrifice the unions, which should have been taking place this coming night, to the splendour of our just cause! Be ye all strong! Be ye blessed!' Ceridwen gave them blessing.

The old priestess nodded her approval, bearing no grudge that Ceridwen had seen fit to take over. She wordlessly signalled her own blessing; whilst the young girl, who should have been their Queen of Beltane, embraced her lover and bade farewell, tears streaming from her lovelorn eyes. Then, remembering her regal role, the maiden took up three torches from the need fire and blessed all before the onslaught.

'Thrice blessed is thrice victorious,' Ceridwen murmured to the menfolk in her family as she embraced each one of them.

'Are you not going to embrace me, Sister?'

Ceridwen gasped. It was Ness, clinging on to Madog for

dear life.

'I thought...'

'I know. You thought I had stayed safely at home with the family. I could not tell Mam I was leaving. I could not face her sorrow. Only Olwenna knew my plan to join you and has sworn to take care of the children. You helped me so much, Ceridwen. How can I not help you now?'

'O Ness! Dear sister. We shall be formidable together!'

Thus heartened, Ceridwen faced the rest of the journey to Segontium, still fearful of what she would face, but finding that the weak feeling in her body had been replaced by the strength and determination contagious from those around her.

When the opportunity came, Marcus was able to make his way towards Lord Geraint without much of a challenge. The Ordovicans seemed to be retreating from the barrage of missiles coming from the fortress walls to the South. Now they were more interested in thrusting towards the northwest and southeast gates. There was a good chance that Marcus and his comrades could gain entry, if the guards to the southwest gate recognised him. He drew level with Geraint. Geraint nodded his assent and called all his men to him with a piercing blast on a high-pitched whistle.

Vipsanius was there atop the tower. He thought he recognised Geraint's ceremonial cloak and then he caught sight of Marcus in a flash of torchlight.

'Plutonius! Instruct the guards to let down the causeway bridge briefly and allow access to Lord Geraint and his men!' Although a small band of painted riders whooped and cried, as though they aimed to attack them as they crossed, they were driven back by a tirade of fiery missiles from the tower.

Marcus was relieved to find himself once more by Vipsanius's side. If the Gods decreed that this was to be his day of death, then at least he would be serving his friend to the end. If they were to be spared, then they would share victory.

'My family, Marcus? What has befallen Rhiannon and Correlia?' queried Vipsanius urgently between commands.

'They are safe across the water to Mona. They are in good hands, never fear.'

Vipsanius threw him a grateful look of relief and pressed on.

Hortensius was incredulous at the speed with which the Ordovican warriors took hold of the fortress from the northeast gateway. Legionaries and auxiliaries were fleeing from the barrage of barracks in that area, scrambling into armour and trying to salvage arms from their besieged quarters. It would be no use now trying to put out the blaze to the forage store. As long as the wind remained a southwesterly, it would be best to let it burn out and defend the rest of the fort. He ordered them to flee to the South of the fort, which had not yet been breached and was less likely to be set ablaze.

'Get yourselves to safety. Head for the barracks to the South of the main street and get the injured to the bathhouse. Take whatever arms you can lay hold on!' The bathhouse to the South had a good source of water from a diverted spring. That would be the best place to send the injured. It would also provide fresh water to help them hold out, until reinforcements arrived.

Hortensius knew that anyone not carrying a shield would stand little chance of survival across the several streets to safety. The Ordovicans seemed to surge across the fort at rhythmic intervals, mowing down any fleeing soldier under the hooves of their warhorses. 'Form a barrage with your shields for each other and get moving! We shall only survive enmasse!' he yelled.

Wave after wave tried to cross the fort to the relative safety of the southwest gate, but not only were the Ordovican warriors fearless, so were their mounts. They charged across the shield barrages and mowed them down as if they were mere scraps of parchment.

They were followed by painted warriors on foot, yelling and daring the soldiers to engage in swordplay. Once distracted by one-to-one combat, they were charged at by warriors in chariots; thrusting spears into vulnerable places; cutting away their legs from beneath them.

Only half the men in the Roman barracks to the North reached the safety of the southern area, where they could join forces with their comrades and rain down missiles and pila from the fortress walls. The rest perished, or worse, were dismembered alive.

The battle raged all night. At one stage, it looked as though the Roman forces would hold the main street and the surrounding buildings of the commandant's house, the workshops and the headquarters, but a fresh surge from the Ceiri, managing to breach the northwest and southeast gates simultaneously, put paid to that.

Eventually, Hortensius managed to reach the southwest tower, where Vipsanius had hoisted the regimental standard and was directing proceedings. He noted with relief that Marcus fought alongside the waging legionaries, hurling pila and lead slingers with deadly accuracy and standing close to Vipsanius. His friend was safe for this moment in time.

Hortensius surveyed the fray. It was getting light. Surely the reinforcements from Kanovium would be arriving soon? The Ordovican warriors had driven the cavalry horses beyond the walls and captured them for their own purposes. He could see a rider now, astride a white mare, his purple cloak billowing behind him, circling the plundered legionary horseflesh with satisfaction.

Now the chieftain reined in and gave commands. Next, he drove with his band of warriors unscathed and swift as the cutting edge of a scythe, through the southeast gate. Hortensius was mesmerized. What would this monster of the mountains do next? He expected Eithig to go for the military headquarters, destroy the regimental shrine and plunder the regimental pay from the strong room. But Eithig had other things in mind. He and his entourage began circling again and again the commandant's house. It was obvious he was searching for a point of entry. There was no need now for torchlight. The glow of a sunlit dawn was making a shy appearance above the summit of Yr Wyddfa. It should have been a perfect Beltane, perfumed by the hawthorn flowers, not this stench of blood and smoke.

'I think it is Eithig,' Hortensius warned Vipsanius. 'No other has a white mare. He is famous for his mount. And look, he wears a helmet with a strange bronze hawk winging flight from it.'

'You are right, Hortensius. It is certainly Eithig riding Gwyngariad, but his men have just ignited their torches. There are at least two hundred of them. The cowards! They are going to try torching the women and children!'

Before Vipsanius had time to give new orders in response, there was a great long blow on the Ordovican war horn, followed by a long low roll on a drum. The warriors ceased their attack and grew still, retreating from their quarry in wary slow motion.

Ceridwen and Ness rode together on dun and grey ponies respectively. Non rode behind them in a supply cart, which had travelled with them from Heli. The adventure was already tarnished by her saddle soreness, so she cushioned herself with a pile of blankets.

On the horizon to the West they could see the smoke beckoning. Non's thrill of the unknown was countered by the sense of growing dread in Ceridwen and Ness. Theirs would be a mission of mercy indeed, ministering to mangled and burned flesh. Ceridwen knew she must be strong for the other two women. She knew the strength would come. Nanw would be by her side; a voice in her head advising; a power in her hands healing. But if Marcus were injured...or worse? What then? How was she supposed to respond, if the source of her happiness were cut down? Whilst he was in the world, there was such hope. They had both walked across the bridge of prejudice and begun to love the other for their true essence. Their physical attraction was so strong that, when they met after a parting, there was a flash of energy between them as they first touched. But at a deeper level they had come to sense the needs of the other, to talk freely as they had never talked to another.

Faced with the possibility of losing Marcus to the next world, Ceridwen felt a great surge of love in her breast. Who would have guessed that from their first meeting, when she was tortured by longings for him and confused by race hatred, she would become so emotionally dependent upon him.

'Ness, does it frighten you sometimes, the way you love Madog?'

'It scares me that I might be widowed young and that it may happen upon this trip.'

'No, I do not mean are you scared of losing him to death, but that you fear your happiness to be totally ensnared in his well-being. If he is unhappy, then you are unhappy. If he is sad, then you are sad?'

'Oh, I cannot allow Madog's swings in mood to affect me. The children must be cheered, whether their father is disappointed with his hunting or no.'

Ceridwen did not know how to reply. It seemed to her that it was Madog who had the steady temperament and Ness who was prone to occasional bouts of testiness, usually due to her Moon phase. Ness obviously loved Madog, for she never looked at another man, but it was not the same as with Marcus and she. She realised with a sense of disappointment that Ness did not understand and never would.

They had only been on the road from Heli by half an hour, when a young woman rider came galloping into view. She was wary about stopping and drew her knife, but when Coll explained their mission, she relaxed a little. The horror of the battle came tumbling from her tongue in torrents, as she warned what they might find, but then she realised that she was losing time and insisted she continue on her way, to get help from Kanovium. She had to do something useful to ease her pain. Coll was equally insistent that she be escorted all the way and it was a reluctant Madog along with Cullen whom he chose for the task. Madog felt secure near Coll. Coll inspired him with such courage. It would be a test to obey his chieftain, but he knew many lives depended upon getting help from Kanovium. He must resign himself to it and take leave of Ness. A swift smile of farewell was all he gave and Ness grew acutely aware of the pain she had inflicted upon him these past few years.

The young woman hesitated suspiciously as Madog and Cullen took up their places alongside her, but her mount, encouraged by the eagerness of fresh ponies from Heli, was eager to be off on the journey and they soon picked up speed; setting out anew to beg rescue. If they rode hard it might take two hours. It would take longer for the troops to come. They had a small cavalry contingent at Kanovium; but, as at Segontium, the majority were foot soldiers.

The early dawn was breaking when Coll and his followers came first to the port at the mouth of the Seiont. The cluster of huts around the shoreline was completely burned out. The men searched for bodies, but found none, until they came across the remains of a rectangular hut, with the scorched bodies of several women and legionaries...the whorehouse.

Could Ceridwen have been mistaken, thought Coll? He could see no children among the corpses and the houses were empty apart from tethered domestic animals, which had perished. He hoped to the Gods the children had escaped and were not held hostage.

The hush of the tide lamented with them, but the distant cries from Segontium, on the smoking ridge above the river, claimed their attention. The battle was still in spate. Eithig was there. Coll could sense it, like a hound scenting its quarry.

The street up to the fort was lined with wooden booths, as yet untouched by fire. Craftsmen's tools lay still where they had been dropped. Stew and victuals, prepared last evening, stood untouched in bowls, their vendors having fled.

'Coll! What think you about our using the booths for temporary beds?' Ceridwen suggested, never taking her eyes from the smoking fortress above them. 'Hedfan could help

Ness and Non set out blankets and bring buckets of fresh water from the nearest well.'

'Choose some other to help you, sister. You cannot shield your little brother from the fight he came to witness and the rescue he came to make.'

'You are right. I must not cheat him of his opportunity to prove himself. Look after him Coll. Guard him with your life.'

'I promise you that much, but you must come yourself up to the fort. I need you to help with your prayers and charms to ensnare our quarry.'

'I have barely ceased praying whilst we travelled. If the Gods are not with us in this, then they have closed their ears to our pleas.'

'Which God or Goddess would not listen to your supplication, sweet voice that you have? Come. We shall both put on our ceremonial robes, so that the warriors will know who we are. They might not have much respect for my position as chieftain of the Celwri, but for you, Ceridwen...descendant of an arch Druid...'

Ceridwen lost no time. As she tenderly pulled the folded garment from her saddlebag, the reds and golds of her ancestral robe caught the first rays of the early Sun. She brushed the threads of gold against her lips and for a fleeting moment inhaled the scent of her grandmother. Ness helped her to pull it over her head then wordlessly released Ceridwen's tresses from their braids. She rearranged the hair about her priestess's shoulders and prayed that the next time she touched her sister's hair it would not be at her funeral.

Ceridwen climbed astride her dun pony and Ness made sure that the folds of the garment splayed across the beast's ample rump. Coll was in readiness too; his cloak of purple and yellow plaid billowing from his shoulders and a circlet of gold glistening in the thick curls of his auburn hair; his burnished shield hanging from his horse's harness and his long sword in readiness to defend himself.

They now headed the entourage from Mona and Heli. Gwilym and Owain returned with their men from inspecting the lie of the land ahead.

'Skirt the northeast gate, where the fires are burning themselves out and head for the southeast gate. Things are quieting there!' Gwilym advised.

Marcus could not believe how quickly the hush fell. The air was pregnant with tension as both sides waited to hear the voice of their leader.

Eithig had nudged Gwyngariad along the *Via Principalis* to where it crossed with the *Via Praetoria*. He reined in immediately in front of the headquarters, to face Vipsanius, whom he could see, standing beneath the eagle standard atop the rampart to the southwest gate. A sea of fresh pila was poised to greet him, but he ignored the threat and paused, the torch still blazing in his hand.

'You see I have your family at my mercy, Vipsanius. How great is Rome to you? Would you sacrifice your women and children for the Glory of Rome? Are you all soldier, or is there a man in that uniform of yours?' he shouted.

'There is no bargain, Eithig! The garrison at Kanovium is already headed here! You are cut off from your retreat to the mountains and cut off from the port! There is no escape for you, especially if you harm the women and children!'

'You speak wisely. I would be a fool to kill my bargaining booty. But, if I were to enslave your wife and children, in recompense for all the misdeeds of Rome, you have a good bargain indeed. Very cheap would you not say? Perhaps you would grant me and my men safe passage, when you see a knife to your wife's throat and a torch to your child's face.'

'My wife and child have sought refuge on Mona. They are not here for you to take. Your spies have misinformed you,' Vipsanius countered.

'Then why' laughed Eithig mercilessly, 'have I heard the shrieking of frightened women and the crying of babes from within your courtyard? Do you deny that there are defenceless creatures within?'

'It is not the first Beltane you have defiled, Eithig!' It was not Vipsanius who answered, but Coll, slowly walking his warhorse from the southeast gate. The warriors recognised his station by the cloak and torc he wore; and the crowd parted in the street, so that he could approach Eithig. He reined in and stopped outside the main gate of the headquarters, then continued his accusation.

'You have defiled the Beltane Rites, seeking to win the hand of our Beltane Queen by treachery. You have condoned the rape and murder of Mona's virgins and been expelled from your land by your own people, who elected me in your stead. I have come to demand your arrest and trial and, if it not be by the court of Rome, then let it be by single combat here...you against me!'

'I, Priestess of Mynydd Llwydiarth, bear witness to the truth of Eithig's crimes!'

The assemblage gasped. The young woman who spoke was uncommonly beautiful and her demeanour regal as she drew level with Coll on her dun pony. The older warriors recognised her Druidic robes and nudged their younger companions with ominous whispers. To offer disrespect to such office was tantamount to defying the Gods. One opposed such office at immortal peril. She was to be respected, believed.

The morning breeze stirred and a crow cawed its greeting to a Beltane Queen. Ceridwen stared coolly at Eithig, sweeping a stray lock of her hair from her face as the breeze caught at her playfully. Those near her recognised Cadoc's ring upon her finger. So...his Druidic wisdom had not died with his death, but had been carried down by the female line. The murmurings and whispering went through the crowd.

Marcus was incredulous one moment; proud the next; then outraged that she should endanger herself so.

'Ye Gods it is my wife! It is my wife and her brother!' whispered Marcus urgently in his friend's ear. 'Vipsanius! Grant me leave to move beside her. I must go to her!'

'Peace. Be still, Marcus. There has been enough bloodshed and she may yet be the one who brings the warriors around. See how they shift uncomfortably before her gaze, like naughty children. She makes them feel badly behaved. I forbid you to move.'

He succumbed to Vipsanius's order, knowing that the situation hung in the balance and that he must not distract the crowd's attention from Ceridwen. Marcus's fear for her caught his throat and unconsciously he reached for the reassurance of her amulet entwined with Leona's locket. He had forgotten it was missing. He felt a dread like a leaden weight begin to fill his body. Breathlessly he closed his eyes in an attempt to bring his fear under control.

It was her voice that prised them open again and, as his gaze fell upon her, his yearning for her yawned like the greatest of chasms ready to swallow him alive.

'The Goddess has seen enough bloodshed and Bel has had his fill of blood this day. No more innocents must die. If there is to be a sacrifice to settle all, let you take me, Eithig. For it was your lust for me was your undoing. Blame all on me and take me as your hostage. Let all others go free!'

This was too much for Marcus and ignoring Vipsanius's orders he began to push his way through the legionaries, easing his way between their sea of swords and shields to the rampart steps. Vipsanius let him go. No one had heard Marcus's whispered request. He did not want to be obliged to arrest Marcus on the count of military disobedience.

Marcus found the steps too crowded with a melee of Roman infantry to negotiate, so he jumped into the only space he could detect and landed at someone's scarred, sandalled feet. They were Dith's feet. Dith knew instinctively where Marcus was headed and beckoned him to follow where he would least be noticed. He led his master, skirting the bathhouse and a barrack building, until they emerged in the main street between the southeast gate and where Coll and Ceridwen had halted. By now Coll's followers crowded the street and Marcus could make out the familiar shoulders of Owain and Gwilym above the rumps of their stocky mounts.

Old Cadwallader, the chief of the Ceiri tribe from the Lleyn, was sitting astride his strangely-painted, black mount and now joined Eithig, advising, warning, his raven eyes challenging, his grey beard carrying weight and authority. The chieftain was heartily sick of the pantomime and wanted to do what he was best at doing - retreat to his mountain fortress, having dealt the Romans a heavy blow. He knew his warriors were outnumbered and could not survive unless there was some room for negotiation. But his men had great respect for any descendant of Cadoc the Druid. This young woman must not be harmed. It would be especially *geas* at Beltane, the most sacred of festivals.

'If you harm a hair of that woman's head you are on your own. My men will not be party to it. We want a negotiated peace that states we walk free, if we agree not to harm the women and children.'

'You would fail me now, Cadwallader? Your wolves' tooth necklace and bearskin cape might proclaim past courage, but you are weak now, weak as a babe at suck.'

'Who is your enemy, Eithig? Do you not realise the worst traitor is yourself. You could not be true to your own penis.'

'I shall do what I do alone and alone take the punishment or the glory. Go and hide behind the skirts of your women. Our coalition never did exist to my mind.'

No one overheard the conversation, carried on, as it was, under breath and beard, but there was much speculation about the guarded facial expressions of animosity flashing between the two chieftains.

Eithig decided he must deal with one problem at a time. Coll had challenged him and must be killed. Then he would think what to do with Ceridwen and whether to negotiate. Meanwhile he must belittle the sorceress in the eyes of his men and goad Coll to anger.

'I would not defile Beltane by taking a queen such as yourself, Ceridwen, who has besmirched the blood of her forefathers by bedding with a Roman. You already have a child by him, I hear, and I would rather not turn the key, where the lock is rusted through already.

'Your sorcery lost me my home and the trust of my people. Let it not becloud the vision of those who are true to my cause!'

Ceridwen, momentarily speechless with fury, was conscious that Coll now leapt to her defence, projecting his voice majestically to the whole assembly.

'Their vision is already clouded, for they do not see in Ceridwen the fulfilment of Cadoc's prophecy '*When the noble bloods of Rome and Druid mingle, as our rowans intertwine, then peace and honour will come with us to dine.*' She was married, by our rites, to a Roman healer, four Beltanes since and has a child by that union. In her is her grandsire's prophecy fulfilled and truly, it is time for peace!'

'If Vipsanius grants us safe passage to the mountains, with Ceridwen offering herself as surety, then there shall be peace and my promise of no more killings,' Eithig challenged, knowing that Coll would not agree.

Coll was about to retaliate by calling into question the validity of any promise, coming out of the mouth of Eithig, but Ceridwen silenced him, by raising her hand in protest and shaking her head. The warriors raised the chant of 'Heddwch! Heddwch!' Let there be peace.

Vipsanius strode purposefully from his vantage point on the turret of the southwest gate, with a heavily armed guard accompanying him. He commissioned a chariot, idle in the *Via Praetoria* and was driven in haste to the junction of the two main streets. The dust skittered, as driver, horse and vehicle, with its commanding passenger, lurched to a sudden halt.

'If Ceridwen is safely returned by nightfall, I shall make sure of your safe escort through the mountain passes, Eithig. What say you Cadwallader? Do you also agree?' probed Vipsanius from the platform of his captured chariot. There would be other opportunities to bring Eithig and Cadwallader to justice. Peace was of paramount importance. There must be no more burning of the fortress. His own wife and child might be safe, but there were women and children in his own house at risk. It was not worth sacrificing their safety.

A glance passed between Coll and Gwilym. They understood each other perfectly. Ceridwen must be protected at all cost. She was the future of their tribe.

'There will be no surety using Ceridwen. I challenge you again Eithig, to single combat and if I win, you and your men will be brought to trial. If I lose, you go free! A simple solution!'

To Vipsanius, Coll's courage was impressive. He was

foolish, even vainglorious, to think he could match Eithig's experience in combat; but the death of the young man would be a valorous one and a sacrifice which would buy precious time and perhaps save the lives of many.

'What say you Eithig? Do you accept his challenge?' queried Vipsanius. 'I swear by the honour of Rome that you will have safe passage to the mountains, if you win?'

'Ie. I accept, with the proviso that weapons shall be long sword only...no shields.'

The crowd drew back to give them an arena of fighting space at the crossroads. Both Eithig and Coll dismounted, handing the reins of their horses to a companion. Hedfan was closest to Coll and took charge of his mount. Ceridwen took Coll's sword, kissed it thrice and gave him silent blessing. She felt the unreality of the moment and could find no certain outcome of what was to happen. She knew she lacked objectivity and that it interfered with her foreknowledge, but she loved her brother so fiercely at that moment - the ferocity of feeling itself would surely affect the outcome?

She noticed an old hag approaching Eithig, a crescent Moon upon her wrinkled brow. The hag began lasciviously stroking his sword and looked pleased with the vibrations emanating from it. Ceridwen noticed it had a stag's horn hilt inset with amber. She tried to summon a prayer to weaken its function, but finding her inner sight confused, resorted to simply praying under her breath, 'Protect Coll, sweet Goddess! Protect Coll at all cost.'

Marcus too noticed the sword. How many people had it unjustly slain, since he saw it first wrought on the anvil at Dindaethwy? Would it be Coll's undoing? He pushed through the crowd, until he stood beside Ceridwen and pressed a reassuring hand into the small of her back. She gasped as she recognised his touch and a surge of hope suddenly strengthened her. Their gaze met but fleetingly, their love for each other mingling with love and compassion for Coll. They willed him to succeed, as now did Cadwallader and his followers.

The combatants faced each other in the bright glare of the

rising Sun. There was no doubt in either of their minds; this fight would be to the death. Coll had no intention of turning Eithig over to the Roman authorities, so that he might escape again. Equally, Eithig saw Coll as a symbol of all who had rejected him, his mother, dying as she did at Einir's birth, Ceridwen preferring the Roman medic to a real tribesman, and his own people who had turned on him and put this pap-sucker in his place. Hatred flashed like knives as they glared at each other.

'No shields!' challenged Eithig, throwing his clattering to one side.

'No shields!' agreed Coll reluctantly, passing his to Owain.

Coll made a cursory bow towards Vipsanius and Vipsanius nodded his approval to commence. Eithig, however, had no such intention. He would never deign to bow to a Roman. Did this not put himself in favour with all the Ordovicans? He expected chanting in his favour, but there was only a tense, anxious silence from all observing.

Ceridwen eased the nose of her dun pony between the two. She took a gnarled hazel wand from her saddle pouch and raised it high, crying, 'To the Gods be the decision and the outcome!' She now trailed it behind the pony drawing a circle in the dusty road deosil. But the old hag in her tatters took an equally gnarled wand from the sleeve of her garment. It seemed to grow longer and animated as she bent and drew the circle *widdershins*, incanting a spell under her breath. She drew tall beneath Ceridwen's glare.

'Just in case you'd a notion to bewitch my master and set the odds a kilter!' she seethed with toothless animosity.

'Enough! Begin!' Vipsanius snapped in irritation, reading the women's actions as a threat to his authority.

The two men stalked about the circle, trying to get the measure of the other. The Sun caught glaringly on Eithig's weapon and flashed a warning to Coll to beware of his back against the Sun. Ceridwen could not bear to look, but continued praying with all her mind for Coll's safety, as the sound of their swords clashing began to rent the air. Both men were fairly equal of body weight, but Coll soon became aware of the sheer force and weight in Eithig's superior weapon. It took longer to wield, but when it came crashing against his own, it took him all his time to remain standing, shaking him and his confidence.

Marcus saw the uncertainty in Coll's stance, as he prepared for the next thrust. 'Speed!' he encouraged him, near enough for Coll to take in the advice. What occurred next was so rapid a sequence that it was hard for bystanders to take in which happened first. Marcus saw Eithig raise his sword with both hands. Coll was physically shaking beneath him and aiming a quick thrust beneath the left rib and up through Eithig's heart. Marcus knew it would land wide. Coll would be cleft in half. Anger burst over him like a tidal wave and, without thought to his own safety, he thrust himself and his own long sword between the two chieftains.

Simultaneously Gwyngariad whinnied and reared, pulling clear of her keeper. She could not only smell Coll, the master she had loved unquestioningly, but she could scent equine friends from Tan Yr Aur. The crowd scattered, fearful of being trampled underfoot and she wheeled around, searching, wild-eyed. Her white coat glistened, splashed with the red wounds she had encountered in battle. She looked awesome, snorting and prancing with her ears flat and her mouth tight. She caught a sideways glimpse of Coll and Eithig slashing at each other. Her confusion, at seeing her two masters clashing in combat, turned to terror. She must find her friends and run with them to safety. Where were they? She could scent them? She jerked her head back, just as Marcus joined the fray and, although the sword made contact with its human quarry, her rearing caused Eithig's weapon to spin in the air. Then, unmistakably, she caught the full scent of Hedfan's grey somewhere to her left and she heard him nicker in greeting.

Hedfan, sitting astride his grey gelding next to Twm, took his chance and caught hold of Gwyngariad's trailing reins as she brushed a greeting against his leg. But the pressing of the crowd had unsettled her and she reared again. The crowd parted once more, not relishing being trampled underfoot. He heard his father shout 'Go Hedfan! Go!' and miraculously a clear way through to the southeast gate presented itself. The reunited horses only needed one word from Hedfan, '*Adref!*' and they broke into a gallop to safety.

Eithig's blow, although thrown aside somewhat by Marcus, was not without consequence. The point of the sword had pierced Coll's shoulder as he dived to escape, and he fell clutching at the wound. Although Marcus was deft enough to block the full force of the blow aimed at Coll, it was his own wrist that took the brunt. Marcus did not feel his injury at first, but, shifting his own sword to his left hand, somehow scrambled to safety beyond Gwyngariad's hooves. The moment seemed etched in his mind in slow motion. He watched incredulously as Eithig's sword turned somersault and landed in the dust at his feet. Only when he bent to scoop it up did he realise his wrist was badly injured. He stared in a dazed fashion at the bone protruding through the hacked flesh.

The majority of the crowd was busy with the panicking horse, but Vipsanius and Cadwallader were riveted to the combat; both holding their warriors at bay, each hoping Marcus would finish it.

The rush of rage, which had brought Marcus to Coll's defence, now turned to fearsome fury. Somehow, he hurled the ceremonial sword skywards towards the staggering Eithig and it homed in, lodging with a great thud into his naked chest. Before Eithig had gasped his last, Marcus pulled the sword from his twitching body, and wielding it high with a scream of rage, cleft the chieftain's head from his body.

A cheer went up from the crowd. Only Eithig's own men remained silently contemplating the ugly scene, held back by Cadwallader's warriors. The old hag organised a pall to take away Eithig's body. As for his head, that was a different matter. Vipsanius ordered it stuck on a pike above the southwest gate, a deterrent to any future uprising.

Ceridwen was tending to Coll when she saw Marcus fall to his knees, then lose consciousness. The next moment she saw Dith approaching his master, tears welling in his swollen, smoke-grimed eyes. He held something in his hands. It was Leona's locket twined about with Ceridwen's own amulet. He bent sobbing and, gently lifting Marcus's head, returned the charm to its owner.

⌘ ⌘ ⌘

CHAPTER XXIII

⌘

WELL BEING

Ceridwen could not fathom how she survived the days that followed. Men died, as she was giving orders to have their wounds tended. Women screamed and lamented, children howled for their fathers and food. The cemetery outside the fortress gates could not contain the bodies. Miraculously the slave house, next to the warehouse by the river, had not been attacked and the miserable inmates were given the task of digging huge pits for the scorched and mangled bodies.

The vendors' booths by the wayside had given temporary beds to the wounded, but Vipsanius ordered the newly arrived troops from Kanovium to erect tending tents, whilst they themselves had to sleep out in the open.

Ceridwen expected to hear grumbling from the men at arms at the hardship of their tasks, but all were so grateful to be alive and considered it an honour to tend their fellow soldiers. However, she was unnerved to hear squabbling amongst her own people.

'Have you no shame?' she admonished. 'We came to our people's aid. Those of us who cannot stomach it should return home!' It silenced a group of perennial whiners from Dindaethwy, who thereafter gave her wan smiles to denote that they were trying to make the best of things.

Coll, thanks to the Gods and Marcus, was still alive and looked as though he may completely recover from his wounds. Owain had given him his undivided attention and they had set off homeward with him two days later. Hedfan had thought better of travelling alone and had doubled back to return with them on his prized Gwyngariad. Marged would be anxiously waiting upon their news.

Gwilym, however, felt it his duty both to stay and protect his daughters and to help Dith tend Marcus. He needed constant care, day and night. Dith had had the unpleasant task of amputating Marcus's right hand. He and Demeter had come to the decision that he would most likely lose the whole arm, if it were not done immediately. It was best done whilst he was still unconscious.

They had honed and scalded a huge axe to attempt a clean chop. Ceridwen had tried insisting she stay with Marcus, but they would not have her near. She might put them off the task in hand.

'Best to let Demeter and me take care of this, my Lady,' whispered Dith, guiding her outside the tent where Marcus lay. 'You shall have plenty of consoling to do when he wakes.'

It was true. Marcus was semi-delirious with pain, when he finally regained consciousness and she held him to her but briefly, before he began writhing about in agony. She plied him with wine and valerian. At first he refused to touch it, splattering the goblet against the hide of the tent wall. But gradually her healing hands soothed and calmed him, enough to make him understand why he must take the wine with its sleeping draught.

Dith had cauterized the wound by dipping the stump in scalding pitch. Hopefully it would seal the flow of blood from the main artery and give Marcus precious time to recover. Until the tar was set and crusted over, it must be left unbound. But each time Marcus caught a glimpse of the red and blackened stump he stifled a scream. He had seen this so many times in others, their disbelief that a limb had gone, escalating the agony of the amputation.

Vipsanius and Hortensius had greeted their wives with relief, but little Correlia had stayed across the water with her grandmother, Lady Branwen, who felt it best to set up a shelter for some of the children, away from the chaos of the burials, the tending of the wounded and the repairing of homes.

Lord Geraint worked in tandem with Vipsanius to ease the chaos and get food and supplies moving again. Not once did Vipsanius belittle the chieftain and his efforts at normalization. It took a strange kind of courage to act contrary to the ideologies of your fellow countrymen and work with the Roman occupation, instead of against it. Geraint had a quiet authority over his men, which came from confidence in the rightness of his actions and gave him an aura of inner strength. Vipsanius had great respect for that and used his own authority but sparingly to countermand anything recommended by Geraint. He did not always find it easy to be business-like with his wife's father, but Geraint made things easier by his professional attitude, always putting the safety of his people first. You knew where you stood with Geraint, even if you still felt the need to call him 'Lord' in his presence.

'You must be at a loss with your surgeon out of action, Vipsanius. Let me send two of my own men, who are extremely skilled,' suggested Geraint.

'I thank you, Lord Geraint. I would be grateful of that. My own medical officers cannot always understand the parlance of the mountain warriors, and we have dozens, left by Cadwallader and Eithig's men, who need special attention, as well as guarding.'

'Leave it to me. We shall nurse them and nurture them until their loyalties become ours. They would not dare to harm the hand that helped them, in case they offended their Gods. But what will happen to Marcus? Will he still have a place in your army?' queried Geraint. He was very fond of Marcus. Next to Vipsanius, if he could choose a son, it would be he.

'I am unsure. It depends how well he mends. His wife seems to cheer him, but, when she is not there, he falls into a strange silence where I cannot reach him, as though he were ashamed; as though the loss of his right hand were some sort of perverse punishment for saving Coll and ridding us of Eithig.'

'If he heals well?'

'Then we shall find him some useful occupation where he can manage with one hand. If he could learn to write with his left hand, then perhaps a job with accounts?'

'You know in your heart of hearts he could not bear that. Could he not teach others his skills and thereby gain some consolation in nurturing others?'

'That, too, is a possibility. But he would have to be based at the main fortress at Deva, the heart of the Twentieth Legion. The Gods shall determine. We think we cast a mould for our lifetime, but when the mould is broken we must create ourselves anew.' They both shook their heads. Both Geraint and Vipsanius knew that neither of them would cope well, if life challenged them in the way it had served Marcus.

Ceridwen knew that something must be done about Marcus. It was almost three weeks since she and Ness had begun their mercy mission to Segontium. They were not really needed now. The crisis was over and the majority of the women from the port had their tending tasks well rehearsed by now. They had spent the last week making soothing unctions and re-stocking Demeter's pharmacy. It was time for her and Ness to go home. But how could she possibly leave Marcus? His amputation wound was healing well and it was obvious that he was going to avoid a dreaded infection. It was the haunted look in his eyes and his lack of interest in things she found frightening.

Gwilym had grown particularly restless the last few days, wondering how they were managing back at Tan Yr Aur. 'Your mother will be fretting and longing to see you both,' he said to Ceridwen, as he relieved her of her wooden pails, on her way back from the well. 'The children will be needing their mothers. Marcus has come a long way. He is going to be fine. We must leave him in the hands of his friends now. They will help him more than we can.'

'How can you say that, Father?' agonized Ceridwen. 'You know that he is despairing inside and, until he allows his grief and anger to dispel, he can never feel a whole man again. We must get him away from this place and home to Mynydd Llwydiarth. There, I can heal and soothe him and make him see hope again.'

'If you prize his happiness, leave him here with his comrades. They know best how to deal with these things. His familiar environment is best.'

'His familiar environment rubs salt into his wounds. He sees others coping with their amputations bravely. Yet he, who was their trusted surgeon, feels he is dying inside. He knows he will no longer be able to do the task he has trained for all these years. The future yawns bleakly for him.'

'Well rather you than me, when it comes either to persuading him, or gaining permission from Vipsanius for his sick leave.'

'Vipsanius will grant it, I vouch.'

Vipsanius was playing with Corellia in the courtyard of the commandant's house. She was newly returned to her parents and Lady Branwen smiled superficially as she chatted to Rhiannon, delighted that Corellia and her parents were safe, but equally stricken for those whose lives had been torn apart. It had been a long day, returning the children to their homes and finding willing carers for the orphans.

'How can you comfort a child when it is bereft of a mother?' she sighed. 'Geraint and I must be responsible for all the orphans now. We have spread them around the families for their nurture. But the boy Taran, the one who came to warn us, he is so distraught he will not be parted from us. Geraint tried to put him with Sunico to learn the art of fishing, but he would not leave Geraint's side.'

'I cannot imagine life for little Corellia without us. She is our ultimate happiness and we hers. It must be terrifying for Taran, with no immediate family at all. Even his aunts were murdered,' sympathised Rhiannon.

'We must take Taran as our own now, but I wanted to reassure you, *Cariad*, that your children will be equally loved and provided for.' Lady Branwen stroked Rhiannon's swollen belly lightly then sighed wearily, 'I must be getting back home to greet Taran and bed him down for the night.'

As Lady Branwen rose in the fading light, Bernice carefully began to light the oil lamps, only half the usual number now, due to low stocks of oil. Then a young woman, with a strangely familiar face, was allowed through the gateway and approached Vipsanius in blessing. She was a priestess no doubt, proclaimed by the crescent Moon painted upon her brow.

Lady Branwen paused. Deep memories from long ago were stirring, memories of paying a visit to a holy well, as a young, love-lorn girl. A priestess called Nanw, with that same lovely face, had beckoned her to look into the mirror of the well, the Full Moon reflecting its silver shimmering light upon its magical water. She had looked down, blocking the moonbeams momentarily and had miraculously seen a smile, a man's bearded smile. Three years later, she had been attending the feast of Lugnasad and had gasped when first she met the eyes of Geraint across the dancing circle. His was the smile she had seen in the well.

Vipsanius motioned Ceridwen through to an inner chamber, where he offered her a comfortable stool and some refreshment, which she declined.

'Before you speak, Ceridwen, allow me to thank you once more for the part you played in turning the situation around. The Ordovicans recognised your authority and therefore believed Coll's words. The outcome could have been so different.'

'The power, vested in me, is for the common good, I believe, and it is the same with you also. I am only saddened that it was not me who was sacrificed, but Marcus,' she replied.

'But Marcus is alive! I spoke to him only this afternoon... surely?

'Marcus looks alive, I grant you, but he is dying inside. His whole life's purpose has been channelled towards his surgery and his healing of others. Now he feels impotent. The men around him bear their injuries bravely and he tries to joke and laugh with Dith, but to no avail. His voice is hollow.'

'What may be done for him, Ceridwen? He and I have been friends through so many vicissitudes, I would not fail him now.'

'Allow me to take him to Mona, home to Mynydd Llwydiarth. There is such healing there and peacefulness. The Summer days coming will cheer him and he shall see his son grow. He dare not give in to sorrow with Llew at his heels. He must set

Llew an example.'

'You are right, Ceridwen. His healing lies in being with you and his son, and so the real Marcus will be returned to us.'

'Perhaps. As he heals, he may choose another path to follow. What shall you do then?'

'His injuries give him the right to leave the army and collect a small pension. But, if I know Marcus, he will not be happy unless he is serving Rome in some way. He could pass on his skills as a surgeon, help with the medical training at Deva?'

Ceridwen found herself trying to hide a wince as he said 'serving Rome', but found another pathway of thought to pursue. 'Neither of us wishes to lose him, Vipsanius. We must not pull him apart in an attempt to keep him by us. If he loses himself...?' The tears came unbidden now, choking her voice as her self-control gave way to an overwhelming wave of compassion for Marcus.

Vipsanius clutched her slender fingers between his own powerful hands. He could feel Cadoc's ring biting into his skin. 'I shall persuade him to come to you for the Summer and I shall persuade Dith to encourage him also. Once he is a man again, then, and only then, must he decide his future!'

'So be it,' she whispered gratefully.

Marcus had complained bitterly about leaving his station. It had been particularly hard to say farewell to Dith. But watching Llew bounding with Luce's kittens in the tall grasses by the river at Tan Yr Aur, he was glad of this respite, glad to leave the rigorous demands of the busy medical routine. He was riding well now, using his one hand. Owain had made him a special shield, which was padded and slid easily upon the stump of his forearm. He was learning once more to defend himself and with that, some of the pride in his manhood began to return.

Daily he practised his fighting skills, wielding his long sword in his left hand. When Owain was too busy with the horses, his nephews, Rhodri, Daf and Rhys were always ready to play at combat. Llew seemed different. He enjoyed rough sports for but a brief time and would rather study the writing his father indulged him in so painstakingly. Was it Heaven sent? Llew seemed to prefer using his left hand. During these long summer days, it would be a good opportunity to teach Llew to form simple letters. Llew was now spending so much time with him, that the boy was even picking up easy Latin phrases and would unconsciously swap from Brythonic to the Roman tongue.

'Pater! Tad! Look at this tree the kitten has climbed. It twines around and around!' called Llew, demonstrating the twining by darting in winding motion among the grassy tussocks.

'Yes. It is not one tree but two, which have seeded in the same spot and now grow as one,' enthused Marcus, lifting the child higher, so that he could pluck down the kitten from the tangled rowans. 'Do you not think they remind you of myself and your mother?'

'You and Mam are not together very often.'

It was a simple, honest observation and it shocked Marcus. If the child had noticed how they had been avoiding each other, then the rest of the family must have recognised it also.

'You are right, Llew. I must do something to remedy that. Come. We shall climb up to *Nain* Nanw's hut. I am sure we shall find your mother there.'

For the last few weeks Marcus had rejected Ceridwen's healing hands, which she had been applying each evening before he slept. Somehow he wanted some credit for healing and rehabilitating himself, and, although he found her beautiful hands soothing and comforting at the beginning of his rehabilitation, he resented how he had become so reliant upon her strength.

'You have brought me through the worst, *Cariad*. Now I must take up the challenge and do the rest for myself. I shall not shrink from consuming your good broth, however. You still have your uses for me, woman,' he joked wryly, playing with the emerald ring upon her finger.

Ceridwen looked at him meaningfully and wide-eyed. 'Is that the only use you have for me?'

They had not lain together once since the uprising at Segontium. It was not that he did not desire her, but he could not fathom how she could possibly desire him; so ugly was the arm that he refused to put around her.

'I ache for you, Marcus, not out of pity, but out of my own need. I see you wrap both your arms around Llew and I wish it were me. They say the shock of amputation sometimes drives away a man's prowess, but I do not understand why you cannot embrace me, at least.'

'O, Ceridwen! What cobwebs have clouded my mind? I thought that you would not want me. I repulse you surely. Look at this arm. It is butchered. How can I claim you as my lover when I am only half the man I was? I am not the man to whom you promised faithfulness.'

'I did fall beneath the spell of your manly beauty, I vouch, but it is your spirit which binds us close, and that shall neither grow old nor become deformed, shall it? It is the part of you which will grow in power and might as we age together.'

'You say such beguiling things. I almost believe you are attracted to me.' He stroked the soft cushion of her right cheek and looked deep into her pained eyes. 'I am sorry, sorry that I have brought you so much unnecessary hurt. I was thinking only of myself.'

'Give me a girl child, Marcus,' she breathed, leaning against him. 'A girl child to whom I can pass my skills; a Guardian of the Light.'

It was a few days after the Lughnasad harvest festival, and in a glorious haze of noonday heat, that Ness and Ceridwen washed out undergarments in the river and hung them on the hawthorns to dry. The small children played upstream of them, jumping the stones and splashing about in the cooling water. Ness was making hard work of the wringing out and, suddenly breathless, lay back on the bank, sighing and looking up at the Sun.

Ceridwen studied her sister surreptitiously and then it came to her...Ness was with child. She stifled a pang of jealousy and sat herself down on the springy grass beside her.

'Ness, you look like the cat to whom we gave the cream. Do

you have a secret to share, perhaps?'

Ness giggled and bit at a blade of grass between her teeth. 'Oh, it is impossible to keep things from you Ceri...When Madog came back from Kanovium with the troops...I was so ecstatic to see him safe. We flung care to the wind. He led me behind the bathhouse...and took me, during some long, boring speech Vipsanius was making to his men.' She giggled once more.

'And your fear of having another child?'

'It is quite gone for the present and I shall not think about it, until this one in my belly is ready to be presented to the world.'

'It is lovely to have my own sister returned to me,' smiled Ceridwen slowly.

'Was I that awful?'

'Horrendous.'

'I am sorry.'

'It could not be helped at the time and time is what you needed for healing to occur.'

'You sound sad and wistful, Sister,' Ness observed. 'You are missing Marcus?'

'Ie. The Summer seems to have fled so quickly, and he has healed so well – enough for father to carve him his artificial hand and for him to master some use of it. I should be glad that he became well enough to return to Segontium, but he has gone without leaving me with child and it will be Winter before I see him again.'

'We shall keep busy. We have the New Year at Samhain, the cattle killings for the winter meat and the pageant to devise for the Winter Solstice. We have each other, Sister. I am not going away from you again. I have been and come back, thanks to you. You have had such patience with me. I do thank you. And I am truly fortunate to have Madog by me so much. He does not visit Coll at Din Silwy quite so frequently.'

'You do not push him away and make him miserable any more. Home is a special place for him again.'

'What do you think of Coll's bride to be?

'Non is young. She will bear him many children I vouch. She is unafraid of hard work and can conquer her own fears. She was a great help to us at Segontium and showed great courage, I thought, in one so young.'

'You are right. Youth is on her side and she is not afraid to learn. Coll could do worse'

'We must sound like two old women gossiping,' laughed Ceridwen, returning to her task of pummelling Llew's soiled linen. 'What made us grow old so suddenly?'

'Life, Ceridwen! Life and the fear of losing it.'

'Perhaps that is why I feel the need is so urgent to beget a daughter. I know your little Rhonwen is willing enough to learn my skills and if I do not, for some reason, beget a daughter, I shall pass all my skills to her. But another child by Marcus would be a sign from the Gods that our union is truly blessed.'

'Ie. I must agree that one child seems a blessing too few, though many must be satisfied with that. You cannot be barren. You have had one child already and Marcus has fathered two at least. They say a wise woman is not always the best counsel to herself. Why do you not visit the wonderful well at Ffynnon Glan and discover what time is most propitious for your desires?'

'You are right Ness. Casting the runes for myself is not working. I keep getting conflicting readings, reflecting my own confusion. I need advice from elsewhere.'

Nain Mali is still there, I hear, helping all who take her food. You could call to see Lady Tangwen at Dreffos on the way back. Owain is bound to have a message for Einir. Go on. Do it. The weather is fine and I shall look after Llew for you and collect your washing before the sea breeze wets all again.'

Ceridwen urged her dun pony down onto the banks of the River Braint. She knew that by following its course through the oak and hazel woodland for about an hour, she would pass the watchtower and ditches of Dreffos to her left. Next she would come upon a standing stone to her right, directing her over a hill and down into a lush valley, whose spring fed the Braint. It was here Old Mali eked out a living, directing the fortunes of the lovelorn. She had a reputation for predicting sure outcomes, using the pure crystal waters of her well, but she was even better at listening and counselling.

Ceridwen slowed her mount and looked down into the little valley of Ffynnon Glan from the standing stone. From here she could see Old Mali's makeshift hut, leaning against an outcrop of limestone. Its thatch badly needed repair; but smoke from a cooking fire declared reassuringly that the old wise-woman was somewhere in the vicinity. It was a perfect afternoon and for a moment Ceridwen was content to pause and breathe the warm, clean air into her lungs. What a vantage point!

She could see the pile of white stones and pebbles covering Nanw's grave, perched on the breast of the headland at Purple Mountain and beneath that the cones of golden thatch at Tan Yr Aur. She could see Dreffos and its watchtower turret, against the backdrop of the mountains on the mainland, and far to the West she could see the wisps of smoke that signified activity at Segontium. Friends, kinsmen, her beloved...all were spread about on this tapestry of landscape surrounding her. She loved them in so many different ways.

It was strange that whenever you felt you were running short of love, your heart would be challenged again and again to pour out more love from its wellspring. Only this morning she had caught herself wondering about the intensity of her love for Llew. How would she be able to match this love that welled so constantly for him, if another child came along? Would she be able to love them both equally? But she already knew the answer and was reminded of a saying of Nanw's, 'Each soul you love is like a different coloured jewel in a crown...they all make up its treasured beauty and cannot be compared, for they are all indispensable to its whole.'

The warmth of the afternoon Sun and the sweet memory of Nanw's words lulled Ceridwen along as she made the last short ride of the journey. Old Mali came out of her hut to greet her, on hearing the hoof beats of the pony and held up her gnarled hands crying, 'Nanw's granddaughter I swear. The likeness stirs memories of our training together. Come inside my humble shelter and take some of my precious water.'

'Blessings Old Mother and thank you for your kindness,'

smiled Ceridwen giving a formal greeting and a sign of blessing. She followed the old hag underneath the awnings of animal skins by her threshold.

'You are a beauty, my dear. Has it brought you great pleasure?'

'I do not witness it, and only use a mirror when I am to perform rites, so that I look the part of priestess. But I see the appreciation in men's eyes. I am not unaware of the effect I have upon them. However, I do guard against misuse of that power, for it is short lived and only there for the purpose of procreation.'

'Good...And it is about procreation you have come, no doubt. You are married are you not?'

Ceridwen nodded, only slightly disconcerted by the hag's directness, but fascinated by the old woman's filthiness. Her thick, brown, woollen tunic was thorn snagged, but unrepaired, stained by food and wood ash alike. Her hair stood about her head in a tangle of matted white, but she had thought to twine some meadowsweet therein to counteract the smell from her unwashed body.

Ceridwen followed her wizened, bent bones into the confines of the hut. It looked tiny from the exterior, but was built around the mouth of a little cave, where a spring emptied lazily into a deep, pebbled pool...Ffynnon Glan, Holy Well. The hide skin over the threshold fell down, shutting out the sunlight, but the flickering of the old woman's fire danced pink and gold music upon the walls of the cave.

Old Mali gestured that she should sit on the willow log between the fire and the pool. She sat quietly waiting for Ceridwen to show her the gifts she had brought for her. Only then would she know how much time she was prepared to spend with the young woman.

'I have brought you gifts of duck eggs, nestling in the straw of this basket, and a pot of...'

'What else?' bargained the wily creature, twitching her head to one side, her beady eyes and sharp hooked nose reminding Ceridwen of a raucous magpie searching for booty.

Ceridwen had come well prepared. Old Mali was renowned

for driving a hard bargain and had been known to put a curse on those tainted with meanness. 'I've brought you some cloth woven by my aunts at Tan yr Aur, and some bronze pins that you might make a cloak or a tunic for fine occasions.'

'And what fine occasions might those be?' she snapped.

'You know you are welcome at all our feast days. Lady Tangwen has offered you her cart to bring you safely to us.'

'I have no need of your feastings and fuss. I fend for myself and perform my own rituals. However, it is fine wool and prettily dyed. It will lie better against my skin than this rough tunic of mine.' She snatched at the bolt of cloth Ceridwen was holding out to her and rubbed her cheek appreciatively against Olwenna and Angharad's handiwork.

Ceridwen waited, her patience taxed, knowing that in no way must she displease the old woman. She found it hard to respect such a dirty and unkempt creature, who had so little respect for her own human temple. But her own thoughts of disgust must be replaced by thoughts of compassion for this elderly soul, who, nevertheless, had dedicated her life to the guidance of others and cared little for riches. She must at least respect Old Mali's life-choice.

At last Old Mali seemed ready. She wrapped the plaid cloth about her and flung some more twigs on her fire, so that it crackled and sparked, like her own voice, when it said, 'Put your right hand in mine that I may read your past and find your desires.' She spat upon her right palm and rubbed the spittle between her hands before offering it to Ceridwen. The nails were yellow with age and embedded with dirt, the fingers gnarled as old hawthorns, and the spittle still shiny, creating pink streaks on the thin, browned flesh of her outstretched palm.

Ceridwen swallowed her revulsion along with her distrust and put her own hand in that of Mali. Mali sighed and relaxed, half closing her eyes against the flickering light of the fire.

She muttered something under her breath...an invocation perhaps to the wise ones gone before. Then she began to speak clearly in the voice of a much younger woman.

'You distrust the will of the Gods in bringing you and your

Roman together. You insult the Goddess, whose name you bear, when you doubt, for she has worked hard to bring your union about. It is meant. You and he are each other's destiny.' She opened her eyes and stared straight at Ceridwen. 'Your union was not created for your own happiness alone, but for peace in your tribe. As you strive for unity, so you will learn the lessons of wisdom...But unity must have its place first in your life...It is the key to the future.'

'You talk as though there is great strife between Marcus and myself. Yet there is no argument between us...just lack of a girl child.'

'And you have need of a girl to whom you can pass your skills? Will the son you have not suffice?'

'Llew will grow to be a man of action. He rides already with Owain and is learning to hunt and fish. He has no interest in my work and sighs and bewails the task when I ask him to help tend the plants.'

'But I see him with scrolls in his hands...What can that be?'

'His father...Marcus has found in him an avid thirst for letters and writing. He has all the rudiments to hand, since Marcus spent the Summer with him.'

'And did you not berate him for teaching him such nonsense?'

'I did not believe it was nonsense; for writing is a good way to send information. Many of Marcus's skills come from the study of books.'

'Books allow magic to fall into the wrong hands. The only way we can be sure of passing on the good, is to do it privately with the chosen initiate. Evil will out, mark my word!'

'Mother Mali, evil is ever present, but I find it is spread most readily by word of mouth and secret gossip, not by medical books and herbals,' countered Ceridwen.

'The memory will fail us if we do not have our skills handed down by rote.'

'I sometimes forget what Nanw has taught me. Perhaps I too should learn to write...the more to make my recipes correct.'

'Good that you stand by your man. Bad that you lower our standards!' Old Mali cried raucously, reminding Ceridwen once again of a magpie.

'I am sorry I have displeased you, but I speak in all honesty my thoughts and I know you would have the truth.'

'I would, but there is much that you still hide from me. Come now. I do not see any issue by Marcus and yet you have a son?'

Tears began to prick at the back of Ceridwen's eyes and she wished now that she had never come. Their secret had remained such, so much so, that Marcus almost believed Llew was his son.'

'There was a wrong done and a wrong righted. Marcus views Llew as his own son. When he was born he only referred to Llew's fathering but once and bade me never speak of it again. He said that sometimes a field is seeded, but then the husbandman dies and the care of the field falls to another, the weeding, the nurture and the gathering of the crop. If he has tended the crop well then the new farmer harvests it with joy.'

'He is wise and compassionate, this Roman. But contention between you will come. Mark my words. It is then you must guard your unity at all cost. You must never be divided in spirit, only in proximity. But come closer...Put both hands in mine and we shall work deeper.'

Ceridwen did as she was bid and a strong silence grew between them. Ceridwen found her compassion rising for the old woman and her own healing energy began to create heat, soothing the stiffened joints of Mali's hands. Mali on, the other hand, relaxed and closed her eyes. It took but seconds for her practised inner eye to see Ceridwen in a burst of light. The star-like rays, of the young priestess's centres of energy, crowned her in a beautiful aura and a turquoise crystalline shimmering spiralled through her, with the rhythm of the sea. Only at her belly was there a darkened patch of inactivity.

Mali focused upon the darkened spot; the blockage of energy, which she knew that Ceridwen had created within herself. She asked the question, 'Why'. The word hovered in the air for a moment, as though exposing itself to the universal source of knowledge. Mali felt herself being drawn into the dark chasm of Ceridwen's barren belly. Her vision stilled and she waited reverently. Then came an insistent reply to Mali's skilled inner ear...'Forgiveness, forgiveness.'

'I have the reason for your empty womb,' she whispered, lifting her eyes slowly to Ceridwen's and gently releasing her hands. 'But it is you who have the solution. Come. Kneel by the well pool and look deep. Tell me; who is it you have not forgiven? Your hatred against this person goes deep and creates a ball of bitterness in your belly. You, of all people, know how to turn hatred about; but perhaps you have buried your hatred deep, deep inside you and have pretended it is no longer there.'

'I do not know who it can be,' said Ceridwen hesitating, for the pictures conjured in the pool would not come clear for her. The smell of the smoke from the fire seemed to fill her head with hazy confusion. Was it Eithig and the terrors he had brought to her family and tribe whom she could not forgive? Was it the Gods for allowing Marcus to be maimed? Was it Marcus himself for entrapping her in his web of love, then abandoning her for his profession? Was it Nanw for leaving her such heavy responsibility? Was it her mother for concealing her true parentage, or sister Ness for making life so difficult for so long?

The picture in the well pool began to clear and she saw herself in a clearing, collecting firewood. Then the idea came to her that each bundle of firewood she collected represented a challenge, some difficulty with which life had already presented to her. She examined each bundle, but was able to lift each one without injuring herself. She saw herself heaving and hauling them, with great effort, onto a huge pyre. Finally, she had shifted all the bundles representing her resentments, or so she thought, and was just about to set the fire alight, when she heard a voice behind her say, 'Look!' A giant stack of sticks had sprung up behind her and she did not know what it represented. Fear was thick in her mouth and her heart was pounding in her chest, but she knew she must turn and face the giant bundle, which had so menacingly sprung to life.

In her mind's eye she made herself move forwards and touch the dry tinder sticks. They fell to either side of her as she pushed her way through them. But the more she pushed aside, the more they sprang up, again and again to menace her way, like a tangled, imprisoning forest. She paused and could see the ugly white panic of her own hands, pushing against the endless fence of sticks. Then all at once she smelled the earthiness of badger set; felt the sensation of her belly scraping along the ground; heard the shrill cry of ravens overhead; felt the piercing thorns of gorse, tearing at her flesh and experienced the thick dread of being smothered, as she gasped for air beneath the wool of her own tunic. She could feel the cold steel weight of Quintus against her bare breasts and heard the scream that rent the air as he thrust into her. She remembered the sickly feel of blood and semen trickling between her legs.

'Come back now, Ceridwen!' the old woman coaxed. 'You have remembered.' Gently Mali pulled her away from the pool, fearful that she would fall into it, for Ceridwen was shaking from head to foot.

'It is not with fear I shake, Mother Mali. It is with anger. There has been a knot of anger within my belly, burning and eating away at my future. I thought Marcus's love had washed away the past, but I have held it here, gnawing at me like an undetected serpent. I know now the man I must come to forgive and the healing I must bring about within myself. Thank you for showing me. Thank you.'

'Ceridwen, what do you here alone? You travel dangerously. Is something gravely amiss?' Lady Tangwen bade her be seated in her fire hall at Dreffos, shooing the hunting dogs away from the hearth and signalling for mead and victuals to be brought. 'You look white and shaken. The glow from your cheeks has gone. Whatever is the matter?'

'I am sorry if I alarmed you. I merely came for news. I have none to bring, except a gift for Einir. It is a carved love spoon to hang at her belt.'

'From Owain?'

Ceridwen nodded and smiled.

'I'm grateful they are not to couple before next Beltane. I

need the time of their betrothal to find another maid. I suppose little Rhonwen is too young?'

'You are right. Ness could not give her up at the moment. She will be needed when Ness has her new babe.'

'There! You do have some good news after all. We did not know Ness was with child again. I shall send some gifts home with you.'

Ceridwen relaxed, enfolded in Lady Tangwen's hospitality and the distance from home helped her put things in perspective. She ate and gossiped with the ladies and became more calm and hopeful. If she could somehow forgive Quintus, she knew her barrenness would disappear. Wanting to do it was half the battle. In time, she was sure her prayers would be answered and the opportunity presented. She watched herself become rosy cheeked and cheerful in the glow of the evening fire. It was a long time, she observed, since she had laughed in such a carefree way. Perhaps she had already shed some of her burden.

⌘ ⌘ ⌘

CHAPTER XXIV

⌘

DEVA

Autumn mists cloaked the mornings now. For Ceridwen, the year seemed to drag itself to a close. She went through the motions of the Samhain New Year celebrations with a feeling of being divorced from her own body. She missed Marcus and her aching longing for him she quenched with herbs that dulled her pain, but also her mind.

She must first bless the cattle before they were culled for their salt beef. She was usually quite emotional at this time, saying goodbye to the beasts she had nurtured or petted, but somehow this year it did not seem to matter a great deal to her. She visited each beast in turn, as it stood quietly innocent by the side of its slayer. The cull was done to all meat cattle simultaneously, so that they should not be affected by each other's distress. An iron bolt was driven down into the brain with one great blow and, as the animal fell unconscious, it was bled from the throat; its blood collected in a wooden pail to be offered at the altar and then sprinkled upon the fields to ensure next year's fertility of the land.

Ceridwen noticed that her hands shook as she made the blood offering. Was it that she felt unworthy to make the sacrifice? Had she not purified herself enough that morning by begging the Gods their forgiveness, wearing a chaplet of rue? Had she forgiven Quintus?

She had tried every spell, she had ever been taught, to dispel the anguish that remembrance of him gave her, but her belly still seemed to ache with bitterness. Even when she buried a little carved figure, representing herself, with a gouged hole between its legs, the ache did not abate.

Perhaps, during the Samhain meditation, when the whole tribe remembered their recent dead and the veil was thin between this world and the next, she would link with Nanw and hear her advice. Her grandmother would know what to do.

The ritual progressed. This year it was the turn of the family at Tan Yr Aur to act out the various roles. The fire danced in the festival clearing. Marged, dressed in a dark brown tunic, stood by the fire with a great basket full of dried herbs; thyme to aid the link between departed souls and bring them closer; rosemary for remembrance; rue for forgiveness. She represented the Spirit of Autumn – the ageing crone, who would go down into the Otherworld for Winter, taking with her the spirits of the trees and plants.

She beckoned to those newly bereaved and, as they stood before the fire, transferred the herbs into their outstretched palms. Gwilym stood forward in his costume and headdress of rustling, russet, oak branches and bound their wrists together, one after the other, tying them together in their grief. They each in turn inhaled the fragrance from the herbs and cast them into the fire.

Then Ceridwen stepped forwards and handed each bound mourner a branch of yew, from the tree that symbolised death and rebirth. She led them to circumambulate the fire and, as they did so, she chanted hauntingly, as simultaneously they swept their grief into the consuming fire with the branches of yew.

'Sweet Fire do burn away the grief
Of man, of woman and child alike,
Who come for healing to your flames.
Take pain and sorrow with your smoke.
Bring memories sweet to comfort's door.
The names of loved ones we invoke;
Their souls to visit us once more.

They repeated it after her and Cullen played a whispering melody upon his pipe, as each mourner invoked the name of their departed one. The whole assemblage chanted the name in unison thereafter, until a pulsing yearning and demanding drew each departed soul nearer. Some fancied they saw the face of their loved one smiling at them from the flames. Some saw nothing, but felt the swish and sweep of protective wings wrap around them.

Lady Tangwen gasped in wonder, as she beheld the spirit of her young son visit her embrace. For a moment it was as if their two souls passed through each other. She had not expected such a visitation. He had been gone from her almost five years, but to behold him now a man was a spectacle her eyes had yearned for. And here he was. He must not have rebirthed, but have developed in spirit to maturity.

Ceridwen stood wistfully apart, mourning herself, for lack of Marcus, feeling only half alive, as everyone, apart from herself, seated themselves and waited silently for her to lead their thoughts in meditation.

She shook herself and sighed, impatient with her own attitude. She should be so grateful that Marcus had survived. He could so easily have died from his wounds. She refocused and began the job in hand; but the words she recited were empty of meaning for her and a picture of Nanw would not present itself to her inner vision, despite the aroma of smoking deadly nightshade, which she swung in her incense burner.

Madog signalled the conclusion of the meditation with slow tapping and then a rap upon his drum. Owain appeared in the clearing, dressed in a costume of Holly twigs that represented the Spirit of Winter to come. He plunged a large, bladed knife into the fire. Then, to a triumphant tune on pipe and tabor, he grinned self-consciously as he ceremoniously cut the mourners' ropes. Symbolically the mourners were now released from their bonds of grief, which they had harboured this last year. Now they could willingly allow their loved ones to rebirth.

Like her grandmother before her, Ceridwen harboured doubts in her own mind about the doctrine of rebirth taught by the ancients, but she dare not breath a word of it to her people, for until she were dead herself she would not truly know.

That there was a world beyond there was evidence enough from the visions and inspirations she herself had experienced; but as to rebirth of a soul into the body of another? That was questionable. Little Rhonwen was endlessly finding the soul of her stillborn sister in the eyes of every new babe, or even a kitten. Angharad and Olwenna both maintained they had memory of being a rich princess in a far off land in a previous life. They even described her identically, in every detail.

Ceridwen had settled their squabble by suggesting that perhaps their weaving skills were being inspired by the spirit of the same, beautiful ancestor. She thought it unlikely that one could share the same soul.

Nanw had maintained the aura of priestess to her tribe, always being confident and self-assured in the presence of others. She was their constant rock upon whom they leaned in the shifting world. Only Ceridwen had been privy to her private thoughts, her human frailties, her own individual questionings and searchings. For Ceridwen it endeared to her even more the memory of her grandmother. Nanw had had the courage to face her weaknesses and had always fought to remedy them.

Ceridwen found herself being drawn away from the Samhain ceremony to Nanw's hut below. She took no torch but allowed the soft light of a hazy Moon to illuminate the pathway downwards. It was past midnight. The owls called to each other across their territories and a bat flew unnervingly across her path between the trees.

She caught her breath as she came in sight of the threshold. A shaft of moonlight caught the face of a man, standing with his face turned up towards the Moon. Was it really Marcus who had come in spirit to be with her as he had promised? She dared not take her eyes from him as she approached, in case the vision disappeared with her next blinking.

'Who walks?' queried the rich deep voice so familiar to her. He had drawn his sword in his left hand, in case he was being attacked, peculiar behaviour for a *sending*.

'It is I...Ceridwen,' she breathed incredulously, moving from the shadows to where he could see her.

There was no ethereality about his embrace. It was rough and passionate, as he flung both arms about her, his wooden hand pressing hard against the small of her back.

'Marcus I had great need of you and here you are. I cannot believe it. I thought for a moment you were a *sending*. How do you come to be here? You said that Winter Solstice would be your next leave?'

'The commandant at the fort above you had a digestive problem he could not solve and there was an auxiliary with a badly knitting femur. They would not come to you for remedy and I was sent for. But it is tidings from Ostia, which bring me to you. I need to speak with you urgently. I came to the threshold to clear my head...to put my thoughts together before I spoke to you.'

'Tell me, Marcus. What has befallen? Why do you need to consult me?'

'My father is dead. There was an uprising of slaves and he was butchered. He was buried two months ago with full military honours, in Thracia where he was stationed.

'My uncle travels from Ostia and is due to arrive in Deva on business this next week. He wishes to meet with me, my wife and my son, to sign the necessary inheritance papers. The estate in Ostia is now mine. I am what we call 'paterfamilias', head of the family, and I must decide what is to be done and how it must be managed.'

Ceridwen was speechless for several moments, unable to comprehend the implications of what he was saying. She searched for appropriate words to respond and found nothing. She knew he hated his father. Pretence at sorrow for his loss would seem so hollow. But would Marcus now leave the army, which was his life, and retire to grow vines upon the family estate? Would she be faced with the choice of choosing her family, her tribe, or Marcus?'

She swallowed and eventually said guardedly, 'I'm sorry to hear about your father. I'm sure he did not deserve such a terrible death.' She was glad the light was too dim for Marcus to read the dread in her own eyes.

'He probably did deserve it. He was vicious when his temper was aroused...a great advantage in battle, but not endearing to his household. I am glad I took after my mother.

'Ceridwen,' he continued, taking her hand in his and leading her to sit next to him upon the log bench within the hut. 'I have some very difficult decisions to make. They must be based on discussion with you and my Uncle Tullius. I have recovered well with your good ministrations this last Summer, but I can no longer perform surgery as I did before. I can advise, I can manage the pharmacy, but my days with the surgeon's knife are over. I could stay with Dith and Demeter, interminably bossing them around. I could teach medical knowledge to students in Deva, or I could retire from the army with a small pension and live well on my estate in Ostia, taking you and Llew with me. You would live a life of ease and comfort. To all extents and purposes, Llew is now my heir. He should learn about his inheritance and be given the skills to manage the estate when I am gone.'

'And I thought the Gods had dealt me a mean dice, giving you to me but thrice a year! Do you know what you ask of me, Marcus? You said you would never expect me to leave my family. You know I cannot abandon my tribe, especially as there is no one trained to take my place. I am not a mere spinner of yarn, whose skills are learned in hours. My whole life has been spent preparing for my role as priestess. You, of all people, should know I cannot leave here!'

'...But Llew? Does he not deserve to see the options which lie before him...to choose where he should live his life?'

'Llew has already had his destiny mapped out for him. Do you not hear him when he talks of being High King, of uniting the tribes of North Cymru?'

'But that is but childish playdreaming, surely? We all want to be great when we are small.'

'In Llew's case he is serious. Remember he has Quintus's

blood and thereby perhaps his audacity, maybe even some of his ruthlessness. We pass him off as our son. But the Gods know differently. Llew is not our property to prod and coax away from his longings. His place is here, with his tribe, his people. One day he will be a great chieftain and bring healing to the land. He will be everything that Eithig was not. He will be a symbol of blood ties between two peoples, the conqueror and the conquered. The Gods have great things in mind for Llew, but they do not happen in Italia, Marcus.'

'Perhaps you will see things differently if you come with me to Deva; get a taste of Roman life; expose your eyes to something other than these mountains and this island,' he suggested with more hope than certainty.

'Why would I want to leave what is familiar and good,' she retorted, 'to be beguiled by stories of foreign lands, of great riches and adventure? Is it not good to be satisfied with one's lot? Is it not destiny to know your place in the scheme of things and know you play a small, but important part in the whole?'

'Not everything we do is destined and you well know it, Ceridwen. We have choices and our life path unfolds the consequences once we have chosen. At least help me choose, by looking at those choices with me. Let not everything in your life be a foregone conclusion.'

'I irritate you like a flea in your clothing. I can hear the impatience in your voice. Things would have been so much simpler if you had never met me, then you could go back to Ostia and marry some rich landowner's daughter and produce many sons for your dynasty.' Ceridwen could hear her own voice alternate between bitterness and despair and she marvelled how so short a time span could conjure such a rift between them.

'We did not wed to find an easy path in life,' Marcus retaliated. 'We found we could love no other, remember? And I have a son. He may not be of my blood, but he is of my soul. Llew and I have always greatly loved each other, since first he put his tiny fist, with total trust, into mine.'

She softened a little as memories came flooding back to taunt her: Llew's chuckles as he had tentatively explored

Marcus for the first time, catching sight of his own reflection in the burnished bronze of Marcus's helmet; their first ride together, with Llew's screams of exhilaration, strapped to Marcus's waist, as they raced a pony along the wide, bleached arc of the nearby beach; Marcus and Llew stretched on their bellies, along the damp stretches of river bank, with flushed cheeks and wide eyes, not daring to breath as they tickled the freshwater fish into submission.

'And Llew loves you and knows you as his natural father. Do not do this to him. I beg of you, Marcus. Do not make him choose between his father and his mother!'

'He does not have to choose. We are his parents and must determine what is best for him. Ceridwen, I have made your family my own and have strong ties with your tribe, but I have another life which calls to me now, especially as I am useless at my trade. I did not ask the Gods to be maimed thus. It changes everything. You must see that, especially as my father left everything to me in his will.'

'You have responsibilities in Ostia; I vouch, just as Llew and I have here on this island. I am not yet married to you by Roman law. I have not promised to follow you to the ends of the earth. You do not own me, Marcus!' Ceridwen had never felt so trapped, except for that moment, which seemed a lifetime ago, in the old badger set. She flinched away as Marcus tried to soothe her.

Gently he countered, 'We are soul mates. You know that, *Cariad*. I cannot believe our paths were meant to cross but briefly. We need each other. We belong together, not existing in a half life a world away from the other.'

'Then you must choose to stay here and work alongside me.' The moment she uttered it Ceridwen sensed the defeat in Marcus. To become her assistant was no life for an ex-military surgeon, maimed though he was. If he stayed with her, his lack of status would wither all that was left of his manhood. She knew in that instant that she would grow to hate herself for standing in his way. Yet she could not bear to lose him. She needed to play for time, to give the Gods their opportunity to work upon the dilemma. In the back of her mind Ceridwen could hear Old Mali's warning.... *'Guard your unity at all cost.'*

At last she said, 'We jumped the flames of Beltane and sealed our passion with a promise to travel life's vicissitudes together. I shall not abandon my tribe, but for one month, Llew and I will travel with you to Deva and make ourselves known to Uncle Tullius. He shall know us for your wife and son and that we have a claim upon your time and prosperity. You have befriended my family. The least I can do is to show some consideration to yours.'

Ceridwen had prepared herself to feel sea sick, but she had been far too preoccupied with Llew's safety upon the merchant vessel to give thought to her own well-being. It had been at first light when they had set sail out of Segontium to make the fourteen-hour journey to Deva. It would be dark when they arrived.

The weather augured well, and once the morning mist lifted, the southwesterly winds gave them good headway in the Autumn sunshine. Ceridwen had never been this far out to sea. She had used the ferries frequently and been fishing once with the family from the shore, but nothing more adventurous. She found herself catching Llew's enthusiasm at exploring the boat, gazing in wonder at the feast of sights; cormorants and seals playing about the rocky outcrops as they skirted Mona; Eryri in the distance, shrouded in a mysterious white cloud; the huge whale shape of the headland of Orme, looming towards them as they headed East.

'Llew, come into my cloak and be still for a few moments. We are getting in the way of the sailors,' Ceridwen ordered as she was given an appreciative smile from a scrawny, brown-skinned deckhand, who was hauling at the boom ropes.

Llew ran into the folds of his mother's new plaid and she rubbed him warmer. They nestled together, sitting on a coil of rope on the stern decking, hoping they would not be disturbed for the time being. Soon, their turn on deck would be taken by other passengers and they would have to return below.

'What will Deva be like, Mam? Will it be full of soldiers like

Segontium?'

'It is ten times bigger than Segontium, and newly built in places. It is very grand and its twenty-six towers and four gateways and walls gleam white in the sunshine. It has bathhouses and buildings warmed with water pipes. Hundreds of people live outside its walls to provide food and skills for the fortress. But here comes your father. He will tell you more. For I have never been myself. I have only listened to the story tellers who say it is awesome.'

Marcus returned from the hold with some wineskins and rough bread cakes to ease their hunger. They would have to wait until they reached Deva for a proper meal. The sailors did not cater for the passenger's needs and had already had their share of salt fish and oyster stew.

Marcus entertained Llew with stories of the wonders of Deva and prepared him to meet barrel-shaped Uncle Tullius, with his shrewd tight-lipped manner and piercing stare.

Ceridwen found it hard to look into Marcus's eyes. The total trust she had in him was gone and she tried to squash her feelings of anxiety. Coupled with this unease was a rising feeling of panic as they sailed out of sight of her homeland. She had never been so far from home before. There, she was important, respected. She felt as rooted to Mynydd Llwydiarth as the trees themselves. But here, out on the ocean, exciting though it seemed, she was just some legionary's woman, soon to be swallowed up in the thronging crowds of a fortress city. Her confidence sapped and she wondered if she would feel out of place in her new Celtic plaid, pinned with her grandmother's brooches. She nervously fingered her grandfather's golden torc, which she had slid around her throat to bring respect to her person. She twisted the rings that she had been given by each member of her family, to pay for any emergencies that might arise.

The boat heaved and creaked as though it was bemoaning her plight. She decided that she must act as though it was the greatest of adventures. Neither Marcus nor Llew must sense her distress. Soon they must descend into the obnoxious smelling hold and be replaced by more passengers. Everyone down there was trying to push near to the sacks of sweet smelling corn at the rear of the hold, or near to the empty amphorae, which would eventually return to Italia to be refilled with wine. However, someone had to be housed near the slop house, a privy curtained off, where passengers could relieve themselves or be sick into the wooden pails provided.

For the next ten hours they would sit shoulder to shoulder with merchants and their families on the piles of sacking provided, relieving the boredom with bawdy jokes and songs.

From time to time the rocking of the sailing vessel was punctuated by shouted instructions from the captain to alter the sails, or take to the oars to help alter course.

Llew had explored the belly of the ship and endeared himself to one of the shackled oarsmen, who sat him between his knees for a while to 'help' him with his task. Ceridwen was suddenly panicked by the thought that the slave might take Llew hostage, but she need not have worried. The wretch was more than satisfied to share the bannock Llew offered him in bribe.

Llew chattered in innocent friendship, not realising that the man understood none of his language. All was smiles and broken-toothed grins.

Towards evening they were becalmed and it took every effort of the oarsmen to help them gain headway. Llew had never seen anything other than an ox whipped before and his eyes grew wide in alarm as the slave gang leader lashed a rhythm upon the boards and took little heed when it cut into the flesh of the oarsmen as he passed.

Marcus obtained permission for them to go out on deck again and it was with great relief that they breathed the evening air, even though it chilled them and made them huddle together for warmth.

There was a faint glow in the sky to the Southeast, as their ship was swallowed by the Dee Estuary. Gradually the outline of Deva itself came into view, lit by a thousand torches.

The sails were pulled down and rolled to some ancient

Latin song growled by the seamen, which even Marcus could not fully understand. Now that they were in the mouth of the river itself they would have to proceed more gingerly, guided carefully by the oars. Flares along the riverbank helped to guide them in and the oil lamps aboard swung and cast their golden light on the tense faces of captain and crew alike.

The merchant boat glided towards its landing stage, like an eagle coming home to roost. Llew was faintly alarmed as the side of the vessel jerked and rubbed along the rope buffers of the harbour wall. But soon all was still. A bridge-like structure spanned the space between the deck and dry land and they were guided ashore, followed by a slave carrying their few belongings in saddlebags.

It was the cacophony of sounds that seemed so strange to Ceridwen and Llew. Deva's port never slept. There were always comings and goings, as long as the weather permitted safe landings. Barges brought stone, hewn from the nearby quarries and clay tiles, made in the kilns at Bovium, down river to the South. Bars of iron ore made their way to the dozens of blacksmiths, forging a living from making simple utensils or repairing arms and armour. Corn supplies, salt meat and fish came in continuously from surrounding farming communities and exotic spices, fabrics and wine made its way from the Mediterranean. More than five thousand troops, tradesmen and their families lived within or nearby the fort. All expected a good standard of living, the hallmark of Roman civilization.

They had landed at the harbour to the southwest corner of the fortress and someone pointed them in the direction of the mansio, an inn near to the bridge outside the southern gate of the fortress. Ceridwen found herself clinging to Marcus. The hustle and bustle at this time of night seemed so alien to her and the walls of stone, with their huge gateways and blazing torches, seemed like gigantic sentinels from some tale of horror. She became aware of an overwhelming smell of wood smoke, as the fires of both settlement and furnaces of the fortress belched heat into the chill of the night.

'I must leave you for a moment,' said Marcus as they neared the raised steps of a temple. 'Women are not allowed into the

Mithraeum, and I must give thanks for our safe landing.'

Ceridwen stood bereft for a moment, with Llew at her knees and the carrier slave panting overdramatically to stress his impatience at this halt in the proceedings. She tried to pray herself, but found that her lips murmured the words meaninglessly.

A gaggle of drunken sailors lurched past, passing lewd comments, pointing and laughing at her in some strange tongue. The slave looked about to flee. She drew Llew into the shadow of the portal and was relieved when Marcus suddenly reappeared.

'Do not be frightened, *Cariad*. There is little crime here. No one will harm a hair of your head. The discipline is very severe.'

She did not believe him, but said nothing, following him along the road to the half stone and timber inn with its russet roof tiles. The courtyard was lit by a central fire, housing a huge spit. The smell of the remains of roasted pig was excruciatingly enticing, but there was to be no time to satiate their ravenous hunger. A smartly dressed slave accosted them at the arched gateway and bade them follow.

'Porcius Tullius has sent me to give you safe conduct inside the fortress. You are fortunate you do not have to stay in this cesspit of an inn, for Tullius is particularly friendly with the legate, Eugenus Aelius. Aelius has requested that you and your family stay as his guests in the *praetorium*.' The slave moistened his lips girlishly.

'That is very unusual...for a legate to fraternise with the riffraff,' grinned Marcus querulously.

'He has heard about your wife, Ceridwen, and is curious to meet her.' The slave's eyebrows lifted and his eyelids fluttered in effeminate innuendo.

Marcus's heart sank. The last thing he wanted was for Aelius to make eyes at his wife and for him to be impotent to protect her from his advances. 'Maybe we should stay at the inn after all,' Marcus suggested. 'It might make matters more simple.'

'You do not have any choice in the matter, Doctor. It was an order from Aelius and you are still in the army, I understand?' the slave replied with deadly seriousness. Marcus nodded, admitting defeat. He still had not made his final decision about retiring. He would need Aelius's permission for any path he chose, for Aelius commanded the whole of the Twentieth Legion.

The slave led them through the twin archways of the south gate, murmuring a password to the guards. The spiked heads of old enemies and miscreants leered from their empty-socketed eyes in the flickering torchlight, from their podiums above the gateway. Llew gripped Ceridwen's skirt for comfort and buried his eyes in her cloak. Marcus seemed preoccupied and did not turn around to lift Llew upon his shoulders as Ceridwen expected. They trailed after him.

It was quieter and more orderly inside the fortress. The street was paved and drained. They passed the bathhouse and rows of barracks, whose occupants were settling down for the night. They quickly came to a crossroads. Ahead of them was a huge imposing building, skirted by pillars supporting a verandah. It was bristling with guards in burnished armour, their torches blazing every ten yards.

Marcus turned to Ceridwen and Llew explaining, 'This is the *principia*. It is the headquarters of the Twentieth Legion. This is where the legionary treasury is housed; the shrine to the Emperor, Severus Alexander; the standards and the great silver eagle, symbolizing the authority of Rome are kept here.'

'Shall we see inside it, Father?' queried Llew in Latin.

'Perhaps,' was all that Marcus was prepared to say right now.

To the right of the *principia* was the *praetorium*, the legate's palace. It was a stone edifice approached by a set of wide regal steps. They were guided through the huge entrance with its ornately carved oak door. Their voices echoed against the tiled mosaic floor and cross-vaulted ceilings. Ceridwen and Llew gaped in wonder. Neither had seen anything so architecturally beautiful, with pictures of Gods and Goddesses picked out in rich colour pigments on the plastered walls. Ceridwen was conscious of resisting the seduction of the man-made beauty surrounding her. She drew an imaginary cloak of serenity about herself and, within its security, stood unafraid and momentarily at peace with herself.

The baggage slave was dismissed and other servants came running eagerly forwards to carry their belongings. A servant brought hot, wet towels to wipe their hands and faces, and at last Eugenus Aelius, chatting animatedly to Uncle Tullius, was seen emerging from the arched entrance of the spacious dining hall.

'Welcome, my friends, to the fortress of Deva. We trust you have had a safe journey?'

'We are delivered safely to your fort and are very grateful,' said Marcus, dutifully standing to attention and bowing his head in deference, then falling on one knee.

'Stand,' ordered Aelius.

'We are very grateful,' chirped Llew, copying Marcus and bringing a wry smile to the chiselled-jawed, bovine face of Uncle Tullius.

'Allow me to present my wife, Ceridwen of Mynydd Llwydiarth, priestess and healer of the Celwri tribe upon Mona.'

For a moment Aelius was riveted by Ceridwen's beauty, rarely had he seen such nobility of carriage and serenity of face in a tribeswoman; but he had not risen to his high status by stealing the wives of others. His was another agenda and it would have to wait until these visitors were refreshed. He held out his ringed hand that she might kiss it, but she deliberately ignored his cue. She dared to smile mysteriously into his eyes and brought her hands to her forehead in blessing, before she clasped his hand between her own in an act of spiritual nurture. He could not guess at her inner turmoil, so practised was she in her role of priestess.

Aelius was taken aback, but not offended. This young woman was obviously unaware of his standing and was simply treating him with hospitality. If he was to use her, he must keep her sweet. He inclined his head in a formal smile and withdrew his hand from her grasp.

'And this is my son, Llew,' said Marcus, pushing him before

Ceridwen and casting a reproachful glance in her direction. 'Kiss the legate's hand as is custom, Llew' he whispered in the lad's ear.

'Oh, never mind these tiresome customs,' laughed Aelius, ruffling Llew's hair. Let us take you through to the dining hall, where you may take refreshment.' As imperious as the Emperor himself, Aelius swept along in front of them, his toga streaming voluminously behind him. He did not enjoy wearing his uniform for dinner. It did not aid digestion.

Uncle Tullius had already embraced Marcus and seemed in deep conversation with him as they went through to dine. Ceridwen caught snatches of the conversation in Latin, something about his brother's death and later mention of the villa and the vine groves at Ostia. It seemed that Uncle Tullius had forgotten to greet her, or perhaps he was already considering himself her sworn enemy.

She watched for the custom of sitting and eating, and arranged herself gracefully on the couch provided, lying on her side. It took all her self-control not to grab at the food and stuff it into her mouth. She was so ravenous. Llew could not wait and was already tearing strips of meat from the roasted lamb's leg he had been served with.

'Wait, Llew. You know it is *geas* to begin eating before your elders,' she admonished.

'Tullius and I have eaten already. Please begin without us. You no doubt have family matters to discuss with Tullius. I must be up at first light to review my men. Perhaps you would excuse me. Lepidus, my servant will look after you and see you to your quarters. I shall meet with you both tomorrow in the *basilica* after you have breakfasted.' With that Aelius swept from the room.

Half-an-hour later, with a full belly and glowing warmth about him, Llew's eyes began rolling and he slumped sleepily on the cushioned couch.

'Perhaps Lepidus will show you to your room, Ceridwen, and your son may be settled for the night. I shall not keep

Marcus long. A brief outline of our business will do for tonight,' said Uncle Tullius, dismissing her with those shrewd narrow eyes which brooked no question.

She followed Lepidus, who carried Llew's sleeping form, up a flight of stairs to an upper gallery, carpeted with rush-woven matting to eliminate the sound of footsteps. He led her to a brightly lit chamber with a double and single sleeping couch. It was a warm room. The heat seemed to be coming from the ornately carved grills in the floorboards, masking the lead hot water pipes.

A marble washstand held a steaming basin of freshly poured hot water and thickly woven cotton towels. The room smelled pleasantly of hot spices and flowers. She motioned Lepidus to lay the boy on the double mattress. She would curl her body around that of her son. Marcus may do as he pleased, when he deigned to join them. She would be sleeping with Llew.

She washed briefly; checked that their baggage was intact; then pulled the luxurious fine wool covers over herself and Llew. Perhaps things would look less daunting in the morning light. She sighed and surrendered to her exhaustion, falling into the obliterating haven of sleep.

She awoke to the morning sounds of fires being stoked, orders given, billycans cleaned, horses whinnying and the tramp, tramp of many feet. The sounds were coming from outside. Marcus was standing by the open shutters, already washed and in his finest red wool tunic. He had given his armour into the hands of Lepidus, who would burnish and polish it so that he would look his best to meet with Aelius.

She had such an urge to heal the rift that seemed to be ever yawning between them and, even though her own happiness and that of the sweetly sleeping Llew hung in the balance, it did not prevent her from feeling Marcus's pain and his tortured indecision.

She tiptoed silently behind him and wrapped her arms about him, feeling his heart pulsing relentlessly within his broad chest. He sighed. She buried her cheek between his shoulder blades. For a moment she felt his resentment that a wife and child so complicated his life, but she also heard him kill the thought with an agonizing longing to be always with them. He was being torn apart.

He knew Aelius would want him to stay at Deva. His training as a surgeon would not then be in vain. He would school the novices in all the grizzly arts of putting the wounded back together again. He knew his knowledge could be passed on to good effect, but how he would cope with the constant reminder and frustration of his disability he could not guess.

Conversely, Tullius was already pressurizing him to retire to Ostia and manage his father's estate personally, joining forces with Tullius in expanding the family businesses and exporting their wine. It would be a good living and would secure a financial future for Ceridwen and Llew. He knew now that she would not go with him to Ostia. He could not expect her to abandon her tribe. It was too much to ask of her. The faint hope he had entertained, that her love for him would override all obstacles, ceased to glimmer in his mind. She would not be Ceridwen if she did not honour her calling. It would be like asking her to change her personality. He realised that now.

'I have not slept, *Cariad*. The weight of decision and knowing what would be best for us all has tortured me all night. The thought of teaching my art at Deva entices me. Through my experience and knowledge others would come to know my skills and benefit would be had all round. My life's purpose would not be empty. But I keep asking myself how I would feel if a novice should bungle a task and I am unable to remedy his mistake, because I am unable to show him with these hands!' He shook them intolerantly before his own face and, then hung his head to his chest to control the burning tears of anger, which sprang to his eyes.

'You will find other ways of demonstrating. Your voice will learn to guide the hands of your pupils,' Ceridwen soothed. 'The Gods will compensate you for your sacrifice. You freed us of Eithig's reign of terror. They will compensate you, mark my words.'

'I am wondering whether my task in this life is done.

Perhaps I have served my purpose and should be put out to grass.'

'Marcus, you are not yet thirty Summers old. Llew and I need you in our lives. You alone bring deep laughter to our eyes. Is that not purpose enough?'

'It should be, I know, but since this dreaded amputation I do not feel worthy of your love. I still feel half a man. I think you would be better off without me.'

'How can you believe that for a moment? How can Llew and I rip out our hearts and throw them away. You have grown to be part of us. Without you we are not whole.'

'You would learn to live without me. I have decided. We must make a clean break. I cannot stay here and know you are but a few hours away from me. It would be torture for us both, and especially as you contest that Llew should come with me. I shall retire to Ostia alone. You will be sent money to make your lives comfortable and I shall sell wine.'

'And may all who drink it choke upon it!'

Llew stirred upon the bed and rubbed his eyes. Their angry words had roused him. He had never known bitterness between his parents before and his anxious little face drew compassion from his mother. Marcus could not bear to look at him and answered the knock at the door from Lepidus, who had returned with his armour.

Once a month, Aelius held court in the *basilica* where he heard petitions and complaints, which could not be dealt with by his junior officers. He sat upon a raised dais, scrolls and wax tablets laid out in precise order before him on a long table. His adjutant and clerk sat either side of him, ready to record any decisions taken.

Ceridwen trailed behind Marcus, who strode purposefully into the building. She dragged an intimidated Llew behind her. Never had he known his mother so speechlessly angry. What had he done that was so bad? Was it because he slept so late and there was no time for breakfast? He dared not open his mouth to ask.

They were halted by the guards at the entrance to the *basilica* and had to state their business and a code number for the hearing. They were ushered through to the pillared hall, where the queue of complainants stretched right around the walls. They joined the tail end of it. The noise and chatter was deafening. A pair of merchants in front of them argued the size of their competing shop fronts, each bringing a piece of rope to signify the measure granted. A guard hovered in case fisticuffs should break out, but suddenly the whole assemblage quieted. The *aquilifer* stood upon the raised dais and struck the stave of his silver eagle standard into the floor.

'In the name of our Lord and Emperor, Severus Alexander, Eugenus Aelius, Legate of the Twentieth Legion, gives ear to your petitions.'

'We shall be here all day,' whispered Marcus grimly; but they were soon sought out by Uncle Tullius, who motioned them to follow him. He had prepared seating for them close to the dais and they found they were second in the queue.

Marcus would have not brought Ceridwen and Llew with him to the hearing had it been his choice, especially after the recent disagreement with Ceridwen, but Aelius had requested their presence. It added to his sense of unease.

The case before them was soon settled and dismissed and it was Marcus's turn to draw towards the dais.

'My plea, Sir, is that the Roman army dismiss me, after my ten years of service, on account of my current disability and injury. I have weighed your offer of serving in the infirmary here as a teacher, but feel that I shall fail in my ability to do justice to the task. I request my pension rights for the time served.'

Aelius paused and cleared his throat. 'Marcus, you have served Rome well and have rid Cymru of a detested offender. You deserve your wish. However, I do strongly disagree with you about your ability to teach. I am sure we would find your expertise invaluable in our infirmary here. I need time to consider your plea and perhaps you too need time to reconsider, to look around the infirmary and see how you would make recommendations. I shall see you again in seven days...However there is a task you could do for me, which might sway me in your favour?' Aelius leaned forward conspiratorially, so that the crowd should not hear him.

'In the infirmary here, I have a dear boyhood friend who is dying. Nothing our priests and doctors can do seems to be able to ease his pain and he has refused to fall upon his sword...says it is against his principles. Your wife has the healing hands, I hear. I want her to see what she can do for this man. I would then be in your debt, you understand?'

Marcus shifted uncomfortably, wondering whether Ceridwen would refuse, or make some excuse. She was not exactly under his control like some of the Roman wives. He motioned her to stand forward and reply for herself. He knew he dared not reply for her.

'I am a priestess and healer, dedicated to easing pain. Naturally, I would be happy to do what I can for your friend. I agree to try in honour of my calling but not as bargain for Marcus's plea.'

Marcus felt shame at the show of disunity between Ceridwen and himself and bit into his lip, hanging his head to conceal his anger against her, aiming to quell the undignified tirade he felt rising within.

Ceridwen smiled inscrutably into the knowing eyes of the legate, then turned and met with the steely gaze of Uncle Tullius. Tullius's porcine, narrow eyes almost disappeared into the puffed cushions of his eyelids. The stare swore enmity. Ceridwen did not frighten him. He had an old crone in his pay who had the power to untangle any spell or curse she could direct at him.

But Ceridwen was wise enough not to be drawn into mental warfare with the influential uncle. She remembered the warning of Old Mali; unity must have first place in your life...the key to the future.

Aelius was shrewd enough to read the situation and did not want anything erupting in his court. 'You have high principles, my dear,' he said cautiously. 'We shall reconvene at my offices in seven day's time. Tullius, you know where to escort them.'

It was necessary to leave Llew in the care of Lepidus, the slave servant, for Marcus had business in the surgery and Ceridwen was due to visit Aelius's sick friend for the first time. They walked side by side without speaking to each other from the *praetorium* to the infirmary. A strained alien formality had crept into their relationship and neither felt able to break away from it.

It was a short walk, the infirmary being the next building to the North of the *praetorium*. It was of rectangular format with an open central courtyard, where patients could be exercised and rehabilitated. The surgery and pharmacy stood either side of the entrance door and a passageway ran around the perimeter, with long barrack-like rooms containing rows of beds opening off from either side.

'I shall be observing in the surgery should you have need of me,' said Marcus with uncomfortable false gallantry. Ceridwen nodded icily, then turned from him to smile at the young boy aide, who had run eagerly to greet them on their arrival.

'Could you lead me to Aelius's friend? He is very sick, I believe?'

'Yes, my Lady! That will be Captain Max. They say he is dying, but it is very slow and horrible for him. Do you think you can help him?'

'I shall try my best. The rest is up to the Gods.'

The boy led her along the herb-fringed corridor skirting the courtyard, until they reached a small private bedchamber at the rear. There were several of these small rooms, where patients, needing constant attention, could be nursed more peacefully than in the barrack rooms.

Demetrius, one of the medical officers met her at the door.

'Thank you for your attention and agreeing to come. We have tried many remedies to help him, but none have worked,' he whispered confidentially. 'He began by being unsteady upon his feet and dropping things. Then he was unable to walk and his speech became slurred. Recently he has been unable to rise from his bed and has had difficulty taking even the most liquid of foods. He is in a great deal of pain. He refuses alcohol and opium, for both give him hallucinations. I am at my wits end to ease him.'

'If my hands can help him, they will,' she smiled reassuringly, then allowed him to lead her into the room.

On a high couch, where he could see the Autumn Sun in the courtyard from a shuttered window, lay a weak, emaciated man. Even in sleep his limbs contorted with pain and his lungs laboured. Ceridwen drew near him. He smelled newly washed and shaven. Someone here was dedicated to keeping him in dignity, at least.

She gazed upon the hollow-cheeked face with rising compassion. This man had been handsome and broad once, vigorous and courageous in battle, no doubt.

She held his hand gently and whispered his name, 'Maximus. Can you hear me?' At first he did not stir, but when she spoke in her normal voice he heard her and slowly turned his head from the window, opening his eyes.

It was then that Ceridwen recognised him and the full horror of the situation assaulted her. Her head reeled. It was Quintus! Quintus Aurelius Maximus! She stifled a cry and backed away. Turning, she ran headlong down the herb passage, knocking against and scattering water pots as she flew. When she finally reached the end of the colonnade, the terrible cry she had been suppressing escaped and rent the air. Men came running, but it was Marcus who caught her as she crumpled by the door.

'No! No! It cannot be! I cannot forgive! I cannot help him!' she sobbed, turning tormented eyes to Marcus.

'Leave us in peace. I shall take care of her,' Marcus ordered the concerned crowd, who had gathered around them. They dispersed reluctantly and Marcus led her shaking to a quiet little shrine in the courtyard.

'What has happened? What gives you such terror, my Cariad?' He stroked her hair and she leaned against his broad chest. He smelled of strength and trust, just as she remembered him before their rift.

Eventually she stopped shaking and was able to tell him that it was Quintus who lay dying in the room at the far end of the infirmary.

'I'm sorry. I do not think I can face him again at present. The terror he put me through came back to me as soon as I read his eyes. Seeing him again has robbed me of every shred of dignity and strength.'

'I cannot expect you to treat him, Ceridwen. It is too much to ask of you. I will get a message to Aelius. There will be no deal. Your well-being comes first.'

'No, Marcus! Perhaps if I can pray...If I can harness the strength of my Goddess and not my own, it should be done. I did not tell you of my visit to Old Mali, the wise old woman who lives near Dreffos. She told me the reason for my present barrenness. My bitterness against Quintus has soured my belly. I must learn to forgive him and start afresh.'

'How can you do that for someone who has ravaged your body and despoiled you so? How is that possible? Surely we should just let nature take its course and allow him to die cursed and in agony. It is his just deserts.'

'He has given us Llew. What a wonderful boy he is. We should thank him in our hearts for giving us Llew.'

'Ie. I cannot gainsay you on that...Is there anything I can do to help you?'

'I need to get to a sacred grove...need somewhere where only the sounds of nature invade my senses...not this mayhem of so-called civilization. I need to heal the shock; to gather my strength; to call upon my ancestors.'

'Come. We'll take you back to our rooms where you can rest and get you some mead to strengthen your nerves. I shall find you your grove and you shall feel in command of your life again.'

Ceridwen stifled the desire to say, 'And how can I ever be in full charge of my life whilst I still love you?'

⌘ ⌘ ⌘

CHAPTER XXV

✥

HIRAETH

Llew saw them return and ran to them excitedly, showing the carving of a wild boar he had made under Lepidus's instruction.

Marcus praised him and said, 'Your mother is not feeling well. We have to let her rest awhile. Come with me and we shall try to find her a place where she might feel better.'

'Perhaps this place seems very strange to her, Pater. I think she wants to go home. Perhaps she has *hiraeth*.' He stroked his mother's hand wistfully, willing a smile to come back to her strained face.

She could not resist his wiles and found she was able to summon a smile of tenderness. 'My, you are wise for your years, Llew. Yes I do have *hiraeth*...a great longing to return home to my mountain and hear the voices of my people around me; have Luce and her kittens rub against my legs and hear the whisper of the trees in the sacred grove. I have tried to be excited about the fortress here and all its wonderful innovations. To be honest, I do not share your wonderful sense of adventure, Llew. I feel like a tree that is uprooted and is dying inside.'

'We shall soon return, all three of us. I know it. Do not be sad, Mam. Aelius will grant Father's boon and then he will be able to come and live with us always.'

Marcus cast Ceridwen a warning look. He was not yet ready to discuss any future plans with Llew, not before he was quite certain that to leave them would be in all their best interests. At present the most urgent priority seemed to be Ceridwen's well-being. It had pushed aside all rational hard-nosed decisions of 'what would be best?'

'We shall see in good time, Llew,' he said. 'All shall unfold. Meanwhile we have several days left here, so shall we go exploring with Lepidus?'

'Yes, I would like to see the amphi...amphi...The place where the soldiers pretend to fight each other. Lepidus told me all about it this morning and promised to take me. They might even allow me to join in!'

Lepidus was garrulous and eager to have an excuse to leave his mundane duties and be their tour guide. Llew's face was alight with excitement. Ceridwen watched all three of them go, but not before she cast a mental cloak of protection around Llew. 'Do not forget your heritage and your destiny, my sweet son,' she whispered soul to soul.

Left in peace, Ceridwen lit an oil lamp and focussing upon its flame, began to pray. She tried to visualise herself being strong and independent of Marcus, a whole being with or without him. She tried to see herself giving of her healing to Quintus with compassion, sending him to the next world forgiven. She knew that this should be her course of thinking, but the conviction that she was worthy of such dignity would not settle upon her. Marcus's announcement that he would live in Ostia without them had shaken her belief in herself. She felt her very faith in her Goddess was disintegrating. She was disintegrating.

'O Ceridwen! My Goddess. Do not desert me now. I cannot even pray properly. Do something!' she cried out angrily.

They returned late in the afternoon, Llew full of exaggerated stories about his training session in the amphitheatre with a young group of legionaries and Marcus with some information about local geography.

Lepidus brought them food up to their room. Ceridwen felt inadequate to face the dining room with its beautifully draped women and their gracious manners. Perhaps another day, when she felt stronger?

Despite her emotional fragility, Ceridwen had not eaten since breakfast and appreciated the salad of oysters and mushrooms washed down with honey-sweetened wine. Llew was not so impressed and spat out the oysters upon his plate with dramatic disgust.

His parents laughed together; the look on his face was so hilarious. 'Here, just dip this bread in the sauce and leave the rest. You can fill up on nuts and honey cakes later on,' smiled Ceridwen.

'I did not think spitting out my food would make you so happy, Mam?' he grinned.

'Eat!' Marcus commanded. Llew sensed his parents relax together and did as he was bidden.

'I found out that there is a forest three leagues to the East,' Marcus continued. 'It was once a Druid settlement, but has been long abandoned. Now there are only the trees and brooks and wild animals to disturb its peace. This very eve it will be Full Moon. Shall I take you there?'

'No. It would be better if someone else were to escort me. I need to find my own strength and not be so reliant upon yours, Marcus.' It was not meant as a rebuke, and Marcus, recognising this, nodded, trying to understand.

'I shall arrange it with Uncle Tullius immediately. He is bound to have someone trustworthy to accompany you.'

Ceridwen's blood froze. That Uncle Tullius wished her out of the way she had no doubt. Perhaps he would take such an opportunity to dispose of her. Ceridwen considered her position; then decided to say nothing to Marcus. To talk of enmity between herself and Uncle Tullius might demolish the tenuous bridge that was being built between them. It was her third challenge. Why did the Gods always arrange things in threes? First, the disunity between Marcus and herself was undermining her whole reason for being; then her fear of facing Quintus, with all the raw memories that entailed, daunted her; but the third...a threat to her life by Tullius. It would only take a fall from a horse, or a foot to slip on the edge of a ravine and it would look like some unfortunate accident.

Once the thought took root in Ceridwen's mind, she became more certain that Tullius would be unable to resist the opportunity. *Hatred never ceases by the arrows of hatred. It shall be conquered only by the darts of love.* Nanw's teaching echoed around her brain. She knew that in all three cases her best weapon of defence was love...unconditional and universal. How could she reach that sacred state that would benefit all those around her? At least she now recognised what she needed to achieve. Perhaps desiring it sincerely was her first step?

Ceridwen pulled Marcus's heavy, woollen, oiled waterproof cloak around her more tightly, and pushed her nervous mount harder against the rain. Uncle Tullius had insisted that he accompany her, along with two henchmen. His company was the last thing she needed, but she took it now as an opportunity to turn around the situation.

Tullius rode before her on his sturdy roan. She could feel his resentment radiating from his back, having to accommodate her by agreeing to this hare-brained scheme. He would not have insisted on coming unless there was something in it for him. Was it to keep in Marcus's favour, or was it to ensure some harm came to her?

Hatred never ceases by hatred. It shall be conquered only by the darts of love. Ceridwen allowed the ancient wisdom to play its music about her mind, hearing the words over and over again in the rhythm of the horses' hoof beats.

The loyalties of the two henchmen had been easily won by her giving each of them the only jewellery she was wearing at the time. They now had nothing to rob her for. She had smiled at them with great love and compassion, giving them the rings and saying to one, 'This might ease your mother in her old age,' and to the other, 'With this you can buy medicines to heal your son.' They did not query how she knew their private concerns, for they had noticed the crescent Moon etched into her brow. They would not dare to harm her for fear of retaliation by her

Goddess. But Tullius was a different challenge. Her smiles of appreciation had not softened him and he had ridden resentfully and grimly into the chill evening rain.

At first they trotted along well-worn roads, avoiding the twin grooves of the cart tracks, but eventually they turned off along a bridle path through a dense, mixed forest. Not all the leaves had fallen, so the trees gave good protection from the wind and rain. The evening scent of wet pines as the rain eased was Heaven's gift to Ceridwen's hungry senses and evoked immediately her relationship with the trees. She requested that they ride deeper into the forest until they reached a small circular clearing.

They all dismounted and the henchmen set about making a fire and a temporary shelter where Tullius could ease himself. Darkness had fallen swiftly. Ceridwen visited the trees, stroking their gnarled bark, holding them in her grasp and imagining their strength and grandeur filling her body. Eventually she found a huge oak and leaned her back gratefully against it. By its girth she guessed it had been here at least two hundred years.

She could see the men on the far side of the clearing, huddled beneath their makeshift awning and feeding the fire. She asked for protection from them and when she was sure it was in place, she allowed herself to drift into the time of the tree. She could feel herself melting into its trunk, drinking sustenance from its roots, taking in radiance from the sky. She drifted back to its youth and felt its struggling yearning as a young tree.

Mesmerized she watched as time fell away and her inner vision began to remember what the tree had witnessed there two hundred years ago. Hazily she stared as the chieftains gathered, their golden torcs about their necks, their plaids pinned with snakes of bronze, their hair limed and white, radiating from their heads like glorious crowns. They were all young and unblemished; all in the prime of fitness; all willing to give their lives to protect their motherlands and their tribes.

They had gathered here to perform the ultimate sacrifice that would please the Gods and rid their land of the scourge of

Roman invasion.

The white-robed Druid priests assembled in a circle around them and she could see their mouths chanting soundless prayers. All waited with bated breath as a closed basket was handed around. Each young chieftain took a piece of bread from the lidded basket, unable to see its contents. As each one received an unblemished piece, the tension mounted until at last, a young man with a novice of a beard, took a piece of blackened bannock. He held it momentarily in his outstretched palms to show the assemblage, then swallowed it quickly to give the signal that he accepted his role as chosen martyr. He was given no time to be afraid. He was bludgeoned swiftly from behind to render him unconscious, then garrotted with a golden wire twisted about his throat. Finally a third priest came forwards with a golden sickle and slit his wrist, so that they might all drink the courageous blood of their chosen sacrifice. He was hailed as King amongst chieftains, and the last life necessary to be sacrificed for the freedom of the realm. But it had not worked. The magic had been fragile against the might of the Roman military machine.

As she watched, Ceridwen was surprised to find not hatred for Rome welling from her heart, but heart-rending sadness. Had the young man truly given his life in vain? *Hatred never ceases by hatred. It shall be conquered only by the darts of love.* That is what the priests had been chanting. Their song echoed down the centuries in this most sacred of places.

As Ceridwen felt herself withdrawing from the scene, she heard Nanw's voice in her head, clear and insistent. *There has been enough sacrifice, enough bloodshed! The love of his shed blood did not prevent the Roman invasion, but it gushed into a pool of spiritual strength in the realm beyond, which those who have the knowledge may always draw upon.*

Your role is to build a bridge between peoples and cultures, to teach your children the art of tolerance and universal fellowship, that they may guide their peoples through the fraught twistings of Fortune.

Fashions in thinking may come go, but your progeny shall carry the light of wisdom in their souls. They shall always protect the ancient wisdom. They shall be Guardians of the Light!

Ceridwen sighed, letting go the breath she had been holding to still the air. It was a moment of great blessing, a moment when she truly began to comprehend the meaning of her existence; her life's purpose. But the message was unfinished. Once more she heard the familiar voice of her grandmother and she responded by stilling her breathing.

For yourself, you have it in your heart to forgive ignorance, to sacrifice your personal goals for the good of your children and your people. You have it in you to be strong. Not for nothing are you the granddaughter of Cadoc and Nanw!

As her words faded the wind hushed and the rain ceased its gentle dripping from the trees. Ceridwen's vision had been full of light. Now, as she returned to the present, she saw the welcome glow of the fire in the gloom and that the three men had fallen asleep.

Above her the night sky cleared and, in a gap through the tree canopy, she saw the Full Moon throbbing in the splendour of silver mystery. 'Thank you my Goddess. Thank you for your blessing and helping me to understand. I am amazed that I needed no ritual this night. Only to feel that I was near you and have the will to do what is fair and just.' As Ceridwen spoke the words, it also came to her that in the future she would not need to physically come to a sacred grove, but could feel the nearness of nature by visiting the rich memories in her mind. Love and gratefulness welled recklessly from her soul, but at the same time she could detect upon the air a faint warning from Marcus murmuring in her ear, *'Be careful, Cariad.'*

Gently she woke the henchmen, who in turn roused Tullius. They doused the fire and offered her the remains of their broth, but she declined, still full of the enlightenment she had received, and in no need of food.

Tullius suggested they take a short cut back. He was cold and grouchy. The sooner he was back in his heated room, bathed and pampered, the better. Ceridwen sensed danger. The path they took was not the easy, rising bridleway they had approached along, but a narrow track alongside a small river ravine. They would follow the river course and ford it lower down. It would take at least a league from their journey. It was not the dramatic valleys of Eryri, but dangerous enough in the dark; the path ahead lit only by their swinging oil lamps.

Ceridwen made prayers for everyone's protection and progress. Henchman one was out in front, Tullius ahead of her and henchman two brought up the rear. She felt her blessings reaching out to the spirit of the river and in return its lushing and rushing calmed and reassured her.

Tullius was becoming impatient. His wise crone had foretold of an accident to his advantage. Surely the Gods recognised that now would be their best opportunity for manipulating a fall? He hummed a tuneless hymn, just to remind them of his whereabouts.

Henchman one became suddenly wary. A stream gurgled heedlessly in front of them across the path. His horse picked its way carefully and the ground held. But Tullius and his horse were almost twice his weight. Perhaps he should throw a line to his master? Then again, there would be no way he would be able to save himself if Tullius and his horse were to fall.

Before he had time to consider more carefully, there came the panic of horse's hooves, as sodden ground shifted beneath Tullius's mount. Tullius cried out, further panicking his horse, which reared and slithered on the wet clay, throwing him from the saddle down the ravine. The horse stood no chance and plunged heavily, breaking its neck, twitching and squealing in agony, but miraculously, Tullius's bulk had protected him and he had rolled and bounced until he came to rest on a tussock of wiry grass. He clung, miserable and gasping, to the steep sides of the valley, terrified to look down, unless a further fall should claim his life.

Ceridwen allowed herself a moment of sentiment for the horse. But she took the situation in hand and ordered the henchmen to line up their horses side by side on a piece of flat ground a few paces from the mudslide.

They roped both horses together and she volunteered as the lightest to climb down the rope to reach Tullius. He would never be able to climb safely out without some help. The horses must be enticed to pull both Tullius and herself upwards very slowly. The henchmen agreed. She was the lightest by far and would give the horses least trouble to pull to safety. They had not the slightest intention of harming her and she knew it for certes.

Tullius was astounded when Ceridwen lowered herself past him to the horse several feet below. She had taken off the huge cloak and had hitched her tunic up above her knees. He had found her disturbingly beautiful before now, so much so, that he had avoided speaking to her in case he betrayed his base longings, but the sight of her lithesome legs did nothing to excite him now; not whilst his life hung in the balance.

She held the horse's head until it breathed its last, releasing it from pain. It took but a few moments, but Tullius became worried then that she would leave him dangling above the river. It would be his just deserts, he knew, but he needed her help above all else. Grimly in his mind he vowed never to think harm to her again and, as if by some silent response, in the next breath she was by his side, encircling his huge chest with the rope. She tied a knot which Coll had taught her and motioned to the henchman, holding a lamp above, to winch him to safety. It did not enter her head that they would leave her there.

Tullius puffed and panted and shouted each time the horses jerked his knees against some rock, but eventually he was pulled to safety. When the rope came down for her, Ceridwen knew she had won her first battle. She cast all three men a grateful smile and graciously, Tullius took her thorn-scratched hands in his and pressed them to his lips. 'The Gods have been good to us, Ceridwen. We are safe indeed. Thanks to your presence of mind. I thought for one moment...'

'That I would leave you there? How could you think that, Uncle? You know I am extremely fond of you? It was important to thank the horse for its services. It was not its fault that it fell.'

'Quite,' said Tullius uncomfortably.

Tullius was still shaken and was quite happy for Ceridwen to take charge. She ordered the henchmen to take turns upon one horse and the other to run behind. She led the way, instinctively following the stream upwards several hundred yards, until they came across the kinder route home. It was gone midnight and decidedly chilly, but Ceridwen had no fear of the now moonlit night. It was her friend.

The next evening, rested and recovered, Ceridwen insisted they all went down to dine. She declined to wear the diaphanous silk stola Uncle Tullius presented her with, but carefully took out the glowing robe of her grandmother's, threadbare in places, but still stunning in shades of red and gold.

Marcus could not believe the transformation in her. She exuded love and confidence in every graceful movement and expression. It was as though coming to Deva had completely put her off balance, but the woodland whisperings had righted her again. He would give thanks tonight at the Mithraeum.

All eyes were riveted upon her as she took her seat in the dining room. She declined to sit as the Romans did. She was no longer afraid to be herself. It felt better to digest her food sitting cross-legged upon the couch and to lift the plate towards her mouth. One concession she did make in her table manners was to make use of the finger bowls and hot wet towels presented to her between courses. She ate heartily, Aelius noted. He had been told of some scene she had made in the infirmary the previous afternoon.

'You are feeling much better, today, Lady Ceridwen?' he murmured between mouthfuls.

'Indeed, Sir! I find your food most wholesome. I thank you for your hospitality. I am sure I shall be well enough to begin treating Maximus on the morrow. You see I encountered him when he was a strong warrior. It was such a shock to see him thus. It quite took my strength.'

'You have but five days left before Marcus makes again his plea. Shall you want to return home immediately after?'

'If you are worried will I abandon Quin...Maximus. I shall not. I shall remain with him unto the end.'

'You do not think...?'

'No. Sadly I know I cannot save him. But I can ease his passing.'

The power, which flowed through Ceridwen's hands, she knew, did not belong to her. It was not her power, but that of the Gods, breathing their energy into the world. Her hands merely became the channel. All she had to do was relax and allow the healing balm to flow, she kept telling herself, as she arrived at the infirmary next morning.

Her breath steamed as she rang the bell at the entrance door. The boy she had seen two days earlier answered and seemed to be expecting her. She had to wait a little outside Quintus's room, whilst his attendant finished his ablutions. Although she felt a little nervous, she drew upon that exterior strength Nanw had said would be available to her.

'Ceridwen, my Lady!' came a welcoming salute. It was Meromic, looking broader and handsomer than ever, now his boyhood gangliness had disappeared. 'I have been expecting you,' he whispered; so as not disturb his master. 'I am sorry I was not here two days ago when you first came. It was remiss of me, but I had a day's respite and slept all of it.'

'You care for Quintus most of the time?'

'Ie. Six days and nights. But Quintus insists I have the seventh day free.'

'You do good work, Meromic,' she smiled as she surveyed the patient appreciatively. He was kept immaculately clean; no mean task in the circumstances.

'I have two slaves to help me. They do a great deal of the lifting between them, but it is companionship he appreciates most. I can understand his malformed speech and interpret their meaning the majority of the time.'

'He seems to be sleeping peacefully now, not like the other day.'

'I tell him stories from my faith and we pray together. It eases him for a while and he seems to gain a momentary peace. I move his limbs about for him at regular intervals and that prevents the pains from shaking him in great spasms. When I am not here...I give my instructions, but I know the care is not quite to the same standard.'

'What happened to your quest for Fiommar? Have you heard news of her?'

'I made constant enquiry when I first arrived and made no headway. Then Quintus became sick and I decided to give up my personal quest, until he grew well. I knew she was never at Deva. We are so alike facially that people would remember had they seen her. I have got into the habit of shaving daily for that reason. Perhaps I have not given up all hope. I pray for her each day.'

'You will be well rewarded for your generosity, Meromic; and I do not mean materially.'

'I am certain you are right. My heavenly Master promises rich rewards in the next world for good deeds. But come closer. Do you wish to begin your treatment whilst he is peaceful.'

'Normally I would not approach him without his permission, but if I have yours then I shall begin.'

Not wanting to disturb the precious period of Quintus's peace, Ceridwen prayed silently, then centred herself for the work she was about to do. She left all her own anxieties behind her and gave all her concentration to channelling white light around Quintus. Her hands worked a little way from his skin, so that her touch would not wake him. She started with his head and worked her way gradually down to his feet. Occasionally he twitched and his eyelids almost fluttered open, but the longer she worked with him, the deeper his relaxation became.

Each organ of Quintus's body responded timidly at first, then vibrantly to her hands. She could feel the heat and tingling in her fingers grow more intense, the longer she worked on each area. It was as though his whole body drank the energy from her hands, as a babe sucks milk from its mother. The Earth Mother was good; She knew how to nurture her children.

Meromic stayed and watched. Never had Quintus slept so long without crying out in pain. When she had finished, Ceridwen washed her hands and motioned Meromic into the Autumn sunshine of the courtyard.

'Tell me, Meromic. I am curious to know why you have

become so loyal to Quintus. You knew the man he was, insensitive and cruel. How came you to regard him with such respect?'

He drew her closer so that they might speak confidentially, fearful that the walls might have ears. 'There was a slave working here in the infirmary. He was a follower of Jesus the Nazarene, the Jewish leader who was crucified by the Romans almost two hundred years ago. He called himself a Christian because he believed Jesus to be the Christ, anointed by the only God to save people from their sins. He told us stories every night; about people forgiven for doing the most horrendous deeds, but who started a new life afresh with God's forgiveness.'

'Did you then become a believer?'

'I did, and was baptised to wash away my previous wrongdoing. But you must keep my secret for me, as I have kept yours?' Ceridwen responded to the query in his eyes and nodded her promise fervently before he continued. 'Christianity is still an outlawed religion, as far as Rome is concerned. For Christians there is no way we can worship the Emperor as a God on his feast days and that marks us as political enemies to the Empire. I would be executed if I were found out. I do not fear death, but Quintus has need of me. I pray all the time that I may see Quintus through his illness and then be led to Fiommar, before I am taken to Heaven myself.'

'I have the knowledge that your God will answer your prayer, but how it will come about, I cannot yet discover,' Ceridwen responded, seeing with her inner eye the wonderful, certain reunion between brother and sister.

'There is more, my Lady. Soon after my baptism, Quintus followed suit, for there was much to forgive in his life. He became Christian and a changed man, with a much higher regard for his men and slaves. We all noticed the difference. It became easy to be loyal to him. We began to talk to each other on a personal level. Neither of us have any family to turn to; in that we are alike. Then he was struck down by this disease. He feels, somehow, that it is recompense for the pain he inflicted upon others. That is why he refuses our medicines and our wine. He thinks it good to suffer so, like Jesus suffered for him.'

'But our medicines are gifts from Heaven, to ease us and make our passage through life the sweeter! Can you not persuade him, Meromic?'

'I think that you might carry the greater weight with him, Lady. He talks of a Lady of the Moon, whom he once wronged terribly. Our God has forgiven him, but I think he can only come to forgive himself, if she could erase his wrong-doing from her heart.'

'I am trying, Meromic. That is why I have come back today. I must conquer my own pain, direct love towards Quintus and watch the consequences. I could tell Quintus I forgive him; but if he does not read it in my eyes, it will be to no avail.'

'This is an opportune time to put right that which is wrong. I know you will succeed, my Lady.'

They returned to Quintus's chamber when they heard the grunting sounds of his stirring. He cried out as he hopelessly tried to reach for some water. Meromic held his head and helped his hand to grasp the goblet and lift it to his lips. His difficulty in swallowing was apparent and it took several attempts before his thirst was assuaged. Only then did he register Ceridwen's presence, his eyes growing round with questions, searching her face.

Ceridwen found herself trying to kill a thought of satisfaction at his predicament. She must remember he was repentant and deserved her forgiveness. She summoned love to flow from the Earth into her feet and up to her heart. At last she felt able to meet his fearful gaze. Then, drawn by compassion, she moved to his side and smiled reassuringly, saying softly, 'I have come to help you, Quintus; not to admonish you. The past is done with and must be healed. Then you will find peace.'

He nodded slowly in response and looked down in shame upon his hands, spread across the coverlet. The hands which had once seized her with such violence were now emaciated and powerless.

'If you will give your permission, I can ease your pain and make you more comfortable. I know you understand the power of forgiveness. Meromic has told me how you became a Christian.' She saw the look of alarm on his face and continued,

'Do not be afraid, your secret is safe with me. I would not betray Meromic. He is needed here to look after you.' She smiled into those same dark eyes, which had so cruelly violated her. Now they were child-like and pleading. He motioned Meromic to draw near and mumbled something unintelligible in Latin.

'He begs your forgiveness, Lady and will submit to any ministrations you deem fit.' Meromic translated faithfully.

'Tell him I am learning to forgive and, if he will accept my healing work and the love which is wrought through it, then I know I shall come to forgive completely.'

Quintus sighed and fell back upon his cushions exhausted. A weight had been lifted from his mind and he was ready to slip into a sleep, which would journey him temporarily away from his pain.

Ceridwen stayed another two hours, sitting on a stool next to his bed, her hands working gently with the purity of the Maiden Goddess, the compassion of the Mother and the wisdom of the Crone. She saw herself as a hollow reed, allowing the magic to flow through her. It had its calming effect on her also. As Quintus drifted and relaxed, so did she. Meromic slept on a pallet on the floor, needy of respite.

She was roused when she heard Marcus's voice, echoing high with anger and frustration down the courtyard cloister. 'You mistake my meaning entirely! Would that I had the fingers to show you. He will die if you leave him thus, trussed up like a stuck pig!'

Quintus jumped awake with alarm, not knowing for a moment what time and place he inhabited; then the pain bit deep again and he moaned. Meromic was by his side, washing the dribble from his mouth and the sweat from his brow.

'I shall return tonight after supper and shall ease you into the night,' said Ceridwen, hurriedly washing her hands and turning anxiously to meet Marcus as he hovered by the door.

'I have done for today, Ceridwen. Shall I make my way back alone?' he said, looking defeated.

'No. I am coming with you and shall return here tonight.' She gave wordless blessing to Quintus and Meromic and taking Marcus by his good arm, escorted him from the building into the fading Autumn twilight.

They did not speak until they were back in the asylum of their private chamber, the golden glow of the oil lamps providing masked shadows for their faces. At first Marcus paced up and down the rush-matted floor, but finally came to stillness, looking without seeing, from their dusk shuttered window. She folded some of Llew's clean clothes into a carved chest, waiting for him to open his heart to her.

'I know myself no longer, Ceridwen. I am ashamed of what I have become – a bitter, twisted reed in the rushes of wisdom. The skin on my arm is healed and smooth, but the scar in my mind still suppurates and stinks.' He turned and leaned in defeat against the pink plastered wall with its fresco of painted fauns and flying lizards, his head tilting upwards, blinking hopeless tears to the stucco ceiling. 'The old Marcus would have patiently guided the novice I worked with today. He would not have allowed a mistake to happen. He would have supervised every move. This Marcus wills the novice to blunder, so he can have an excuse to rail and rant. I fail both patient and novice miserably.'

'You use the novice to ease the volcano of your anger. Sometimes you hiss and smoulder when you are about Llew and myself, but in the arena of your work you erupt.'

'The young men in your charge are blistered by the lava of your tongue. Your anger needs to erupt where you can do no harm. Go to the Mithraeum tonight and take your trouble to your God. Give it to Him to carry. If he is a good God, He will do it willingly for you.'

She led him to their bed, as silken in her movement as the bronzed ripple of the coverlet. 'For now I can think of only one immediate remedy,' she whispered as she stroked the pain from his eyes and drew him to her.

Llew could not wait until suppertime. He must tell his parents about his adventures with Lepidus; how they had joined in the games of the legionaries, practising for their Ludi Plebeii, the feast in honour of Jupiter; how he had joined one of the charioteers in a race around the arena, the trundling of the wheels knocking the breath out of him, the danger exhilarating him at the same time. He ran ahead of Lepidus and rang the bell of the infirmary.

The door was opened by the fresh faced boy, whom he had glimpsed before with his mother. He did not wait to be allowed in, but ran past the flabbergasted youngster and poked his head around the surgery door. There was a group of men prodding at a very bloody body on a table, but no sign of his father. His parents must be with Maximus.

'Hey, stop!' shouted the door boy, but Llew did not hear. He was running with all eagerness towards the room where he knew his mother had been working. Wait 'til they heard what he had been doing. 'What courage!' his father would say. 'How clever, my little princeling,' his mother would coo at him and he would grow a little taller with pride.

He stopped short of the open door to Max's room. Meromic's coaxing voice could be heard as he spoon-fed Quintus, half the contents of each spoonful re-emerging as Quintus struggled to swallow. Llew's eyes widened, transfixed upon the face of someone. He seemed to him to be a very old man being treated like a baby.

Equally stunned, Quintus raised his hand, a signal to Meromic to stop feeding him and stared long and hard at the boy in the doorway; a boy whose face he had seen before, long ago in his own childhood, when he had stared at himself in his mother's mirror.

Quintus's mouth gaped and Llew stepped back in momentary horror.

'Do not be frightened. You must be Llew. Your mother is very proud of you and says you are very brave,' Meromic reassured him. 'It is Captain Max's illness makes him look so. Really he is a handsome, strong warrior. Come near to the bed and be introduced.'

Marcus and Ceridwen lay upon the bed satiated and exhausted, cradling each other with tenderness and savouring their closeness, to be remembered in the days of separation to come. It had been the first time that Ceridwen had made love to Marcus, completely commanding their love play and he had been content to allow her to take control of his life for a few moments. He certainly had no control over himself at the present time and allowing her that power had given him momentary respite from his agonising indecision. His love for her and longing to be near her had grown more intense since his initial resolve to move to Ostia. Imagining being apart from her had begun to torture him, especially after the danger Uncle Tullius had exposed her to. His indecision hovered like a vulture over its prey.

Meanwhile, Llew was enjoying every new experience he encountered under the supervision of Lepidus. But the boy had the annoying habit of relishing thoughts of their return together to Mynydd Llwydiarth, to recount their escapades to Owain and Coll.

He ran into Marcus's arms now, as a breathless Lepidus returned his charge to their chamber.

'You will never guess what I have learned to do today, Father! I cannot wait to show Owain when we all get home.'

Marcus and Ceridwen exchanged wordless agony. They both knew Marcus must no longer put his decision on hold. Llew must be prepared if Marcus was to leave.

For now they allowed Llew to draw them into his world of new discovery, making suitable noises of parental encouragement as they prepared to go down to dinner. Ceridwen bent to adjust Llew's bronze-studded, leather belt, girthing his clean tunic. She smiled up at him. He was still chattering excitedly about the day's events, his hazel eyes animated and his darling dark curls bobbing about his head.

Suddenly, she had a vision of him grown and handsome, a golden torc about his neck and a Celtic chieftain's plaid about his shoulders. From that moment she ceased to fret about Llew's future. She knew the Gods had prepared a path for him and was content. It was Marcus who concerned her most.

Lepidus had warned Llew to say nothing of the visit to Quintus, on pain of refusing to take him on any more adventures. He did not want it known that the boy could escape him so easily when he had his safety in trust. It was something that disturbed Llew. He was unused to keeping secrets, but the old man in the bed had been scary, with those wide eyes and the gaping mouth, threatening to devour him. Perhaps Lepidus was right and he should say nothing of the encounter. Ceridwen said he was brave. He did not want to disappoint her by telling her how frightened he had been.

Two more precious days sped by; as Ceridwen treated Quintus and eased his pain; as Llew explored more and more, with Lepidus, the way of life for a Roman soldier; as Marcus advised and taught at the infirmary, calmer now, but no happier about his task. At night he and Ceridwen lay in each other's arms as though waiting for the decision to be made for them, their life together hanging in the balance.

Three days later they were at supper in the dining hall with Uncle Tullius. Ceridwen detected an air of joviality about him. He seemed to be talking and making plans as though Marcus had finally decided to return to Ostia. She smiled politely back at him and noted that Marcus was careful to include a great deal of 'If I were to...' and 'Perhaps'. Aelius was not present, as some pressing business took him to the offices, but his wife and children made efforts to please their guests, his daughter accompanying her singing with her lute and her younger brother playing hide and seek behind the pillars with Llew, once they had permission to leave the tables. Their boyish laughter echoed about, competing with the music. It seemed pleasant and yet to Ceridwen surreal.

Aurora, Aelius's wife, smiled graciously under her blonde, waved wig, piled high with coils and curls upon her head. She spoke slowly to Ceridwen in Latin, never having deemed it necessary to learn Brythonic.

'We are so grateful to you, Lady Ceridwen. I hear you have eased Maximus a great deal, since you began your work with him. Aelius visited him last evening. He was very peaceful.'

'The work I do is intensive and the magic comes stronger the more I use it,' Ceridwen responded. 'Do you not find your little boy comes to you when he falls and wants you to hold him and take away the pain?'

Marcus translated for her and Lady Aurora replied again in Latin, 'I have not had that pleasure, unfortunately, for his nurse takes care of those sort of things. But I notice, when I have one of my headaches from too much red wine, that my own hand eases the pain.'

'We all have a little healing in our hands, but it is like any skill. Those who practise it have it the greater. The Earth Goddess is good.' Again Marcus translated.

'We name your Earth Goddess Cybele,' smiled Aurora. 'You must come to my room and see the shrine I have created for her.' Aurora always found that the tedium of fortress life could be relieved, by impressing the guests with her good taste.

But she was not to have that pleasure. There was a bustle of consternation about the entrance to the dining room, as Meromic himself came urgently to see Ceridwen.

'Excuse my interrupting your pleasant meal,' he said breathlessly, 'but Maximus labours in his breathing and does not seem to hear me.'

'I shall come immediately. Please excuse me, Lady Aurora. It may be wise to send a message to...'

'I shall send for Aelius post-haste. He will wish to say farewell to his boyhood friend.' Aurora rose abruptly, needing no interpreter this time, and bade the boys be hushed. Ceridwen sped to the infirmary, Meromic at her heels.

'That young man! Extraordinary! Quite a girlish face! Remarkable! I would swear I have seen it before,' slavered Uncle Tullius to Marcus with a mouthful of grapes. He motioned a slave to refill his wine goblet. 'Now I remember who he reminds me of...a beautiful slave girl. I bought her in Lugdunum and shipped her off to Ostia to look after my wife. What was her name?'

'It was not Fiommar by some chance, was it Uncle?'

'That's right. By Jove! How did you know?' Tullius spluttered, the gulp of wine he had taken finding no way down his gullet.

'Ceridwen told me that the reason Meromic always shaves his face is to be recognised as Fiommar's brother. When they were youngsters they were sold into slavery and have been parted from each other for many years. He has been searching and praying he would find her once more.'

'Well if he can pay me a good price for her and my wife agrees to it, we shall see them reunited perhaps.'

'Perhaps,' Marcus replied, unimpressed by his uncle's level of generosity. Still he supposed a well-to-do merchant did not become wealthy by giving away anything or anyone of value. He would think on it. Now he had his father's inheritance, it empowered him greatly. Once he was again in Ostia he would look into the matter. For now he needed to get Llew to his bed. Ceridwen was usually the one to sing him to sleep, so it could be problematic.

Llew dragged his heels and pouted a little at being taken away from his new playmate, but he was tired and grateful of his bed.

'Stay with me, Pater, until Mam comes back,' he pleaded as he snuggled beneath the warm blankets. The oil lamp guttered, its flickering revealing the fear in Llew's eyes.

'She might be a while, Llew. I shall stay with you, but do not expect me to sing,' Marcus chuckled softly into his ear, nuzzling his curls.

Llew closed his eyes and sighed, gripping Marcus's hand tightly. He willed himself to fall asleep, but kept seeing the face of the sick man, Captain Max. It would not go away.

'Pater...Will *Taid* become a baby before he dies?'

'What a strange question! Where did you get that idea?'

'We went to the 'firmry to find you and I saw Meromic feeding Quintus Maximus with a spoon. The boy at the door said he was dying.'

'Hmm. Not all deaths are so. Some people slip into the next world with little effort and others go gradually. It is a little like being born. Some babes come quickly and some take their time. It is down to the Gods and their will how and when your grandfather will die,' Marcus explained, hoping that would satisfy Llew.

'I would like to die quickly; maybe fighting for my homeland, like a soldier. Ffynan sings a song about how our forefathers died gloriously for our tribe.'

'Not all fighting is for the best. You shall learn that as you grow,' murmured Marcus stroking Llew's head as the boy relaxed and gave in to his exhaustion. At last Llew's eyelids drooped and closed and his breathing slowed. For a moment Marcus could see a resemblance to Crispian. Perhaps Crispian would have looked like this at such an age. He admonished himself for being fanciful.

'I grow weary of putting together mangled bodies, which others have maimed. My calling seems less glamorous by the day...just necessary,' he sighed to the walls. Then he unstrapped the artificial hand Gwilym had made for him, turned and laid upon the bed and encircled Llew with his stump of an arm. He was too tired to think and needed to escape into the world of deep sleep.

Quintus was unconscious when Ceridwen drew by his bedside. He did not respond to her washing his brow, but his breath came in rasping spasms, as his lungs heaved grotesquely. She instructed Meromic to hold his feet with all the respect he could summon and, after drawing energy from the Earth and the Heavens, she placed her right hand above Quintus's chest, hovering so that the weight of it should give him no burden to carry. The other hand she placed upon the crown of his head, willing his spirit to have the confidence to release its hold upon his body and flee to the Cauldron of Life.

Meromic was not too distraught to be fascinated. His trust in Ceridwen was complete. Had he not known the work of her hands at first hand, the time she had healed him upon Mynydd Llwydiarth? It took but two minutes for Ceridwen's skills to relax Quintus's body and release him from the laboured breaths. Meromic felt a strange drawing of energy from his own hands. Quintus was using him also.

Ceridwen sensed his wonder and said softly, 'We are

midwives, Meromic, easing his passage.' He nodded, understanding. She watched as she became aware of a pink aura about Quintus growing in depth and warmth. He was sinking into the womb of the Earth Mother, cocooned by her love and compassion.

They were interrupted by Aelius's rushing into the sick room. He signalled for Meromic to remain where he was. 'No need to stand upon ceremony, Meromic! Max has need of you.'

Aelius stared at Ceridwen. Such beauty, not seductive, but celestial, like the statues he had ordered anew for the *basilica*. Ceridwen read his hesitation as awkwardness around death, which indeed it would have become the very next minute.

'Sir, come and befriend Max in his passing hours. Sit close and talk to him of your boyhood days and camaraderie,' she whispered gently with quiet authority. He found himself obeying and pulled a stool near to Quintus's left ear. At first he found it hard to remember how their friendship had begun. Then he recalled how he had first encountered Max, at the top of a citrus tree in the family courtyard, aiming fruit at him with teasing laughter. He had marvelled at Max's agility and aimed to emulate him.

Once he began, the memories came flooding back to him; how his own mother had agreed to take in Quintus Aurelius Maximus, when his mother had abandoned him for her lover; how his mother forbade him to play with Max, because he was not of their status. How sweet it had been to meet in secret. The danger of being caught had made their friendship bond the more exciting.

To the droning of Aelius's boyhood memories Ceridwen worked on. Later, Aelius had a slave play soothing harp music and another bring food and wine for them. But Ceridwen only paused to take sips of water. For three hours she stayed thus, until she could hold her arms above Quintus no longer.

Meromic insisted she rest and he attempted to continue her work. She took a walk into the quadrangle and appreciated the scents of familiar herbs like those she grew at Cae Gwynion, but within ten minutes the dying man began his laboured breathing again and she had to return to soothe him.

Just before dawn, Meromic and Aelius allowed themselves a conversation. Ceridwen heard Aelius say, 'It is all arranged.' She assumed they were talking of Quintus's funeral, a smart military affair, no doubt, with much marching and salutation to celebrate Quintus's loyalty to the Emperor.

It was then that Quintus's body gave a great shudder and a final gasp. Meromic cried out, 'Sweet Jesus save him and guide him to everlasting bliss!' He began to mutter a prayer he said every day, but in the panic of the moment some of the phrases eluded him...

'Our Father, Who art in Heaven, hallowed be Thy name. Thy Kingdom come...Thy will be done on Earth...Forgive us our wrongs and those who have wronged us! Deliver us from Evil!'

For a moment Aelius was drawn into his own grief at Max's passing, but then Meromic's prayer began to impinge on his consciousness. Had he not exclaimed, 'Sweet Jesus!' Had he not uttered some prayer similar to one he had heard Christians chant as they were executed?

'You are a Christian!' he barked at the crumpled auxiliary, sobbing now upon the dead man's chest.

Ceridwen left Quintus's side and stood between Meromic and his legate. She looked steadily into Aelius's eyes and said, 'Maximus was the Christian. Meromic only thought to give him the prayer he would have wanted. He was obeying his master. That is all. Now, would you like to emulate your boyhood friend?' It came to her that at some time in the future Aelius would espouse Christianity, but not at this moment, not when his whole life and livelihood revolved around serving his Emperor. Aelius was as dumfounded by her regality, as he was at her intervention.

'Meromic,' she scolded gently. 'Come outside to the courtyard brazier and recover yourself. Aelius needs some private moments with his friend.' She drew Meromic past the speechless legate and out into the chill air of dawn.

'I wished him a sweet meeting with his Lord. He did truly turn about his life and endeavour not to sin,' Meromic quavered, swallowing and slowly recovering his composure.

'And you may have turned about your life. What were you

thinking of? You called upon Jesus. You chanted the Christians' prayer. Are you so eager to die?'

'No....I...It was just that the most important task was to give Quintus the farewell he needed. I threw caution to the wind. You lied for me. Thank you. I shall not be able to deny I am a Christian, if Aelius questions me again, but thank you for caring.'

'You are young and strong, Meromic. Now your task is to find Fiommar, not to die a martyr's death.'

'God's will be done. If I am to die for my Christian Faith, then, perhaps one day, Fiommar may hear of my courage and become a Christian herself.'

'It shall not happen so. You will meet Fiommar again in this life and it shall be a joyous reunion,' she reassured him. He shook his head in disbelief. They shivered as the wind got up and were glad when Aelius summoned them into the sick room once more.

Quintus Aurelius Maximus looked at peace; his struggle over; his face serene. Initially, Aelius could not meet their eyes. He too had shed tears and he felt it unmanly to have submitted to them.

He cleared his throat and muttered gruffly, 'I do not want any tittle-tattle about Max's being a Christian. Is that understood? If it became general knowledge, I would be obliged to throw his body to the dogs outside the fortress. I have prepared for his internment just beyond the north wall and I shall arrange a suitable memorial stone. Do not mention the matter again, either of you.'

They both knew what might happen to them if they disobeyed and nodded their consent. Aelius did not wish to open the grave of worms that was Meromic's beliefs. He trusted he had judged the situation well and that secrecy and diplomacy would win out.

He sighed and was about to dismiss Ceridwen, when he remembered Quintus's will. 'By the way, yesterday, Max had me draw up a new will for him. He has no heirs and has a pension and savings to disperse. He took quite a fancy to your son, Llew. Said he reminded him of himself as a boy and wished to be his patron. He has left money in trust for Llew's education and has requested that Marcus manage the fund. The rest of his effects go to Meromic and the infirmary, in recognition of the care they have given him.'

Ceridwen took some moments to digest the information. She tried to think when Quintus might have glimpsed Llew, but could not summon it to mind. She had purposely tried to shield Llew from a meeting with his blood father, but the Gods had contrived otherwise. Despite the pain, Quintus must have been perfectly clear of mind when he came face to face with Llew. She grasped what a shock it must have been for him to realise, on his deathbed, that he had a son. He had tried to make amends with this last bequest and she breathed thanks to the Gods for that blessing. Mischievous children could be trained from their errors, but she had never encountered before, an adult who had changed so dramatically for the better. There was hope for the human race yet. Her eyes met Meromic's and he smiled back at her. They both knew, in that moment, that her forgiveness of Quintus was indeed complete.

As she walked through the infirmary and out into the stirring sunrise of the paved street, she felt lighter, as though she were floating a little above the ground. Today, whilst Meromic prepared Quintus for burial, she must take matters in hand and encourage Marcus to talk through his decision. Was he going back to life in Ostia to manage his vineyards? Or was he going to take up post as assistant tutor surgeon here in Deva, honouring them with an occasional visit at Tan Yr Aur. They had but two days left before the final decision was to be offered to Aelius. Llew must be prepared to leave Marcus whatever happened, with the promise of occasional visits. As Llew's legally recognised father, Marcus could demand that Llew accompany him back to Ostia. But she knew Marcus would not prise him from her. It would kill everything between them and he would not risk that. Now there was Llew's education to discuss and she was prepared to negotiate some Latin tutoring, as long as his own culture was equally recognised.

She entered their chamber soundlessly and, although she was exhausted, she sat upon a graceful seat opposite the bed and watched the magic of the morning light creep over the faces of her husband and son. Marcus was curled protectively about Llew's form and she could sense that, in his sleep, it was the ghost of his right hand that offered love and protection.

Marcus stirred first and sat up, rubbing his eyes against the light in a boyish fashion. She waited for him to focus upon her, then said quietly and firmly, 'Marcus. Quintus is dead. My work here is done. You have two days before you give Aelius your decision, but I have a greater need of it now, if I am to prepare both Llew and myself. What say you?'

He sighed. 'I must be honest and say that I do not feel I belong here. Whether I could become accustomed to it, so that I could be nearer to you and Llew, I do not know. Perhaps I should try for your sakes. I long for Ostia as you long for Mynydd Llwydiarth, but, without you and Llew with me, there would be an emptiness...'

'Your options are unhappy ones, unless Llew and I are to be made unhappy. I cannot bear to be the cause of your pain,' she winced.

'Look, you have finished your task here and I can take a day from work. It is a holiday today. The festival of Ludi Plebeii in honour of Jupiter demands games and banqueting. Let us just enjoy this one day as a family and tomorrow I shall give you and Llew my decision. Then we shall make the necessary preparations. Please...Let us enjoy this precious time together.'

Her protest was changed into acquiescence as she saw Llew stir and heard Lepidus knock upon their door with early breakfast.

'Ludi Plebeii! Ludi Plebeii!' chanted Llew, who had sprung up with miraculous energy and was bouncing up and down upon the mattress. He became even more excited when he learned that Marcus and Ceridwen were to accompany him to the games and races. The only way to stop his whooping and whirling was for Marcus to fell him on the bed, their bodies a laughing, giggling tangle.

Ceridwen decided to enter into the spirit of the day. No

415

matter what was to follow in their lives, today would be a time to treasure always. When they were old they would remember it; a day streaming with late Autumn, golden sunshine and they would, once again, hear the roar of the crowds urging on the racing charioteers.

At the arena, made from the huge parade ground outside the east wall of the fortress, they made themselves comfortable on the tiered wooden benches, reserved for officers and their families. They were glad not to be in the jostling melee of the stands. Lepidus had provided them well with a picnic, warm rugs and a running commentary of explanation for Llew.

'That is the marker for the feet of the javelin throwers. Look! That gap in the palisade is the entrance for the athletes. The charioteers will come from the stables by east gate. Their racetrack is being marked out now. They must skirt the standards which you see being driven into the ground by those soldiers.'

Llew was entranced and stood upon the bench, craning his neck to see over the heads of the crowd. Ceridwen sat between her loved ones, her right hand in Marcus's and her left hand steadying Llew. Lepidus sat protectively on Llew's left. But Ceridwen hardly noticed when Aelius opened the proceedings and commanded the trumpets to sound. She was totally engrossed in remembering the first time she had ever set eyes upon Marcus, when he had brought Hedfan safely home. She remembered the sweet agony of their first embrace; his courage in winning her at Beltane; their night in the fragrant bower and the amazing love Marcus nurtured for Llew, binding all three of them so close. She savoured each memory with relish, rejecting anything that did not give her delight and pride. It was an indulgent feast of the most delicious sweetmeats of her life.

Only when Aelius's voice rang out, to dedicate the most dangerous of the chariot races to the memory of his friend Quintus Aurelius Maximus, did Ceridwen spin back to the present.

Everyone stood for a minute of silence to remember the bravery of Quintus. Ceridwen looked at Marcus's profile and etched it into her memory; so noble in its stillness; so handsome, his dark hair curling a little at the nape. Beloved! Did he really know how much he meant to her? Then she smiled at Llew. He was emulating Marcus, standing to attention with a serious expression. How she adored him.

'Thank you, Quintus! Thank you for my wonderful son,' she thought to herself, noting there was no bitterness to sour her emotion. She would always remember this moment...the three of them a family.

The tension was taut. The crowd stilled as the five highly skilled charioteers drove their teams of horses to the starting line. Then Aelius dropped his white kerchief and they were off at breakneck speed. Lepidus had betted most of his secret savings on the charioteer with the green plumed helmet and black steeds, but Ceridwen noted that, despite his years, Llew could spot good horseflesh.

'The roans are better,' he said matter-of-factly.

The race was a nail-biting seven circuits of the arena, jostling for a place to the outside of the circuit, where it was easiest to turn the bends and control the horse teams. The menfolk were riveted to the action, cheering and yelling with lusty inhibition; whilst Ceridwen chose instead to watch her husband and son, drinking in their excitement; sharing their mutual glances of glory, as the charioteer with the roans battled and weaved his way to victory, as though responding to the rhythms of a well-rehearsed dance.

The crowd went wild; their cheering so deafening that Llew clamped his hands about his ears. The victor dismounted and bowed before Aelius. He approached his legate and took off his helmet to receive his wreath of laurel. Ceridwen stared at the young man facing her, thirty feet below. At first glimpse, she thought the man to be ugly, with his lower jaw protruding pugnaciously. Then his features settled to her focus and she gasped in recognition...Coll!

He bent and accepted the wreath offered by Aelius and, as he rose, looked straight at her and smiled. A ray of sunlight from the South suddenly broke through the ranks of white wisp cloud and illumined his face. The crowd roared in appreciation of his victory. Never had anyone witnessed such a performance.

Ceridwen was speechless for a moment, puzzling how Coll had emerged here at Deva, master of charioteers.

'I lost!' shrieked Lepidus, striking himself upon the forehead. 'All my ill-gotten gains down the sluice. What an idiot I am! Never gamble Llew.'

'Your man had no chance against my Uncle Coll's team. I told you. Lepidus, which team would win,' grinned Llew, puffing his chest out importantly.

'You are in error, Llew,' Marcus corrected. 'The victor was Cassius Aquila. I met him only two days ago, when he came to the infirmary for some liniment.'

Ceridwen's heart froze. So Llew had the sight just as she did. There was no doubt about it. It had been a *sending*. Coll must be in need of her. She would pray for him. The sooner she could get home to Mynydd Llwydiarth the better.

Gwilym and Hedfan, along with a small escort of men from Din Silwy, were met with suspicion as they drew up to the Deva Bridge, spanning the river close to the south gate of the massive fortress. Even though they had hidden their weapons in their saddlebags and looked harmless enough, they were searched and questioned brusquely.

Gwilym did not realise that the resentment, emanating from the disgruntled faces of the guards, was more to do with missing the games, than having to search their party.

'Dismount and empty your bags upon the ground,' yelled the most senior of the bunch, their swords drawn and their shields ready against attack. Gwilym's contingent sighed and obeyed. Their knives and axes would have to be left here in trust until they were ready to leave; but had been indispensable in protecting them upon the horrendous two day journey across the Straits of Menai, up the Pass of Sychnant and crossing the river Conwy to push North to Deva.

They were weary, but had travelled whilst their light had held, the sombre urgency of their mission propelling them into unfamiliar territory. Gwilym took two bronze sistertii from the drawstring bag at his belt, but he could tell, by the expression on the guard's face, that he would charge at least three to look after their belongings. He knew the guard was taking advantage, but he had no heart left in him to barter.

During the arduous, cold, inclement journey, he had rehearsed over and over again what he would say to his daughter. He thought he had the measure of it. But once the drizzle and mists of the hills were behind him and the afternoon Sun broke the clouds to illuminate their destination, his mind had turned into a quagmire and his courage had sunk into his boots.

Now, any hope of gaining speedy entry into Deva, relieving some of his miserable anxiety, was immediately dashed.

'You will have to wait here for the next hour, whilst the arena is emptied. We cannot have you getting lost in the crowds whilst they are exiting the games.'

Gwilym looked puzzled. He did not understand the guard completely.

Hedfan, who was more proficient in Latin, explained; then began pacing the entrance to the bridge, as though his shoes scorched his feet. It was not his feet that sorely hurt. Gwyngariad had carried him well. It was tears of despair he was trying to hold back. At last they trickled unbidden, and he turned away from his comrades to save face.

Llew sat upon Marcus's shoulders as they made exit from the arena, holding back from the main throng of the audience, who were marching home for supper, or anticipating a wallow in the bathhouse. He chattered incessantly and Ceridwen smiled at Marcus. What a wonderful day it had been; so memorable in many ways.

'Can we go to the river and watch the boats, Pater? We could buy some supper from one of the booths and I can watch the fire-eater.'

'Who said there would be a fire-eater?' laughed Marcus up at him.

'Lepidus said there is always feasting and fire-eating after the games.'

'That is right, little man, but not until the evening draws in. That is when the revelry begins in earnest,' grunted Lepidus struggling with the baggage of their picnic, which they had not long since finished.

Neither Ceridwen nor Marcus wanted their carefree mood to end, so they agreed to turn down towards the river beyond Southgate. They walked briskly to combat the chill breeze, Llew bobbing above them like a young crow peering from its nest.

'I spy a cargo ship and men unloading her onto a barge. There's Uncle Tullius! I can tell it is he by his gold tunic. He is bossing people about.'

'Only Uncle Tullius would dream of missing the races in preference to work,' laughed Marcus.

'Look by the bridge! A white horse! It is Gwyngariad and Hedfan...Taid is there too!'

For a moment Ceridwen was sure Llew was mistaken; or perhaps he was experiencing another *sending*. But a minute later, when Marcus had broken a passage through the crowds, her heart leapt. A great rush of joy at beholding her father and brother was tempered by fearful anxiety. They would not have come unless something terrible had happened.

Gwilym and Hedfan stood like standing stones as they watched Ceridwen, Marcus and Llew head towards them at the gateway to the bridge. Marcus lifted Llew down from his shoulders, so that he could run like a battering ram to his grandfather and Gwilym folded the boy to him, staring meaningfully at his daughter.

'We vouch the good conduct of these travellers,' said Marcus to the chief guard, with whom he was familiar. Marcus expected Gwilym and his companions to come with them across the bridge, but he still stood motionless, staring into

Ceridwen's questioning eyes.

When at last he spoke it was hardly audible. 'I have bad news, Ceri. Just as you left for Deva, a message came from Din Silwy that Coll was sick with a fever. Your mother went to tend him. His body turned purple all over and breathing became hard. He complained of a headache and could barely swallow the herbs Old Betw and your mother offered him. They could do nothing for him. He was dead within hours.'

'No!' she cried. 'Coll! Oh sweet brother! He smiled on me just a little while ago...a *sending*. Why did I not know his need of me? Why did the Goddess hide his pain from me? Nanw could have told me. I should have been there to nurse him. I might have saved him!'

'You could have done nothing. It all happened so swiftly,' Gwilym countered. 'I have much to discuss with you and Marcus.'

Marcus was almost as shaken as Ceridwen. Coll had been like a brother. Since he had saved Coll's life at Segontium, they had become particularly close. He could not help thinking what a cruel twist of fate had come about. He had lost a hand to save Coll and now, just six short months later, Coll was dead.

He was glad when Uncle Tullius, drawn by curiosity, left his work by the boats and came to take charge.

'I am sure Aelius will accommodate you, once he knows the situation. Follow me,' Tullius said and with a modicum of self-importance led the way into the fortress.

True to Tullius's prediction, Aelius gave Gwilym and his men hospitality in the *praetorium*. However, it was a large shared guest room that offered little privacy. Ceridwen decided to take Gwilym and Hedfan up to their bedchamber. Lepidus would arrange refreshment and they could talk privately; privately, that is except for Llew, who would not be parted from his grandfather's side and refused point blank to go and find his playmate.

'Leave him be, Ceridwen. The boy will come to no harm being party to our discussion. It concerns him as well,' said

Gwilym gravely, tenderly drawing Llew to be seated by his side.

'Because of fear of contagion, Coll was cremated several hours after his death,' he continued, Marcus and Ceridwen, Hedfan and Llew hanging upon his every word. 'Old Betw presided in your absence, Ceridwen. We sent him to the Underworld with great honour at Cae Gwynion. We summoned all the members of farmsteads in our tribe. After the ceremony, we held an emergency meeting to discuss whom we might choose to be chieftain.

'We were all in agreement that Llew should one day take the place of his uncle. In him is Cadoc's prophecy fulfilled. He is of Roman and Celtic blood, noble and already wise for his years. He will grow to be a Keeper of the Peace. He will safeguard our future.

'Meanwhile we choose Marcus to run the affairs of the Celwri, for he has shown great courage and wisdom. Will you accept our decision as your own, Marcus? We would be greatly honoured.'

Marcus was dumbstruck. He had never thought to be invited to such honour, never dreamt he would be accepted into the Celwri tribe as a clansman and asked to be their chieftain to boot.

Ceridwen's heart lifted. The God's had turned Coll's death into an opportunity for Marcus. As one door had closed, another had opened. She willed him to respond, not daring to speak. It must be his decision alone.

Marcus looked at his feet, dust laden and carrying his past upon them. He looked into the large, round eyes of Llew, who did not as yet fully understand the implications of the discussion and who sat uncommonly still. If Llew was to be an important part of the Celwri tribe's future, then it must become his future. The boy was not his by blood, but by Mithras, the same spirit coursed through their veins. To be Llew's mentor and tribal leader would be a new beginning, a new challenge and one he might grow to relish.

The silence in the room was unbearable. Ceridwen held her breath.

'Yes. I accept. If Aelius will dissolve my contract with the army, I will be your temporary chieftain, until Llew comes of age.'

Hedfan and Gwilym congratulated him and slapped him upon the back. Then Gwilym knelt at his feet and wiped away the dust with his arm. 'My Lord.'

'Do not bow to me, Gwilym. You are my true father. I only hope that I may do you justice as a son,' said Marcus sincerely, bringing Gwilym to his feet. Gwilym's joints creaked with age, but the new hope in his eyes had suddenly transformed his face with youthfulness.

Ceridwen smiled a slow smile of greeting. The Marcus she once knew was returning to her, the polarity of his life choices no longer pulling him away from her. They embraced and Llew pushed between them.

'You are coming home with us, Father,' the boy said with satisfaction. Then Hedfan and Gwilym too were gathered into the circle of comforting arms. The decision was finally made. Ceridwen fancied she saw the spirit of Coll watching approvingly from the painted fresco of the wall. All would be well.

The following day sped by like lightning. Aelius reluctantly released Marcus from his contract with the army. They were losing a good surgeon, but he knew he could count upon Marcus to keep the peace upon Mona. That must be worth its weight in gold, or copper as the case might be with the mining industry there. It might prove useful to have allies in the safeguarding of Parys Mountain to the West of the island, which still yielded good ore.

Uncle Tullius was initially furious about Marcus's decision and saw it as treachery to the family; until he was appeased by the settlement Marcus had drawn up legally. Tullius's eldest son was to be given the task of overseer to the estate in Ostia and would run the affairs there in Marcus's absence. He would take a handsome profit, but would ensure the rest was ploughed back into the business. Uncle Tullius was to keep

Marcus informed of progress. Marcus knew that his uncle would take financial advantage of the situation, but he did not care. As long as the people's livelihood on the vine estate was not threatened, he was content.

Marcus put in a good word for Meromic to be transferred to the legion guarding the port at Ostia and drew up the necessary papers for Fiommar's freedom to be bought. Marcus thanked Aelius and his wife Aurora copiously with amphorae of Uncle Tullius's choice wine and leave taking was brief.

It was decided they would journey back to Mona on horseback via Kanovium. An army contingent bound for the fortress would be a guarantee of safe conduct through the hills and valleys of North Cymru.

Autumn mists plagued their progress and played games with time, deceiving them into thinking they had come far, when really they had travelled but a short distance. Llew wanted to shiver and complain, but something his mother had impressed upon him the previous evening stuck in his mind. 'Young princelings take no heed of their own desire, but grow to put the tribe before all else.'

He had been distraught at the thought of leaving Lepidus and Ceridwen had to appeal to his sense of pride, so that he could act with some dignity in saying farewell. They had rehearsed it until he was familiar with what to say to Lepidus.

'One day you will be chieftain of the Celwri and you must begin to take charge of your emotions and not let them ride you. You will make it unbearable for Lepidus if you cry. You must be brave and act the warrior. Afterwards you may give in to private tears.' Llew had smiled wanly in response to her. He always wanted to please his mother.

'Besides,' she had continued, 'Owain and *Nain* will be waiting for you with Luce and her kittens. They will want to hear all about your adventures.'

It was after noon by the time they rode through the steep, fearful valley of Sychnant and dropped down to the coast at Abergwyngregyn. By the time they reached the ferry point and bade farewell to their military escort, who had to return to the fort at Kanovium, the mist had begun to clear and a watery sunshine spangled the sea with its glittering mystery.

A scrawny, toothless ferryman shook his head.

'Ohh...'Tis too dangerous! We must wait until the tide goes out. The confluence of the currents, swirling about Mona, meets where you see the white foam. Two hours and we shall be able to take you over. You may as well eat and take your ease for a while.'

Marcus wondered how the toothless wonder managed to eat his own stringy meat stew. No doubt the delay in the crossing would give the ferrymen a good opportunity to make profit from the fare they were offered by the beach fire. They ate and warmed themselves. Gwilym bantered with the ferrymen. Hedfan took Llew to find weird and wonderful seashells and Ceridwen and Marcus began to walk together, a relief from the saddle soreness.

'I want to show you a special place,' said Marcus. 'I think you will like it! Come on!' he shouted, breaking ahead of her and turning to encourage her up the valley.

They passed the hut settlement with its busy forge and pushed higher, climbing the winding path, running alongside the rushing waters of Rhaeadr-fawr, swollen with recent rains.

They disturbed some wild ponies grazing amongst the forest trees and felt drunk with the fresh smells of the vegetation. They were breathless and warm now from their efforts and Marcus helped Ceridwen up the steep hillside, until they drew clear of the forest belt.

'Look. Turn around,' he said, his eyes smiling.

'It's Mona!' she exclaimed. 'We can see the whole island so clearly from here!'

'There's Mynydd Llwydiarth, your sacred mountain.'

'Oh Marcus, how I long to be home; to behold the faces of my family; to see Cae Gwynion and its creatures; to visit the Holy Ground and Coll's grave.'

'A few short hours and we shall be there and I shall be there with you.'

'You made such sacrifice for Coll, but his sacrifice was the greater. Whenever you feel the lack of your hand, remember how Coll would have you live your life...with great joy in its blessings.'

'You and Llew are my blessings. Living life with you both is going to be so enriching!' Marcus enthused, hugging her close.

'And when you visit your friends at Segontium and have Dith beg you to stay, will you not tire of us?'

'I shall enjoy their camaraderie and value it still, but I shall come home to my family and my mountain, where I belong. Come, we must climb higher. There is more to show you.'

The river twisted and turned up and up, the sound of rushing torrents drawing them on, until they skirted a grassy outcrop and beheld the falls. Sunbeams danced rainbow crystals through the raging foam of the waterfall.

'It is wonderful! I have never seen such power. It is glorious!' she shouted above its roaring.'

'Be careful you do not slip on the stones,' Marcus warned as she ventured closer, balancing precariously from mossy rock to rock. 'What are you doing?'

She had begun to take off her clothes. 'What does it look like? I am going to bathe!'

'You are mad. You will freeze!' he warned.

'Not if you come into the water with me! Where is your courage?'

She screamed with the shock as the water hit her body.

Someone had thought to strap boards at the foot of the falls, so that the level decking made it easier to shower. Wooden pegs, driven into the rock crevices, made it safer to keep one's balance, as the force of the water hit.

A minute later, having tugged off his clothes with impatience, he joined her on the platform, his left arm clinging to one of the pegs and his maimed right arm about her. They raised their faces to the torrent and felt its power beat upon their limbs. There was magic all around them; in the curtain of sunlit water; in the smell of the wet rock and in the raging roar of the river, as it thrust and surged into the bed of rocks below.

Marcus drew her body close. She was his ice queen; her skin white and glistening, her nipples teased proud by the spray; her eyelids drooping seductively and her mouth parting in temptation. Instinctively he lifted his right hand to stroke the beautiful curve of her cheek. Oblivious to the cold, his fingers caressed her and lingered upon each feature of her face. Her eyes were closed, but she felt his touch and nuzzled and kissed his hand in response. Then he embraced her and kissed her full on the mouth. Thrilling to the sensation of having a whole hand once more, with which he could explore the treasures of her body.

He gathered her up in his arms and carried her beyond the foam, laying her down on his woollen cloak on the mossy bank. She enfolded him in its warmth as he came down to her. They writhed together in exquisite torment, teasing and arousing each other, until she felt the need to take him into her would make her burst. She pushed against him and they rolled together. For a moment she paused to look into his strong, dear face, so full of yearning.

Then they were caught in a rhythm so urgent with passion, that the sound of the waterfall fell away, and all they could hear were their own cries of ecstasy, strangely mingling with the cry of an eagle overhead.

They stilled, lying together and not wanting to part just yet. Ceridwen closed her eyes and felt a whisper of starlight brush down her and settle in her belly. She knew at that moment she had conceived. It was a girl-child spiriting its way into her womb; a girl-child, thirsty for the secrets of old; thirsty to know the ways of healing and the paths to spiritual growth; a Guardian of the Light.

Ceridwen hugged the knowledge to her. There would be time enough to tell Marcus when they got home and were established in their new routine. They sat up and she sighed, allowing the wind to play with wisps of her hair. Reverently, wordlessly, they parted and dressed for the journey down to the ferry. Tenderly, she strapped on his artificial hand, her father had made so skilfully. He smiled in appreciation. He was content. The magic would visit him from time to time and he

427

would feel whole again.

'Let us go home,' he said, offering her his left hand to steady her down the path.

'Yes. Let us go home.'

⌘ ⌘ ⌘

Epilogue

⌘

One magical winter morning, as our family walked through the forest at the top of Mynydd Llwydiarth (Purple Mountain) on the island of Ynys Môn (Anglesey) in North Wales, we came across some pines steaming their frost into the glorious winter sunshine. We paused to watch the mist swirl and dance, gazing over to Snowdonia. Although only five hundred feet above sea level, the vista was incredible.

Lower down the track, as the view urged us on, we came across a little white cottage for sale and fell in love. Six months later we moved in, incredulous of our luck at finding anywhere so beautiful. So began my fascination with the area and promptings from the rocks and forest behind the house captivated me into doing some historical research.

Market day in the town of Llangefni, in the centre of the island, was full of amazing encounters with local artists and regular folk searching for a bargain. The local hostelries were the places to find the characters, weather-beaten farmers and traders, earnestly practising that Welsh tradition of anecdotal competition...all in Welsh, which at that time escaped my understanding. You couldn't help noticing how many Welsh people had Roman noses, nor how many of the women had that 'Italian look'. These weren't your typical tall Druids of the folk tales. Were these people descended from Romans?

It got me ruminating about British history in general and about how we are all of very mixed race, descendants of wave after wave of intermarriage between settler and invader.

I wasn't quite prepared for living on Anglesey. Although I lived there for 23 years of my married life, for a long time I felt a little estranged from the 'indigenous' Welsh community. It wasn't until I seriously started studying the Welsh language and its history that I began to feel truly part of it.

It was the time of the burning of holiday homes. Welsh Nationalist Extremists had had enough of the English moving into their rural villages and making them ghostly places, with their empty holiday retreats. I began to ponder the insecurities of a land invaded and wondered a great deal about the Roman invasion of Anglesey, or Mona as it was called, two thousand years ago.

For the first time in our married life I began to put down roots. We renovated the cottage and settled into our idyllic mountain retreat one and a half miles from the village of Pentraeth.

Down a mountain lane from the cottage was a convenient bus route for the children and myself to get to work and school, and it was only a fifteen-minute commute for my husband to get to his office on the mainland at Bangor University. My job of running the kindergarten at a delightful private school in Llansadwrn was wonderfully rewarding, but kept me well occupied with little time for myself.

However our idyllic life was in for a shock. I developed chronic fatigue syndrome and an old injury to my spine was exacerbated by it; so much so, that I could not walk without screaming.

Giving up a job I truly loved, with people and pupils I truly loved, was a tremendous spiritual battle. I needed to find another life goal. Peculiar as it might seem, I did not feel daunted. I felt protected and that my disability had come to me for a reason.

I decided that whilst I was bedridden I would research the novel that I had always wanted to write. As a member of the Baha'i Faith I had always been fascinated by the link between all religions and the unity of their Divine source. So, in order to be truly satisfying to write, the novel would have to lead me towards some form of spiritual research. Given where we lived on Anglesey, it seemed appropriate to delve into ancient Druid teachings.

It took two years of research and ten years of writing in short periods in the morning, when my brain was able to function. I propped myself up at the desk on a kneeling stool and began the task. I did all those mechanical things you are supposed to do when writing a novel, researched it avidly and charted its plot and characters. However, a very curious thing began to happen. As I began to immerse myself in the plot and characters, my planned story began to evaporate and was replaced by the promptings of its main heroine, Ceridwen, the Druid priestess of my story, who, I was convinced, had truly lived and worked near the site of our cottage.

'Where Rowans Intertwine' can be read simply as an historical novel or its spiritual lessons can be applied to today. We are all such products of mixed race, culture and language. That is why I have chosen a period in history around 230 A.D. - a time when the strain of Roman occupation was still deeply affecting the descendants of Druids on the island of Mona (Anglesey).

The initial title I chose was 'Guardians of the Light' - a reference to how spiritual virtues and skills are passed down from one generation to another. However, I discovered, ten years into the writing, that a computer game and subsequently a series of novels had been developed using the same name. 'Where Rowans Intertwine' therefore became the new title and refers to the prophecy of one of the novel's characters, Cadoc, Ceridwen's grandfather: *'When the noble bloods of Rome and Druid mingle, as the rowans intertwine, then peace and honour will come with us to dine.'*

The Druids believed that the rowan tree gave protection from enchantment and that the trees watched over the spirits of the dead. Sprays of rowan were fixed to cattle sheds and rowan hoops put around the necks of animals in need of protection. Branches were often put upon the main door of a house or worn about the person. The rowanberry carries a pentagram, an ancient symbol of protection, so the tree is entirely appropriate to feature in the title of the novel.

Besides, the title reminds me of the avenue of intertwined rowans, which lined the driveway up to our idyllic cottage.

The magic depicted in the story is not fantasy but is based on practices passed down from mother to daughter over the centuries. I have experienced some of this at a personal level. Although being brought about by ritual in the novel's context of time, these days it can be achieved through a heightened sense of consciousness and spiritual awareness. This has been confirmed to me over many years of my own practice of Baha'i prayers, meditation and Reiki healing.

The Druid's Holy Place was always a mountain, where groves of sacred trees were established as a living temple and a clearing established for sacred rites. Near our mountain cottage were some struggling oak seedlings and a bluebell wood, competing with the pine forest, which had been planted to provide quickly grown timber during the Second World War.

Tacitus, the Roman chronicler, tells us that the sacred Druid groves were demolished with the Roman invasion of Mona; but do their progeny live on 2000 years later, I wondered? The more I researched, the more I became convinced that we were living on the ancient site of a Druid training school. And so this tale was born, woven like Celtic plaid from fact, imagination and inspiration.

⌘ ⌘ ⌘

More information about Margaret Grant can be found at:
margaretgrantauthor.wordpress.com

Made in the USA
Charleston, SC
21 October 2015